About the Author

Stephen B. Cooper is from a working-class background from the North East of England. He is a singer-songwriter, writer and poet with a knack for the unusual.

Dedicated to my brother Simon Cooper and his wife Caroline, for bullying/helping me through the darkest days of cancer.

Stephen B. Cooper

THE FISCHERS
VOLUME 2

MARRIED TO MAYHEM

AUSTIN MACAULEY™
PUBLISHERS LTD.

Copyright © Stephen B. Cooper (2017)

The right of Stephen B. Cooper to be identified as author of this work has been asserted by him in accordance with section 77 and 78 of the Copyright, Designs and Patents Act 1988.

All rights reserved. No part of this publication may be reproduced, stored in a retrieval system, or transmitted in any form or by any means, electronic, mechanical, photocopying, recording, or otherwise, without the prior permission of the publishers.

Any person who commits any unauthorized act in relation to this publication may be liable to criminal prosecution and civil claims for damages.

A CIP catalogue record for this title is available from the British Library.

ISBN 9781786294326 (Paperback)
ISBN 9781786294333 (Hardback)
ISBN 9781786294340 (E-Book)
www.austinmacauley.com

First Published (2017)
Austin Macauley Publishers Ltd.
25 Canada Square
Canary Wharf
London
E14 5LQ

CHAPTER 1
A RHINO HAS TWO HORNS

It is one year to the day since the Fischers were wed. Mark and Pyah sit around a camp fire in the middle of the African desert. The fire sparkles as the embers rise into the midnight sky. The flames dance to the music of an old song quietly playing on the old radio Mark had brought.

"Happy anniversary, dear," Mark kisses Pyah as the clock strikes twelve, "one year and you haven't killed me," he laughs.

Pyah strokes his face, "Yet. I haven't killed you *yet,* my dear," she corrects him, chuckling to herself.

Mark reaches around to un-holster his gun.

"It's loaded," he says, handing it to Pyah with a wry grin.

Pyah takes the gun, pulls the magazine then breaches the barrel, pulling the round from the pipe,

"Oh, I think we can do better than that," she says, pointing the gun down between his legs, "hope that's loaded!" she teases, raising her eyebrows.

Mark takes his gun back, reloads the round, places the magazine back and puts it on safety. He then holsters it and stands up. Taking Pyah by the hand, looking deep into her eyes he pulls her slowly to her feet. The flames reflect in her green eyes as he pulls her slowly into his arms. In the silence of the African desert Mark can feel her heart quicken. Her breath warms as he gently touches her lips with his. A sudden breeze moves her hair across his face as a tingle of anticipation courses down her spine, raising the hairs on the back of her neck. Mark brushes her hair from her face,

"Well we are definitely alone," he murmurs, kissing her neck while running his hand over her buttocks, "not a soul for miles."

Pyah arches her neck, "What you want to get down to it right here? Right now?"

Mark nods, "Yep, never done it under the stars and we can't get interrupted, it's impossible."

Pyah pulls his head back, "Oh I think you may have just given that the kiss of death," she says, smiling cautiously, "tempting fate, you know we are going to get some company now."

Mark shrugs, then gently teases the zip down at the back of her frock. He tentatively pulls the straps forward, down the front allowing the frock to slide over her breasts and fall to the ground. He steps back to admire her perfect form as she stands bold in the firelight, the shadows dancing across her body while the glow highlights her angelic white lace thong and bra.

Pyah tips her head. "I love the way you still look at me," she tells him, holding her hands outstretched, "as if you had never seen me undressed before." She takes him by the hand, pulls him forward then starts to unbutton his shirt, "You do realise there are wild animals out here."

Mark mockingly growls at her, "What? Apart from me you mean?" He sweeps her up into his arms then starts to walk to the motor home.

Pyah points at her frock on the floor, "The other wild animals might get it."

He bends down to let her reach for it then walks back to the motor home. As she reaches out for the handle they hear a shuffling noise coming from out in the desert.

"Told you there were wild animals out here," Pyah said, quickly opening the door as Mark cautiously looks around.

"Either that or someone has come out on a dogging trip," Mark quipped, stepping quickly into the motor home and fumbling for the door while Pyah sniggers under her breath, "romantic I must say."

The motor home has mood lighting. Pyah reaches across to switch it on as Mark stumbles towards the bed, nearly dropping her.

Pyah clings on for dear life laughing aloud, "Looks like someone is getting old!"

Mark regains his footing, "I'll show you who's getting old, missy," he says, throwing her on to the bed "the only thing I'm getting hold of tonight is you."

He rips his shirt off, beats his chest and drops on top of her as she wraps her legs around his waist. Mark slides his hand under her back to unclip her bra as she pulls herself forward to kiss him. Lowering her back onto the pillow he gently pulls her bra forward and drops it on the floor beside the bed. Pyah reaches down, unclipping his trousers, neither one saying a word as they both look adoringly into each other's eyes. Mark kisses her neck as she pushes his trousers over his hips. He runs his hand down over her breasts then down to her hips to gently persuade her thong over her thighs. Mark kicks his shoes off then kneels before her as she teases his trousers down to his feet allowing him to drop them on the floor alongside her bra. The firelight flickers through the curtains across his chest as Pyah strokes her hands across his torso to pull him gently down into her bosom. The passion rises as does his manhood while Pyah runs one single fingernail up his spine then spreads her hand through his hair.

The motor home gently sways as Mark places his lips against Pyah's, "Feels like it's getting a bit windy."

Pyah grasps a handful of his hair, "Don't spoil the moment," she tells him, pulling his head back to give him a stern look, "if you fart I'm rolling over and going to sleep."

The motor home sways a little more as Mark attempts to pull back the curtain, "No I mean it seems to be getting windy outside," he says as the motor home rocks violently.

Pyah sits up, "That's not the wind, my dear," she says, shuffling across the bed, "something is pushing the van," she surmises as she attempts to see out of the window.

Mark reaches down to grab his gun, "What or whoever it is, is going to get an ass full of lead."

Pyah grabs his arm, "I wouldn't do that if I were you," she warns, pulling him towards the window, "looks like we've got a young female rhino with an itch." Taking Mark's gun away to put it on the pillow she continues, "Trust me you're just going to vex her with that and then she'll attack the van," Pyah pats the bed, "best we just sit and watch, let her finish then she'll be on her way."

Mark smiles at Pyah, "How come you're such an expert on rhinos all of a sudden?"

Pyah kisses his cheek, "I did some light reading before we came."

Mark puts his arm around her waist, "So how can you tell it's a female?"

Pyah closes her eyes, "It only has a horn on its head."

Mark starts to laugh, "So does that make her a dickhead?"

Pyah puts her hand over his mouth, "Loud noises spook black rhinos."

Mark pulls her hand down and whispers, "How the hell can you tell what colour it is in the dark?"

Pyah shakes her head, "It's nothing to do with the colour, you numpty," she sighs, "she has a shorter neck than a white rhino and black rhinos are solitary."

Mark raises his finger, "So white rhinos hunt in packs?"

Pyah lifts a pillow to her face to laugh into, "You're not too bright at times, dear husband," she observes, gently slapping his forehead, "they're vegetarian, they don't hunt."

Mark just shrugs and looks out of the window. After a short while the rhino saunters over to a nearby tree to scratch. Pyah pulls the curtain back to watch as the young rhino stops, turns around and sniffs the air before rubbing herself against the tree. After a quick scratch she prances around a little then trots off into the night.

Mark lies back on the bed pulling Pyah back into his arms, "That lady needs a hobby, or a man."

Pyah rolls on top of Mark, "I don't think that a man would be any good to her," she comments, stroking Marks penis, "in fact I don't think that even you are big enough to satisfy her," she says sniggering then pecking him on the cheek.

Mark gently slaps her buttock, "You know what I mean, another rhino, a man one."

Pyah lifts herself onto her hands, "bull."

Mark gives her a look of confusion, "What you don't think she wants a shag?"

Pyah shakes her head laughing, "Dear, they're called bulls, male rhino's," she points out, batting her eyes at him.

Mark points at the window. Then down at his genitalia "Oh, bull as in male not as in bullshit," he says, pausing while the penny drops, "gotcha."

Pyah kisses his chest, "Now I on the other hand," she begins, walking her fingers up his chest and onto his neck, "I need a man," she continues, placing her finger gently in his mouth, "so you going to show me a man and what he can do or are you just going to ask stupid questions on the mating habits of the black rhino?"

Mark slowly slides his hands up the inside of her thighs as she arches her back, pushing herself up off his knees. Mark slowly slides into her as she throws herself forward. A torrent of red hair cascades in an arc above her then gently rests like a veil shrouding Marks head as their lips meet. Mark's torso heats to fever pitch as Pyah tenderly rocks back and forth across it. The perspiration lubricating between them as it vaporises through the rasping passion. A rush of blood flushes Pyah's whole being as the tingle of ecstasy raises the hairs across her skin. The feeling of euphoria envelops Mark bringing him to the brink of intensity, holding off for that moment when Pyah is ready to explode as she feels him rise inside of her. The warmth of juices seep with a spasm of resounding pleasure signifying to Mark she is ready as he erupts inside of her to climax in a harmonious rush.

Pyah moans softly laying gently down onto his chest as he brushes her mass of hair from his face. He rolls her delicately to the side, onto the welcoming cool, cotton sheet as they both gasp intensely. The rush of adrenaline abates into an ambient air of serenity without suppressing an electrically stimulated atmosphere of passion.

The couple lie together for five minutes before Pyah stands up, "Well I'm having a shower," she announces, nudging Mark before he falls asleep, "don't suppose you can put clean sheets on that?" she asks, pointing down at the bed, "I don't want to sleep in a sweaty bed all night."

Mark just groans, pulling a pillow over his face. Pyah tuts then heads for the shower.

Mark sits up and places his hand where he laid, "Oh, Jesus that must have been good," "then sniffs his own arm pit, "oh for Christ's sake," he swears, cringing at the smell of his own B.O. He pulls the pillow cases off, then the sheets and flings them into the wash basket. Then he replaces them with fresh ones just in time for Pyah to come out of the shower.

"Oh my god you've actually changed it?" she exclaims, rather surprised as she reaches for the hair dryer, "Well don't think you're getting back in it until you smell as fresh as those sheets."

Mark raises his eyebrows then smiles as he silently saunters past, kissing her shoulder on the way into the shower. It isn't long before he is finished and drying himself on the way back to bed where Pyah is laid in a sound sleep. Mark slides effortlessly into the bed and spoons her, finding himself soon nodding off into a comfortable slumber.

CHAPTER 2
WHEN BULLS COME A-COURTING

The morning comes around swiftly breaking daylight through a crack in the curtain. The sound of bird life brings Pyah out of her slumber as she gently removes Marks arms from around her. She leaves him to rest a while as she gets her regular morning shower. While she is showering a faint whiff of bacon drifts through into the cubicle. She silently steps out of the shower to poke her head out of the bathroom door where Mark is stood naked with just an apron on at the hob making breakfast.

"Well this is a first," she comments, walking up behind him and putting her wet arms around his waist, "to what do I owe the pleasure?"

Mark drops the fish slice he's holding, "Jesus woman you're all wet," he exclaims, pushing the pan off the flame and turning around, "just thought you could have your breakfast while I was having a shower then we could get out of here and on the road."

Pyah sniffs at him, "Yeah you could definitely do with a shower," she agrees, putting her arms around his neck, "seems this heat doesn't agree with your sweat glands," she chuckles, "I was going to ask if you fancied jumping in with me but I don't think there is enough room for both of us."

Mark gives her a kiss then turns back to the hob, "Well, by the time you've dried yourself and dressed this should be ready."

Pyah heads back to the bathroom while Mark serves up. Pyah sits at the table as Mark places her breakfast in front of her then heads for the shower. In the shower, he manages to soap himself down and starts to wash his hair when ***BOOM*** the whole motor home moves about two feet backwards.

"What the hell was that?!" he yells, trying to wash the soap from his eyes.

Pyah gets up as her breakfast is sent reeling off the table by the van being bounced backwards another two feet.

"MARK!" She runs to the front of the van to open the cockpit curtain and is sent flying into the driver's seat, "Mark!"

Mark rushes out of the shower trying to rub the soap from his eyes, fumbling for his gun, "What the hell is going on?!"

Pyah is on her hands and knees in between the front seats "We're being forcefully moved; I think?" she answered, trying to get to her feet as the van is hurled back another two feet.

Mark can just make out a large grey blur through the front windscreen of the motor home, "What?" he queries, trying to aim his gun with one eye through a soapy haze, "What the fuck is that? An elephant?"

Pyah manages to get to her feet, "Put the gun away you loon!" she calls as both of them are sent flying to the ground again by the movement of the van, "It's a rhino,", she explains, scrambling towards him on her hands and knees, "a fucking big, big fucking rhino and I think it's having a romp with the van."

Mark hands the gun to Pyah, "Here, shoot the damned thing I got soap in my eyes."

Pyah hands the gun back as the van starts to rock sideways, "You'll just aggravate it with this," she tells him, trying to get to her feet again, "put it away, he'll be finished soon."

Mark puts the gun on safety, reaches up and drops it on the floor, "Shit. If I shoot it in its dick it'll be more than aggravated," he claims, rubbing his eyes, "it'll think twice about shagging our van again and how the hell do you know it's a male?"

Pyah tuts as she falls to the ground again, "Same reason I know you won't be able to shoot its dick. It's shagging the van," she says, rolling her eyes up into her head, "it's got its dick buried in our radiator grill."

Suddenly the motor home is still and a stomping of feet can be heard. Pyah gets to her feet and looks through the curtain to see the rhino prancing around like a young antelope. It shakes its head then prances some more

"I think the van was a good shag," she laughs, looking back at Mark, "I think you can go and finish your shower now, by which time we should be able to get out of here."

Mark splashes some water on his eyes then takes a quick peek through the curtains, "Shit you weren't kidding when you said he was a big fucker," he observes, looking down at his gun, "this might have tickled him, glad I didn't shoot him," he reasons, then quickly returns to the shower.

Mark rinses himself off and is just starting to dry himself when the van starts to rock sideways again, "Oh shit, tell me he isn't shagging the van again?"

Pyah looks out of the side window, "No, he's rubbing up against it."

Mark wraps a towel around his waist and comes to the window, "What the hell is he doing that for?"

Pyah shrugs, "Don't know maybe he's wondering why she ain't responding."

The rhino takes a couple of steps backwards then gently headbutts the wheel of the motor home. Mark quickly grabs a pair of boxer shorts and tries to put his feet into them as the motor home is sent sideways and bringing Mark to his knees, rolling down the centre, bouncing off the bottom cupboards, "Screw this for a lark," he mutters as he manages to drag the boxers up around his waist, "if we don't get the hell out of here we won't have any wheels to get out on."

Rushing to the driver's seat, Mark grabs the keys from the centre console as he is flung into the seat by the sudden sideways movement of the van, "Oh shit, hot, hot, hot," he complains, bouncing off the hot leather seats.

Pyah rushes down the aisle with a towel as Mark is trying to start the van while keeping his body off the hot leather. She pushes the towel under him, "Better move your arse," she warns, looking out of the passenger window, "I think the engine noise spooked him," she continues, strapping herself into the seat, "INCOMING!"

The van is sent hurtling sideways about three feet, "Yep, he's definitely pissed off now," Mark says as he violently steers the van into the skid, frantically trying to hold it upright on the dirt road. He slams it into first gear and holds his foot on the accelerator, spinning the wheels and leaving a plume of sand and dust exploding into the air as the van careers down the desolate track. Mark drives the van into second gear without lifting his foot off the accelerator, sending the rev counter into the redline as the tires try to get grip.

"What's he doing now?" he asks, trying to catch a glimpse out of the wing mirrors.

Pyah leans forward, looking back through the side window, "He's lining up for another run," she says, but Mark knows what's about to happen just by the way Pyah has planted her feet firmly against the dashboard to jam herself against the back of her seat, "INCOMING!" she yells as she grips the bottom of her seat.

Mark just has time to brace himself and start to steer into the slide as he sees the rhino impact the rear quarter through the wing mirror. Again, the van is sent barrelling up on two wheels into a sideways slide. Mark manages to hold it together, getting all wheels back on the dirt then throwing it into third gear while the van violently jumps forward as he dumps the clutch anxiously looking for the next attack. Pyah has lost sight of the rhino but then Mark catches a glimpse on his side of the van as it comes in at full speed. It just grazes the rear panel of the van causing it to skew slightly. Mark knows by this that the rhino has reached its top speed and he can now outrun it. Keeping his foot firmly planted he drops the van into top gear just in case and gives a big sigh of relief.

Pyah looks out of the back window, "We're not out of the woods yet," she warns again as she unbuckles her seat belt, staggering down to the back of the van, "yeah I can just make him out through the dust. You may have outrun him for now but he's still coming."

Leaving the rhino in a dust cloud they travel as fast as Mark dares for about a mile and a half when Pyah starts to sniff the air, "Oh my God, what is that smell?!" she exclaims, putting her sleeve over her face.

Mark cringes as the smell reaches his nostrils, "Jesus!" he yells, trying to waft the smell from his nose, "smells like a rancid rat has crawled up a camel's arse and died."

Pyah baulks as she sniffs at the air intakes, "It's coming in through the vents," she declares, grabbing the edge of the towel Mark is sitting on to cover her face, "have you damaged the engine?"

Mark nervously taps the gauges, "Nope, everything is reading right, water, oil," he replies, covering his mouth with his hand.

Pyah starts to roll down the window but then hurriedly rolls it back up, "Shit, its worse out there."

Mark starts to slow down, "I think I better pull over just in case."

Pyah quickly unbuckles her seat belt, "Hold on," she says, grabbing a pair of binoculars then walking down to the back window, "we don't want that bloody randy rhino charging up on us while you're out there checking."

Mark slams his foot back on the gas, "Yeah better give it another half mile or so," he agrees, sending Pyah flying down the van.

"Oh for Christ's sake," she huffs as she lands face down in what's left of her breakfast and slides through it. Pyah quickly sits up, turns around to see her breakfast plate hurtling towards her. "Oh shit," she says as it lands firmly in her lap, rolls across her hip and is sent crashing into the wall behind her, shattering.

Mark turns to see his wife sprawled across the floor, legs akimbo, "Sorry darling," he apologises as he slams the brakes on, causing Pyah to slide forwards over the breakfast beans, firmly smearing them across her buttocks.

Mark can feel the daggers from Pyah's eyes without having to look as the van comes to an abrupt sliding halt. Mark tries to pretend he hasn't noticed as he jumps out of the van, rushing around to the hood, "Can you keep an eye out for that rhino while I check this, dear?" he asks, trying his hardest to sound not to condescending.

Pyah huffs as she awkwardly gets to her feet, "Dickhead." She struts out of the van trying to appear dignified and looks through the binoculars, "Bollocks," she comments, turning to Mark, "We ain't got much time so whatever you have to fix do it quick," she tells him as she watches him turn around to vomit at the side of the desert track.

Pyah looks through the binoculars to see the rhino about a mile out trotting along sniffing the air, coming in their direction, "You haven't got time for that dear, whatever it is fix it and let's get the hell out of here. I reckon we have about two minutes, three at the most."

Mark slams the hood down, "Trust me, dear, I can't fix that," he says, then rushes around to jump in the driver's door.

Pyah quickly climbs in, "Don't say can't," she says, panicking to get her seat belt on, "please tell me we can get out of here."

Mark starts the motor, "There's a map in the glove box, find the nearest place where we can get help."

Pyah flicks the glove box open, "OK what the hell is wrong with it and how far have we got?" she asks, spreading the map out on her knee.

Mark reaches for a tissue, "That big bastard shot his load all over the radiator," he informs her, blowing his nose then spreading the tissue out, "and that's what it looks like except the heat is melting and boiling it. We need to get some detergent or something."

Pyah glances across at the tissue then starts to roll the window down, "Oh you dirty bastard." The pungent odour caresses her face as she violently vomits out of the open window. Pyah glances back, "I think you better get your foot down, dear," she warns, seeing the rhino getting very close to ramming range, "looks like our mating partner has got the scent again," she adds, turning to give Mark a worried look.

Mark glances over his shoulder, "Oh shit," he says as he can see the rhino through the rear window getting up to his top speed and gaining on them.

Pyah grabs Marks gun, "Fuck it," she announces, then heads down the van, "incoming," she says but Mark manages to get the van up to speed just enough to outrun the rhino.

Pyah aims the gun at the rhino as its horn comes within inches of the back of the van before it runs out of steam and gives up.

CHAPTER 3
WHEN DEODORANT JUST WON'T DO

"Looks like it's given up, for now," she sighs as she staggers back down to the passenger seat and pulls out the map, "there's an outpost about thirty or forty miles down this track," she says, stabbing at the map, "maybe someone there can help."

Mark takes the map off Pyah and throws it into the back, "OK, take over the wheel while I get some clothes on."

Pyah's eyes widen, "You're kidding, right?" she says disbelievingly, looking down at her own messy attire.

Mark shakes his head, "No I'm not," he says, waving his hand at her, "at least you're not sticking to the seat." His back makes a slurping noise as he prises it away from the hot leather.

Pyah stands up and walks back to the wardrobe, pulls out a t-shirt and throws it at him, "I'll get changed, then I'll take the wheel," she tells him, grabbing a fresh set of clothes for herself to carry into the bathroom.

Mark raises his arm, "Marvellous, just bloody marvellous," he mutters as he awkwardly pulls the t-shirt over his head as the van skews over the road.

Pyah sticks her head out of the bathroom door, "What the hell's going on?" she asks as Mark regains control of the van plonking Pyah down on the toilet.

"Oh it's just me trying to get this fucking t-shirt on while driving at breakneck speed over a road full of craters the size of the sea of tranquillity, dear, don't worry your little head about it, I've got this!" he spews hostile sarcasm at her, "you just take your time and make yourself look beautiful for the rednecks at the outpost, don't mind me," he whines, holding the steering wheel with his legs while he struggles to put his arms through into the t-shirt.

Pyah quickly finishes getting changed then rushes to his side, squeezing between the driver's door and seat, "OK you moaning old git," she says, shoving him off the driver's seat. "I'm here, you go and get your whining arse changed," she tells him as she slides him off and sits on the driver's seat, "Christ this seat's wringing wet."

Mark gives a smug self-satisfied grin, "Well you should have waited," he gloats, waving his hand at her nice clean clothes, "now you're just going to have to sit in my sweat and get changed again when I'm finished."

It takes another change of clothes, some antibacterial wipes and about forty-five minutes to reach the outpost. The first thing they come across is a cross between an armoury, a haberdashery and a supermarket. The sign above the door reads *"White and Wong's General Dealers."* As they pull up a gentleman in khaki shorts, a khaki shirt and a wide-rimmed leopard skin hat walks out to greet them.

He waits for them to disembark before speaking, "Morning! White's the name, James White but you can call me Jimmy," he starts, wafting his hand in front of his nose, "what can I do for you good people? Smells like you been shagging a rhino."

Pyah held her nose, "Yeah tell me about it," she says, walking straight into the store, "don't suppose you sell air freshener?"

Jimmy points to back of the store, "Think you're going to need more than air freshener, my dear, what happened?"

Mark lifts the hood, "A big bull rhino shagged our van," he explains, pulling a towel up to his face, "did you say your name was Jimmy White?"

The guy walks over to the front of the van, "Yeah, like the English snooker player," he says laughing out loud "where did this happen?"

A voice comes from an upstairs window, "The closest you ever came to playing with your ball was at the French Lettuce across the way!"

Mark looks up to see a Chinese girl hanging out of the window then across the street to what looks like an old western saloon hotel named the French Lettuce.

Jimmy puts his arm around Mark's shoulder, "That is my good lady wife and partner in crime," he says, pointing up "what went," he says, chuckling to himself.

The Chinese girl throws a slipper down at him, "Take no notice of him, dear. I am his wife but my name is Mary White. When we met," she says, pointing down at the sign "it was Mary Wong, as you can gather."

Jimmy picks up her slipper "My pet name for her, what went Wong… get it?"

Pyah walk out of the shop with a can of air freshener in her hand, "How much is this?"

Jimmy walks over and takes the air freshener off her, "Told you this is no good, I'll have your van cleaned," he says, walking around the back, "looks like he got a few runs at you too," he continues, then he walks into the middle of the road, "how long ago did you say this happened?"

Mark walks out to him, "About three quarters of an hour, thirty to forty miles back."

Jimmy sucks his finger then sticks it into the air, "Don't suppose he lost interest, did he?"

Pyah steps forward, "No he bloody didn't," she answers, wafting her hand across the hood of the van, "chased us for about a mile and a half before we outran him but he was still coming last I saw of him," she continues, putting her hand up to shade her eyes, "that's why I would like to get this cleaned off and get the hell out of here before he catches us."

Jimmy shouts in African and two young boys come running from the back of the store with large chemical sprayer. Jimmy instructs them in African as they head down the road out on to the desert track.

"They'll spray for about a mile out that should throw that big bastard off your trail," he tells them, walking into the store, "if not this should sort him out," he says, pulling a long gun out from behind the counter.

Pyah grabs the gun, "You can't kill it, they're endangered."

Jimmy pulls the gun back, "I ain't gonna kill it," he explains, holding up an explosive round, "shoot these at its feet, scares the hell out of it and disorientates it, he'll soon give up and run."

The van is taken to an old livery stable, washed down and repairs are set about while Mark and Pyah are introduced to the owner of the French Lettuce. Sonja Fabich, forty-five-year young French madam, standing five-foot nine in her four-inch stiletto boots, "Welcome to the French Lettuce."

Pyah shakes her hand, "Why the French Lettuce?"

Before Sonja can answer Jimmy butts in, "Because that's the way she pronounces letters," he says, sniggering to himself, "French Letters, French Lettuce? Get it?"

Sonja slaps the back of his head, "Take no notice of him, he made the sign up outside, the name stuck and brings in plenty of business," she tells them, placing her arms around a young African girl that appears beside her, "why fix what isn't broken? That's my philosophy." Sonja pecks the African girl on the cheek, "Go and prepare a drink for our guests," she says then taps her gently across the butt.

Pyah follows the African girl to the bar, "So what do they call you?" she asks.

The girl lifts a glass from behind the bar "Aabida, but Sonja likes to call me Mimi," she replies, giving Pyah a churlish look.

Pyah smiles provocatively at Mimi "I'll just have a coke if you don't mind," she says, turning to Mark "do you want a coke, hun?"

Mark is still engrossed with Sonja, "Yes please," he says without averting his eyes from her.

Presently Jimmy walks back into the brothel, "Your boy has arrived. He's scampering around about three quarters of a mile outside town."

Sonja cringes at Jimmy, "Town?"

Jimmy loads his gun, "Yeah I like to think of it as my little town and you wouldn't want a fucking big rhino coming in disturbing it, would you?"

Sonja rushes to the door, "A rhino? What the hell does he want, shit he is a big bugger."

Jimmy lifts his gun, "Seems he's developed a crush for their motor home," he chuckles.

Sonja looks at Mark, "You had a run in with that?"

Mark nods as Jimmy fires a round at the rhino's feet. The rhino turns tail and runs. Jimmy loads another round and fires at the rhino's feet again, "Well that's the last we should see of him," he says and then places his gun behind the door to retire for a long cool drink with the Fishers, Sonja and Mimi.

CHAPTER 4
THE BEAST WITHIN

The sun is just tipping its head over the horizon in Los Angeles as Carl Sinclair, the Fischers' boss is gently pulled from his slumber by a stimulating tingle through his genitals. Through bleary eyes he sees the covers moving slowly up and down across his lap.

Lifting the cover he smiles, "Morning darling," as he looks down at his fiancé Sarah, unable to respond as she has a mouth full of his penis.

"Hm hm," is her only response, briefly opening her eyes, batting her eyelids at Carl then closing them sensually as she slides a finger into his anus.

Carl sighs then lies back on the pillow with his arms behind his head, relaxing to enjoy the moment. Remembering a year ago, coming home alone, after a late night he would be waking up to an alarm at seven o'clock, rushing around to get dressed and leaving the house at half past with a slice of toast in his mouth to get to the office for eight. His cholesterol would be running extremely high from days of stress, stress, stress. The bliss of a carefree life in a loving relationship, leaving work at work and waking up to a blowjob every morning. A nymphomaniac fiancé that likes to be in control in the bedroom insisting that she does all the work, just the way he likes it. Sarah waits till she can feel his excitement rising then backs off to prolong his ecstasy kissing his lower abdomen. He can feel her lips pressing against his skin as she works her way slowly up his torso teasing with her tongue.

A mass of blonde hair emerges slowly from under the cover, "Morning sleepy head," a dulcet tone resonates as she pushes her lips against his before he can reciprocate.

Straddling him she reaches down between her legs to guide his penis into her then slides softly back onto it. Grinding gently back and forth, she pushes herself up off his shoulders, biting her bottom lip. Her head tilted and her eyes closed soaking up the euphoria as Carl reaches slowly to place his hands softly on her hips. Sarah, a rush starting up her spine, clasps his hands to bring them up onto her bosom forcing Carl to grip her breasts tightly as she starts to quiver and grind erratically across his lap. A gentle spasm turns into a jerk. The jerk turns into a thrash. The thrash turns into a frenzied maniacal flailing as screams echo throughout the house. Carl relaxes back in the knowledge that when she has finished she hasn't finished as she throws herself forward growling through fiery eyes, a shroud of blonde burnishing the evilest of looks, "Do your worst," she sighs as she launches herself onto her back dragging Carl on top of her.

Carl always relishes this bit in anticipation. Her only rule is that he leaves no marks where they can be seen, below the elbow, below the knee and above her shoulders. The rest is fair game so long as he doesn't leave a permanent scar. He's tried ramming into her as hard as he can almost doing himself a mischief. He's tried biting her, scratching her, even used sex toys on her, not the normal sex toys either, some of the real brutal ones but still hasn't managed to quell her inner animal. The night before he managed to secrete a couple of his ties onto the top bed post and hide them between the mattress and the headboard. Now he throws her hands back pulling the pillows forward to slip her hands into the ties.

Sarah grins wildly as she looks up at him tying her wrists, "Ooh this is new," she breathes, her body still oozing perspiration as she pants erratically in anticipation.

Carl presses his lips against hers then bites her bottom lip, gently pulling away to start kissing her neck. He moves slowly down her breasts like a tiger stalking its prey he bites her nipple gently grinding his teeth across it. Slowly he strokes between her breasts with his tongue till he comes upon the other nipple, pulling it into his mouth then retracting his head to lift her back by her breast clean off the mattress. Sarah squirms, moaning in rapturous delight as the tingle of pain sends a spasmodic ripple down her torso.

Carl presses his lips against her solar plexus rubbing his cheek down her torso on to her abdomen. Dropping his shoulder between her thighs while wrapping his arms around her hips to bury his head firmly into her vulva.

Sarah gapes her mouth to gasp a lungful of air as she wrenches her head back onto the pillow, arching her spine in euphoric pleasure.

Carl drops softly off the end of the bed while running his lips the full length of Sarah's leg placing her big toe in his mouth to gently suck upon it. Reaching down under the bed he reveals another tie. Pulling the tie up he places it over her ankle then pulls it tight.

Sarah lifts her head slightly to watch him tie her other ankle, "Now what are you going to do?" she asks, raising her eyebrows and widening her eyes with shameless expectations.

Carl stands bold, "Ooh I got me some ice-cream and strawberries and stuff," he says, crawling up to straddle her, "I think I might have me a breakfast feast right here," he adds, kissing his finger then pressing it against her breasts.

At that the phone rings. Sarah cringes, "Do not answer that."

Carl picks up the receiver then immediately drops it, "Sorted," he says as he starts for the door.

The phone rings again. He walks back to it and picks up the receiver, "GO AWAY!" he shouts down the receiver then slams it down, "If it rings again I'm just ignoring it," he decides as he heads down the stairs to the fridge.

His mobile bleeps to tell him he has a text, then the phone rings again. He grabs a tea towel and starts to drop tubs of ice cream and jars of syrup in it. Standing up he rushes to the phone as it is still ringing, "I'm busy!" he screams down the phone.

The voice on the other end just manages to say, "It's the F.B.I, check your texts," before he slams the phone back down.

As he re-enters the bedroom the phone starts to ring again, "Fuck 'em," he declares, dropping the towel full of goodies on the bed, "if it's a problem they can't solve themselves then they ain't much good... pffft F.B.I?"

Sarah grins at him, "You've had five texts since you went downstairs."

He opens the ice cream as the phone is still ringing. Trying to ignore the distraction he starts to spoon it on to Sarah's breasts. He receives another text.

Slamming the tub of ice cream on the bed next to her he picks up his mobile, "For fucks sake," he says, flicks it open, then stops rigid as he reads the text.

Sarah shakes her head frantically, "Don't do this to me, if the F.B.I ruins my ice cream sundae I'm going to kill someone."

Carl picks up the ringing phone with one hand and shows Sarah the text with the other.

Sarah starts to struggle as she reads, "$10,000,000 bounty for Pyah and Mark Fischer's heads," she bites at her bindings, "untie me."

Carl reaches across with his free hand and unties one of Sarah's hands as he talks to the F.B.I., "Who placed the bounty?" he asks, bringing the phone closer to Sarah so she can hear.

The agent tells them, "We think it came from the De-fuer sister."

Carl puts the phone on loudspeaker then goes to untie Sarah's feet while Sarah unties her other hand. The agent asks where the Fischers are at the moment.

Carl looks at Sarah, "As far as we are aware they should be in Paris, France," he answers.

The phone is silent then, "Whereabouts in Paris, France?"

Carl shrugs at Sarah. Sarah shakes her head in disgust then tuts, "Four Seasons, George V."

The phone goes silent for a while, "I'm presuming that's a hotel?"

Sarah is in the bathroom cleaning the ice cream off herself, "YES IT'S A FRICKING HOTEL," she yells as she starts to pull the cases from off the wardrobe tops, "We'll get in touch with a friend of ours in London," she says, dragging clothes out of drawers, "you see if you can get us a flight out of here."

Voices can be heard in the background on the phone. "There is a long haul leaving for Lille, France in two hours so we're going to try to commandeer two seats for you. It's the best we can do. Our agent will meet you at the airport with your tickets good luck," the voice says, then the phone goes dead.

Carl sits on the edge of the bed staring at the text as Sarah slaps him on the back of his head, "You just going to sit there or are you getting dressed?"

Carl stands up, "Guess we're going to France then," he states, then heads for the shower.

Sarah throws the clothes in the cases, "You better make it a quick one," she calls as she starts to lay some fresh clothes out on the bed for them, "what do you reckon the weather will be like in France?"

Carl scrubs himself down quickly, "Better pack for cold," he answers, rinsing himself off, "best safe than sorry," he adds as he jumps out to dry himself.

When Carl comes back into the bedroom Sarah is still naked on the phone with Lacey as he walks over and gently slaps her across her buttocks.

She spins, "Not the right time," she scolds, scowling at him then turning back to the phone, "Oh he's still feeling randy and although I could definitely go a few more rounds with him I think we have bigger fish to fry."

Carl skulks around the bed hanging a pet lip off his face muttering to himself, "at least you got to cum once."

Sarah covers the receiver, "Did you say something?" she growls at him.

Carl looks at his feet, "Nope," he says, then picks up his boxers, a little boy lost demeanour all over him.

Sarah tuts then turns back to the phone, "He's sulking because his tractor didn't get a full service."

Carl can hear Lacey's raucous laughter over the phone, "I hope you disturbed her in a sound sleep or the middle of a shag."

Sarah hangs up the phone, "Here you might need this," she says, throwing a vest at him "Lacey say's its cold in Europe," she explains, then struts to the bathroom.

Carl slips the vest over his head, "What did she say about the Fischers?"

Sarah sticks her head back through the door, "She's got a friend in Interpol that's going to the hotel to check on them," she tells him, turning back to the shower, "and by the way it's two in the afternoon in London so she's at work. The only shagging she's doing is on a computer," she adds, giggling to herself.

Carl puts his trousers on, "More than I'm getting," he mumbles to himself.

Sarah's keen hearing picks up what he's saying, "You still griping?"

Carl sits on the bed to put his socks on, "No dear, just checking that I have two socks."

Sarah quickly showers then exits the bathroom still dripping, towel drying her hair as she walks over to her bedside cabinet to look at the clock, "We've got an hour and three quarters to make that flight so stop whingeing and get dressed."

Carl is stood fully dressed looking down at himself, arms outstretched, "I'm done while you're still posing around in your birthday suit."

Sarah throws the towel on the bed, "Are you going to be like this all the way to France?" she asks as she walks around the bed.

Carl backs into a corner terrified that she is about to kick the shit out of him, "No dear, I'll behave," he promises as Sarah stands right up against him invading his personal space in a menacing manner.

She stares right into his eyes, not a word spoken as he raises his arms and tries to back up through the wall. Still staring at him she reaches down to his fly to unzip it. His heart starts to race, all manner of evil running through his mind as he sees the calm fury of a woman scorned burning in those sadistic eyes. She reaches into his boxers as he twitches in submissive anticipation, adrenalin rushing through his veins contemplating the punishment that she is conjuring up, "Erm... I," his mouth dries as she places one finger over his lips pulling his penis slowly out of his trousers then slides down his body to kneel at his feet.

He looks down at her as she stares at it, "Honey, I-" her head snaps back up to glare into his eyes as the words retract quickly back into his head. "Oh shit," he mutters, closing his eyes to silently pray for some salvation.

Her stare slowly returns to his penis as she softly places her lips around it. Carl opens one eye and drops his gaze to see Sarah's head moving back and forth. He gasps a sigh of relief then slumps into a relaxed state of ecstasy as his penis becomes fully erect to reach a swift climax.

Sarah finishes him then stands proudly smiling, wiping her mouth, turning to strut back to her side of the bed. She gets dressed without a word as Carl checks his penis for damage before putting it away then finishes his packing, silently grabbing the passports to follow her out of the house into the car.

Carl puts the luggage in the trunk then gets into the driver's seat before speaking, "What's the plan?" he asks tentatively, wondering if they are still in boyfriend/girlfriend mode or employer/employee mode.

Sarah turns with an electronic pad in her hands, "We have to meet the F.B.I agent at the airport, once we land in France an Interpol agent will be at the airport to meet us to give us some Intel on the Fischers."

Carl relaxes in the knowledge that he is now in charge.

CHAPTER 5
ANYTHING FOR A QUIET FLIGHT

When they get to the airport a man gets out of a prominent black sedan then walks over to them, "Carl Sinclair?" he asks, holding his hand out to show an F.B.I. I.D to Carl.

Sarah takes the I.D, "Don't mind if I check that?" she asks, flicking her pad open to check the F.B.I database, "Yeah that seems legit," she concludes, handing it back to him.

Carl shakes his hand, "This is my personal security," he says, introducing Sarah, "Sarah Louis, she may be petite but trust me you mess with her and you die," he says, giving a little chuckle.

The agent shakes her hand, "Pleased to meet you," he greets, smiling, "my wife is about your size, we always say, good things come in small parcels but so do nuclear bombs and look at the devastation they cause," he adds, kissing her hand with in trepidation.

Sarah gives him a smirking leer of distain, "We're told you have some tickets for us?"

The agent reaches into his pocket to produce two tickets to Lille, "Your flight leaves in half an hour, the flight has already been called but we've put it on hold for you," he tells them as a buggy pulls up to take them to the gate. "Good luck," he says as he gets back in his car to drive away.

Sarah sits in the buggy, "Creep," she says, shuddering, "made my skin crawl," she continues as Carl sits beside her to put his arm around her.

She takes his arm from around her, "Let's keep this professional in public, if you don't mind Mister Sinclair,", she says, putting emphasis on the working relationship.

Carl puts his hands on his lap then leans across to whisper in her ear, "Pyah and Mark are members of the mile-high club you know."

Sarah's head snaps around "I DON'T THINK SO MATE," she yells, scorning him publicly, "you can get stuffed!"

Carl pouts, "I was just saying."

Sarah shuffles away from him, "I don't care what you were just saying," she starts, grimacing at him,

"*that* is one club I am NOT becoming a member of," she continues, patting his lap gently, "even out of office hours, so you can just dream on," she adds sternly, turning to look straight forward in the direction of travel.

Once at the departure gate they are swiftly boarded and taken to business class to be seated so the flight can get under way. The flight is quickly brought to cruising altitude. The seatbelt sign is turned off and while the pilot introduces himself the air hostesses do their rounds, making sure the passengers are comfortable. A hostess reaches Carl's seat, leans in to discretely hand him a note and asks if she can get him and his good lady anything from the trolley.

Sarah sniggers, "I'm his P.A but yes I would love a cup of tea, black, no sugar please."

The hostess reaches back to the trolley to produce a cup "Earl Grey?" she asks, lifting a box of tea bags.

Sarah nods happily, "Ooh yes that would be lovely, thank you."

Carl is still engrossed in the note that he was handed as the hostess leans forward, "Would sir care for an aperitif?"

Carl hands the note to Sarah, "Err, pardon?" he says, stumbling his words.

The hostess lifts a small bottle of whisky, "A drink before your meal?"

Carl looks at the hostess then down at Sarah's tea, "Erm, no thank you I'll just have a coffee, White, two sugars, thank you."

She hands him his coffee then a menu, "I'll come back when you're ready to order," she says, then walks to the seat behind them.

Sarah reads the note silently. It reads, *"We suspect your phones have been tapped and you're being followed. We are in first class and will be watching. Do not acknowledge us when you land. We are not here, if you know what we mean. Cramer and Fargo of the F.B.I."* Sarah brings out her pad and types, *"No mention of where we're going or anything related to our mission till we get into the hotel room,"* then hands it to Carl. He nods and drops her a wink. She rolls her eyes then shakes her head, silently sighing.

When they land at Lille, surprisingly they see no sign of Cramer or Fargo.

Carl whispers to Sarah, "Seems our friends have learned some stealth."

Sarah drops her head and closes her eyes in disgust. Walking ahead of him she tries to ignore the comment. They get a cab to the hotel while Sarah tries to make small talk keeping Carl away from the subject of their mission. Once in the hotel they are led to the penthouse suite by a bellboy. He puts the luggage on the bed.

Sarah quickly tips him then shuts the door behind him, "You're not too bright," she starts then her head snaps around as the bathroom door opens.

Cramer is standing with his finger firmly pressed against his lips. Sarah puts her hand over Carl's mouth before he can ask Cramer what he is doing here. Cramer beckons them both into the bathroom, closes the door behind them then turns the shower on, runs the tap and switches an electric razor on, dropping it in the sink.

"You made the reservation over the phone," he says, reaching into his pocket, "you even requested the penthouse. So, we got here first to scope it out," he explains, smiling smugly "just to see if it was bugged."

Sarah gives him a condescending look, "I think you're being a bit paranoid," she tells him, reaching to turn the tap off.

Cramer stops her, "Well we've found two up to now and Fargo is in the bedroom looking for more," he informs her, returning the condescending look, "so when you go back out there just act normal and talk about what you would normally talk about when you're on your own."

Sarah shrugs. "OK," she says, then walks back out of the bathroom.

Cramer turns the shower off, the razor off and the tap and then follows her.

Carl flushes the loo for good measure then follows "So honey, what's the plan?" he asks.

To his surprise Sarah spins, grabs him by the lapels and pushes him down on the sofa, "Well I was thinking we might get a little romance in before collecting the info from our friends," she says, straddling him.

Cramer shrugs and nods as he goes to the bedroom to help Fargo. Carl is dumfounded but couldn't say a word if he tried with Sarah smothering him with kisses. He pushes her back,

"Slow down girl, let me catch my breath first," he says, frantically pointing at the bedroom door.

Sarah bites his ear then whispers softly, "He said normal. For when we're alone."

He pushes her back again looking at her with terror in his eyes, "Hang on," he says, knowing that she means what she is proposing, "I don't think this is the right place or time for THAT," he argues, still frantically pointing at the bedroom door.

Sarah tilts her head, "OK," she agrees, then drags him up by his tie leading him to the bedroom, "Maybe you're right," she opens the door and waves at the two agents to leave, "this is the right place and who gives a damn about time," she says, pushing Carl down on the bed.

Cramer taps her on the shoulder then points at the bedside lamp showing her a listening device attached to its base.

Sarah nods while Carl tries to climb off the bed, "Oh shit," she breathes as she drags him back on then flings her arm across to smash the lamp against the wall.

Cramer stands on the bug then whispers in her ear, "Don't make it too obvious, there are two in the living area and another on the balcony."

Sarah holds Carl down and pulls Cramer close, "I'll leave those alone so they can hear what I want them to hear," she says, giving him the thumbs up then shooing him out of the room.

Carl pulls her in close, "OK he's gone can we get back to civilisation?" he asks, hoping this is a show she is putting on for the benefit of the two agents.

Realisation starts to dawn that this isn't a show for anyone as she drags his buttons off his shirt, "Now you just lay there like a good little boy and let me do my thing," she says, tearing his vest straight down the middle, "when I'm finished you can take up where you left off at our house."

Carl reaches up and pulls her down by her hair, "What about the bugs?" he growls as quietly as he can.

Sarah bites his neck, "If this place is bugged then our home probably was and if it was then this is what they'll expect."

Carl lies back, rubs his mouth with his hand "Oh shit, so you're going to have your wicked way with me."

Sarah sits up, smiles and nods. Carl lifts his head, "Right here? Right now?"

Sarah keeps smiling, nodding and biting her bottom lip as she drags his belt from around his waist, "You may need this in a minute," she says, placing it in his hand.

He throws his hands out to the side submissively, "Don't suppose there is any use in struggling?" Sarah shakes her head with the naughtiest of grins across her face as she pulls his trousers down, throwing them to the floor, then slipping his boxers off leaving him butt naked all except his socks. She licks his scrotum, running her tongue up his torso as she ultimately straddles his hips slowly gliding his penis into herself.

Carl knows at this point he has to just lie there, try to relax enough as to not climax but stay erect and let her do her thing, "No point in fighting it I suppose," he says as he pulls a pillow under his head.

She grips his wrists to pull them under her skirt forcing him to grip her panties then pulling them sideways to rip them off. He reaches beneath the front to sashay them gently out as she lifts off him before lunging down on him to grind forward with her pelvis. She then pulls his hands up to her breasts wrapping them over her blouse top so he can pop the buttons while she places her hands on his chest to support her lunges. He drags the buttons off one by one, launching them across the bed, then shimmies the blouse off her shoulders to fling it across the room. Sarah eyes are closed as if in a trance as she moans and sways in her own little euphoria. Carl reaches up to the front of her bra, heaving it forward, struggling to snap the elastic as Sarah reaches around her back, eyes still closed to unfasten it then lifts his hands onto her breasts as he grips tight to pull her forward into his mouth.

She moans with delight, "Bite," she says in a dulcet husky tone. Carl grinds his teeth across her nipple then sucks as much as he can into his mouth, bearing down with his teeth to allow them to rasp across it as he retracts away. She lifts to enhance the sensation of pain fused with pleasure as her body ripples to a climactic shudder exploding her juices from within.

Momentarily her sweat drenched body drops across Carl's as she gasps a few breaths, then she wraps her legs around his to haul him on top of her as she rolls on to her back. She grasps the belt off the pillow, binds her wrists with it and lifts them to the headboard, "Your turn," she says, giving him a sultry pout as she thrusts his pelvis against hers with her ankles.

Carl lifts himself up onto his hands to start driving into her with all the force he can muster. Her head slams into the pillow as her neck cranes backwards, "Yes... HARDER!" she yells as she slams her hips forward, "thought you were going to get ice cream," she adds, drawing back then lunging her hips to meet his thrust.

Carl bites his lip as he hammers into her, "In a minute."

There is a knock at the door. Sarah wraps her legs around his waist as he stops suddenly, "Ignore it," she says, trying to push him into her, "just fucking ignore it."

Carl drops forward on to her then starts to thrust, building speed as the door knocks again, "ONE MINUTE," he calls, trying to hold the grunt that's building in his lower gullet.

He carries on pummelling his groin against Sarah's, almost at the point of climax as the door knocks yet again, "I SAID IN A MINUTE!" he yells as his body starts to twist and writhe as he uncontrollably spasms through his ejaculation.

Dropping forward to relax in her perspiration he gasps one breath of elation as the door knocks again, "For FUCKS SAKE I'm coming," he says, lifting himself of Sarah, "can't you people just wait for two fucking seconds while a man enjoys the moment," he complains, storming towards the door.

He flings the door wide, his rage blinding him to the fact that he is still butt naked except for the socks on his feet, "Oh it's you," he says as he looks upon Lacey standing with one hand on her hip, the other draped by her side holding an electronic tablet.

Lacey gives him the once over, looking down his naked body then back up to his face, "Nice socks," she comments, raising one eyebrow.

The realisation hits him as he darts back behind the door for cover, "Shit," he says, looking for something to cover his embarrassment as his erection mizzles.

Lacey struts in past him handing him the tablet. Written on the tablet is *"I know the room is bugged"*. She tips her head slowly staring into the bedroom to watch Sarah endeavouring to untie her hands. She walks into the bedroom, flicks the buckle open on the belt, then walks back out as Carl rushes past her with the tablet pressed firmly against his genitals. She calmly walks into the breakfast area, "Don't mind if I make myself a cuppa, do you?"

Carl reaches into the wardrobe to get two dressing gowns, tossing one to Sarah then quickly donning one himself. A rosy glow is still on his face as he enters the living area, "I'll have one if you're making it," he says, trying to act nonchalant, "to what do we owe the pleasure?" he asks, placing the tablet at her fingertips.

Lacey pushes the tablet away with a tea towel, "It's ok you can keep it," she says, looking down at what he had covered with it.

He picks it back up to hand it to Sarah as she exits the bedroom, "I saw it," she says shimmying away from it.

She walks up alongside Lacey, "I'll have one too," she says, pulling her dressing gown tight around her neck, "if you don't mind, black, no sugar."

Lacey glances around at her, "Hmm I used to have a jumper that colour," she says, flicking Sarah's chin, "cute."

The pale pink flush on Sarah's face turns into quite a burnished glow, "Excuse me but I don't, well, I mean to say that's, err, you," she stammers, flicking her finger between Lacey and herself "no offence but I'm not one of those," she says, rushing her words then dropping silent in anticipation of the retaliation.

Lacey hands her a cup of tea, "Don't know what you're missing," she tells her, then sidles away with a smug grin on her face.

Carl picks up his cup, "Wouldn't mind seeing that myself," he comments, then slinks towards the bedroom as Sarah gives him the evilest of condescending glares.

Lacey starts tapping in her tablet then holds it up to Sarah. It reads, *"bet this is making good listening."* Sarah stops dead, shock all over her face, "SHIT I forgot all about that."

Lacey pats the sofa beside her to beckon Sarah to sit next to her. Sarah moves sideways across to a separate chair, "I told you I'm not that way inclined."

Carl walks out of the bedroom, "Forgot about what?" he asks with a confident debonair swagger.

Sarah holds the tablet up. Carl gives a conceited approving nod then sits on the arm of the chair next to Sarah, "Are you going to get dressed honey?"

Sarah stands up, "I think that's a dammed good idea," she says, giving Lacey a superior smile as she pulls her dressing gown back up around her neck.

Lacey stands, "Do you need a hand dear?"

Sarah's head snaps around, "Not bloody likely," she says, eyes wide, showing utter disgust at the mere suggestion. She scurries off to the bedroom making absolutely sure that the door is shut behind her.

Lacey makes small talk with Carl, her eyes firmly fixed on the bedroom door as Sarah reappears in her best business suit buttoned up to her neck with a skirt just above her knee.

She sits directly opposite Lacey, "So, where were we?"

Lacey sits forward, "Well, thought we could go for a coffee to discuss the situation," she says, peering straight up Sarah's skirt, "is that a set?" she asks, pointing between Sarah's legs.

Sarah looks to see where she is pointing, "Oh for Christ's sake have you no shame," she complains, getting up to storm into the bedroom.

Lacey shrugs, "Only wanted to know where you got it from."

Sarah whips the skirt off, "If you're referring to my underwear," she says, sticking her head back out of the door, "yes it's a set, sussy, bra and knickers from Spice."

Lacey blatantly stands, walks over to the door and sticks her head in, "Where's that then?"

Sarah is frantically pulling a pair of trousers up, "Shit, do you mind? Can't a girl get some privacy?" she says, struggling as the trousers ruffle on her thighs causing her to lose her cool, "it's in Los Angeles," she says quietly, tears starting down her cheek.

Lacey walks over to her, "Calm down," she says, lifting Sarah's chin, "I was only teasing," she adds, reaching down to gently unruffle Sarah's trousers, "first time I've seen the ice maiden defrost."

Sarah gives a snorted chuckle, "ICE MAIDEN?" Reaching for a tissue from the bedside cabinet she asks, "Who the hell came up with that?"

Lacey lifts Sarah's trousers around her hips, "That's Pyah's pet name for you," she tells her, tucking her blouse into them, "she used to call you it when you were best of enemies but it stuck," she explains, fastening the buttons, "yeah she means it with best of affection now. Trust me if anyone else calls you it they better start to run."

Sarah peers into Lacey's eyes, "You're serious, aren't you?"

Lacey nods, "That woman loves you the way only a sister could love," she says, putting her hands on Sarah's shoulders, "I envy you."

Sarah steps back in amazement, "Whoa, I thought she loved *you*?"

Lacey shakes her head, "No, she's *in* love with me, and Mark of course, but she would die for you."

Sarah's eyes fill and Lacey leans forward but Sarah swiftly puts her hand over Lacey's mouth, "No," she says, stepping backwards, "admiring my underwear? that's ok but what's inside it belongs to him," she adds, pointing towards the door.

Lacey shrugs "Can't blame a girl for trying?"

Carl pops his head around the door frame, "I don't mind sharing."

Sarah leans around Lacey, "Well I DO," she protests, giving him a stern look, walking towards him, then pushing him out of the door, "we are going for coffee," she says, turning to Lacey "Ain't that right?"

Lacey waves her on then follows silently as they leave the suite.

CHAPTER 6
KNOWING WHICH WAY THE WIND BLOWS

The hustle and bustle of the Parisian night life was just getting under way as seven pm came around. Sarah, Lacey and Carl decide to stroll down the avenue outside the hotel to a small wine bar Lacey spoke of.

Partway down the avenue Sarah stops to admire a picture in a tattoo parlour window as Lacey walks up beside her, "Wouldn't have took you for the kind that would like a tattoo?"

Sarah gazes at a picture of a geisha girl, "No I just like that picture," she says, tilting her head then looking down at her thigh, "mind you if I had the guts I wouldn't mind one."

Carl pops up behind her, "Go for it."

She pecks him on the cheek "Anything I want," she turns to Lacey "no matter what I say, if I want something he just agrees, or just gets me it."

Lacey puts her hand on Carl's shoulder, "You know she would look lovely in a gold-plated Lambo," she says, trying to hold back the sniggers.

Carl gives Lacey a serious kind of smile, "If she wants one then I would give a diamond encrusted Lambo," he says as he cuddles Sarah from behind, "I'd have to sell a few shares like but she's worth it."

Just then a gang of bikers, twenty strong, pull up in front of the tattoo parlour. The leader dismounts, then approaches the tattoo parlour, "Bonsoir Mesdames, Monsieur," he greets in a slightly English accent.

Lacey walks over to his bike, "Hayabusa? Nice."

A young girl sat pillion takes off her crash helmet, "You're English," she says, breeding spewing out of her English accent.

Lacey strokes the petrol tank, caressing the custom paintwork with her fingertips "You're a bit young to be a biker's moll," she observes, noticing the girl is only about fourteen maybe fifteen years old.

The leader walks around the other side of his bike, "This is my daughter," he says, presenting his hand for Lacey to shake, "Davis Shuanasi, as I said. My daughter is Paula Shuanasi. Pleased to meet another Brit. Where are you from, we hail from Notting Hill."

She shakes his hand, "Lacey Raven out of East Molesey, pleased to meet you."

Realising this is a well-bred man and his daughter, Sarah's prudish first impression dwindles unnoticed as she approaches the girl, "Sarah Louis," she introduces, offering a hand, "and what is a pretty young girl like you doing flying around France on a big bad bike," she says, cracking a smile.

The girl politely takes Sarah's hand, "Paula Shuanasi, pleased to meet you," she says as she dismounts the bike, "my dad doesn't go flying around. He obeys all of the laws of the road."

The rest of the bikers go towards a nearby wine bar while Davis and his daughter stand chatting to Sarah and Lacey. Suddenly a grey Peugeot van screeches to a halt in the street. The door of the van is slid open while two men armed with sub machine guns start to riddle the area with gunfire. Lacey grabs Paula, spinning her around, throwing her to the ground to lay on top of her, covering her to protect her from the gunfire. Sarah kicks Davis's legs from under him then throws him around her, dropping him to the ground as the bullets rip into her back pushing her down onto him. Carl dives behind a nearby car for cover. The van's door closes as its speeds off in a cloud of tyre smoke to disappear around a corner.

All of the other bikers come running out of the wine bar as Davis lifts Sarah's limp body to feel around her back where the bullets hit. Surprisingly he finds no blood as she starts to rouse.

She lifts her head, looking him straight in the eyes, "Kevlar," she explains, picking herself up off him to brush herself off.

Davis pushes himself up onto his elbows, "Nice move little lady," he compliments, making a twisting motion with his hands. He suddenly stops, looks under the bike, across to his daughter with Lacey laid motionless across her.

Paula tries to push Lacey off staring at her dad, "I think she's dead," she cries, as a stream of blood runs down from the middle of Lacey's spine on to the floor.

Davis jumps to his feet, "Don't move her sweetheart," he orders as he rushes around to check her pulse, "no, sweetheart, she's not dead but she is badly injured," he says, flicking his phone out to call for an ambulance.

He very carefully lifts Lacey as Sarah pulls Paula out from under her. Lacey gives a groan as Davis lowers her gently to the ground, "Shit that hurt."

Davis starts to apply pressure to the wound. Lacey's head turns to look up at him, "And so does that."

Davis smiles at her, "Sorry, hun, but I got to stop the bleeding."

Lacey drops her head onto the floor and closes her eyes, "Did anyone get the registration number of that fucking van?"

Carl's head pops up from the car he is hiding behind, "I did."

It isn't long before an ambulance arrives followed by a stream of police with Interpol in tow.

Davis pulls Sarah to one side as they load Lacey into the ambulance, "Under normal circumstances I could presume this had something to do with the mongrels I'm chasing but," he starts, tapping Sarah's Kevlar vest, "what with the Kevlar, Interpol, American and British accents, I'm guessing C.I.A maybe?" he continues, then swinging around to Lacey, "British secret service?"

Sarah gives him a wry grin, "Close, she's S.I.S but we," she says, pointing at herself and Carl, "are a privately-owned security firm," she tells him, pulling Carl in by the arm, "Davis Shuanasi meet Carl Sinclair, Carl Sinclair meet Davis Shuanasi."

Davis shakes Carl's hand with vigour, "Damn, Sinclair security," he says, pulling him in for a hug, "you looked after my niece Toyah Woodrow," he mentions, chucking Carl on the shoulder, "the singer, about three years ago, top job too, good man."

Carl smiles at him, then remembers who he is talking about, "Yeah my main man took that job, believe it or not that's who we're looking for now," he says, lifting his arms, "gone A.W.O.L. and has no idea there's a hit squad after him," he explains.

Sarah slaps him across the arm then looks away in disgust. Carl starts to walk towards the Interpol guys, "Guess I better shut up then?" he pouts, with his head hung low.

Sarah looks up at Davis, "OK, I'll show you mine if you show me yours," she says, then winks.

Davis gets her meaning, "Well my wife stumbled across an illegal arms deal purely by accident and they killed her for it," he explains.

Sarah slumps down on his bike, "Wow."

Davis sits beside her, "Now I'm hunting them down and they know it. That's what I assumed this was about," he says, waving his arm around at the debris, "an African group with some sort of French connection," he finishes, turning to face her, "your turn."

Sarah cautiously looks in his eyes, "OK," she agrees, standing up in front of him, "we took down an arms dealer about a year ago, killed him. Now his psycho sister wants revenge," she tells him, looking up at the sky, her eyes filling up, "that bitch has put a ten-million-dollar bounty on the head of my best friends and I have to find them before she does," she explains.

Davis pulls Sarah in for a cuddle, "Shit," he responds, patting her back, "you probably think this is stupid but have you tried to call them?"

Sarah pushes away from him, "Oh they've gone completely incommunicado, don't want to be disturbed for their first wedding anniversary," she sniffs, wiping the tears from her eyes, "all we know is they are SUPPOSED to be staying at the Four Seasons, George V hotel but they booked it and never turned up."

Davis stands up, "So what do these friends look like and what are they called?" he asks, beckoning one of his gang over.

Sarah takes out photos of Mark and Pyah, "This is them about four months ago, their names are Mark and Pyah Fischer."

Davis takes the photos, "Don't know about these two but a couple by the name of Fischer booked into the same hotel as we were staying at last night," he stares at the photos, "they had a similar look but she was nowhere near as bonny as your friend," he comments.

The other gang member approaches Davis as Davis turns "What did they call that hotel we were at last night?" he asks, handing him the photos, "she isn't the same woman as that arrogant bitch by the name of Fischer is she?"

The biker looks down at the photo "Les Jardins de la Villa and no, this one I definitely would, who is she?"

Davis grabs him by the lapel "A very good friend of mine," he snarls, then releases him.

The biker apologises then walks away. Davis takes a photo of the photo with his phone, "I'll keep my eye open," he promises, handing Sarah a piece of paper, "here's my phone number," he pecks her on the cheek, "you better go and see how your friend is," he comments, then stands their mesmerised by the photo of Pyah.

When the ambulance arrives at the hospital it's quickly ascertained that Lacey's wound is a through and through with no damage to any vital organs and the bleeding is nearly stopped but she will have to stay in overnight. Interpol stands guard outside her room while Carl and Sarah set off to the hotel, Les Jardins de la Villa.

While en route Sarah receives a call from Cramer, "I heard Lacey has been shot, how is she?"

Sarah smiles, "Oh she's ok, tough old bird that one. But don't you dare tell her I said that."

Cramer laughs down the phone, "My lips are sealed, any way we got a lead on Pyah's visa card."

Sarah stops him. "Don't tell me, Les Jardins de la Villa."

The phone is silent for a few seconds, "How the hell did you get that? Have you found them?"

Sarah shakes her head at the phone, "Sadly no. A reliable source tells me that apparently there are a couple of imposters using Pyah and Mark's names and we're on our way there to catch the bastard and find out what's going on."

Cramer can be heard shuffling paper, "OK how long before you get there? We'll meet you. Just give us ten minutes."

Carl and Sarah arrive at the hotel minutes later and sit outside waiting for Cramer and Fargo. As they are waiting a tall redhead and rather bland looking man exit a taxi to enter the hotel. Sarah gets out of the car, "Sod the F.B.I. I'm going in," she insists as Cramer and Fargo arrive behind her.

"Too late. Is that them?" Carl steps out of the car.

"Looks like it," Fargo steps in front of Sarah, "no point in going in there half cocked. We wait and follow them to their room. Then we can question them in private without a scene, OK?"

Sarah agrees as they walk into the hotel. They see the couple enter the lift as Cramer presents his I.D. to the desk clerk "That's the Fischers isn't it?" he checks, pointing at the lift as the lift door shuts.

The clerk nods as Fargo leans over the desk, "So what room are they in?" the clerk taps on the keyboard in front of him then spins the monitor pointing at a room number.

As they start for the lift Cramer turns back to the clerk, "If you want this to stay discreet you won't do anything until we leave, comprende? Including warning them."

The clerk nods, then resets his screen. As Cramer turns to follow Sarah he notices the bullet holes in her jacket, "What the hell happened here," he asks, stroking her back.

Sarah glances over her shoulder at it, "Moths. Fricking big moths."

Cramer shuffles up beside her, "OK, if that's what you want me to believe, but it's the first time I've known moths to use sub machine guns."

CHAPTER 7
RIDE 'EM COWBOY

Sarah hits him as they both start to snigger. In the hallway, just down from the room a maid is collecting laundry as Cramer approaches her to flash his badge, "You speak English?"

The maid stands up, "Oui monsieur."

Cramer points at the room, "Have you got a key for that room there?"

The maid glances down the hall, "Oui monsieur, I have a master key."

Cramer takes it from her, points at an open door then draws his gun. The maid scurries into the empty room as the four approach the room with the imposters in it. Cramer uses the electronic key to quietly open the door then sidles in followed by Fargo, Sarah and Carl bringing up the rear. Two coats are strewn across the floor followed by his pants, her skirt his shirt her blouse then her bra leading to the bedroom door.

The door is slightly ajar as Cramer pushes it slowly fully open to reveal her pants laid on the floor next to his boxers and socks. She is strapped to the bed, face down with a pile of pillows under her abdomen, raising her in the middle while she thrashes, screaming, "Yes, yes, yes, big daddy, shove it up there. Ram it in," as he is taking her from behind.

Slapping her buttocks with all his might while holding his other hand aloft shouting, "Yeeehaa ride 'em cowboy."

Cramer notices the man is wearing a holstered six-shooter. Pointing his gun directly at the man's head, Cramer pushes the muzzle against the man's neck and pulls the hammer back. The man stops rigid slowly raising his other hand above his head while Sarah walks around the bed to crouch down where the woman can see her "Mrs Fischer I presume?"

The woman tries to look back at the man, "Err what's going on honey?"

Sarah pull her gun and places the barrel about two inches in front of the woman's face, "I asked you a question."

The woman looks cross eyed at the end of the gun, "Mrs Fischer, well yes and err well actually no," she starts to pull at her restraints as tears of fear run down her cheeks, "Look lady I just get paid to do this. That Mrs Fischer paid me because I look like her. All I got to do is hang around Paris pretending to be her for a couple of weeks. Whatever you want her for it has nothing to do with me," she pleads as the colour drains from her face, "she said she needed to disappear for a while, that's all, gave me her credit card and told me I could spend five hundred bucks a day no more. I'm just doing my job. Please don't kill me."

Sarah tuts into the air, "I'm not going to kill you," she says, putting her gun away, "I'm her best friend and I need to find her NOW!"

The colour starts to come back into the woman's cheeks, "You're not going to kill me?"

Sarah shakes her head, "Nope, just need to know where they are."

The woman wipes her nose on the sheets, "She didn't tell us. I swear."

The guy coughs, "I did see a map with Gibraltar and Africa marked off, sticking out of her purse."

Cramer pushes the barrel into the guys neck, "Well you better keep that to yourself," he warns, then holsters his gun. "Oh by the way I would lose the I.Ds because there's an assassination squad looking for the Fischers," he says lightly then turns to walk out of the room, "y'all have a nice day now."

Sarah bends down to the woman's face, "Where's the credit card?"

The woman points at her bag on the bedside table, "In there."

Sarah finds it quickly, then pockets it while she leaves the room, "Bye y'all."

All she can hear as they leave the hotel suite is the woman screaming, "Don't just sit there crying, untie me you fucking freak."

Sarah soon catches up with Cramer, "What the hell did you tell them all that for?"

Cramer stops and turns to Sarah, "If an assassination squad finds them do you think they're going to ask questions before identifying their dead bodies?"

Sarah looks back at the room, "You think that the killers will still assume that THEY are the Fischers?"

Cramer just nods then walks on as Sarah pauses, "OH SHIT."

Carl stops to wait for Sarah and Cramer then links arms with Sarah, "You do realise who you're here with?"

Sarah stops dead unlinking arms with Cramer, "It's ok, you go ahead we'll catch up," she tells him, then turns to Carl, "Damn, do I see a little green-eyed monster rearing its ugly head?"

Carl puts his hands on his hips, "NO, you see a fucking jealous fiancé making sure his fiancée isn't about to fuck some jumped up agent."

Sarah gives a very wide smile "Lacey is an agent and you were willing to let me fuck her."

Carl places his hand in front of her "Whoa that's totally different. She's a woman and she ain't going to be sticking her dick up you."

Sarah laughs out loud, "Trust me, she'd probably stick more than a dick up me. Probably comes with batteries like."

Carl storms off, "I'm not having this conversation."

Sarah stands fast, "I'm teasing…oh!" she says, then starts to walk after him "I'm just flirting. If I can charm a gay, then I can charm anyone."

Carl stumbles as he tries to stop and turn at the same time. Sarah laughs as she stops, placing one hand on her hip, "You got more chance with Cramer than I ever had."

Carl's eyes widen, his mouth agape, "He?" he asks, pointing back at the lift doors, "nahh?"

Sarah nods smugly. Carl looks back then at Sarah, "But he's an F.B.I. Agent."

Sarah tips her head then raises her eyebrows pouting. Carl is lost for words, "You're imagining it, Cramer?" he protests, dropping his hand in front then letting his wrist go limp, "but he's like," he stutters, puffing his chest as he flexes his biceps "a proper man's man."

Sarah adopts a camp pose, letting her wrist go limp. Carl strolls back to her pretending to be in deep thought, "So do you reckon him and Fargo are, you know?" he asks, cupping his hands together and rocking them back and forth.

Sarah shakes her head "No, he's a closet gay," she says, then starts to make her way to the lift.

Carl scurries after her "What's a closet gay?"

Sarah stops, "He likes women and their company but is in denial to his attraction to men!" she spouts, then pulls him into the lift.

Carl puts his hand on his chin, "So you reckon he's not getting any either way?"

Sarah pushes the button for the ground floor, "Probably not. He's probably celibate."

Carl stares at the ceiling, "Wow," he mutters, then pulls Sarah into a cuddle.

Sarah kisses him, "So the plan now is, we go see how Lacey is, then you take me back to the hotel room and we really give them something to listen to," she explains but Carl seems confused. Sarah huffs, "You're going to shag me like you have never shagged me before and I'll take it as an apology."

A twinkle comes to Carl's eyes, "Sounds like fun."

Sarah rubs her hand across his dick, "Ice cream and all."

When they arrive at the lobby Cramer is waiting for them, "HI, I'm on the way to see Miss Raven," he greets, his hands firmly pressed into his pockets, "I was just wondering," he puts an anxious hand across his chin, "well I know this isn't really the time and all but is she seeing anyone?"

Carl turns to Sarah, "HAH," he says, a big smug grin across his face, "you were wrong."

Sarah puts her arm around his waist and digs her nails discretely into his side, "Just a second," she excuses, pulling Carl to one side, "you mention one word or even give an inkling of our suspicions and you ain't getting nothing, bud."

Carl tries to pull her hand off him, "But you're wrong, I wasn't going to say anything, but you're still wrong."

Sarah digs her nails in again, "No I'm not. It's a cover, trust me," she declares then walks back to Cramer, "we were just going to see her but if you want to go we'll wait for an hour. You can give her our regards," she tells him, patting him on the shoulder, "and no, as far as we know she isn't seeing anyone."

Cramer thanks them then scurries off to the hospital. Carl and Sarah walk to their car, trying to appear calm and serene.

CHAPTER 8
SUSPICION AND ICE CREAM

Once in the car Carl drives to the hotel as fast as he can. They virtually run all the way to the room. On entering the room Sarah grabs the "*do not disturb*" sign. Writes "*under no circumstances*" followed by "*if you want to kill us you'll have to wait*" across the bottom then places it on the outside of the door, "Just a precaution," she says as she swings a chair in front of the door, "You never know," she continues, taking her and Carl's phones to switch them off, "you got an hour, show me what you got!"

Carl rushes to the fridge and grabs a handful of tubs - ice cream, syrups and spreads - then comes back into the room.

Sarah has taken her jacket off, "Ooo this looks like fun," she sighs, closing her eyes with her arms outstretched, "hit me with it."

Carl drops everything but the ice cream on the chair, rips the lid off, sticks his hand in, and scoops a large dollop out. Sarah waits then opens one eye to see him fumbling, undecided as to what to do with it, "Err..."

Sarah grabs his hand and thrusts it down her bra, "Use your imagination man," she tells him, grabbing his other hand and placing both of them on her blouse top, "go for it."

He rips her blouse wide open, "YES!" he cries, digging into the ice cream again then shoving it down the other breast.

Sarah grabs him by the lapels as he pushes a hand full of ice cream into her mouth then pushes his lips against hers, reaching into the tub as he slops the mess all over her face with his mouth. She unfastens her skirt allowing it to drop to the floor. He rams his hand full of ice cream down her pants as she presses herself against him pulling his jacket down off his shoulders, "What about the syrup?" she breathes.

Carl reaches for the syrup, still trying to keep his mouth firmly pressed against hers while shaking his jacket off his arm. Sarah rips his shirt wide open as he presses against her, squeezing the syrup above them, allowing it to dribble in between their bodies as they frantically grip each other, hands flailing all over, spraying dessert everywhere. Sarah grabs him by his belt to drag him into the bedroom, ice cream dripping from her bra, running down her abdomen and over suspender belt to join with the mess oozing from her pants to run down her legs, "Feeding time me thinks," she purrs, giving Carl the dirtiest of smiles as she throws herself on to the bed dragging him on top of her.

She wraps her legs around his waist, pulls his shirt down his arms to throw it across the room then unfastens his belt, flinging that the other way.

Unzipping his trousers, she teases, "Time for you to come out to play," she reaches down into his boxers to grip his extremely erect penis, "ooo we are excited, aren't we?"

Carl pushes his trousers and boxers down to his feet, then pushes them off with his feet flicking his shoes off in the process. She grabs the last of the ice cream to slap it on her torso as Carl slides down her body taking her pants with him. Starting at the bottom of her thigh he runs his tongue up the inside to her vagina, then slides his tongue gently into her as she wriggles with delight.

"I'll never look at an ice cream sundae quite the same again," she breathes, pushing his head in between her legs as she drops them over his shoulders.

Carl licks the ice cream off her abdomen then sticks his tongue in her navel, "I never noticed before but you have a very deep inny," he mumbles as she crunches her legs up around his head giggling, "shit that tickles."

He licks all the way up between her breasts onto her neck then slides his penis into her, "Guess what I'm going to do now?" he grunts, leering perversely into her eyes.

She grabs a mass of his hair, "Whatever it is make it quick we're running out of time."

Carl picks her up by her waist then flicks her over on to her stomach, grabs some pillows and starts to push them under her abdomen, "I'm going to ride you like a bucking bronco," he tells her, then heads towards the wardrobe for some ties.

Sarah turns to him, "We haven't got time to tie me down. I'll grab the headboard and pretend. Remember we have to get showered after this."

Carl sulks a bit then runs back to the bed, jumps on it behind her and rams himself in to her, "Yeeehaa, ride em cowboy," he crows.

Sarah pulls her legs up around the pillows, "JESUS that's my ass you fucking idiot!"

Carl stops, "Oops couldn't tell with all the ice cream," he says, then starts to pull out.

Sarah reaches around, "You liar, but seen as how you're in it just take it slow. Fuck this is weird."

Carl is stunned, "What, you're going to let me?"

Sarah nods, "The amounts of times I've stuck my finger up your arse, I'm surprised you haven't tried it before. So, make it quick but take it slow if you know what I mean?"

Carl pushes some ice cream down around his penis as he slowly slides it in to her. She groans and twitches, holding her hand against his thigh to make sure he doesn't enter too quick. Once he is all the way in he starts to retract.

Sarah grabs the pillows, "Urgghh shit, feels like you're pulling my guts out. Back in back in." Carl is silent but pushes forward again then back out.

Sarah stretches forward, "Faster," she instructs, so Carl starts to speed up.

The ice cream lubricates well as Carl can feel himself coming to a swift climax, jerking in a spasmodic fashion. Sarah grips tight on to the sheets, "Oh fuck, Jesus, didn't think it would be like this."

Carl drags himself out of her and drops over her body amidst the perspiration, ice cream and syrup. His legs have turned to jelly as his abdomen twinges, "I'm getting too old for this shit," he claims as he rolls over onto his side "no pun intended."."

Sarah stand up, "You haven't got time to loll about. We need to get showered before we go to the hospital," she reminds him, mincing out of the door, "shit that stings. I don't think we'll be doing that again," she adds as she heads into the bathroom to sit on the loo.

Carl staggers to his feet, overexaggerating the struggle into the shower. Sarah tuts at him, "When you have finished there, can you go to my bag and get my haemorrhoid cream?"

Carl nearly falls over trying to turn in the shower, "Haemorrhoid cream? What the hell are you doing with haemorrhoid cream?"

Sarah drops her head, "I use it on my eyes. It shrinks the bags under them but in this case I'll be using it for what its designed for…Stopping my ass from stinging."

Carl starts to giggle, "You use ass cream on your face?"

Sarah slowly looks up at him through evil eyes, "Do you want to keep that?" she asks sweetly, pointing down at his dick. Carl winces then covers it up with his hands. Sarah looks back at the floor, "Well hurry up and go and get it."

Carl quickly showers himself then grabs a towel on the run to her bag. He retrieves the cream then hurries back to her, "There you go dear, does it really hurt that much?" he asks but she just glares at him so he retreats to the bedroom to get dressed.

Soon they are all sorted and heading for the hospital.

Cramer arrives at the hospital to see Lacey conscious holding Davis's hand, "Oh I'm sorry I'll come back later," he says then turns to head back out of the ward.

Lacey sits up as Davis chases after him, "Hey man, you're not intruding. In fact, we were just talking about you," he says, putting his arm around Cramer's shoulders, "the lady in there has quite a thing for you."

Cramer stops and looks straight into Davis's eyes, "Don't shit me man… you were holding hands."

Davis smiles, "I was just thanking her for saving my baby girl's life, no one can replace her mother."

Cramer shakes Davis's hand, "Thanks man," he tells him, then walks back in the room to present Lacey with a bunch of red roses.

Lacey takes the roses, "Next you'll be asking me out on a date," she teases, giving him a sultry smile.

Cramer's face flushes, "Well, err, I, err."

Lacey puts the roses on the cabinet beside her, "I accept," she says, then beckons him closer with her finger.

Cramer leans cautiously across the bed. Davis stands up and discretely walks out of the room as Lacey pulls Cramer by his tie and kisses him, "As soon as this mess is cleared up, you and me?"

Cramer nods frantically, "But first I got some news, apparently the Fischers are in North Africa."

Davis hears him talking from outside the door, "You know, I might be able to help you there," he offers, walking back in the room, "my brother in-law is over there, chasing up the South African connection to my little problem," he explains, folding his arms, "I could give him a bell to see if he can help you?"

Lacey shakes her head, "Seems our problems are at different ends of a big continent... thanks but I wouldn't want to inconvenience you."

Davis walks over and takes Lacey's hand, "Apparently he may be chasing an arms convoy into North Africa so it won't be an inconvenience," he says, pecking her on the cheek, "anyway, he would probably, personally come and drop a thank you card off in your hand for taking a bullet for his niece," he adds as he pulls his phone out of his pocket then leaves the ward, "I'll go and get a coffee while you two young love birds have a chat," he declares, leaving Cramer blushing again.

Davis is mulling around the main entrance with his coffee when Sarah and Carl arrive, "See you may have tracked your friends to Africa?"

Sarah heads towards reception, "Don't suppose you know what ward Lacey is on?"

Carl stops to talk to Davis, "So how's things going with you?"

Davis shouts to Sarah, "She's on thirty-two," then turns to Carl, "I'm fine. Paula's fine and my brother in-law is going to keep an eye out for your friends in Africa. So, everything is just peachy at the moment."

Carl shakes his hand, "Well, we got to go. Catch up with you later, unless you're coming back to the ward?"

Davis declines the offer "I thought I would give Lacey and Cramer a moment," he explains.

At that Sarah stops and turns back to Davis, "Cramer is up there with her? And they're, you know, having a moment?"

Davis smiles and nods, "Oh, you should have seen the jealousy in his eyes when he caught me holding her hand," he says, shaking his head, "I had to quickly explain I wasn't interested. You should have seen the relief on his face," he goes on as he sits down, "yeah brought her a dozen red roses. Don't know where the hell he would get them this time of night like."

Sarah sits next to Davis, "Better give them a bit of time then," she concurs, patting the chair next to her, "come on you might as well sit and wait with us," she adds, looking at Carl.

Carl slumps down next to her, "You mean we could have, thingy, stayed back at the hotel a bit longer, if you get my drift?"

Davis leans forward to look around Sarah at him, "Were you two doing naughties?"

Sarah slaps him across the arm, "Do you have to?" she giggles, smiling through a blushed face.

Carl smugly smiles, "You have no idea."

Sarah slaps him across the arm, "Don't even think of teasing."

Davis slides forward on his seat turning to Sarah, "Well, I wouldn't have taken you for that type of girl."

Sarah slaps him across the arm again, "Stop it, you pair of bastards," she objects, then stands up, "I think that Cramer's had enough time," she decides, then hurriedly scurries towards the lifts.

Davis stands up and high-fives Carl, "You old dog, good on you," he congratulates as they casually saunter to the lifts.

Sarah pouts holding the door for them, "Well come on then or you're using the stairs."

When they get to Lacey's room Cramer is just kissing her goodbye, "I'll check on you before you leave," he promises, then heads for the door, blowing her a kiss on the way.

Sarah rushes to her bedside, "OK come on give," she starts, sitting on the bed next to Lacey, "what's with you and him? Are you an item? Is he coming to see you in England? Are you going to move to America?"

Lacey puts her hand over Sarah's mouth, "Whoa, slow down girl you'll have me wed with kids before I get out of this bed."

Sarah pushes Lacey's hand down, "Well I could go and get a priest, you are Catholic aren't you?" she offers, sniggering like a schoolgirl.

Lacey gently taps her on her lap, "Stop it, you bitch," she says, sniggering back.

The doctor insists that Lacey stays in for observation overnight but will be allowed out in the morning so long as she takes it easy. Carl and Sarah make plans to go to Africa for all three of them, totally against the doctor's recommendations.

CHAPTER 9
BLOOD LUST

The sun is blistering high in the African sky as it strikes noon. All the shutters are closed while shades are lowered. Even the animals are taking a siesta out of the searing mid-day heat.

Mark turns to Sonja, "Don't suppose we could have a shower? Looks like we ain't going nowhere till it cools down a bit."

Sonja waves at Mimi, "Can you show these good people to an empty room dear?"

Pyah stands up, "Won't be a mo, just going to get a fresh set of clothes," she says.

But as she starts for the door Sonja stops her, "There's a couple of kimonos in my room should fit you and your husband," she offers, leading her behind reception into her living quarters.

Mimi takes Mark's hand to lead him up the stairs, "Would you like a hand?"

Mark stops dead, "I think we better wait for my wife if it's all the same to you," he says, pulling his hand away.

Mimi gives him a sultry look, "You're not shy, are you?"

Mark takes a few steps back, "Err no," he fumbles, finding himself in un-chartered territory, "it's just that I like my women a little bit more mature," he tries, trying to be as tactful as he can, "I'm not sure what the laws regarding minors are in this country but that's a little bit more than frowned on where I come from."

Mimi huffs then walks over to her clutch bag laying on the bar, takes out her passport, and shoves it into Mark's hand, "Take a look at the birth date."

Mark looks to see she is in fact twenty going on twenty-one years of age.

She pulls it back off him, "That's why the men like me, they think they are getting a fourteen-/ fifteen-year-old."

Mark walks around her, "WOW, sorry, but it still wouldn't feel right," he says, then sidles towards reception.

Mimi follows him slinking like a snake, teasing him with a girlish chuckle, "A man with morals, now that's a first."

Pyah comes out to see Mark backing up, trying to climb over reception backwards, "Oh aye, what's going on here," she asks with a devilish smile on her face, "you been charming the children now?"

Mark smirks at her, "She ain't no kid, she just looks like one. I've told her WE are not interested."

Pyah runs her finger across his chin, "But it's ok to eye up a young maid then?"

Mark raises an inquisitive eyebrow, "Oh, you have a good memory when it pleases you."

She walks in front of Mimi, "So how old are you?"

Mimi passes her the passport, "Twenty," she says, pointing at the birth date.

Pyah spins, "She's legal, cute and willing, what's your problem?" she asks, laughing out loud.

Mark's face turns serious, "You would actually let me go with a prostitute? No way I'm ever going to pay for it."

Mimi steps out from behind Pyah, "Oh I think I could give you a freebie," she says, looking over to Sonja.

Sonja smiles and nods. Pyah strokes Mimi's cleavage, "You telling me you would turn down the chance of this nubile young ebony flesh for a few morals?" she asks as Mimi provocatively lowers the front of her dress.

Mark struts towards the stairs "Look, I only want a shower, a cold shower quite frankly," he says, putting his hands in his pockets, "you, WOMEN, do what you want but keep ME out of it," he huffs, then proudly walks up the stairs with his nose in the air.

As he gets to the top of the stairs Pyah throws a kimono at him, "You may need this."

He picks it up then turns to them, "I don't suppose you're going to tell me which room I'm going to?"

Sonja steps forward, "Number six is empty, hun, third on the right," she tells him, then starts to chuckle, turning to Mimi and Pyah, "you two are wicked."

Pyah leans on the reception desk, "Oh, I'll just wait to give him time to get undressed then take her up with me," she says, pointing at Mimi.

Sonja turns back to the door behind her, "I'm keeping well out of this," she declares as she stops and turns with an evil grin, "unless you want a hand," she adds, then shakes her head, opens the door to walk through it and closes it behind her.

Mark enters room six rather cautiously, checking behind the door, "Hello, anybody there?" he asks, pushing all the doors open in the room. Once he is satisfied that no one is occupying the room he drops the kimono on the bed to start to get undressed, walks into the bathroom, turns the shower on and steps in, "Ahhh peace at last," he sighs as the warm water trickles down his body soothing as it goes.

He can smell the pungent odour of that rhino embedded in his skin and his hair. On the shelf is a complimentary tube of shower gel, shampoo and conditioner. He reaches across, takes the shower gel, picks up a fresh scrunchy and suds himself down. Then he picks up the shampoo, squirts it on his head and starts to rub it in.

All of a sudden another pair of hands reach in, takes the scrunchy and starts to wash his body. His eyes are full of soap as he carries on washing his hair, "Wondered how long it would take you?" he says, then spins as a voice that he recognises but is not Pyah's answers,

"Well, couldn't let you think I was abandoning you."

Mark backs into the corner as he can hear Pyah giggling in the background, "Get her out of here," he says as he tries to rub the soap from his eyes while covering his genitals with a tiny flannel, water splashes across his face as the soap goes in one eye, "Shit, that hurts," he moans; Mimi is still rubbing his leg with the scrunchy, "will you get off me woman?" he demands, pushing her hands down.

Mimi stands with her hands on her hips, "Oh so NOW I'm a woman, what the hell are you complaining about, you're, we're not doing anything illegal."

He turns to face the cubical wall, "It still don't feel right."

Mimi rubs his buttocks, "So, keep your eyes closed and think of England."

He puts his hands on the wall above him, dropping the flannel to let the water run over his face in submission, "You can wash me, that's it."

Mimi turns to Pyah who gives her the nod then winks at her. Pyah strips off to climb in the shower with Mark, "Don't know what all the fuss is about," she says as she notices Mark is not in the least bit excited. "Ohh looks like someone is asleep," she coos, taking his penis in her hand.

Mark slaps her hand, "And he is staying asleep thank you," he says, turning to Mimi, "a wash, that's it."

Mimi's eyes widen as she sees the size of his manhood, "Oh my god, never seen one like that before," she says, swallowing "even my country men would be jealous. Shit, you're huge."

Pyah taps her on the shoulder, "You should see it when it wakes up," she says, spreading her hands to about two feet and smiling.

Mimi licks her lips then strips down to her bra and knickers, "Wouldn't want me to get them wet now would we?" she says as she rubs her body against Mark's back, reaching around for the shower gel.

Pyah strips off completely, steps in, then sidles around to the front of Mark, kissing him seductively. Mark keeps his hands firmly planted on the tiles in front of him, "Now, now, not in front of the kids."

Pyah chuckles, "This really does bother you doesn't it? Told you, she ain't no kid."

Mark twitches nervously as Mimi suds his back, then slides her breasts down to his buttocks. She washes his legs with one hand while discretely slipping her bra off with the other.

As she runs her soaped hand up the inside of his thigh Mark reaches down to stop her, "I think that's my wife's territory thank you."

Mimi puts her hands on Marks shoulders "Is this ok?"

Mark relaxes a bit, "A... ha," as Pyah crouches down to wash the front of his legs, while reaching around to pull Mimi's panties off.

Pyah starts to rub his penis as Mimi pushes her body against his spine, wrapping her arms around to his chest.

Mark stands rigid, "Please tell me she has still got her underwear on?"

Pyah shakes her head slightly as she pops the end of his penis in her mouth. Mark steps back slightly, pulling away from Pyah then spins to see Mimi naked, closes his eyes, then turns quickly back to Pyah, "Oh shit... oh shit, shit, shit, shit, I've been ambushed."

Pyah wraps her arms around him, "Relax," she says, pecking him on his lips, "you're acting like a little virgin," she adds as Mimi wraps her arms around him from the back, kissing him on the shoulder blade.

Mark twitches again, "It's alright for you two, I feel like an antelope caught between two lions."

Mimi gently bites his shoulder, "Lionesses, if you don't mind," she corrects, cautiously moving her hand down to his penis as it comes up to meet her hand, "ooo seems someone has eventually woken up."

The door to the bathroom slowly opens. Sonja is stood watching, "Looks like someone is having a good time," she greets, placing one hand on the door frame, "enough room for a little one?"

Mark pushes his dick down, grabs a towel, then scurries out to the bedroom, "That's it, out, ALL of you," he demands, assertively pointing at the door "all I want is a bloody shower, what does a man have to do to get some peace around here?"

Sonja slinks towards him, "You're not shy are you?"

Mark picks up a pillow, "No, I AM NOT," he cries, threatening her with the pillow, "I just want a bloody shower, IN PEACE, ON MY OWN, thank you," he rants, pointing at the door again, "now all of you, that includes you," he adds, pointing at Pyah, "OUT."

Pyah and Mimi pick up their clothes and towels, then skulk towards the door pretending to sulk, then run out of the room giggling as Mark walks after them turning to Sonja, "You too."

Sonja slinks up to him, taps his bum, then walks out of the room turning to wink at him, "You don't know what you're missing," she says, then drifts down the hall while Mark shuts the door and locks it.

Sonja turns to Pyah, "That room's empty," she says, pointing at another door, "if you want to finish your shower off."

As Pyah opens the door Mimi walks up to her, "Would you like a hand?"

Pyah tips her head, "What the hell, why not?" she decides, stepping to one side to let Mimi go in first, "I know you're of age and it's been a while since I had some young nubile fresh meat."

Mimi looks into her eyes, "Don't say it like that, sounds as if you're about to devour me."

Pyah lifts Mimi's chin, "I might yet," she says, pecking her on the lips, "I am hungry," she adds, smiling provocatively.

Mimi sniggers then walks into the room while Pyah shuts the door behind her. Sonja walks past the door on her way downstairs, taps on it to say, "I want her back in one piece if you don't mind," then glides down the stairs, smiling.

Pyah throws her clothes on the bed but Mimi has dropped hers by the door as she walks to the bathroom to turn the shower on.

Mark walks into the shower checking the door cautiously before relaxing to a nice warm solitude of silence. Once he has finished he dresses, then leaves the room to go to the bar for a relaxing brandy. On his way past the room that Pyah and Mimi are occupying he can hear Pyah singing '*Ebony and Ivory*', he strolls past smiling.

Pyah stands in the shower facing the controls while Mimi stands with her breasts laying against Pyah's spine. Pyah turns the control from the drench setting to the waterfall setting allowing the water to cascade between her body and Mimi's. Mimi reaches around Pyah to pick up a large sponge from the rack with some shower gel. Soaping the sponge, she then starts to caress Pyah's breasts, allowing the suds to gently run down Pyah's torso into her waiting hand.

She slowly lifts it to Pyah's other breast, where she cups and fondles her nipple. Pyah reaches behind to pull Mimi's hips in close, pushing her buttocks against Mimi's hips. Mimi kisses Pyah's shoulders, allowing the water to run off them into her waiting mouth to taste Pyah's scent as she gently moves her breasts against Pyah's spine. Pyah slowly turns to meet Mimi's gaze as she presses her lush red lips against Mimi's, sharing the water in her mouth as their tongues entwine. Pyah lifts her hands on to Mimi's shoulder blades pulling her up into a full embrace as Mimi runs her hands along the length of Pyah's spine, lifting them through Pyah's hair, pushing her tongue in to Pyah's mouth. Pyah sets one arm around Mimi's upper back while gliding the other down her spine, over her lumbar then in between her buttocks to gently slip a finger in to Mimi's anus. Mimi's eyes widen but then close to accept the unexpected pleasure, lifting her legs to wrap around Pyah's waist. Having Mimi's weight now firmly balanced on her hips, Pyah's hands are free to roam as she ventures around to Mimi's tiny breasts then down to her vagina, teasing her clitoris as Mimi starts to sway with delight, rocking back and forth to Pyah's rhythm. Pyah comes away from Mimi's mouth to caress her neck with her lips, softly biting, pulling Mimi's flesh into her mouth to taste it. Mimi cranes her neck to allow Pyah full access, akin to a vampire's prey under the spell of the night. Pyah's thoughts are running on auto pilot as a carnivorous longing begs her to bite down hard through Mimi's jugular. Pyah retracts for the fear that she might, then places Mimi against the cold tiled wall lifting her by her thighs to gain access to her breasts. Pyah draws the whole of Mimi's breast into her mouth resisting the urge to bite but suckle, trying desperately to get the vampiric thoughts from her head.

Pyah's body surges with hot blood coursing through her veins, tempting her, *"what would it be like?"* she thinks, her eyes raising to Mimi's exposed throat, vulnerable to an unsuspected attack. Pyah closes her eyes pulls her mouth slowly from Mimi's breast, leaving only the nipple to suckle on while gently sliding two fingers into her. Mimi softly rocks as she bears down on Pyah's hand then groans as she drops forward onto Pyah's head tightening her embrace as she orgasms to a sultry quiet whimper pulling Pyah's head into her bosom. She lifts Pyah's face to kiss her on the forehead then glances deep into Pyah's eyes as Pyah closes them and drops her head low as if in shame.

Mimi brings her legs straight as Pyah allows her to glide tenderly to the floor, Pyah's head still bowed low, Mimi steps back, "What's wrong?"

Pyah gazes deep into her eyes, "Nothing," she says, chucking Mimi on the chin, forcing a smile before turning to exit the shower, "I just…. I think I'll save it for Mark."

Mimi pulls her back by the arm, "Is it because you didn't finish?" she asks, tipping her head, "'cause if it is I think I can soon remedy that," Mimi can feel Pyah trembling as Pyah moves back in to press her lips against hers, "are you sure you're ok?"

Pyah stands with a smug smirk, "If you must know, I've never had an experience like that before," she says, stroking Mimi's face, "where I've had to stop myself from doing something I might regret."

Mimi drops her hands onto her hips, "Like what?"

Pyah starts to walk away then turns, "Like eat you," she says, laughing towards the ceiling as she picks up a towel to dry herself.

Mimi stands silent not sure if Pyah is being serious, "I hope that's just lust I see in your eyes?"

Pyah slinks towards her, "Oh its lust, my dear," she says, a condescending quiver on her lips, "but not the type of lust you're thinking of."

Pyah picks up her Kimono, throws it around herself then glides out of the room leaving Mimi puzzled and confused.

CHAPTER 10
UNREQUITED PREY

Mimi gets dressed in deep thought, while Pyah graces the stairway to find her husband sat at a dining table in his kimono. A cup of tea before him and a docile faraway grin of pleasure spread across his face. Completely unaware of Pyah's approach, in a little world of his own. Pyah wonders if he has taken something but then hears something. As she approaches she lifts the table cloth that drapes to the floor to find Sonja on her knees with Mark's penis deep in her mouth. Sonja gives Pyah a sideways glance, forces a smile, then gives a thumbs up. Pyah gives a consenting nod, drops the cloth then heads towards the kitchen to make herself a coffee leaving Mark blissfully unaware of her presence.

As Pyah is pouring her brew she hears a familiar grunting as Mark is brought back to the world with an ecstatic ejaculation. Pyah peeks around the door to see Mark slumping over the table sweating profusely, grunting through a strained expression of burgundy pleasure. His hips thrusting forward in time with the agitated twitching of his head as he grips on to the table cloth dragging it slowly towards him before relaxing his head on the table in front. Sonja crawls out from under the table on hand and knee then stands wiping her mouth with her fingertips to place them in her mouth in the most provocative of fashions, turning to meet Pyah's gaze. Both ladies smile with raised eyebrows then turn. Pyah finishes making her coffee as Sonja kisses Mark on the forehead, then heads for reception only to bump into Mimi exiting the staircase.

Mimi follows Sonja behind reception, "Looks like you enjoyed that as much as he did."

Sonja links arms with Mimi, "He's got a hell of a cock on him," she says, leading her into her living quarters, "so how was it with Mrs Fischer?"

Mimi unlinks their arms, "She's a really good fuck," she confides, arriving at a table with a decanter of brandy and a set of glasses on top, "I've never felt quite so vulnerable though," she adds, pouring two glasses.

Sonja sits on her chaise lounge, "What do you mean, vulnerable?" she asks, patting the cushion beside her to invite Mimi to sit.

Mimi sits and hands her the glass, "Well, the whole experience felt dangerous and out of control, I don't mean frantic frenzies, out of control," she explains, sipping at the brandy, "I mean, well, it felt like she was going to do something all the way through it."

Sonja sits forward, "Like what?"

Mimi shrugs, "That's it, I don't know, it's hard to explain, but when we finished I looked into her eyes and I know this sounds silly but I swear for a moment at the back of her eyes I saw the hand of Satan reaching out from the depths of hell."

Sonja's eyes widen as her jaw drops. Mimi sniggers, lifting Sonja's jaw, "Funny how I felt no fear, just a sense of anticipation, as if I wanted it," she continues, sipping at her brandy again, "it was probably just my imagination going into overdrive in the heat of passion."

Sonja takes a large drink, "Yeah, let's just hope so," she says, gulping at her brandy, "last thing I want is to start believing in demons, ha ha," she adds, forcing a laugh, "she did say she might eat you," she remembers, relaxing to the thought that Pyah was probably winding Mimi up.

Mimi turns to gulp at her brandy, "She did, didn't she? Nahh," she dismisses, shaking her head as she realises that Sonja is pulling her leg. They both giggle, finish off the brandy and Mimi gets up to pour another, "I'm not the one eating someone else anyway," she mutters under her breath.

Sonja flicks her legs up on the chaise lounge, "I'd be careful missy or you might find yourself sleeping alone tonight."

Mimi turns with a sultry look, "What?"

Sonja waves at the brandy, "I heard what you said," she says, beckoning her to bring the brandy over, "I'm not that deaf," she points out, smiling a knowing smile.

Mimi sits next to her and cuddles in like a small child as Sonja wraps her arms around her kissing her on the top of her head, "Mamma's little baby."

Pyah brings her coffee to the table next to Mark as he has just caught his breath, "Would you like to be alone with your debauchery or would you like a coffee?"

Mark raises his head slowly, "I've just had a very pleasurable experience," he gloats, a smug grin across his face.

Pyah sets her coffee on the table, "I know, I saw the stupid faraway look on your face," she says, sipping at her coffee, "she still only got half of it in though."

Mark sits bolt upright, "How the hell?" he asks, taking Pyah's cup, sipping from it then handing it back.

Pyah sniggers, "While you were in the land of the blow job fairy I took a look under table to see Sonja with her teeth out and your cock in her gob."

Mark drops his head into his hands, "Oh you're joking, she had her dentures out?"

Pyah nearly chokes on a mouthful of coffee, "No but it brought you off your little cloud for a second."

Mark shakes his head violently, "Oh got that image in there now... you had to ruin it didn't you," he complains, slapping himself on the forehead, "so how was it with the CHILD?" he asks, trying to poke back to regain some sort of edge.

Pyah sips her coffee, smiles a shameful smile, then looks at the floor silently. Mark gets up from his chair, walks around her and lifts her chin, "Whoa, what the hell happened?"

Pyah bites her lip, "Well... Nahh it doesn't matter," she decides, then pulls away from him. #

Mark crouches down in front of her, looking up into her eyes, "OK give, what have you done?" he asks, a fatherly overtone to his voice.

Pyah places the cup down and slips her hands in between her legs, "I nearly bit her."

Mark stares blankly, "And?"

Pyah shakes her head, "NO, I really nearly bit her," she worries, tears forming in her eyes, "I had her jugular in my mouth and all I wanted to do was rip it from her neck and drink from her flesh."

Mark steps back, stumbling on to his bum, "Whoa, you actually wanted to," he places two fingers to his neck, "and," he lifts his hand to his mouth as if to drink, "like a vampire?"

Pyah nods shamefully as Mark stands, walks towards reception and picks up a chain he noticed earlier, "Catch," he says, tossing the chain towards her.

Pyah catches the chain, a silver crucifix dangling from it, she tips her head in puzzlement then looks at Mark. Mark raises his eyebrows, "Just checking."

Pyah realises what he means, smiles a girlish smile, then launches it back at him, "You better watch yourself matey or I might have your blood by the end of the night."

Mark places the chain back behind the desk, "The amounts of times I have had your neck in my mouth and thought, what the hell? Wonder what it would taste like?" he tells her, walking back to her, "it's a natural thing, I hope, either that or we are both potential VAMPIRES," he adds, laughing a dirty guffawing laugh as he pulls her into a warm embrace, "silly bugger."

Pyah slaps his butt, "Don't tease, I've never had that before."

The night is closing in as Jimmy walks into the dining room "Well your van is all cleaned, repaired and ready to roll," he says, looking out of the window at the sunset, "but I wouldn't suggest setting off till morning. That sky looks full. Possible storm on the way."

Pyah walks to the window, "How much would you say Sonja would let us have a room for the night?" she asks, turning to Mark, "unless you would like to stay in the motor home tonight dear?"

Mark shrugs, "Makes no difference to me," he says, waving towards reception, "whatever takes your fancy I suppose."

Jimmy walks to reception, rings the bell and waits. Sonja appears, "And what can I do for you, you randy old git?"

Jimmy gives her a leering once over, "Not that I wouldn't but it's our guests," he says, raising his eyebrows, "they're wondering how much for a room for the night?"

Sonja places her chin on her hand as Pyah and Mark approach, "Well the usual fee would be fifty dollars a night but seeing as though you have given so much pleasure to my baby and me you can have it for twenty-five," she declares.

Jimmy raises his arms in disgust then turns away, "I would have thought you would give them a freebie," he says, turning to give her a dirty look as he leaves, "tight fisted old battle axe."

Sonja looks at Pyah and Mark, "Girl's got to make a living," she says, shrugging as she spins the register and hands them a pen, "you could always sleep in that van of yours," she points out, looking around them at the night sky, "but I wouldn't want to be out there on a night like this."

Pyah and Mark walk towards the door, look out at a clear red sky, then Mark turns back to Sonja, "Yeah, Jimmy said there's a storm brewing but I can't see it."

Pyah steps forward, "You're not just saying that to get us to stay, are you?"

Sonja tips her head, lifts the pen and hands it to Mark, "It's completely up to you, I'll say no more on the matter."

Pyah pushes past him, "What the hell, it's only twenty-five dollars and we get to sleep in a big comfortable bed," she reasons, grabbing the pen to sign the register.

Mark takes the pen off her, "Who said you're going to get any sleep?" he asks, then signs in, "we'll still have to go and get some fresh clothes out of the motor home for the morning though," he says, and off they set.

When they come back, Sonja takes them upstairs, along the hallway bypassing both of the rooms they have already seen into another room set aside for VIP's and dignitaries, "This is our presidential suite," she explains as she opens the door to a room with an emperor size four poster bed draped in black lace edged with red satin.

Pyah stands gobsmacked for a moment, "Wow, now this is what I call a bedroom," she comments, turning to Mark, "I want one."

Mark blows air through his teeth, "And where am I supposed to get the money to afford it let alone find the space to fit it?"

Sonja strokes Marks face as she leaves them to it, "Enjoy... oh and if you need anything there's a pull cord next to the bed," she adds, turning to lean around the door frame, "and I do mean ANYTHING?"

Pyah gently pushes her out of the door laughing, "Oh I think I've got that covered," she says, closing the door then running to launch herself onto the bed, spreading herself out on it, "Oh this is gorgeous," she sighs, moaning with delight.

Mark struts around the bed, "Excuse me, but I don't suppose I'm invited to your little fantasy, am I?"

Pyah looks up at him, "I feel like a queen."

Mark looks down at his kimono, "Yeah, so do I in this get up," he says, sticking his hand out with a limp wrist.

Pyah laughs out loud, "Just got an image of you in a skirt singing, *'I want to break free'*."

Mark crawls on to the bed and pins her down by her shoulders, "you really think that I am like that?" he says, growling in fun, then attempting to bite her nipple through her kimono.

Pyah rolls him onto his back as her hair cascades across his face. He spits and splutters, getting a mouthful as she lifts the flaming red mass back across her brow, brushing it back down her spine. Dropping down to lunge at his mouth, she presses her lush red lips against his. Biting his tongue as he thrusts it in between her lips. Pulling back then letting go, she stares down at him, "So you want to play rough?"

Seeing the impish glint in her big green eyes as they sparkle with devilish anticipation, Mark grasps her wrists, "That all depends on whether you're going to suck the life force out of me, or whether you're wanting to make love?"

Pyah sits up, "If you're just going to take the piss," she huffs, pulling his hands off her wrists, then folding her arms to show she is upset at his insult.

Mark raises to his elbows, "I know I shouldn't but I'm sure I saw that Emily Rose for an instance," he says, placing his hands on her waist, "unnerved me slightly, taking the piss is the only way I can handle it."

Pyah stands up over him on the bed, "Well don't," she warns, towering over him, "or I will let her loose, then you're in shit creek pal," she says innocently, smiling a girly smile as she undoes her kimono, "now are you going to show me some love or what?" she asks, dropping the kimono to the floor.

The sunset glimmers through the open window, casting an auburn shimmer across Pyah's body, highlighting her every curve as Mark looks on in admiration, "That colour suits you," he says, seductively unwrapping his kimono.

Pyah studies her body in the scarlet cast, "Hmm it is quite fetching, isn't it?" she agrees as she drops to her knees to help him disrobe, "doesn't look too bad on you either," she mentions, running her hands down over his chest onto his abdomen as she straddles him.

Mark holds her hips as she starts to delicately work her pelvis across his penis, "Hmm, looks like someone isn't afraid of the big bad Emily Rose," she teases, referring to his manhood.

Pyah slides forward on his now fully erect penis, lifting to allow it to gently penetrate her as she drifts back on to it moaning with a euphoric wince. Mark closes his eyes to drift into the ambiance of the moment allowing Pyah's mood to engulf him, surrendering to her serenity. He discretely reaches across to calm the light as not to disturb Pyah in her tranquillity as she leisurely drifts into an atmosphere of unadulterated solitary rapture. Mark has never before experienced her in this state as he lies back to capture the contentment in this moment with her. Mark soon finds himself moving instinctively to Pyah's motions as the pair silently reach a soft contented climax.

Pyah lies across Mark without a word as he caresses her in a warm embrace. Soon they can hear the wind tapping at the shutters bringing them from their light slumber. Mark crawls out of bed to approach the window. "Oh, you should come and see this," he says as Pyah appears by his side.

The sun has set leaving a subtle glow on the horizon, hindered by only a haze of desert dust whipping up from the ground.

The desert appears to be dancing as the isolated undergrowth sways to the exploits of the wind, twisting one lone tree in the distance as it fights to keep its poise. Jimmy can be seen closing his storm shutters before coming to Sonja's to bar the hotel against the impending storm.

Soon the outpost is locked down as Sonja taps on Pyah's door, "Can I come and close the shutter before storm hits?" she asks.

Mark wraps a sheet around himself, "Yeah come in."

Sonja enters, goes straight to the window and pulls the shutter closed. Dropping a bar across them from the inside, she says, "There we go, all cosy for the night, shouldn't bother you now," smiling as she leaves the room, "The kettle is on if you can't sleep,", she adds, closing the door behind her.

Mark slides into bed next to Pyah as she snuggles down into him, closing her eyes with a little moan of contentment. Mark embraces her as she lies her head across his chest then closes his eyes as the both drift off into a silent slumber.

Suddenly they are awoken by a crashing sound. The sound of something pounding against the side of the building as the wind can be heard howling through the outpost like a siren.

Mark turns to Pyah, "Do you fancy that cuppa now?"

Pyah looks up at him with bleary eyes, "A little wind isn't going to keep me awake but if you want to go?" she says, shrugging as she pulls the blanket back for him.

Mark climbs out of bed, "I can't sleep in this and I'm only going to keep you awake," he says, pulling a dressing gown on, "think I will take her up on her offer," he decides as he walks towards the door.

A rush of wind slams into the hotel lifting the bars on Pyah's shutters rattling them with a horrifying racket. Pyah jumps out of bed, "Wait for me," she calls as she drags a dressing gown from the drawer, running after Mark.

Mark stands at the door giggling to himself, "Suddenly thirsty eh?"

Pyah throws her arms around him, "NO, freaking shitting myself is what I am!"

Mark cuddles her, "A little wind won't keep you awake eh?" he teases as they both chuckle and head for the kitchen.

Sonja, Mimi, Jimmy and Mary are all in the kitchen drinking hot chocolate. Two cups are waiting, already prepared in anticipation of Pyah and Marks arrival.

Sonja picks up the kettle, "Drinking chocolate? Cocoa? Coffee? Or maybe something a little stronger?" she offers, pointing at a bottle of bourbon on the counter.

Pyah picks up the bottle, "I'll have a coffee if you don't mind," she requests, sitting at the breakfast bench.

Mark sits next to her, "Yeah, me too," he says, dragging the bottle around to the middle of them, smiling at Pyah.

Sonja pours them both a coffee as they top it up with bourbon, "Hmm this should do nicely," Pyah sighs, sipping at the alcohol laced coffee.

It isn't long before Pyah is resting on her arms, which are laid across the counter in front of her, drifting into a quiet slumber as Sonja disappears to return with a thick heavy sleeping bag. Mark picks Pyah up and Sonja lays the sleeping bag on a wide counter as Mark lays Pyah on top of it. The group chatter till the early hours of the morning as the storm abates.

Mark sweeps Pyah into his arms and heads off to bed, lowering her without rousing her, then covering her to slip in beside her as the sun caresses the horizon.

CHAPTER 11
GUNSLINGERS-R-US

The next morning Pyah awakes at nine am to take a shower, leaving Mark to sleep on, then goes to sort out the motor home for their journey ahead.

As she pulls it alongside the hotel Mark is standing on the front steps stretching, "Hmm what a lovely morning."

Jimmy calls him across to the general store, "Here, I might have something of interest to you."

Mark enters the store as Jimmy takes him to an unobtrusive door to the side of the store, "I noticed that little pop gun you have and thought you might want to borrow something with a little more clout," he says, opening the door to an armoury.

Jimmy hands him a buffalo gun, "This should do for anything you may come across."

Mark hands it back, "No, I don't think I need to be doing any hunting and this will do for any trouble I might come across," he declines, patting his Glock, "thanks for the offer though."

Jimmy shrugs, "Take a look, you never know what might catch your eye."

Mark heads for the door, uninterested, when something does catch his eye, "Is that a quick draw rig?" he asks, bringing Jimmy's attention to a holster hanging behind the door.

Jimmy reaches up to the holster, then under a counter to reveal a six shooter, placing it on the counter in front of Mark.

Mark picks it up, "Wow, a long colt too," he exclaims, tipping his head, "bloody heavy, and is that an extended fanning hammer?"

Jimmy reaches behind him, "You certainly know your guns, this one was my son's before he passed," he says, then opens a door to a shooting range, "care to pop off a few rounds?" he offers, leading Mark into the range then lifting a hinged post about twenty-five feet away with a target attached.

Jimmy points at the revolver, "That ain't been modified for competition though that's why it's so heavy, shoots real rounds not like those blanks those fairy boys shoot."

Mark loads the chamber with six rounds, places the gun in its holster, then draws it as fast as lightning, fanning the hammer to score the edge of the bullseye.

"Nice," Jimmy raises one eyebrow, "the boy can shoot too, I'm impressed."

Mark spins the gun around his finger then places it back in its holster to draw it again. He scores a perfect bull this time, "Twitches to the right a bit but I could get used to this."

Pyah hears the gunfire and come to investigate, "Boys and their toys, might have known."

Mark hands her the gun. Pyah has trouble cocking it and, with the hair trigger, fires one into the ground in front, sending her reeling backwards.

She hands the gun back to Mark, "Think I'll stick with my berretta," she decides, then draws it quickly, unloading ten rounds into the centre of the target.

Jimmy walks to the target, "Holy shit, remind me never to challenge her to a gun fight," he remarks, laughing, as they leave the store.

Mark turns to Jimmy, "How much do I owe you for this?"

Jimmy shrugs, "You can borrow it till you come back this way," he says, rubbing his chin, "I presume you are coming back?"

Mark nods as they say their goodbyes then they go off into the desert once more.

CHAPTER 12
MERCENARIES DON'T COME CHEAP

Sarah, Carl and Lacey arrive on the six am flight into Nador International Airport, Morocco. Stepping out from an air conditioned aircraft, the morning sun seems to seer the air around them as a waft of hot wind takes their breath away. The perspiration streams from their pores, drenching their clothes which stick to their skin as the sweat rolls down their bodies. The dark concrete of the runway softens their shoes as the heat moves up through their soles.

Lacey flicks off her stilettos but quickly puts them back on, "Shit, that's hot," she yelps, unbuttoning her blouse as far as she dares.

Sarah takes off her jacket and unbuttons her blouse, "Damn, never thought I would be baring my all to the world," she comments as she slips her bra off under her blouse, then pops it into her hand luggage.

Carl takes his jacket off to place it over his head while they walk to the terminal, "It's only early morning, just wait till it gets towards noon," he tells them, wafting himself with a pamphlet, "you think *this* is hot."

Sarah takes out some wet wipes, "Oh, he's a bundle of laughs," she remarks, handing Lacey a wipe.

They quickly get into the cool terminal as Sarah flops on the nearest seat, "Oh that's better," she sighs, reaching across to a convenient water cooler, "the problem is we've got to go back out in it once we clear Customs."

Lacey plonks herself next to Sarah, "Oh let's just enjoy the moment before venturing out in that again."

Carl decides to soldier on through Customs, "I'll wait for you on the other side," he tells them as he disappears into the crowd.

Once Sarah and Lacey have gone through Customs they find Carl at the airport bar sipping on a large cold beer, "I presume you two wouldn't say no," he greets, pointing at a couple of glasses on the bar, "apparently that hire car firm doesn't do off road vehicles," he adds, pointing at a rental car booth,

"we have to go out of the airport and down to the second intersection to the right of here," he indicates, pointing to the right, "then turn left and we can't miss it."

Sarah gulps at her drink, "How far?" she asks, then gulps at it again, "Because if its more than a hundred yards I ain't going nowhere," she declares, finishing off her drink then rattling it at the bar man, "again young sir," she orders, turning back to Carl, "you go get it and bring it back here, oh and make sure it's air conditioned, oh and don't go getting some rusty old wreck, oh yeah and no leather seats, don't want my arse sticking to no leather in this heat thank you," she rattles off as the barman brings another cold beer. Sarah winks at him, "You'll do for me, just keep 'em coming till I tell you."

Lacey downs her beer in one, "It's OK, I'll go with him," she says, linking arms with Carl as they set off, "I think I know what us women need," she adds, trotting off out of the airport, leaving all the luggage with Sarah.

As Sarah is slowly getting a tad tipsy, a young man comes up to her and starts to give her a bit of flannel, appearing to chat her up. She notices another in a reflection moving slowly towards her bags, "You know young man, I do like a bit of flirting but if your mate gets one more inch closer to my luggage then I'll blow both of your balls off and feed them to him," she says casually, turning to look the other straight in the eye, "I ain't that drunk," she smiles, moving her jacket to reveal her gun then smiling as they nonchalantly walk away.

She decides it's time to turn to Coca Cola with ice and manages to down two more before Lacey arrives back, "Looks like we struck gold," she declares.

Sarah stumbles off her seat, "Get a good car then?"

Lacey catches her, "Not only that but I think you're drunk."

Sarah nods passively, "But I am sobering up," she says, lifting her glass of coke.

Lacey giggles at her, "Well, I have some good news and some bad," she says, dropping all the luggage on a trolley, "seems Pyah and Mark rented a motor home from the same place."

Sarah sits on the trolley, "Onward James," she instructs, waving her hand in front, "I hope that is somehow in some weird sort of way the bad news coz I hate real bad news."

Lacey shakes her head, "Seems our killer squad are about four hours in front of us."

Sarah jumps off the trolley, "Oh for fucks sake," she swears, giving herself a sobering shake then dragging the trolley to the door as fast as she can, "we better get a freaking move on then."

Carl is sat outside the airport in a convertible "Like?"

Sarah stops dead in her tracks, "Oh, you stupid idiot," she exclaims, walking around the car, "how the hell is this supposed to travel round a desert?"

Carl jumps out of the car, "It ain't!" he says, lifting the trunk lid, "it's just supposed to get us to a small private internal air strip just outside of town," he explains, nodding confidently, "they'll fly us into an outpost that they think Pyah and Mark were heading for, THEN we'll pick up a vehicle and go from there?"

Sarah helps him and Lacey load the luggage, "Suppose it's a plan," she agrees, walking around the car then plonking herself in the rear seat, "betcha didn't come up with it all on your own though?"

Carl drops his head, "No, it was Lacey's idea," he admits, then plonks himself in the driver's seat, "Seems our Mercs hired a couple of four by fours about three thirty this morning and were asking about the Fischers," he tells her as he sets off down the main drag, "guy thought they looked like hunters, said they seemed a bit shifty so he didn't tell them anything but as soon as we showed him us in the wedding photo he gave us all the info he could," he continues, then he turns to head out of town.

Lacey is sat in the back with Sarah, "Yeah, apparently there's only one road out of here in the direction he thinks they went but it hits an intersection about seventy miles out," she says, brushing the hair from her face, "so those Mercs have a fifty/ fifty chance of taking the right route," she explains, pulling a bottle of water from a bag, "let's hope they go the wrong way, because otherwise this is going to be tight."

It isn't long before they are at the airfield explaining the situation to the pilot.

He takes them to a helicopter, "Usually I would fly you out in that," he says, pointing at a Lear jet, "but this can drop you right outside the outpost where I can wait for you if they're not there."

Sarah opts for his suggestion and they're soon in the air, heading for the outpost. The pilot flies as high as he can in the hopes that he may see something of either the Fischers or the mercenaries.

As they fly over the intersection they can see a dust cloud off to the right, "Well, if that's your Mercs they're heading in the wrong direction," the pilot says, pointing down at them, "should take them about ninety miles out of their way and give you about an hour and a half to two hours' head start on them."

He quickly drops to the ground, hoping they haven't been spotted, then heads towards the outpost. Once at the outpost Jimmy heads out to the chopper to greet them. He welcomes them but is surprised at their story. He tells Carl that the Fischers set off the previous morning and he isn't sure which route they would be taking. He telephones all the possible places that Pyah and Mark could turn up at, giving them the info he has but no one has seen them, "Seems your young friends have done a disappearing act but if they turn up my mates will call, so you can go and get them."

Sonja turns up, hearing most of the conversation, "Looks like we got us a bit of a pickle and the only thing I can suggest is you stay here till they're found."

Jimmy pats his rifle, "And don't you worry about those mercenaries."

Carl puts his hands on Jimmy's shoulders, "I don't think that's a good idea," he confides, tipping his head to Jimmy, "these guys are trained professional maniacs, best thing you can do is stay well clear."

They tell the pilot to head back to the airport before taking a room at the hotel, "We'll just pretend we're normal safari customers when the bad guys arrive," Carl decides.

Sonja takes them to the hotel to get settled hoping they hear from Mark and Pyah before the mercenaries arrive.

She puts Sarah and Carl in the VIP suite then Lacey in an adjoining room. It isn't long before they are all unpacked, downstairs, trying to enjoy a pleasant cool drink in the midday heat when Jimmy walks in toting his buffalo gun under his arm, "Looks like trouble heading in from yon side of town," he warns.

Sarah turns to him, "Just try and act normal and put that bloody thing away!" she instructs, pointing at his gun.

Jimmy turns to skulk out of the door as two four by fours pull up outside the hotel. Seven burley men dressed in camouflage get out carrying sub-machine guns, strolling into the hotel as if they own it.

The head man walks over to the bar, "Seven beers, when you're ready, woman," he orders, dropping a wad of money on the counter.

Sonja ignores the woman remark while she draws the ale from the old-fashioned pump, "Will that be all YOUNG sir?" she asks in her best sarcastic tone.

The second in command plonks himself on the bar, "Ain't seen one of these places in a while," he says, sniffing at the air, "where's the girls?" he asks, laying across the bar towards Sonja, "don't tell me you're the only one."

Sonja backs away from him, "Sure I don't know what you mean."

The Merc flicks her under the chin, "I know a brothel when I smell one, so don't come it with me honey," he warns, jumping down, holding his arms out and spinning, "bring on the totty," he says, then walking over towards Lacey, "don't suppose you want to oblige?" he asks, running his hands through her hair.

Lacey glares at him, "No dear, I'm just a paying customer, JUST LIKE YOU."

The Merc steps back, "Whoa, a limey, what you doing so far from home honey?"

Sarah steps up, "We're on safari," she explains, sitting next to Lacey, "how about you, hunting?"

The lead man walks over to her, "You could say that," he says cagily, sitting on the table in front of her, "don't suppose you've seen a lanky red head and an office boy 'round these parts recently?"

Carl leans forward, "Son, the only women hereabouts is the madam," he says, pointing at Sonja, "and these two beauties here," he goes on, pointing at Lacey and Sarah, "as I'm a bit partial to a bit of red head you think I would have noticed one."

Sarah's head slumps as the head man walks over to him, "Now who said anything about a woman?" he demands, lifting his gun towards Carl, "I said a lanky red head," he says as he grabs Sarah, pulls her up in front of him and shoves the gun under her chin.

The phone rings. Sonja answers it as the second in command snatches it off her and lifts it to his ear, "Hello?" he says, then aims his gun at Sonja.

The phone is momentarily silent then a voice says, "Are you the boss?"

The Merc holds the phone out to the head man, "It's for you."

He pushes Sarah back into her seat then walks over to the phone. Two mercenaries walk outside while three stand guard over Sarah, Carl and Lacey. The second in command flicks his legs over the bar to sit teasing Sonja at gunpoint.

The head Merc answers the phone, "Mr Fischer I presume?"

Mark is on the other end, "You have me at a disadvantage."

The head Merc smiles smugly, "Although my name is unimportant I think you should know the name of the man that has your life at his disposal, it's Alfred Heart but you can call me Alf."

Mark pauses momentarily, "So what is it that I can do for you?"

Alf gives a raucous laugh, "You can let me collect the bounty that's been placed on your head, I don't ask too much do I?"

Mark thinks for a moment, "Can I first ask who placed the bounty and second how much it is?"

Alf taps on the bar, "The bounty is ten million dollars for your head and ten million dollars for the head of your pretty little wife," he says, pausing for a response then carrying on, "as for who, well she said you'll know her, Denier De-fuer, name ring a bell?"

This time Mark gives raucous laugh, "Definitely a fruit loop that one, her marbles are scattered from here to Mombasa, I wouldn't trust her as far as I can spit."

Alf flicks his teeth, "We'll see, if she don't keep her side of the bargain then her head's the next to roll but first let's talk about your situation."

Mark sighs, "So what's the plan? You chase me all over Africa and I do the running, see who gets fed up first?"

Alf laughs, "No, no, no, you're going to come here and duke it out with me and my men, otherwise your raven-haired bitch friend and her compatriots die in a hot sweltering desert where no one will find them."

Mark thinks, "Tell you what, I'm at Goby Springs, why don't you come and get me?"

Alf laughs out loud again, "That puts you about three and a half hours out, I'll give you four to get here then I start shooting people, you drive that piece of shite you got into the middle of this outpost, where you and the redhead get out so I can see you, then we take it from there. You got till five pm then I'm gonna take that old git with the elephant gun into the middle of the road and put a bullet in his head then every five minutes on I shoot another, five pm!" he yells, then slams the phone down.

The second in command drops down behind the bar in front of Sonja, "So, there must be some nubile young flesh here, I mean what's a brothel without girls," he says, stroking his gun down Sonja's cleavage.

Sonja plays to him, "I could show you a good time," she coos, tempting him with her feminine wiles, "got a bed just through this door."

He smiles at her "I BET you could too, but I prefer a girl to a hag."

Alf walks across, "Keep your mind on the job," he tells him, then turns to Sonja, "he asked you where the rest of your staff are?"

Sonja pouts, "I sent them on a short break as this is our slow season."

Alf turns to his second, "Go and check the rooms," he orders, pointing up the stairs, "if there are any up there bring them down, ALIVE!"

The second heads upstairs but finds no one, then comes to the top of the stairs, "All empty, seems she's telling the truth," he says, then slides down the banister.

Alf stands in the middle of the room, "Well, looks like we got some time to kill," he pulls out a radio and puts it to his mouth, "you get any sign you call ok?" he says into it, no one can hear the response as he has an ear piece. He walks outside to the two standing guards, "Watch for that old fool, make sure he don't do nothing stupid with that fire stick of his," he says, tipping his hat to Jimmy who's leaning against the door frame of his shop.

CHAPTER 13
GUNFIGHT AT THE FRENCH LETTUCE

The hours seem to drag, but just before five Alf's radio goes off, "OK, looks like showtime, one of them jumped out about half mile back and is trying to flank us," he says, pointing at his second, "get out back to cut them off."

The motor home stops about two hundred yards out as Alf walks over to Jimmy pointing his gun, "OK old man, reach for that rifle and I blow your head off."

Alf grabs Jimmy by the arm to march him into the middle of the road, "Let's just hope for your sake this goes as planned," he says, pushing his gun under Jimmy's chin then looking at his watch, "two minutes and we see if they're willing to let you die."

At that the motor home starts moving slowly towards him, building speed steadily. By the time it gets to him it's travelling at about fifty miles an hour, skews across towards Jimmy's shop, then comes to a sliding stop across the main thoroughfare just past Alf and Jimmy. The driver's door, which is on the opposite side, opens. A pair of women's feet can be seen underneath as she exits the vehicle to slowly walk around to the back.

A young African girl appears around the rear of the vehicle as Alf's second radios him, "I have the Fischer woman."

Pyah walks up to the second with her hands in the air, her empty gun in one hand and the magazine in the other, but, before Alf can warn him that Mark is there as well, Mark stands from his hiding spot behind the second to shoot him in the back of the head with his gun silenced.

Alf pushes Jimmy forward, points his gun at him, and smiles. At this a barrage of lead comes raining down from the upper floor of the general dealers. Mary has a nine millimetre Ingram pointing in the general direction of Alf, spraying the floor with bullets.

The two guards outside the hotel start blasting the window where Mary is as Jimmy runs for the store's front door, diving through it for cover. Once inside he heads for his secret armoury, grabs two Uzi's and a small bag of magazines. He heads out of the rear exit to head for the side of the hotel.

Once there he starts to climb through the window into Sonja's bedroom. Mimi is hiding behind a screen with a table lamp and attacks him as he climbs in, "Jesus, woman, it's me," he says, backing her off, "grab these," he instructs, handing her the guns, "now get back where you were before you get hurt," he says, taking the guns back off her.

Pyah and Mark enter a window on the other side of the building, bringing them into a store room. They open the storeroom door at the same time as Jimmy opens the door behind reception.

When the shooting starts the three men that are guarding Lacey, Carl, and Sarah head towards the door to give covering fire. Lacey and Sarah jump up. Sarah reaches up her skirt for a small lady gun in a garter holster while Lacey pulls her berretta from the back of her skirt belt. Heading for the reception counter they both start firing at the guards near the door. The guards turn to spray towards them as they dive over the counter. Sonja is cowering behind it as Jimmy leans out to drag her in to her living quarters. Pyah and Mark rush out, sliding behind a sofa while firing at the mercenaries. Alf ducks into an alcove just outside the door as his men take cover behind some chairs just inside the door.

Lacey darts across the room to Mark and Pyah, "Shit, I'm just about out of ammo," she moans, firing the last few rounds in her gun.

Pyah hands her a clip, "Make it count because I only have one more," she tells her as Jimmy throws the two Uzis across to her. Pyah hands Lacey the last clip then picks up the Uzis, "Oh, these should do nicely."

Mark kisses her, "Now would be a good time to see Mina Harker, if you know what I mean."

Lacey looks puzzled as Mark shakes his head, "Private joke."

Sarah is pinned down behind the reception, lifting her gun to show Pyah that it's empty as Jimmy throws the bag of clips to Pyah. The mercenaries start unloading at Sarah.

Seeing this Pyah fills with rage as Mark shoots blindly over the sofa. Pyah looks at him, "That does it, they woke the vampire lady," she says as she stands tall with both Uzis, the fires of hell blazoned across her eyes cutting through everything in front of her.

As the mercenaries try to get cover they are dropped one by one. Alf makes a rush for the reception desk, diving behind it he lands next to Sarah. Sarah slaps him frantically but he punches her then grabs a mass of her hair lifting her up in front of him. All of his men are dead as he backs through the bodies using Sarah as a human shield, "If anyone so much as twitches I'll kill her."

Pyah drops the empty clips out of the Uzi's, "You so much as hurt her and I swear you'll suffer a very long and painful death, this I can promise you."

While Pyah is talking to him, Lacey crawls out into the store room, then jumps out of the window heading for Jimmy's shop. She comes alongside the motor home where the young African girl is sat, desperately but unsuccessfully trying to cock Marks six shooter.

Lacey smiles, "I'll take that, thank you," she says as she picks up the holster to put it on. She lifts the girl to her feet, "Go and find some where to hide," she tells her, then starts to walk around the van.

As Alf backs slowly out of the hotel he checks the store windows, "If anyone is up there still, you shoot and I'll take her with me. I die, she dies, get it?"

Lacey is about to step out when a rumble can be heard in the distance.

Alf lifts his radio, "What the hell is that?" he asks, then rips the ear piece out, throwing it to the ground, "say again," he says as the rumble gets louder.

A voice on the other end is distorted but Alf can make out, "It's a bunch of bikers heading your way, about thirty-five or forty of them."

Alf marches Sarah to his four by four as the biker gang pulls up across in front of Jimmy's store. The lead biker gets off his bike, puts a stogey in his mouth and nonchalantly struts toward Alf.

Alf points his gun at the biker but the biker just stares at him, "I'm looking for a woman about six feet tall, legs that go up to about here," the biker indicates with his hand under his chin, "raven black hair all the way down her back," he continues as he lights the stogie, "she's supposed to be travelling with a boring old fart and a girl that looks a little bit like her," he says, pointing at Sarah.

Lacey steps out from behind the motor home, "You must be Irish?"

Irish looks her up and down, "Hmmm, legs to your armpits and long, long, raven black hair, you must be the raven?" he checks, nodding his head in approval, "my brother in-law's description doesn't do you justice."

Alf shoves his gun under Sarah's chin, "Excuse me!" he says, getting slightly irritated, "I have a sniper aiming right in here so if any of you decide to stop me not only is she dead but so are some of you."

At that, one of the bikers drops to the floor with blood gushing from his head.

Irish whirls his hand in the air as two bikers start to doughnut their bikes to cause a dust cloud for cover, "Now your sniper can't see us."

Lacey walks towards Alf, "How about we see how much of a man you are," she suggests, patting the revolver. "You win, you walk away unhindered, but you leave my friend."

Alf laughs, "You're shitting me, right? Like I'm going to give up my insurance just like that."

Lacey cricks her neck, "Well, if I have to shoot her to get to you I will," she says, lifting the gun slightly from its holster then dropping it, "but I won't kill you, because there's a lanky redhead in there who would love to cause you some serious pain, so what's it going to be - I shoot you then she gets you, or we go one on one and may the best man win, I'll even let you draw first," she offers, stepping out into open space, "what's the matter? you frightened of a girl?"

Mark, Carl, Pyah and Jimmy come to the door as Alf throws Sarah to one side, drops his machine gun and unclips his side arm, "Whenever you're ready, bitch!"

Lacey smiles at him, "After you."

Alf reaches for his gun, but doesn't even get it clear of the holster before Lacey has the six-shooter drawn, fanning it to unload all six rounds into his head.

Irish slowly starts to clap as the rest join in.

Lacey takes a bow, "We still have a sniper out there," she says, pointing out at the desert.

Irish sends his gang off to search but when they get to where the sniper should be its just flat desert. No tracks. No sign. Irish goes after them as they scour the open waste, then one of them spots a small mound with some twigs growing out of it. One of the twigs seems a bit thicker than the rest and is totally horizontal.

As he approaches Irish stops him about twenty feet from it, "Just shoot it."

The biker shoots the mound causing it to explode, sending shrapnel everywhere. Luckily no one is badly injured. The only surviving evidence is a small metal plate with a fox's head in the shape of a V engraved into it. They go back to the hotel.

Irish walks over to reception, "What's left out there seems to be the remains of a remote-control rifle and the only thing that left is this," he throws the little plaque on the desk, "seems it was meant to be found."

Carl picks it up, smiles, and shakes his head.

Lacey takes it off him, "Do you recognise it?"

Carl taps it, "I was in Vietnam with a guy that used an emblem very similar, but it can't be him, he's dead."

Sarah stands in front of him, "Are you sure?"

Carl laughs, "Oh yes, he died twelve years ago," he says as he walks around the desk, "I was a pallbearer at his funeral, open casket and all, put him six feet under while me, his missus and the thirteen-year-old daughter stood and watched. Trust me he's dead."

Irish leans on the desk, "An apprentice maybe?" he suggests, reaching over to grab a bottle of scotch, "or a brother, maybe the kid?"

Carl shakes his head, "Nope, he took a land mine out in Vietnam, then him and his missus dropped off the face of the earth, didn't hear from him till he was dying of cancer. Turns out he was in the middle of the Australian outback just watching life go by."

Irish lights up a stogie then takes the bottle to one of the sofas, "We'll probably meet this sniper again, then I got a score to settle."

At that Jimmy comes running in, "They've shot Mary, she needs an ambulance or a doctor or something, I can't stop the bleeding," he cries, tears flooding down his face.

Sarah runs back to the store with him, "Phone for an ambulance while I try and stabilise her."

When she gets there Mary is semiconscious with four bullets in her chest, "Shit, she's losing a lot of blood," she says, placing her hands on Mary's wounds to apply pressure. "Here hold this there," she instructs, giving Jimmy a towel to hold on Mary's wounds.

Pyah rushes in, "A surgeon's on his way but he won't be able to get here for about thirty minutes."

Sarah throws a towel at Pyah, "Can you apply pressure on here while I find something to remove these bullets?"

Pyah applies the pressure with Jimmy as Sarah starts to look around, "You got any surgical spirits or the like? Maybe a set of forceps and a scalpel I don't suppose?"

Jimmy looks up at the ceiling, "Err, yeah, surgical spirits behind the counter downstairs, Scalpel in the craft ware, right in front of the counter, err, there's a first aid box near the spirits and some long-nosed pliers on the back wall with tools, will that do?"

Sarah dashes off, "Marvellous."

While she's down there she notices some ink hypodermics and some clear tubing, grabs everything she needs then heads back upstairs, "Don't suppose you know what blood type she is?"

Jimmy thinks "Err, yeah she's AB negative."

Sarah raises her hand to the sky, "Thank you, God."

Jimmy looks at her, "What? I thought that was a rare blood type."

Sarah unravels the tubing, "Yep it is, but it means that she can take any type of blood in a transfusion," she says, attaching the hypos to the ends, "now all we need are some willing donors, at the rate she's losing it we're going to need a lot."

Pyah rolls her sleeve up, "I'm your first customer."

Sarah sticks the needle in the spirits then into Pyah's vein, clamping the tube as the blood starts to flow "don't suppose you have a clamp for this?" she asks, turning to Jimmy.

He points at a desk lamp behind her that's clamped down. She gets the clamp, puts it on the tube then feeds the other needle into Mary's arm, "Looks like we might just get through this," she says, then pours spirits over Mary's wounds, "let's see if we can get these little bastards out of her," Sarah picks up the pliers, "sorry Mary but this is going to hurt."

Jimmy stops her, "I got some ether downstairs if that's any good?"

Sarah kisses him, "Bloody great, if you have some dust masks we can put her under."

Jimmy rushes down, bringing dust masks and ether. Sarah puts a dust mask over Mary's mouth then slowly pours the ether onto it. Mary is soon under so Sarah extracts the bullets. All the bikers wait in line to donate their blood.

The sound of a helicopter landing outside is a welcoming sound as a surgeon appears at Sarah's side, "Well, looks like you're doing a top job there, young lady, well done."

Two paramedics arrive with a gurney and lift Mary onto it, "She's not out of the woods yet but it looks like you may have saved her life."

Local police arrive. Lacey shows her MI6 credentials, so they do a clean up and leave Lacey to it. Jimmy goes to the hospital with Mary as everyone else has a drink in the hotel.

Lacey pulls Pyah over to the bottom of the stairs, "How are you?"

Pyah kisses her, "I'm fine but I did have a moment the other day," she says as she starts to explain what happened with her and Mimi.

Lacey laughs, "So that's what Mark's Mina Harker remark was all about? Scary."

Neither of them notice Mimi walking around them with clean sheets for the upstairs rooms, "Yeah, scared the shit out of me too," she chimes in as she strolls up the stairs.

Lacey takes one look at her then turns to Pyah, "You didn't?" she says, pointing at Mimi, "she's only a kid."

Mimi stops, turns, and raises her eyebrows, "I'm nearly twenty-one," she points out, then struts up the stairs.

Lacey stands with her mouth agape, looks at Mimi then turns to Pyah, "She's twenty-one?"

Pyah smiles, "Almost, it's a wonder she didn't start firing her passport at you."

Irish walks over to them, "So ladies, what's the topic?"

Lacey points up at Mimi just before she disappears into one of the rooms, "The hooker, she's twenty-one you know," she says, laughing.

Irish takes his stogie out of his mouth, "That's a hooker?" he asks, taking a couple of steps up, "Whoa, might have some of that later."

Lacey pulls him back, "What you would rather pay for it?" she asks, taking his stogie and puffing on it.

Irish puts his hand in the air, "My brother in law said you were taken, some F.B.I. Agent or something?"

Lacey takes his hand, "Not yet I'm not," she says, pulling him up the stairs, puffing on his stogie.

Pyah stands there smiling, "Just remember that hole in your shoulder."

Lacey stops, "Won't be a minute," she says, then walks back down to Pyah and slaps the dirtiest full on kiss on her.

Irish raises his eyebrows, "You can join us if you want," he remarks.

A voice comes from near the reception, "Now she IS taken," Mark says as he steps out.

Carl turns in his seat, "And you can keep your eyes off the little cute one, she's mine," he says, sipping his whiskey.

Lacey walks up, grabs Irish's hand and drags him up to the nearest available room. She pulls him in, hangs the, do not disturb notice outside, then shuts the door, "Usually I like to undress a man but, what the hell, get your kit off," she tells him as she just about drags her clothes off.

Irish quickly and proudly obliges, "Whoa, girl. You can leave the stockings and sussy on, I prefer it, and damn girl you got long legs."

Lacey slinks over to him, "All the better to wrap around you."

He looks at the dressing on her shoulder, "What's that?"

Lacey puts her hand over it, "Got shot just before we came over here, but that's not the hole you should be worrying about," she says, dragging his mouth on to hers then pulling back slightly, "you can do whatever you want, so long as you don't start this bleeding again," she tells him, patting her wound.

Irish looks into her eyes, "Anything?"

Lacey nods, biting her bottom lip, "Ah ha, so long as you leave no marks anything goes."

Irish is a bit shocked, "I like a bit of kinky but I wouldn't go that far."

Lacey grabs his butt, "Oh, I don't know, once you get started you never know what you might fancy, if I want you to stop I'll tell you."

She pushes him backwards towards the bed but he stands his ground, "Oh, we like it like that eh?" he says as he grabs her wrists, lifting them above her head and pushing her back against the door. He places his legs one either side of hers to keep hers closed, pinning her against the door, then leans his torso against hers while pressing his lips against hers, flicking the back of her teeth with his tongue, "Ooo you do like it rough," he comments, forcing his erect penis in between her legs.

She moans with delight, closes her eyes, then gently bites his tongue. He reaches down to grasp at her breast squeezing her nipple to her obvious satisfaction as she runs her nails down his spine. He doesn't flinch but pulls one of her legs out around his waist to ram his penis as far into her as he can, slamming her against the door with his hips. Still she moans with pleasure. He then spins her around to face the door, grasps a handful of breast with one hand and thrusts the other between her legs, pushing his hand into her to hold her while he pushes his penis into her anus, and still she just moans in ecstasy, "Wow, you are a kinky bitch."

At this she decides to speak, "Are you going to talk all night or fuck the shit out of me sometime soon?"

He picks her up by her breast and vagina spins her around and walks to the bed still thrusting into her as she reaches around to grab his butt laying her head back on his shoulder, mouth agape, gasping. He reaches the bed and tosses her like a rag doll onto it. She groans as she lands, still face down, grabbing the brass head stead as Irish climbs on top of her, forces her legs apart to thrust his penis into her. He lifts himself up with one arm while wrapping his other around her waist, bringing her up to her knees then pushes her shoulders down sliding his hands back to her hips.

He can feel himself coming to the point of ejaculation as Lacey turns her head to him, "No, not yet," she says, pleading with him.

He is past the point of no return as he starts to spasm and groan. Lacey reaches under herself to rub her clitoris for all she is worth as to climax with him. When he has finished he pulls out, then flops on the bed beside her, panting. Lacey stays in the kneeling position groaning as she is left to finish herself alone.

"Well that was nice," she says in a sarcastic tone as she rolls over with an air of disappointment.

Irish rolls on to his side, looking her straight in the eye, "Yeah, it was good, wasn't it?"

Lacey tuts, then gets out of bed, gets dressed, then heads downstairs, leaving Irish completely oblivious to her frustration.

Carl is still mulling over the fox head plaque, "Wouldn't mind meeting this sniper myself, see what his story is?"

One of the bikers steps forward, "Probably gone running to that crazy bitch that sent him."

Carl flicks the plaque in the air, "Yeah, if only we knew where she was," he says, shaking his head.

The biker catches the plaque, "Oh, that's easy, she's at a little town just down the north-west coast, called Tan-Tan," he says, sitting next to Carl, "that's where we were heading when we got the call about you, she's brokering some arms deal. That's why Irish's sister was killed. She found out about it. She sent the info to Irish before they killed her though and now he wants Denier De-fuer's blood."

Carl stands up to rush to the general store. There he grabs a map then rushes back to the hotel, "OK chaps, looks like we're going on a duck hunt," he says, slamming the map down on the counter, "tomorrow we head for Tan-Tan," he tells them, pointing at it on the map, "and kill us an arms dealer to get this fucking bounty lifted."

CHAPTER 14
SHOOTOUT BY THE SEA

The desert sun peeks its red glow over the horizon as Carl squints at it through bleary eyes then turns in the bed to Sarah, "Oh shit where's she gone? What fricking time is it?" he asks himself as he reaches for his watch, "Oh God, half three, what the hell are you doing awake Carl?" he reprimands himself, tapping himself on the head.

He slams his head back into the pillow, shuffles about for a bit then sits up, "Are you in the bathroom?" he shouts, but he gets no response.

He gets out of bed, puts a dressing gown on, then heads downstairs. Half way down he can hear voices coming from the kitchen. Its Pyah, Mark, Sarah, and some of Irish's gang discussing how they are going to get Denier De-fuer.

Mark is sat at the head of the table, "You know she's going to have a rather large entourage all armed to the teeth?"

Pyah is stood at the grill cooking bacon, "Yeah, but I don't think Jimmy will mind us borrowing some of his armoury."

Lacey is sat on Irish's knee, "Well, we can take it all, I think we're going to need it and we do have two new vehicles, courtesy of our dead Mercenaries."

Carl walks in, "Jesus, couldn't this wait till morning?"

The whole group turn in unison, "It is morning."

Carl places his hand on his head, "NO? Morning doesn't start till seven am, just because the sun is getting up doesn't mean we have to."

Sarah walks over to cuddle him, "You go back to bed then and I'll wake you before we go."

Carl shakes his head, "And every time I turn over you won't be there, I've kinda got used to you being there and when you're not I can't sleep."

Sarah turns to Pyah, "Fill me in when I get back down," she says, walking Carl back out the door, "I'll just go and tuck him in."

Carl stops her, "Very funny, do you think I'm some sort of kid like?" he spins her around and taps her across her butt, "you go and play with your friends I'll be down when I get dressed."

While he is gone, Mark and Irish have a good look at the map, discussing the best route.

Mark spins it around, "Well, if we go out on to the N6 At Figuig till we hit the N17."

Irish follows up the map, "Yeah, into Tendrara, we should be able to pick up the N19 up to Taourirt."

Lacey leans across, "That's taking us up country and Tan-Tan is down here," she points out, pointing further down the map.

Both Irish and Mark give her one of those 'this is a man thing' looks, then Irish slides her finger back up the map. "A2 to Rabat," he says, tracing the route with Lacey's finger, "A3 down the coast to Casablanca," he continues, then he smiles at her, "where we might stay overnight."

Lacey jumps off his knee, "Think I'll go and help the girls."

Mark pulls the map around, "Thought we might push on through?"

Irish shakes his head, "Even on the bikes that's an eighteen-hour journey," he explains, looking over to the girls, "they're going to need sleep and rest before we get there, and you ain't going to be able to flog that camper," he adds, pointing out the window to the motor home.

Mark peruses the map, "Yeah, even flogging it it's going to be tomorrow night, best take our time."

They all head over to Jimmy's shop to empty his armoury.

Carl tries to have a kip but finds himself tossing and turning. He eventually gets back up, gets dressed then heads downstairs. It's all quiet as he saunters around the deserted hotel calling out, "Oh shit, where the hell is everyone?" he asks, getting an eerie sense of isolation.

He looks outside to find all the vehicles present, then investigates the kitchen, empty, there's no sight or sound of anyone, "I'll bet the bastards have gone back to bed," he stands mulling it over, "but then where would Sarah be?"

Just as he's starting get a sense of panic and his mind starts to imagine the worst, Pyah comes out of the store with an arm full of guns, "Thank shit for that," he exclaims as he runs out the front, "thought you lot had been abducted by aliens or something."

He then goes to help load up the four by fours. Soon everything is prepared and Sonja has made food for the journey. Last minute checks are made, it's now six am as they all set off in convoy. Once they reach Taourirt they stop off for refreshments before pushing on to Rabat.

As they have arrived at Rabat after six pm all the women are tired from the journey so it's decided to stop over for the night to make an early start for Casablanca the next morning. The girls refresh themselves, doll themselves up, and decide to have a night out exploring the local cuisine. Mark, Carl and Irish plonk themselves at the nearest bar to make battle plans when Mark gets the strangest feeling they are being watched. No one looks out of place so when they leave Mark unobtrusively waits outside to see if anyone follows, "Hmm, must be a bit of paranoia," he decides, then heads off to see if he can catch up with Pyah.

The girls have already eaten when he catches up with them so he grabs a kebab from a local vender then strolls along the main drag, hand in hand with Pyah. Lacey and Sarah start to feel a little bit like gooseberries so they decide to head back to the hotel. Carl and Irish are at the hotel bar when they get there but instead of joining them Sarah stands shaking.

Lacey stares at her, "What's up hun? You cold?" she asks, then goes to wrap her jacket around Sarah's shoulders, when Sarah suddenly launches herself at Lacey, slaps a kiss on her lips then runs off blushing all the way to her room.

Lacey follows but when she gets there Sarah is crying her eyes out, "Whoa what's all this?"

Sarah spins away from her, "I'm sorry I didn't, well you know, I couldn't help it I just, well, oh for Christ's sake ever since you saved my life I've wanted to do that but just couldn't summon the courage."

Lacey sniggers, "What and you thought it would offend me?" she asks, spinning Sarah around, "me, the woman that's been trying to get into your drawers ever since we met," she points out, laughing out loud. "it's not as if it's a secret that I like women."

Sarah looks deep into Lacey's eyes, "Yeah, but it is a secret that I like you, that way, that is."

Lacey blows air through her teeth, "Yeah right, I knew all along, you just needed the right incentive to come out of your shell," she says, pulling her into a gentle embrace, "the way you look at me and Pyah, I hate to say this but it's kinda obvious, well to me and Pyah anyway," she says, laughing out loud again, "the way you used to pretend to despise her. All along she knew you just hated the way you felt about her."

Sarah stands with her mouth agape, "What, you mean Pyah knows how I feel about her too? Oh shit," she says, closing her eyes then walking to the window, tears rolling down her cheeks, "what the hell am I going to do?"

Lacey wraps her arms around her, "Oh I think I can think of something."

Sarah spins, "No not that, what the hell am I going to do about Pyah?"

Lacey tips her head, "Well, I wouldn't do anything, just do what you're doing now and leave it at that, the time will come and everything will happen as it's supposed to," she says, then she kisses Sarah.

Sarah reciprocates but starts to twitch nervously as Lacey's hand drifts down across her breast. Lacey's hand carries on down around Sarah's spine till she comes to her skirt button, flicking it open. She kisses Sarah's neck as she stealthily unzips her skirt allowing it to drop to the floor. Lacey's hand drifts back up under Sarah's blouse into the small of her back as she pulls her into a close embrace. Sarah's hands twitch as she places them gingerly on to Lacey's shoulders. Lacey lifts her up off the ground and carries her to the bed, placing her gently on the cold cotton sheets. Straddling Sarah, Lacey unbuttons her blouse as Sarah looks anywhere but straight at Lacey. Quivering with uncertainty Sarah allows Lacey to tease her blouse and bra away.

Now looking deep into Lacey's eyes through the shroud of raven black hair she can see Lacey's pupils expand to the width of her iris. Her eyes like black coals, seducing every inch of Sarah's soft white skin as the little pools of sweat congregate in the delves on her body. Lacey runs her hands down over Sarah's torso sliding herself down the bed to gain clear access to Sarah's panties. Sarah nervously opens her legs the slightest bit consenting their removal as Lacey pushes them to her feet. Lacey kisses Sarah's trembling thighs as she gently forces them open to reveal her vagina. Lacey gazes up at Sarah in a sultry fashion as she tenderly flicks her clitoris, then slowly plunges her tongue deep into Sarah.

All of Sarah's fears and uncertainties dissipate at that very moment as a tingle of pleasure rushes through her body. She lifts her legs over Lacey's shoulders as her head reaches back, craning her neck while arching her spine as Lacey lifts her up by her buttocks, pushing her hands around to place them on Sarah's hips, as Sarah's pelvis twitches, then spasms, turning slowly into a full on thrust. Sarah reaches down to grasp two hands full of Lacey's hair as she grits her teeth, groans, then screams with pure ecstasy. Her head thrashes from side to side as she squeezes Lacey's head between her thighs, then drops to the bed, her hands over her face, "Oh shit, never had that done to me before."

Lacey crawls back up to meet her eyes, "You mean to tell me that Carl has never had oral sex with you?"

Sarah slams her hands down on the wet sheets, "No, well yes, but he's never done, *that* to me, you know," she confides, giggling, "when he does it, it's pleasant, if you know what I mean," she continues, grasping Lacey's face to recklessly kiss her.

Lacey pulls back, "Oh, and what I did wasn't pleasant?" she asks, trying to look stern.

Sarah knows she's winding her up, "Oh, that was more than pleasant."

Lacey stands up, slips out of her own clothes, "Oh, trust me, I've only just started," she says, then slides back on to the bed like an animal stalking its prey.

Sarah pulls the sheet up over her breasts in fun, "Oh, please, Miss Tiger, don't eat me, I'm such a small morsel, you would hardly be satisfied."

Lacey gives a snarl, "Oh, I'm going to do more than eat you," she promises as she quietly growls, "I'm going to show you some pleasures that only a woman can show. Welcome to the girls' club," she says as she pulls Sarah's hand down between her legs.

She closes her eyes with delight as Sarah slips two fingers into her, "You do realise I haven't got a clue what I'm doing?"

Lacey opens her eyes, stares deep into Sarah's, "Oh, you don't realise what you do know, young lady. All you have to do is think about what would give you pleasure then do it to me."

Sarah tickles Lacey's clitoris while she thinks then reaches up to place Lacey's nipple in her mouth, "*hmm not as difficult as*

I would expect, I can do that," she concludes mentally, giving herself a proud inward smile, thinking "*just experiment Sarah.*"

Lacey gently but firmly grasps Sarah's breast then slides her hand down between Sarah's legs to play. After an hour of pure unadulterated lust both girls lay back on the warm damp sheets looking at each other.

Sarah makes the first move, rolling on to her front, "So, are we going to have a shower then go and join the others?"

Lacey looks up at her, "Yeah, I think they'll be wondering what's happened to us."

They step into the shower to wash each other, giggling like a couple of school girls gossiping, then get dressed to return to the men.

CHAPTER 15
A CHANGE OF HEART

Pyah and Mark walk in to the bar just as Sarah and Lacey sit with a couple of Bacardi and cokes. Mark walks over to the men, a smug grin on his face, kissing the other two girls on the head as he passes.

Pyah orders a drink then sits with Sarah and Lacey, "So how has your night been?" she asks airily, not really with it as her head is obviously in the clouds.

Lacey leans forward, "Looks like you had a good night?"

Pyah just smiles and nods, then sees the smug smirk across Sarah's face, "Looks like I'm not the only one that's been getting her passionate ways tonight," she says, pointing at Sarah.

Lacey lifts her glass, "Oh, we've had a bit of fun, you might say."

Pyah's eyes widen as she nearly chokes on her drink. Her head snaps around to Lacey, then to Sarah while still pointing her glass at Lacey, "You? You haven't?" she sputters, spinning her head to Lacey, "You two were? You? While me and Mark were? You? WOW," she continues, lifting her glass to salute Sarah "welcome to the girls' club!" she concludes, reaching across the table to give her a peck on the cheek, "so when am I invited?"

Sarah blushes into her glass, "Tonight is Carl's night I'm afraid, but we'll see," she says, taking a sip from her drink, "mind you, I usually demand my way with him, won't he get a shock when I just let him get on with it tonight?"

All three girls lift their glasses to each other, chinking them together. Sarah smiles "to the three buffeters," she toasts, giggling as Pyah and Lacey crane their necks back at her, "MUFFKETTEERS?"

Pyah's head droops as Lacey shakes hers in dismay, "Where the hell did you get that from?"

Sarah shrugs, "Better than being a Sith lord," she comments, looking over at the boys.

Lacey giggles at her, "Yeah, mine's Darth Maul, two minutes of Mauling and wham bam thank you, mam."

Sarah spits her drink out laughing, "Mines Darth Toto, too scared to do anything and starts shaking even if I say fetch."

Pyah stares at her, "Toto? Isn't that the dog out of the Wizard of Oz?" Sarah nods. Pyah thinks for a moment, "I suppose mine's Darth Vader, dark, mysterious and evil with some good still in him."

Lacey sips at her drink, "Yeah, and with a dick the size of a light sabre I suppose it makes him the chosen one, as I well know."

Sarah nearly chokes on her drink again, "What, you've seen it?"

Pyah casually announces, "She's had it both ways," she says, pointing at Lacey's mouth, then at her vagina.

Sarah sits back stunned, completely speechless. Pyah stands up and saunters over to the bar shrugging, "Would either of you care for another?"

Sarah lifts her glass, "Yeah, make it a whisky, straight, and make it a large one."

Lacey sits there chuckling to herself, "Don't worry, you're safe with Carl. It's just a special bond we have and it just happened."

At that the boys decide to join them. Carl sits down next to Sarah, "So, what you lot gossiping about?"

Sarah looks deep into his eyes, "You don't want to know, trust me, you don't want or need to know."

Carl squints at her, "You're probably right, I don't think I want to know anyhow."

Later that night Sarah climbs into bed next to Carl. Carl waits for her to get started as usual but she just rolls over to him and says, "Well? Are you going to make love to me tonight or what?"

Carl sits up, "What, no rampant onslaught first?"

Sarah shakes her head, "Nope, just make love to me," she says, laying there looking up at him with adoring eyes.

Carl cautiously kisses her, then kisses her breasts, still watching her face for any signs of fury. He slowly places his leg between hers, "Don't know what you girls were talking about, but if this is the result I definitely condone it," he tells her as he starts to make passionate love to her.

Sliding in to her, he kisses her neck as she lifts his head and gazes into his eyes, "What would you do if I told you I fancied someone else?"

He stops dead. "Well, I suppose we all fancy someone else at one time or another," he answers, then carries on, expecting her to push him on the remark.

She kisses him instead, "What would you say if I told you I fancied another woman?"

A big grin comes across his face, "Well, now that's a different matter."

She kisses him again, "What would you say if I told you I was shagging another woman?"

He stops dead again and looks at her with a disappointed frown, "I wouldn't be too happy."

Sarah's head drops on the pillow, "Why?" she asks, hoping she hasn't done the wrong thing.

Carl smiles at her, "Well, if you have shagged another woman you could have at least invited me, even if it was only to watch."

Sarah slaps him across the arm, "OK, what if it just happened?"

Carl kisses her breasts again, "Well, if it just happens again then stop, think, then come and get me."

She slaps him again, "What if it was Lacey?"

Carl's head jolts back, "Now that's a different matter altogether."

Sarah gives him a confused look, "Why?"

Carl huffs, "Have you seen the size of that Irish? If he found out I was watching his missus shag my missus, well, let's just say I wouldn't like him to find that out."

Sarah gives him a little girl lost look, "Well, what's wrong with him watching too?" she asks, teasing Carl.

He climbs off her and gets out of bed, "I don't think so," he pouts, then stomps into the bathroom, "I don't care how big he is, if I find out he's seen you in the buff I'll smash his face in, no man gets to look at my missus's body except me. You want to shag other women that's fine by me. I'd like to watch but not with you and Lacey, or you and Pyah come to think of it, cause I know if you're shagging Lacey it won't be long before you're shagging the other one," he rants as he comes out of the bathroom and climbs back into bed, "before you know it, all the men are watching all the women shagging, wanting to join in, changing bloody partners and it turns into a fucking swingers party, no fucking thank you, I ain't sharing you with no other man or woman if it means some other bloke watching," he elaborates, pouting, "don't care what you say, you might be the boss in the bedroom but I'm putting my foot down on this one, NO," he climbs back on top of her "and that's final, rant over, now can we make love or what?"

Sarah hugs him, "Glad we cleared that up," she says, giggling at him, then kissing him passionately before rolling him on to his back to slide down his abdomen, "relax, while I take away your frustration, trust me I won't let any other man even look at me," she promises, then slips his penis into her mouth.

Carl lies back and starts to relax to enjoy the moment, "It's not the fact that I don't like men looking at you," he explains, placing his hand gently on her head, "in fact I love it when men leer and gawk at you. I just proudly hold your hand and feel, like, ten feet tall, as I know you chose to be with me not them."

A tear comes to Sarah's eye as she comes back up the bed, "You know, I won't be able to do this if you keep making me cry, you soppy git."

Carl grimaces at her in fun, "Excuse me, who you calling soppy and what the hell are you doing up here? Did I tell you to take that out of your mouth? Have you finished? No, now get back down there and fucking suck bitch," he orders, giving a masterly nod.

Sarah licks his torso, "Ooo, I didn't think you had it in you, I'll go and finish then, oh masterful one," she says, as she pops his penis back into her mouth.

Carl just lies back and enjoys taking his time. It takes about quarter of an hour before he reaches his climax, by which time Sarah is drowned in her own sweat and her legs are starting to ache, but she doesn't complain. She just rolls over as Carl spoons her, then they soon fall asleep.

They wake up the next morning to the sound of Pyah singing in the shower with the window open. Sarah gets into her shower, opens the window and starts to chat to Pyah.

Suddenly Sarah hears Lacey's voice, "Don't mind if I cut in, do you?"

Pyah spins to see Lacey stood buck naked behind her, "Irish taking all the room in your shower like?"

Lacey steps into the shower with Pyah, "Yeah, the fat bastard takes up all the bed, then he gets up early, spends about an hour in the shower, god knows what he does in there? He's worse than a woman."

Mark saunters into the bathroom all bleary-eyed, "You talking to yourself in there?" he asks, pulling the cubical door open and looking down at Lacey, "you're not my wife. Where the hell is my wife?" he grumbles, turning back to the bedroom grumping to himself.

Pyah steps out from behind Lacey, "I'm here, you daft sod."

Mark sits on the bed, "Yeah, I figured that, but it's a bit crowded in there for another one."

Lacey sticks her head out, "Oh I don't know, I think we could fit a little one in."

Sarah's voice comes through the window, "Thought you said he weren't little?"

Pyah leans out of the window, "Shhh, he doesn't know we told you that."

Then Carl's voice comes booming through, "Who the hell are you talking to, honey, this is not a secret escapes ad."

Sarah sticks her head out of the shower, "Pyah's shower is on this adjoining wall and I can just about touch her out of the window, so we're just having a girly morning chat is all."

Carl stretches, "Oh, well you get on with it but hurry up, I need a shower, I stink, feel sorry for the maid when she comes to change this bed."

Soon the girls are downstairs, tucking into breakfast while the men shower. As the girls finish, Mark and Carl appear, "Haven't you ordered us any?"

Sarah shakes her head, "Nope, get your own," she tells them, looking around them, "where's Irish?"

Lacey stands up, "Oh, he'll still be preening himself, got more toiletries and beauty products than a model that one."

Mark stares at her, "You're joking? A big bad biker like that?" he says, laughing.

Lacey clicks her teeth in disapproval, then nods as the girls head out for a walk.

Once outside Lacey pulls a packet of cigarettes from her purse, sticks one in her mouth and lights it as Sarah walks over, "Didn't take you for a smoker?"

Pyah sticks her head around Sarah, "Only now and then on a morning," Lacey says, whining, "secret smoker you know," she explains, squinting at her.

Sarah takes the packet, "Don't suppose I can have one, can I?"

Lacey nods as Pyah stands, mouth agape, "Not you too?"

Sarah puffs away happily, "Been about three years since I had one of these, usually have one at Christmas, prefer a good Havana though."

Pyah cringes, "A cigar? You like a cigar?"

Lacey spins around, "Oh, yeah, a good Cuban," she agrees, nodding in approval, "nothing like the smell of a hand rolled Cuban."

Pyah walks away in disgust, "Yeah, they stink," she remarks as she heads down the main drag.

Lacey takes quiet note of a black sedan parked down one of the side streets, then hurries up to Pyah, "It's probably nothing, but did you see that black car down that street we just passed?"

Pyah sprays herself with deodorant, "Yeah I did, it was parked there last night when me and Mark came back from our walk. Doesn't seem to fit the area does it?"

Sarah trundles along, "What you two conspiring about?"

Pyah sprays her with a touch of deodorant, "We're just commenting on the black car around the corner."

Sarah stands still, "What black car 'round what corner?"

Lacey drags her in between her and Pyah, "You need to get your head together instead of on his dick."

Pyah links arms with her, "I was just telling her that it was there last night."

Sarah stops again, "What was there last night?"

The two girls drag her forward, "OK, I'll start from the beginning and go slow for you," she says as she explains her suspicions.

When they get back to the hotel they tell Mark and Carl. Mark turns to Carl, "You know, I had a funny feeling we were being watched all night, I just couldn't pinpoint them."

When everyone has eaten they set off on the road again. Pyah sits in the back of the motor home with the other girls, looking out the back to see if they are being followed. Every now and then Pyah thinks she sees the black car and tells Mark, but Mark can't see it.

They have been on the road for about an hour when the black car comes into plain view about quarter of a mile behind them, approaching fast. Mark radios Irish to inform him so Irish lets three of his bikers drop back. The car pulls into the side as the bikers pull up a few hundred meters ahead of it.

Irish radios his men, "What's it doing?"

They watch, "It's just sat there."

Then all of a sudden one of them goes down as the other recklessly tries to turn his bike around while radioing Irish, "We're being fired on, some fucking sniper has us pinned down," he relays as he drops his bike to roll in to the roadside behind it.

Irish and the rest of his gang turn around to head back, reaching the two men as the car comes hurtling up, firing on them. Irish's men draw their machine guns to return fire as Irish pulls over to try and cover his men. Something comes flying through the air as he drops his bike in the sand "GRENADE!" he yells, pulling his man to his feet to push him down a small ravine.

The grenade blows Irish's bike to smithereens, shrapnel is flying all over the place as his men speed through to try to catch the car. Irish radios his men, "Looks like they're trying to split us up. Get back to the Fischers and find somewhere to take cover."

The men spin around to head back to the Fischers as a bullet comes out of nowhere ricocheting off Irish's helmet. Irish and his man Sims are both pinned down. Every time they pop up to try to locate the sniper the result is a bullet whistling past them at very close quarters.

Mark finds a small shanty town about a mile down the road, he pulls over as the bikers arrive and commandeers one of the bikes. Pyah tries to stop him, "Where the hell do you think you're going?"

Mark reaches into the back of the four by four, "A sniper has Irish pinned down, where the hell do you think I'm going," he answers, pulling a Dragunov rifle from the back of the vehicle, "you know I'm the only one here that can use this and as it's his only chance, what would you do?"

Pyah kisses him, "Be bloody careful."

Mark smiles, "As always," he says, then heads off into the desert to flank Irish.

Irish radios Mark, "I think my sniper is out at sea, there's a little cove a couple of hundred yards away. Not sure but I think he's in a boat out there."

Mark manages to get up behind Irish and Sims, then travels into them on foot unobserved. Sims has a Kevlar helmet that he's been putting on the top of the dune in front of them to try and get a fix on the sniper. Mark hangs back as he sees Sims putting the helmet back up again, "Got you, you little bastard," he mutters, spotting a small dinghy through his scope.

It's sat in the cove about half a mile away from Irish. Mark takes a shot at it then runs in toward Irish. As he lands next to Sims he startles Irish, "Where the hell did you come from?"

Mark smiles at him, "Hello to you too," he hands Sims his binoculars, "here stick these up under your hat and put it back up there."

Sims does as he's told as Mark pops up at the other end of the dune. Mark takes a couple of shots at the boat, hoping to hit something. The boat speeds off, but as they are about to leave the car comes back down the road. Mark turns his gun on it to shoot the driver as the car barrel rolls across the road bursting into a ball of flame. Irish and Sims grab Sims's bike to head back to the rest of the party while Mark heads back into the desert to retrieve his bike.

Soon Mark catches up with Irish just as they're coming up to the shanty town. Irish notices men on the roof sneaking up on Pyah's position, "You got company," he tells her over the radio, "there's a couple of dozen coming over the rooftops at you from the south and they look well-armed."

Pyah and Lacey dish out the weapons as Irish's men circle around the shanty town, trying to catch their hunters by surprise. Mark gets himself down in a prone position to pick a couple off. As he does, Irish notices a few of the Mercs drifting off into the desert to try and outflank Mark, "Won't be long," he informs Mark, "seems we have some uninvited guests trying to crash our little party," he says, patting his gun before heading off into the desert to wait for them.

Mark pinpoints a few for Pyah, Lacey and Sarah, then picks the odd one off himself. Irish comes across the six that were trying to get behind Mark. He shoots three of them before his gun jams. The other three drop their guns, thinking it would be more fun to kill him bare handed. Irish smiles at them, "Oh, you have got to be kidding me," he takes a stance, "you do realise there are only three of you, ha ha ha," he crows, laughing out loud as the biggest charges at him with a large knife.

Irish sidesteps, grabs the knife and thrusts it up through the guy's ribs, then spins to the next one, "Bring it on."

This one pulls out a rather large machete and starts to swing it around as the other sidesteps around Irish. The guy thrusts at him. He catches the machete by its handle and shoulder charges the guy to the ground, spinning to throw the machete at the other guy, hitting him full in the chest. Irish stands up, grabs one of the Mercs' guns then shoots all three for good measure.

He returns to Mark with all the Mercs' weaponry, "Look what I got," he says, a big smug grin on his face.

Pyah, Lacey and Sarah stay close to each other through the narrow walkways of the shanty town. A few of the mercenaries have dropped down and are now creeping through the streets. Pyah hears footsteps. She signals to Lacey and Sarah to go around the back and come in from behind. Sarah and Lacey silently scurry off while Pyah waits. As she is about to pounce out, a gun man appears above her blasting down at her.

She ducks into the shed to shoot through the roof, killing him. The other Mercs approaching rush Pyah as Sarah and Lacey come around the corner, guns blazing, slicing the Mercs in two with a barrage of lead.

Irish's men are up on some dunes at the edge of the little town. They have a clear view of most of the rooftops, giving them the opportunity to pop off the few remaining Mercs trying their surprise assault.

Two Mercs have found a small hut on the rooftops and lay in wait for any unsuspecting quarry as Irish spots them. He points the movement out to Mark. Mark takes careful aim, waiting for one of them to just stick his head out. Sarah walks underneath them. Mark exhales, "Come on. Just twitch," he says as one of them crawls out of the shadows.

Mark puts a round straight through his head as Sarah spins to blast through the roof of the shanty hut. She empties a full magazine into the rooftop hut as Pyah and Lacey appear beside her blasting. Eventually the guy in there falls through the door landing next to his partner, DEAD. The girls give each other a high five and turn to Mark who gives them a thumbs up. Mark stands to walk back to the shanty town as Irish radios his men.

The town is cleared, checked and Sarah breaks out a bottle of whisky to celebrate.

There's no sign of the sniper in the boat as Mark and Irish stand looking out to sea, "Must have gone scurrying back to his master with his tail between his legs," Mark says as he lifts his glass to Irish. It isn't long before they are back on their way to Casablanca

CHAPTER 16
ENVY IN CASABLANCA

The evening air is hot and close when they reach Casablanca. The humid temperature sticks their sweat drenched clothes to their bodies. Irish leads them straight to the cool underground car park of the Kensi Tower hotel. "Guess this is as good a place to stop over as any," he says as he and his men park their bikes, "it's a bit expensive but when you want the best and I'm presuming you want the best," he continues, turning to Mark as he and Pyah climb out of the motor home into the fresh air-conditioned car park.

Mark fans himself with his hand as Pyah spins in the middle of the air-conditioner flow then lies down on the cold concrete floor, "Oh, I think I'll sleep here tonight."

Sarah is laid on a bunk in the back of one of the four by fours as Carl steps out, "Oh, it's a lot cooler out here honey," he calls, walking over to Mark.

Sarah sits up, "You could have come and helped me out, you miserable so and so."

Carl rushes back, "Sorry dear, here, let me help you."

Sarah sees Pyah lying on the floor, rushes over, then lies down beside her, "Oh, that's the best idea you've had in ages."

Only a few of the bikers notice Lacey has ridden in on one of the motorbikes as she rides past Carl, Sarah, Pyah, Mark and Irish. They are stunned to silence as she parks the bike up.

Mark turns to Carl "I thought she was with you."

Carl turns and shrugs, "I thought she was with you."

Irish walks over to her, "Wow, you ride, NICE."

Lacey dismounts, "I got an R1 at home so this piddling little thing isn't really classed as riding, is it?" she asks as she looks down at the seven fifty she's borrowed, "figured it was the coolest way to travel, especially with your skirt hitched up and the wind blowing in at your knickers," she explains, sniggering as she walks over to Pyah hitching her skirt back down.

Pyah looks up at her, "Dirty mare," she reprimands, giving Lacey a wry smile.

Lacey sits next to her, "You're only jealous because you didn't think of it."

Pyah laughs out loud, "I wouldn't dare get on the back of one of those things, let alone ride it."

Lacey leans down to her whispering, "It's nearly as good as sex," she confides, pecking Pyah on the cheek, "in fact, sometimes it's better," she adds, glancing up at Irish, then giggling with Pyah and Sarah.

Sarah sits up, "I'd get on the back with you," she says, placing her hand on Lacey's lap.

Pyah sits up, "I think it's about time we tried to book into this place and see if we can get some sort of shower."

Sarah stands up, "Oh, yes please," she says, helping Lacey to her feet.

Lacey brushes the back of her skirt off, "All for one and all that," she declares as the three link arms with each other to waltz into the hotel. The boys follow, admiring their arses as they swing from side to side, swaying in a uniform dance.

All of the men head straight to the bar, leaving the girls to book in. Luckily, there are plenty of rooms available so Pyah, Sarah and Lacey head for one. Once inside the room, Pyah strips off as Lacey heads for the balcony to stand in the cool sea breeze, "What a view."

Sarah follows her out, "Yeah, it's a good job we're so high up or everyone would be getting a hell of a view," she comments, pointing at Pyah prancing around naked.

Lacey looks at Pyah, "Ooo, that's a damned good idea," she agrees, then strips right there on the balcony.

Sarah blushes with a shocked look on her face, "You can't be serious?"

Lacey shrugs, "Like you said, we are way up in the air where no one can see us."

Pyah walks out, "Oh, its nice out here," she comments, giving Sarah a once over, "come on girl, get your kit off, stop being such a stick in the mud. You only live once," she says, sniffing at her clothes, "trust me, you need a good airing too."

Sarah timidly steps back inside the room and strips. The two girls watch, laughing as she covers her boobs to take her bra off. Pyah steps forward to lower her hand, "Oh, for Christ's sake woman, let it all hang out."

Lacey puts her head over Pyah's shoulder, "You know she's got better boobs than us?"

Pyah steps back, "She's got a nicer shape than us," she says spinning Sarah.

Her and Lacey say in unison, "nicer ass too."

Sarah turns back and taps both of them on the shoulder, "Stop teasing, you bitches, or I'll get dressed and go down with the lads."

Pyah grabs her by the shoulders, "Whoa, I ain't kidding, what are you? About a twenty-two-inch waist?"

Sarah looks a little disgruntled, "I'm only a twenty actually."

Lacey puts her hand out, "Exactly, I'm a twenty-five."

Pyah spins, "Snap. And what size are those, thirty-four C?" pointing at Sarah's boobs.

Sarah nods sheepishly. Lacey cups her own, "Thirty-four D."

Pyah licks her finger to rub her nipple, "Yeah me too, with a thirty-two-inch hip. No curves, just long legs thank god."

Lacey walks around Sarah, "Cute, perfectly shaped little bundle, and you call us bitches, hmm."

Pyah walks over to Lacey, "Kiss me!"

Lacey shrugs, "OK," then kisses her.

Pyah rolls her eyes into the back of her head, "NO, KISS me!"

Lacey gives Pyah the most passionate kiss she can muster then Pyah walks over to Sarah, "OK, your turn."

Sarah steps away, "Why?" she asks, shaking her head.

Pyah steps forward, "Just indulge me, it's an experiment."

Sarah puckers up, then kisses Pyah. Pyah pouts, "Is that how you kiss Carl?"

Sarah frowns, "NO."

Pyah tips her head, "Derr, now kiss me."

Sarah starts to kiss Pyah, then for some reason gets horny, wrapping her arms around Pyah with a full-on snog. It takes Pyah's breath as she pulls away, "Whoa, she's a better kisser than you," she says, pointing at Lacey before strutting into the bathroom.

Lacey follows her, "Excuse me, I want a reprieve," she says, then kisses Pyah again, "better?"

Pyah shakes her head. Lacey walks out of the bathroom in disgust. She grabs Sarah and kisses her, "Put some effort into it then," she demands, so Sarah does the same to her as she did to Pyah.

Lacey walks into the bathroom wiping her mouth, "See what you mean," she agrees, splashing some water on her face as she clears her throat, "she's better than you too."

Pyah looks up at Lacey. "I kind of figured that."

They walk back to the door as Sarah is stood in the middle of the room smiling, they pop their heads around the door, "Bitch," they declare, then attack her with the pillows.

They battle her on to the bed then dive on top of her as the pillows burst open. Feathers are everywhere.

Pyah licks Sarah's boob then licks Lacey's, "You know she even tastes better than you."

Lacey licks her own arm then licks Sarah's boob too, "You're right, bitch," she says, then attacks her again with a surviving pillow.

Pyah pins Sarah down while they're all giggling, "Quick, get her drawers off," she instructs as she pushes her mouth against Sarah's.

Lacey drags Sarah pants off, then rams her tongue straight into her as Sarah and Pyah become entangled in the throes of a passionate kiss. Pyah kisses Sarah's neck then down on to her breast while Lacey comes up her abdomen to meet Pyah at the other breast. Sarah looks down at them, "You know, I would have killed someone if they had suggested this a few weeks ago but it just feels so natural now and damn I'm enjoying it," she laughs, giggling to herself, "fwar, me, a bisexual?"

Lacey comes up, "Oh shut up and enjoy then," she says, then sticks her with a kiss whilst plunging her fingers into Sarah's vagina.

Pyah stays where she is, suckling on one breast while fondling the other. Sarah doesn't quite know what to do with her hands at first but then thinks, "*Fuck it*" and slides one into Pyah's vagina and the other into Lacey as they both moan with their mouths full as she inserts two fingers in them.

Pyah comes up to Sarah's neck kissing it all the way to her ear as she whispers, "She likes her arse smacked you know."

Lacey hears her, "Hmm hm," she hums and nods while still kissing.

Sarah pulls Lacey back, "Seriously?" she asks, wide eyed, "you too?"

Lacey seductively bites her lip, "Ooo, nothing like a good spanking I say," she says, then spins her arse toward Sarah, "go for it."

Sarah wallops her right across her cheek, "I prefer to have someone across my knee," she tries to say while Lacey plunges her tongue into her mouth.

Lacey pulls back, "Yeah, nothing like giving and receiving I say."

Sarah wallops her again, "You can do me later."

Pyah sits up, "You keep that shit between you two, you pair of kinky bitches."

Sarah and Lacey stop what they are doing, sit up, and look at Pyah. Sarah pouts "Says the girl that instigated this whole love triangle, pffft kinky bitches?"

Lacey leans across to kiss Pyah, "And didn't you tell me you were spanking some cop woman before?" she checks, flicking Pyah's chin, "and totally enjoyed it? Giving orders like a dominatrix," she adds, raising her eyebrows.

Pyah blushes slightly, "Yeah, well, when someone likes pain you give them it, I just don't like pain," she justifies, tipping her head, "it's for the birds, fucking scary birds like."

Sarah turns to Pyah "Talking about scary, what's this Mina Harker thing? The vampire lady? I heard Mark calling you it at the hotel."

Lacey laugh a raucous laugh, "Oh, she wants to bite someone."

Sarah spins, "Who!?" she demands, a little tremble in her voice, "and why?"

Pyah strokes Sarah's face, "Take no notice of her sweetie, I just had a moment with the African girl, that's all."

Sarah sits back smiling, "What kind of moment?" she asks, a curious look on her face.

Pyah gives Lacey a look of intent, "Big mouth. Well, I had her jugular in my mouth and had to pull away for fear that the temptation to bite was going to overpower me, if you must know," she says as she turns to sit on the edge of the bed.

Sarah throws herself backwards on to the bed, "And you call us kinky?"

Pyah spins quickly, jumps on top of Sarah and pins her down, straddling her, "If you don't shut up I might just bite you," she warns, glaring deep into Sarah's eyes.

Sarah raises one eyebrow, "I might just let you," she says, taking Pyah by complete surprise as she jolts her head back, releasing Sarah. Sarah sits forward, "Gotcha!" she says, then starts to laugh.

Lacey wipes her brow, "You fucking had me there for a moment too," she says, sighing, "thought I was just about to enter the fucking twilight zone for vampires," she goes on as she lies back on the bed, "I like a good spanking, but shit you two were getting a little too scary for my liking, vampires? SHIT," she says, then rolls over onto her front.

Pyah leans forward quickly and bites one of her buttocks while Sarah bites the other. Lacey jumps off the bed, "Whoa, you two stay away from me, you crazy bitches," she warns as Pyah and Sarah fold with laughter.

Lacey picks up one of the half empty pillows and smashes them both with it, "Stop it," she reprimands, then bursts in to laughter on the bed next to them.

They decide it's about time they got ready, but first they need a shower as the feathers are sticking to their sweaty bodies. As they take their suspenders and stocking off they find feathers inside them. Sarah tuts, "Shit, these things get everywhere."

Pyah starts to laugh, "You ain't kidding," she says, pointing at one stuck in the crack of Lacey's arse.

Sarah folds over, "Jesus, woman, you laying an egg there or what?"

Lacey looks in the mirror, then starts to cluck like a hen, strutting around the room and into the shower. The other two follow.

Soon they are ready, dressed and on their way down to see the lads. Before they get there they quickly check each other for feathers or any other sign of a sexual nature that might give away what they have been up to. Sarah doesn't care, "I'll be telling Carl what I did, it might make him jealous, that's if you don't mind?" she checks and the other two shrug.

Lacey puts her hand on her heart, "For Christ's sake, don't tell Irish, and tell your blokes not to say anything to him either, don't want him getting any ideas."

CHAPTER 17
WHEN ENEMIES SPLIT

The boys are in the bar with Irish and his gang, having a good old chin wag about the battle that had just taken place. Seeing who has biggest bragging rights when the girls walk in dolled up to the nines. The conversation stops dead as the room drops into complete silence. All three girls are dressed in very short sparkly dresses as Pyah puts her arm around Mark, "You going to take us out on the town then?"

Sarah ruffles Carl's hair, "Yeah, we think you should hurry upstairs, get suited and booted and treat us."

Lacey struts her stuff in front of Irish, "Unless you boys want to stay here bragging about who has the biggest dick, all night," she shrugs, pecking Irish on the lips, "we can always go and have some fun of our own," she tells them as all three girls head for the door.

Mark shouts the barman over, "Can I have three scotch and sodas please," he orders as he stands, offers his seat to Pyah then steps back, "I'll be back down by the time you have finished your drink, dear," he says, walking towards the lift, "are you two bumpkins coming, or am I taking the girls out all on my own?"

Carl power walks after him, "Don't mind if I do, young sir."

Irish just sits there, "Sorry to be a bore, but party, dancing, flashing lights, and glitter not exactly my thing," he says, tipping his head to his drink, "but you go and enjoy, I'll be alright with the lads," he adds as he walks over to his crew to revel in their celebrations.

It isn't long before Carl and Mark are dressed in their best and on their way back downstairs. Mark decides to walk down the ornate staircase to make an entrance rather than just come out of the lift. Halfway down the stairs he stops and looks over the banister rail, "I don't fucking believe it."

Carl looks over then back at Mark, "Don't believe what?"

Mark points down at two females at the other bar, "If I'm not mistaken, that's Denier De-fuer."

Carl nearly snaps his neck trying to take another look, "You have got to be shitting me, what you going to do?"

Mark pulls him back, "I'm going to go and say hello, you coming?"

Carl blows air through his cheeks, "Suppose," he agrees, following Mark down the stairs.

As they reach the bottom, Pyah and Sarah spot them and wolf whistle. Mark puts two fingers up to signal he will only be two minutes, then walks into the other bar, "Well, I'll be damned," he remarks, sitting right next to Denier, "thought that was you, heard you been looking for us."

At that, the other woman turns to face him and Carl. Carl squints, "Don't I know you?"

Denier spins on her stool, "My dear, I would like to introduce mister Carl Sinclair, Carl meet-"

Before she can finish Carl interrupts, "Elleon Vixter," as a tear comes to his eye.

Elleon looks stunned, "Are you the same Carl Sinclair that brought my daddy home from Vietnam?"

Carl drops his head, "And helped to bury him in that god forsaken outback."

Elleon's eyes flood, "I'm sorry," she says, then turns, takes a large brown envelope out of her back and throws it on the bar in front of Denier, "I don't hunt my friends or my daddy's friends," she tells her, then heads for the door.

Denier picks up the envelope and walks after her, but when she gets to the door Elleon has completely vanished.

Carl walks up behind Denier, "I think those aborigines taught her that one," he comments as he pushes past her to go to see Sarah.

Mark stays seated at the bar, "From what I can make out she's good."

Denier huffs, "Ten a penny, when I've dealt with you, I'll deal with her."

Mark gives a raucous laugh, "If what Carl tells me about her father is half of what she is, then I'd say you have a big problem, if you decide to go after her," he tells her, standing up and walking to the door, "but your first problem is going to be getting out of here, alive."

Denier pulls out a compact, "Oh, I don't think that's my problem," she replies, dabbing her face as the door closes behind Mark.

Mark bumps into Pyah as he is returning. Pyah is in one hell of a hurry, "Where the hell is the cow?"

Mark stops her and Lacey as she comes rushing up while Carl is trying to hold Sarah back, "Just think about it honey, please."

Mark gives him an evil stare, "What the hell did you have to go blabbing your mouth off for?"

Pyah pushes his hands off her, "What the hell you protecting her for?"

Mark shakes his head, "Because she has about eight armed men surrounding her and I don't really want to go up against them unarmed, plus I think this is a really nice hotel and I wouldn't want to spoil it, would you?"

The girls stop, think for a moment, then agree not to go in and shoot her. Mark walks over to Sarah, "She doesn't know you, does she?"

Sarah pulls a face, "Never met her so I presume not, why?"

Mark stands back, "Well, I would like you to go and keep an eye on her for a few minutes while I try and sort something."

Sarah shakes her head, "And?" she asks, lifting her hands, "what happens if she leaves?"

Mark gives her a gormless look, "Improvise, follow her, use your cell phone, I don't know, I won't be long," he tells her, then rushes off with Pyah.

Sarah saunters into the bar, walks past Denier to a stool three seats down, sits and calls the bar man, "White wine please barkeep."

As the bar man pours her the wine she pulls out a cigarette case, "Don't suppose you have a light too?" she asks, putting a cigarette in her mouth.

Denier's hand appears beside her with a lighter in it, "American?" she asks Sarah.

Sarah takes the cigarette out of her mouth, looks down at it, then back up at Denier, "Yeah, err no actually it's British," she says, putting it back in her mouth to light it, "but I do smoke the odd Marlboro Light."

Denier titters, "I meant you," she clarifies, flicking the lighter closed, "are you American?"

Sarah draws heavily on the cigarette, "Nope, Canadian," she answers, blowing the smoke out of the side of her mouth.

Denier sits next to her, "Oh, whereabouts in Canada?" she asks, sliding the lighter back in her bag.

Sarah takes a sip from her wine, "Oh, just a little town in British Columbia called Prince George, you probably won't have heard of it, no one ever has."

Denier leans on the bar, "Route sixteen, near the Stuart River provincial park, you'll be surprised where I've been," she says, slipping the cigarette out of Sarah's hand to take a puff before handing it back, "What street?"

Sarah takes another puff, "Saint Patrick's, you know it?"

Denier takes a cigarette out of her case, "Lower quarter, yeah I know it, got an acquaintance lives off Domano boulevard."

Sarah realises that Denier is coming on to her, "Well, I just came in for a swift one, my husband will be wondering where I am," she reasons, and starts to drink her wine quickly, "it's been nice talking to you."

As she starts to stand up Lacey walks in and slinks past her and Denier to sit right at the end of the bar. Denier's eyes follow her all the way down.

Sarah looks over her shoulder at Lacey then back at Denier, "Friend of yours?" she asks, pretending to have no knowledge of Lacey.

Denier smiles at her, "You could say that."

Sarah shakes Denier's hand, "Well, it's been nice, I might see you around," she excuses, then saunters towards the door.

When she returns to the group Mark and Pyah reappear, "What you doing in here?"

Sarah tuts at him, "Lacey's in there with her, she was coming on to me."

Pyah shakes her head, "I didn't think that Lacey was that stupid, fancy coming on to you in front of that bitch."

Sarah puts her hand over Pyah's mouth, "No, that bitch was coming on to me when Lacey walked in," she corrects, smiling, "Lacey went to the end of the bar and I pretended I didn't know her, I think De-fuer bought it."

Mark pulls a tracking device out of his pocket, "I don't suppose you can get this on her?"

Sarah takes it, "How?"

Mark shrugs, "Go back in, tell her you've lost something, look around the bar, ask the barman if he's seen it, then try and slip that in her bag or something."

Carl taps her across the butt, "Improvise, dear."

Sarah takes a pen out of her bag, writes her mobile number on a card, then walks back into the bar. She walks back up to

Denier, "Hope you don't mind, but if I've read this right you may want this," she says and hands her the phone number.

Denier smiles, "Oh you read it right," she says, then kisses Sarah.

Before Sarah can put the device into her bag, Denier walks off to the ladies' room. Sarah stands for a moment then decides to follow. As she enters the ladies room the door at the other end shuts, "Damn, missed her."

Lacey walks in behind her, "Did you give her your number?"

Sarah nods, "But I was supposed to get this in her bag," she says, showing Lacey the device.

Lacey flicks Sarah's nose, "Hopefully she'll call you, then we should get a fix on her."

Sarah kisses her, "Genius," she praises as they both walk out of the ladies and back to the boys.

Sarah hands Mark the device back, "Sorry, I had no chance."

Lacey steps forward, "Yeah, but she'll probably phone her if I know that look she gave missy here."

Carl puts his arm around Sarah, "Then we can just ask her where she is I suppose," he suggests sarcastically.

Sarah closes her eyes in disgust, "No, then we get a fix on her phone," she corrects, shaking her head at him.

Mark raises one eyebrow, "Or you could just ask her."

Sarah leans forward, pecks Mark on the cheek, "We'll see," she says as Carl pulls her back.

"Ahem, we'll have none of that, thank you," he says sternly, stamping his authority.

Sarah starts to walk to the bar, "If you only knew," she teases, smiling a sultry smile.

Carl scurries after her, "Excuse me," he starts, gently pulling her back by her arm, "if I only knew WHAT?"

Sarah reaches up, pecks him on the cheek and whispers in his ear, "Later, my dear," then tries to walk away.

Carl gets a bit flustered, "No, DEAR, now," he says, leering back at Mark.

Sarah pulls his face back to her, "Don't worry dear, I haven't shagged him and I'm not about to, so just wait," she instructs, then orders a large Bacardi and coke.

Carl's anger turns to perverse curiosity, "You know something about him, don't you?"

Sarah kisses him, "NO, just wait, I'll tell you later, when we're alone."

Carl pushes her drink into her hand, "OK, drink up and we can get alone," he says, tipping her drink towards her mouth.

Sarah puts her drink down, "Patience," she tells him, then takes a sip, "aren't you having one?"

He turns to the barman, "I'll have a scotch, straight, somehow I think I'm going to need it."

CHAPTER 18
RESTAURANT FOOTSIE

Mark suggests they go and have a meal at a little restaurant he saw on the way in. They go and hand their keys back into reception. Pyah pulls the receptionist to one side, "I'm afraid we've made a bit of a mess in our room," she apologizes, handing him a fifty-dollar bill, "don't suppose you could send a maid up to clean before we get back can you, please?"

The receptionist pushes the bill back towards her, "It's ok madam, that will be seen to before you return."

Pyah pushes the bill back, "We had a pillow fight and when I say mess I mean *mess*, give this to the maid, I can only apologise," she explains, winking at him.

He takes the bill, "I'll see to it that she gets it," he promises, smiling through a minor blush.

As they leave the hotel they catch a glimpse of Denier and her entourage disappearing out of town, heading back towards Tan-Tan. Mark turns to the girls, "Don't worry, we'll get her," he assures them, then starts walking backwards with his hands in the air. "It's a beautiful night, let's just enjoy it and have some fun."

Sarah links arms with Carl on one side, Lacey links arms with him on the other side. Pyah links arms with Lacey, then pulls Mark in on the other side.

Carl starts to sing, "We're off to see the wizard," and they all turn to stare at him.

Mark gives him a sideways look, "NO," he objects, shaking his head.

Carl shrugs, "OK, so where's this gaff you're taking us too?" he asks and Mark points at a little restaurant about one hundred yards down the road on the corner, "looks good to me."

As they walk in, a maître' d approaches, "Table for five?" he checks, taking their jackets, "would the ladies care for a beverage before ordering?" he asks, handing them a wine list, "and the gentlemen something from the bar maybe?"

Sarah hands the wine list back, "I think we'll all have something from the bar thank you," she says, turning to the other girls.

Pyah and Lacey nod in agreement. The maître d collects a drinks menu from the bar and hands it to Mark, "When sir is ready to order, I'll just be here," he tells him, pointing at a small podium to the front of the restaurant.

After ordering, the food quickly arrives. Mark and Carl start to tuck in as Mark stops dead. He has one foot that he knows is Pyah's creeping up his leg. This doesn't faze him, but when another creeps up that he knows isn't hers, that's a different matter. Both Lacey and Sarah are within reaching distance and when he looks up both are smiling into their food. He also notices that Carl seems to be in the same predicament. Carl is smiling at first as Sarah starts to play footsie with him, but another foot joins in as he starts to blush openly. He swallows, then unbuttons his shirt slightly.

Mark looks at him, "Getting a bit warm there, mate?"

Just for fun Mark slips his shoe off, then runs his foot up Carl's leg. Carl jumps up, "OK, that does it, I know that's you," he accuses, pointing at Mark, "flipping big clodhoppers," he rants, looking around at everyone else, "and I know one of them was you," he continues, pointing at Sarah, "at least I hope it was, but which one of you two are playing silly buggers?" he demands, pointing at Pyah and Lacey.

The maître d' walks over, "Is there a problem, sir?"

Carl shakes his head, "No, just this lot having a little fun at my expense, don't worry I'll get them back," he says as he calmly sits back down.

Every now and then someone touches Carl's leg all throughout the meal so he openly looks under the table to see who it is. Finding it's Sarah he sits up, "That's OK then," but if it's someone else he grabs their foot to stab it gently with a fork, "that'll teach you," he says, smiling.

Soon the taking the piss out of Carl turns to jovial banter on all quarters, as the whole group become merry on the alcoholic beverages. Before long the meal is finished, coffee has been drunk and brandy has been consumed to the point of uncontrollability, when the management very tactfully asks the party to leave.

They submit to the restaurants wishes, bid the staff a good night, then head back to the hotel via the scenic route, to the discontent of some locals trying to get some sleep.

When they get back into the hotel Sarah suggests a good strong coffee before retiring so they head to the bar. Irish and his men are still there, discussing a plan to get Denier, when the group descends on them.

Carl inadvertently hears them mention Denier's name, "Oh, we were talking to her earlier," he mentions as the alcohol shuts his brain off, "and the Vixter."

Irish turns to him, grabs him by the lapels and pushes him against the bar, "And you didn't inform us," he says, growling, "where the fuck is she?"

Sarah makes a move to try and stop him before Carl says anymore, but Carl's brain still isn't engaged, "She left after the Vixter quit on her, I think she's gone back to Tan-Tan."

Sarah catches Carl as Irish throws him to one side. Irish turns to Mark, "If you're going to keep things from us then this arrangement is terminated, you're on your own mate," he says, walking out of the hotel with his men in tow.

Irish gets on his bike and heads towards Tan-Tan leaving the group in dismay. Lacey steps forward, "Good riddance I say," she says, picking up a drink that one of them had left, "they were attracting too much attention anyway."

The group mulls on this for a moment, then agrees with her. Pyah orders a coffee, "We're probably better off without them, plus they'll probably give us a distraction," she reasons, turning towards Lacey, "you said he was a lousy shag anyhow," she adds, laughing.

Lacey wraps her arms around Pyah, "You're not kidding there, wham bam thank you, mam," she says, looking around at Mark, "I don't suppose," she starts, pausing momentarily to give him a puppy dog smile, "I can sleep in your room tonight? And I do mean sleep because I don't feel like being alone tonight."

Pyah turns and smiles at him. Mark shrugs, "Don't see why not, I'll just sleep in your room and let you two get on with it," he reasons, taking a sip out of Pyah's coffee, "I'm too tired to argue," he yawns, then kisses them both goodnight and heads up to the room.

Sarah links arms with Carl, "Yeah, we're going to call it a night too, sleep well," she tells them, a touch of sarcasm in her voice, "see you in the morning," she says, then drags Carl away from the bar, grumbling under his breath.

When Sarah and Carl reach the room, he is just about dead on his feet so she drops him on the bed, pulls his shoes and trousers off then covers him up, "Big drunken lug," she comments, then sits in a chair to read a book.

Sarah is tired but restless. The book just isn't doing anything for her so she creeps out of her room to head for Pyah's room, "Hope they're still awake," she mutters under her breath as she creeps along the hallway.

When she reaches Pyah's room she quietly puts her ear to the door. Silence is all she can hear from within so she gently opens the door, "Can I come in?" she asks, whispering into the darkness.

She switches the light on to find an empty room, "Damn, they're not back yet," she walks over to the bed to stare at it, contemplating whether or not to just get in, "fuck it, Goldilocks would just jump in," she decides, then strips off completely naked and climbs in, "shit I hope Mark doesn't come back," she hopes, adrenaline coursing through her veins, "God, I feel like a naughty child."

After waiting for what seems like an eternity she starts to feel a little drowsy. Her body calms as the alcohol takes over while the adrenaline rush peters out. Soon she is sound asleep. Pyah and Lacey return to the room to find her snuggled down in the sheets. Quietly, they undress as one gets in to the right of her and the other gets in to the left. Pyah switches the bedside light off, "Night all."

Lacey turns hers off, "Yeah, night, hun."

They both gently snuggle down to spoon Sarah, all three reassuringly safe in each other's arms.

The morning soon comes around as a knock on the door bring all three girls out of their slumber. Sarah stretches, "Go and see who that is, honey," she says, her eyes still firmly closed.

Pyah leans over to peck her on the lips, "Anything for you, sugar."

Sarah sits up rapidly, "Shit, I forgot about that," she says, looking to see if Mark is in the bed with them.

Lacey sits up, to the relief of Sarah, "I'll get it, bet Mark ordered her breakfast," she guesses, pointing at Pyah, "who is it?" she asks as she gets out of the bed to slink over to the door.

A voice from behind the door calls out, "Room service, madam."

Lacey opens the door to a young man who immediately averts his eyes to her nakedness, then rolls the trolley in, looking down at his feet, "Where would madam like it?"

At that Pyah jumps out of the bed, "That's a leading question if ever I heard one, especially to ask her," she remarks, giggling at Lacey.

Pyah looks at Sarah who has the sheets firmly pulled up around her bosom, "You not getting up then?" she asks, laughing at Sarah as she tries to drag the sheet from her.

Sarah has a firm grip on the sheet and is under no circumstances going to relinquish them, "Get off, you bitch," she says, giggling as she tugs them back.

Lacey is now stood right behind the young man, running her hands over his shoulders, teasing his mortification, "Now, where would madam like it? Hmmm, let me see."

Pyah saunters around the front of him, "Do you think he could accommodate two?" she asks, brashly flaunting her naked body to his tightly closed eyes.

Lacey looks around at Sarah, "Or even three," she suggests, blowing a kiss to Sarah.

Sarah's eyes widen, "Don't go bringing me into your sordid little fantasies, you want to shag a baby then you go ahead, I'm quite happy with the big muscular brute that I have," she declares, giving an evil grin, "if he finds him in here he'll probably rip his legs off and eat them raw."

The young man fumbles for the door with his eyes still firmly closed, "Sorry ladies, but it's more than my job's worth and I, I, have other people to serve," he excuses, rushing out of the room.

Pyah and Lacey collapse on the bed in fits of laughter. Sarah slaps both of them, "You wicked bitches."

Pyah turns to her mouth agape, "Us?"

Lacey slaps her back, "Yeah? My boyfriend is a muscle-bound animal that'll rip your legs off if he catches you?" she reminds her, dropping back on the pillow.

Sarah drops next to her, "Well, it's the only thing I could think of to get him out of here, away from you two vixens."

Pyah straddles her, "What you mean is, get him out so he didn't see those pert little tattas," she says, stabbing at Sarah's boobs.

Sarah picks up a pillow and bats Pyah with it and Pyah grabs the pillow, "I don't think so. Cost me fifty bucks to get his room cleaned after last night."

Lacey sits up, "Shit, I never noticed."

Sarah looks around, "Bloody hell, bet they had a hell of a job, like."

Lacey gets out of bed, walks over to the trolley and lifts the lids on the food, "Wow, two full English's? Anyone hungry?"

The other two get out of bed as Sarah walks over to the door with a sheet wrapped around her to lock it, "Just so we don't have someone walking in on us," she explains, then proudly drops the sheet to the floor.

Lacey turns to look at Sarah, "You know, I don't know which looks tastier, the food or her."

Pyah walks around Sarah, "Hmm, it is a difficult one."

Sarah tries to ignore them and walks straight to the food, "If you're not going to eat this, I sure as hell am," she says, grinning from ear to ear, "now stop messing around, there'll be plenty of time for that later. I'm starving."

Pyah turns to Lacey, "You heard that, we're on a promise. She said we could, later."

Sarah's head drops, "Bastard!" she complains, muttering under her breath. Lacey strokes Sarah's bum as Sarah pushes her hand off, "Later, ok?"

They soon devour the food, shower and get dressed. All three head out of the room and bang on the other's doors, "Come on, you lazy sods, it's morning, we got a lot to do and little time to do it in."

Mark's door is locked but Carl's door is open so they charge in to jump on him. Soon he is forced to get up, get dressed and help them to try and wake Mark up.

After a short while and a few complaints from other guests they decide to leave him to head downstairs.

Downstairs they bump into Mark, who has been up for hours preparing the motor home and the one four by four that Irish left.

CHAPTER 19
WHEN A STORM BLOWS

The sun is low in the sky as the gentle sea breeze dances across the surf up to the coastal road. Mark has the window rolled down, his arm relaxing on the door as the radio blares out to the sound of '*Who Wants to Live Forever*' by Queen, "Seems like a good day to die," he comments, laughing at the empty road ahead.

Pyah gives him a snide look, "A good day for a killing would be better," she corrects, sipping at a can of coke, "you do realise she'll definitely be expecting us and we have no back up now?"

Mark taps on the steering wheel, "That's the beauty of it," he explains, smiling a cheesy smile, "that Irish is probably there by now. If he travelled all night, he should already be giving her hell and that's our distraction."

The penny drops with Pyah, "And we don't have to worry about that sniper anymore, I like it."

Mark taps her on the thigh, "If Irish has found her it also means we don't have to go looking."

Pyah picks up the two-way radio, "You there Carl?" she asks, looking back at Carl and Sarah who are driving the four by four.

Sarah picks up the radio, "Yeah, we're here. We were just wondering what the plan is."

Mark takes the radio, "Not over the air, we'll pull over in about an hour then discuss that, ok?"

Carl takes the radio, "Roger wilco and out."

Sarah slowly turns to him, "ROGER WILCO AND OUT?" she exclaims as Pyah walks to the back of the motor home to pull funny faces at them out of the rear window.

Sarah picks up the radio again, "Can you put your wife back in her straightjacket please, she's distracting my driver," she says in the poshest English accent she can muster and the whole group starts to laugh, "well, it's nice to see everyone in good spirits," she comments as she puts the radio down then picks it back up, "roger wilco and out," she says, giggling at Carl.

Carl leans across to her, "You're a bitch but I love you," he says, kissing her as the vehicle skews across the road.

Sarah takes the wheel to correct it, "Keep your eyes on the road. I love you too, dear," she tells him in a rather mothering fashion.

Carl raises his eyebrows, "So, how come I slept alone last night?"

Sarah flicks his chin, "AWW, did the baby miss mamma last night?"

Carl slowly turns his head, "Actually I did," he says, trying to put a serious face on, "woke up and you weren't there so I spent HOURS traipsing the floors looking for you. Worried sick out of my head fearing the worst," he continues, his lips involuntarily turning up at the edges, "I was frantic," he finishes, shaking his head then bursting into a snigger.

Sarah licks her lips, "OK, let mamma remedy that," she coos, undoing his fly.

Carl reaches down and grasps her hand, "Whoa, what you doing?"

She lifts his hand back on the wheel, "Relax and drive," she commands as her head goes down into his lap, "the road is empty and no one is going to see, so just enjoy it. I know I will and, Jesus, I'm feeling randy as fuck, so don't even think about stopping me."

Carl scans the roads in front and behind him, sighs, "Oh, shit, what the hell," then relaxes to let her do her stuff."

Pyah is still looking out of the rear window of the motor home, "Nah, she can't be..." she says, then rushes back to the radio, "excuse me but what's Sarah doing?"

Mark turns to her, "How the hell should I know?"

Pyah lifts the radio, "I'm not talking to you," she says, pointing at the radio, "don't ignore me. Why has Sarah got her head in your lap?"

Carl comes over the radio, "What a stupid question."

Pyah's jaw drops as she rushes back to the rear window, "She is," she says, shouting to Mark, "she's giving him a blowjob right in the middle of this, err, empty, road," she declares, looking around to see absolutely no traffic for miles.

She slinks back up to Mark. Mark sees her in the rear-view mirror, "You can forget it. Knowing my luck, you'll get down there and a cop'll appear or you'll wake her up," he says, pointing at Lacey asleep in the back.

Pyah walks up behind him, "Aww? Come on, I haven't had any this morning and she's, well, you know, we get caught they get caught," she whines, sliding her hand down over his chest and on to his trousers, "please?"

Mark tuts into the air, "If I see anyone coming, you get straight back up," he says, leering at her.

She kneels in the gap between the seats and slowly, seductively, takes her time pulling down his fly. Mark can just see Sarah's head bobbing up and down through the rear-view mirror as Pyah slowly slides her mouth around his penis, "Well, this should make the journey go faster," he comments softly, placing his hand on Pyah's head.

Pyah peeks up at him, "So long as it doesn't make you come faster," she responds, sniggering to herself.

The radio crackles, "Oh, by the way, were you two holding down that button on purpose?" Carl's voice comes ringing out of it.

Pyah nearly chokes as she realises she is sat on the radio. Mark covers his eyes guffawing out loud, "You numpty, he heard everything."

Pyah shrugs, "He can't say nowt, he's doing the same," she reasons, then carries on happily sucking.

Mark turns off the coast road deciding to head for Marrakech, "Think we might just make it for lunch, what would you like, oh sorry you're already eating," he says, laughing out loud, then getting on the radio to Carl to tell him the joke.

No one else finds it funny. Carl answers, "There's a nice little market stall thingy there that sells good streetside food."

Mark strokes Pyah's head then puts the radio to his mouth, "Do they sell hot dogs ha ha," still no one laughs, "oh fuck you all I thought it was funny," he pouts, then quietly gets on with his driving, admiring the countryside.

In fact, he gets so engrossed in his surroundings that he becomes a bit slack as Pyah bites him, then sits up, "What the hell can be so much more interesting than this?" she asks, pointing down at his dick while looking out of the window.

The sun shimmers across the desert on the edge of a sandstorm, "Ah that could be a problem if its heading this way," Mark pops his penis back in his trousers, then gets on the radio "have you seen that mate?"

Carl is completely oblivious to his surroundings, listening to the music and enjoying his blowjob, "Seen what mate?"

Pyah takes the radio, "Sarah! I would stop what you're doing and look out your window to the right."

Mark sees Sarah's head pop back up as she grabs the radio, "Oh shit, err," she says, looking around and scanning the horizon, "are we going to pull over to ride it out?"

Mark takes the radio, "Yeah, as soon as I find a safe place to stop," he tells her, just at that moment he comes up to an old abandoned petrol station, so they pull in.

Carl and Sarah join them in the motor home, "Well we ain't sitting in that thing, it's full of holes."

Pyah makes sure all the windows are shut while Sarah puts the kettle on. The sandstorm is upon them in seconds. Carl pulls back one of the curtains, "These things don't last long anyway," he says, looking up to see the sky disappear, "ten minutes, tops."

One cup of coffee and twenty minutes later Mark turns around to Carl, "Ten minutes, tops?" he says incredulously as the sand still batters the side of the motor home.

Lacey eventually wakes up, "So, what have I missed?" she asks, looking out the window, "ooo pretty."

Pyah and Sarah are playing cards by torchlight, "They're like two cats on hot tin roofs," they tell her, referring to the men.

Lacey tuts, "Just sit down, you're making us uncomfortable," she says as she joins in the card game, "don't suppose one of you could make me a nice cuppa, could you? I'm parched," she asks, yawning, "I had the strangest dream. You two," she says, stretching, "were giving them two a blow job."

Sarah and Pyah start to giggle. Lacey looks at them a bit disgruntled, "OK, what's the joke," she grumbles as the answer pops into her head, "you weren't?" she asks, pointing at where she was laid, "while I was asleep?" she huffs and plonks herself down with her arms folded, "and I missed it," she pouts, sulking, "you could have woken me."

Pyah leans forward, "I bloody shouted it loud enough from the back to the front," she says, pointing at the rear window then the driver's seat.

Lacey leans forward then pushes Pyah's shoulder, "LACEY I'M GOING TO SUCK ON SOMETHING DO YOU WANT TO HELP?" she yells at the top of her voice.

Mark and Carl turn to each other, shrug, then turn back to the storm.

Pyah grins at Sarah then turns to Lacey, "Well, they're both there, all you have to do is ask."

Lacey sticks her tongue out, "Now you're just trying to make me feel like a two-bit whore."

Sarah drops her head into her cards, "Nothing two-bit about her," she remarks, sniggering under her breath.

Lacey struts up behind her, "But you still calling me a whore, you little minx?" she demands, grabbing Sarah's boobs from behind.

Sarah flings her head back, "Depends on how much you're going to charge me," she says, looking straight up at Lacey.

Lacey grabs her by the cheeks, "Oh, I think we could come to some sort of agreement," she flirts, then plants her lips firmly on Sarah's.

The boys sit in the front seats as Mark turns to the girls, "OK, looks like its lifting, might still get a late lunch yet," he says as he switches the engine on, puts the van into drive and steps on the gas, "oh, for crying out loud," he complains, switching the engine off, "looks like we're going to have to dig it out," he sighs as him and Carl are forced to climb out of the passenger side door.

The wind is still howling but the sand has abated as Mark hands Carl a shovel off the back of the van, "You start at the front and I'll do the back," he instructs, banging on the side of the van, "don't suppose you three would like to help?"

Lacey bangs back, "Don't suppose you want a kick in the ass?"

Pyah stands up, "What do you want? I ain't digging."

Mark opens the passenger door, "Well, you could sit there and drive when I tell you."

Pyah huffs, then sits in the driver's seat, "Say when."

Lacey straddles her with her back against the steering wheel, "When."

Pyah grimaces, "I'm supposed to be driving."

Sarah comes and sits in the passenger seat, "This I've got to see," she says, resting her chin in her hand with a curious look on her face.

Pyah's eyes turn, then her head, "See what?"

Sarah crosses her legs, "Just how you get her into gear and turn her on and rev her up from that position?" she says, completely deadpan. Pyah reaches out to her as Sarah slides back in the seat, "No, keep your eyes on the road," she says, tapping Pyah's hand, "and your hands on the controls."

Mark taps on the windshield, "When you ladies have quite finished with your roadside tutorial, can we try this now?"

Lacey rolls down the window, "You can try me any time," she says, licking her lips at him.

Mark points at the van, then at the road, "Van, road," then towards Marrakech, "lunch," he says, shaking his head.

Pyah starts the engine, puts it into gear, then slowly rolls it out of the sand. Carl jumps in the four by four as Mark relieves Pyah of the steering wheel.

It isn't long before they're back on the open road. Sarah and Pyah are finishing off their game of cards while Carl is grumbling over the radio about being alone as Lacey walks up behind Mark. She slips her hand down his shirt and kisses his ear before he realises it isn't Pyah, "Oh, shit, woman, what the hell you trying to do? Get us killed?"

Lacey swings around in front of him and straddles his lap, "Aww, but I'm horny and we both know Pyah don't mind, do you?" she checks, shouting back to Pyah.

Pyah is engrossed in her cards, "Whatever," she says, waving her hand then slamming her cards down, "hah, gotcha, gin!"

Mark tries to look around Lacey at the road, trying to seem uninterested, "What about-"

Before he can finish Sarah sits in the passenger seat, "Me? It's ok, I've already eaten," she tells them as she looks out of the side window.

CHAPTER 20
A GROWING

The coastal road ahead is straight and empty with sunlight drifting across from the coastline horizon. Mark's distractions forcing him to concentrate hard on his driving. Mark makes a point of complaining but doesn't stop Lacey as she unzips his trousers.

Sarah turns to switch the radio on, then her eyes widen catching a glimpse of Marks penis, "Oh my fucking god," she says, swallowing, "I knew you were big, but holy shit man, that is one hell of a, a hell of a, wow."

Pyah saunters forward, "Oh yeah, you ain't seen his anaconda, have you?"

Mark starts to blush slightly but still makes no attempt to prevent anything. Pyah realises that Lacey is climbing on, "Err, hang on a minute, we were only going down on them," she says as Lacey slides all the way down onto it, "what you're doing is fucking dangerous."

Lacey grabs her by the lapel and pulls her into a full-on snog, "He can see around me."

Mark smiles and nods.

Pyah leans around him, "And if you were concentrating on your driving you shouldn't be hard."

Mark grins at her, "So do you want to drive?"

Pyah huffs, "I don't think so mate, pull over and I'll show you what I want."

Sarah stands up, "Oh, for Christ's sake, get a room, I'll fucking drive," she says as Mark relinquishes the wheel to her, picking Lacey up, still inserted, and walks back to the bed.

The van slows slightly as Sarah sits down, then Carl comes over the radio, "Have we got a problem? Why are we slowing down?"

Sarah picks up the radio, "No, there's not a problem, you just carry on and follow me."

Carl thinks for a moment, "Why are you driving, hun?"

Sarah dares not tell him the real reason, "Coz the others are sorting something out in the back for a minute," she says, looking back as Pyah is sitting on Lacey's face, "jammy cow," she adds under her breath, thinking how she could convince Carl to at least let her try that dick just once.

The van starts to rock gently from side to side as Sarah tries to compensate hoping Carl doesn't notice, "OK you three, what's going on? And don't tell me Sarah is driving coz you're sorting something in the back," Carl demands, banging the radio against the steering wheel, "if my suspicions are correct, the only thing getting sorted are sexual parts, am I right? Don't ignore me, you should never ignore a sexually frustrated man that was almost there when that fricking sandstorm hit," he rants, banging the radio again, "answer me or I'll come 'round you and cut you up."

Sarah picks up the radio, "Yes dear, they are shagging but you can't, YET," she says, taking a deep breath, "don't worry babes, I'll make it up to you in Marrakech," she promises, smiling at the radio.

The radio is silent for a few seconds then Carl speaks, "OK, but I'm not a happy bunny, Marrakech right?"

Sarah blows a kiss through the rear-view mirror, "Love you, won't be too long now," she says, sighing, then turning to the other three, "the things I do for you."

She turns back to the road ahead, catches a glimpse of the romp in the rear-view mirror, then decides to close the curtain behind her, "I got wing mirrors and that's just too much of a distraction," she declares, eyes fixed firmly on the road, "KEEP IT DOWN BACK THERE!" she calls, trying her hardest to block out the moans and groans of sexual ecstasy.

She puts her hand down her own pants "No," she says, pulling it back out, "keep it for Carl," she reminds herself, scanning the horizon for something to take her mind off things. She picks up the radio, "I spy with my little eye something beginning with, S."

Carl picks up the radio, "You have got to be kidding me, right?"

She groans, then picks up the radio, "Just humour me."
Carl huffs, "SEX."

Her head drops, "Outside the fucking van!!! That's why I'm doing this, a distraction."

Carl scans the outside, "Derr, sand."

Sarah smiles, "Nope," she replies.

Carl thinks, "Err sky?"

Sarah smiles again, "Nope."

The mic is silent for a few seconds then he concedes, "I give up."

Sarah's head drops again, "No, you can't give up that easy, indulge me."

Carl looks out of the window, "All I can see is sand and sky, oh, and a fucking motor home," he says, still looking around.

Sarah starts to giggle to herself, "try harder."

Carl rolls down the window, looks behind him, then in front and up in the air, "OK, you're going to have to give me a clue."

Sarah picks up the radio, "You looked everywhere but there?"

Now Carl is very confused, sticking his head back out of the window to scan around again, "There's fuck all else out there."

Sarah kisses her hand, "Fucking geniuses," she says, praising herself before answering him, "where did you look, behind you, yeah, in front, yeah."

Carl shakes his head, "And up in the sky."

Sarah waves her hand at the radio, "Exactly. Where didn't you look?"

Carl looks at the radio without keying it, "How the fuck should I know, you stupid woman," he mutters, then composes himself, keying the mic, "give me a minute."

He looks out of the window, "OK, I looked up. I looked back. I looked forward. I looked both sides but, I didn't look down, oh for crying out loud you smart arsed bitch, is it shadow?"

Sarah smiles, "Yay, about bloody time. Your turn."

Carl closes his eyes, "Oh shit," he says, then looks outside, pointing out at the horizon, "what the fuck?" he ponders, then it hits him, "OK, got it. I spy with my little eye something beginning with M."

Sarah shakes her head and immediately shouts, "Mirror."

Carl is silent for a few seconds, "Fuck off."

Sarah is jumping in her seat, "Was I right? Ha ha."

All Carl can say is, "YES."

Sarah squints forward, "Oh, you are going to like this one but you'll have to be quick."

Carl scans the horizon again, "OK, go on then."

Sarah squeezes the radio, "I spy with my little eye something beginning with M."

Carl immediately responds, "Mirror?"

Sarah shakes her head, "NO you dope, hurry up, I'll give you a clue. We're approaching it."

Carl looks at the back of the motor home, "Excuse me, but all I can see in front is your arse."

Sarah waves him on to her side, "So come 'round a bit."

Carl drives out from behind her, "SEX, SEX, SEX."

Sarah laughs, "That'll do. It was Marrakech but SEX will do," she says, turning to the group in the back, "we've arrived, so you lot better do the same unless you want an audience."

As they pull into Marrakech they notice a large contingency of police. The police have congregated outside the hotel they were planning on staying at. There is also a large group of motorcycles parked. Lacey notices these motorbikes seem to belong to Irish and his crew, "Knew he'd start some trouble without us to keep him on the straight and narrow, I'll bet he started a bar fight," she says.

But then ambulances start to arrive as a police officer stops Sarah from proceeding any further, "Sorry madam, but you have to find another route," he says, waving her into a side street.

Sarah hangs out of the window, "We're supposed to be staying at that hotel."

The policeman walks over to her, "You can't stay there tonight, there's been a gun fight and the hotel will be closed until further investigations have been made," he points back down the street, "there are a few boarding houses back down the way if you still need to rest up for the night but I suggest you move on in the morning unless you know something about this."

Sarah shakes her head, "How would we know anything about it we just arrived," she says, then she picks up the radio, "Carl back it up, we're heading back over."

Carl comes back over the radio, "What's going on?"

Sarah looks back to Mark as Mark is already heading out the camper door. Sarah keys the radio again, "Don't ask any stupid questions, Mark's heading your way so sit and wait quietly, then back it up and head to that B&B behind us."

Mark jumps in the four by four, "Looks like Irish may have done the job for us but we don't want to give the cops anything more than we have to so just turn around and head for the B&B."

Carl quickly spins the car around, "So you reckon De-fuer could be dead?"

Mark shrugs, "We'll find out soon enough, but let's get the hell out of here first."

They park around the side of the farthest boarding house, then go to book in. Once in the room they break out some binoculars. Looking out of the window Lacey throws the binoculars on the bed, "Damn! He was a pain in the arse but I wouldn't have wished that on him."

Sarah picks up the binoculars, "What?" she asks as she looks out of the window.

Lacey points at a body being loaded into an ambulance, "That's Irish, he's dead."

Sarah looks, "How can you tell, his face is covered?"

Lacey sheds a tear, "That's my bracelet he's wearing, the bastard stole it before he left."

There's a knock at the door. Pyah opens it, "Oh, it's you," she says.

Elleon Vixter walks in, "Thought you might need an update before I head off."

Carl spins her around, "Is that bitch dead?"

Elleon shakes her head, "Nope, he missed and paid the price with all but four of his men," she says, walking across to the window, "yeah, she was long gone before he even arrived, they were waiting for you but when he arrived without you they had to revise their plan," she explains, throwing a piece of paper at Carl, "your names have been added to the bounty," she tells him, pointing at him and Sarah, "and a crew of bounty hunters are staying at the boarding house at the end of this block just waiting for you to stick your pretty little heads out when those cops leave."

Lacey grabs the paper, "Where's my name?"

Elleon smiles, "She ain't interested in you, not sure why, maybe it's something to do with you being MI6?"

Lacey puts an arm around Elleon, "Oh, trust me, she's going to be very interested in me, by the time I'm finished," she says, then walks over to Pyah, "so are we staying or we going to sneak out before those Mercs get wind that we're gone?"

Carl turns to Elleon, "How many are they?"

Mark steps forward, "Whoa, big feller, what you thinking?"

Carl tips his head, "Just wondering if we could maybe take 'em out before anyone realises, is all."

Elleon starts to laugh, "Dad always said you were crazy," she says, patting Carl on the back, "there's twenty-five of them spread over three B&B's, you got no chance."

Carl looks at the floor, "OK, we take 'em out in the desert and pick 'em off one by one?"

Mark points his finger at Carl, "Now that's not a bad idea, especially if we have two snipers at work," he says, giving Elleon a knowing look.

Elleon puts her hands in the air, "Ain't my fight anymore, sorry but I'm out of here," she says, turning towards the door, "just thought I'd give you the heads up, I think Dad would have at least wanted me to do that," she adds, blowing Carl a kiss then waving as she leaves.

She stops in the doorway, "Oh, by the way, do you have any idea what De-fuer is buying down at Tan-Tan?"

The group turn to her as Sarah steps forward, "Yeah, weapons I should think."

Elleon steps back in, "She's still trying to carry out her brother's plan, VX gas? Ring a bell?"

Lacey smiles, "Yeah, he was planning on using a case we took back to smuggle it in to America but she doesn't have the case anymore," she says smugly, walking over to tower over Elleon.

Elleon steps around Lacey, "Yeah, right. Trust me she ain't going after just the USA anymore, she plans on firing a VX rocket at all the main parliamentary seats in Europe, including the UK and the Pentagon, and the White House amongst others."

The whole group steps forward. Mark pushes through, "How many rockets is she purchasing, for Christ's sake?"

Elleon starts to walk towards the door again, "Twenty-four, and they ain't the little ones," she tells them, then disappears, leaving a group with that dead inward feeling lingering in their guts.

Carl slumps into a chair, "Shit, we have to stop this psycho bitch."

Mark rushes out after Elleon but she has gone. He walks back in, "This shit is getting serious, she ain't after revenge like we thought. This bitch has been reading too many spy novels. She's after world domination. Would you believe it?"

Lacey starts to laugh, "And we thought Guy Fawkes was a nut."

Pyah walks to the window, "OK, I got a plan," she says, turning back to the group, "she ain't here, she's at Tan-Tan right?"

Mark nods, "Yeah, but she ain't going to be there when we get there."

Pyah cuddles him, "But those killers don't know we know that and are probably going to follow us when we leave if we leave now."

Sarah steps out onto the balcony, "That's if they see us leaving."

Pyah steps out, "Oh, they'll see us, trust me. That's the idea," she turns to Lacey, "you ride a bike, you think you could steal one of them without anyone noticing?"

Lacey blows air through her teeth, "Pffft, please. You think they are that intelligent? Cops and Mercs have one thing in common. No brain," she says as she heads out of the door, "I think I know where you're going with this, won't be long," she promises, then she's gone.

It isn't long before she returns, "Done. It's in the back of the four by four," she says as she goes to pour herself a drink, "I'm presuming I stay until they follow you, then head to Tan-Tan?"

Pyah kisses her, "You got it, girl. You should be able to get there long before we do, radio us and give us a sit-rep."

Carl sits up, "So we ain't getting cleaned up and I don't get no rumpy pumpy?"

Sarah walks over, "Sorry hun, but the world needs us," she says, kissing him on the cheek, "but I will make it up to you."

Carl grunts, "If we survive," he remarks, tapping her bum, "you know I'm supposed to be the boss of this organisation?"

Mark stands in front of him, "OK, our leader, what do you suppose we do?" he asks, smiling at Carl.

Carl shrugs, "How the hell am I supposed to know? That's what I employ you lot for," he says, laughing as he grabs Marks hand for a lift to his feet, "let's get this show on the road and you two geniuses can fill me in on your plan on route."

Everyone except Lacey piles into the two vehicles, drive slowly past the rest of the boarding houses then take the route around the back of the hotel toward Tan-Tan.

134

CHAPTER 21
SANDCASTLES AND SNIPERS

The sun is high and the heat is blistering as the group head out for Tan-Tan. Lacey watches for about five minutes, "OK guys, your package is headed your way," she tells them as the Mercs head out after them.

Mark and Carl floor it towards a little village on the map while Lacey waits to make sure it's clear to head out. The bike Lacey stole is capable of off road so she sets out over the desert while Mark pulls into the village to hide. About five minutes later, the Mercs come trundling past in convoy. As soon as it's clear. Sarah and Pyah head back towards Marrakech with the motor home while Carl and Mark head out after the Mercs in the four by four with the Dragunov and a bucket load of ammo.

Carl starts to pray, "Hope this isn't the last thing we do," he says as Mark heads off into the desert, "they should have figured out by now that we have doubled back." Pulling up behind a large dune about a mile off the road. Carl peaks over the dune. "Oh shit, here they come," he warns, sliding back down.

Mark brings the gun up to his shoulder, "As soon as I start shooting you drive out there," he says, pointing into the desert "as fast as you can."

The Mercs arrive back at the little village, approaching cautiously. Mark takes careful aim at the lead car driver then shoots. A perfect headshot as the vehicle swerves all over the road. The rest of the Mercs skid to a halt, jump out of their vehicles and take cover behind them. Carl drives off into the desert like a mad man. One of the Mercs sees the dust cloud and jumps into a vehicle to go in pursuit as Mark takes careful aim, allowing him to get onto the sand before ventilating his head, "Two down, twenty-three to go," he mutters, then moves location.

Another Merc takes a sniper rifle and makes a run for the back of the dunes. Mark unfortunately doesn't see this as he gets a bead on one of the Mercs head sticking out from another vehicle. He takes careful aim then shoots, killing the Merc, but is surprised by a bullet glancing off the Dragunov from behind the vehicle that's now stranded in the desert in front of him, "Shit, how the hell did he get there?" he curses, popping his head out quickly then back in as the sniper shoots.

Mark rolls to the side then takes aim, only to see the Merc's head splattered by someone else's shot. Mark scans the desert to see the Vixter down behind another dune about a mile and a half out. She salutes him then disappears.

Mark pops his head back up and looks at the corpse through the scope, "Damn, she can shoot," he comments, then turns his attention to the rest of the Mercs as they scatter into the village, "twenty-one and I'm still here," he sighs, looking at the dent in the side of the Dragunov, "hope this thing still shoots," he says as he takes aim again, seeing one Merc running down a small alley.

Mark pulls the trigger, missing the Merc's head by about six inches, "Your lucky day, pal," he remarks as he recalibrates the sights.

Carl has driven for about four miles in a straight line when he realises Mark didn't give him any instructions except drive that way as fast as you can. Looking into the desert as he pulls up he asks himself, "OK, now what?"

He sits there for a moment then decides to head back, "Shit, I know I'm probably doing the wrong thing but what the hell, who wants to live forever-," he pulls up abruptly, "I fucking do, what the hell are you doing Carl, they are trained killers. That's what you got Pyah and Mark for," he reprimands himself, contemplating turning back around to head back into the desert, "oh, that's smart, you're liable to get lost and die out here," he continues, fumbling around looking for the radio, "oh, shit, Mark took the radio," he realizes. as panic starts to creep in.

All of a sudden, a voice rings out, "What the hell you trying to do, get yourself killed?"

Carl jumps out of his skin, "Jesus Christ, woman, don't need Mercs to kill me off or this god forsaken desert to swallow me up when I got loons like you trying to give me a heart attack," he complains, sighing a sigh of relief as the Vixter sticks her head in the four by four.

"Nice set of wheels, man, so what's this part of the plan?"

Carl looks out into the waste, "You know, I think they think I might be in the way so they just decided to get rid of me," he suggests, shrugging, "he said drive out here very fast."

Elleon walks around, gets into the passenger seat and points to the right, "Then what? Oh, my vehicles that way."

Carl starts to drive, "Dunno. All I got was drive out here."

Elleon shakes her head and smiles, "And you did it without question?"

Carl slowly turns his head, "It's what I do, yeah. I'm the boss but they do the thinking when it comes to keeping me alive and up to now it seems to be working."

He comes over a small ridge where there is a sand buggy waiting. Elleon gets out of his vehicle, reaches into the buggy and throws Carl a compass, "If you head due south for about ten miles you hit the road to Tan-Tan," she directs, pointing out to the desert, "don't worry about your mate, I'll pick him up if he's still with us," she says as she drives off in the general direction of Mark.

Carl looks down at the compass, "Well, he didn't say anything about coming back for him and I got three quarters of a tank of fuel so Tan-Tan here I come," he decides as he watches Elleon disappear, "yeah, he's in good hands," he nods, setting off due south, the compass stuck to the dash with duct tape.

Mark starts to work his way towards the village through the dunes as Elleon appears beside him, "Jesus, woman, do you have to do that?"

Elleon starts to giggle, "Yeah, Carl just said the same thing, funnily enough."

Mark stops, "You've seen Carl?"

Elleon sits down, "Yeah, I sent him to Tan-Tan with a compass. What exactly was the plan where he is concerned?"

Mark sits down beside her, "You know, I never really gave it much thought. Figured he would drive for a while, then turn around and come back. Just needed him out of the way, babysitting him and shooting baddies gets a bit difficult."

Elleon looks over a dune, "So, now you're just going to walk in there blasting? Hell, of a plan."

Mark gives a sarcastic smirk, "I wasn't going in blasting, I was just trying to get a better view."

Elleon stands up, "Tell you what, you wait here and keep watch, see if you can pick a few off. Won't be long," she says as she heads off behind another dune, disappearing again.

Mark looks around to see she's gone, "I would love to know how she does that," he comments as he sticks his gun over the top, with the village in plain view.

Elleon appears about half a mile to his side, up on top of one of the dunes, fully naked, "Shit, what the hell is she doing?" he asks himself as he looks at her through his scope, "cute little body like."

Just then she fires a round in the air and starts to dance on the top of the dune. Mark spins his gun back to the village, "Oh shit," he curses as one of the Mercs pops up with his gun aimed at her, "and she calls me stupid," he says, shooting the Merc as he fires at Elleon.

Elleon sees the muzzle flash, diving down behind the dune for cover, "OK, that didn't work," she says, quickly getting dressed.

Mark is still watching the village as three of the Mercs come out of the side to try and outflank Elleon. He shoots them in quick succession, "OK, that's another four, err, that makes, ooo, nineteen to go."

Suddenly Elleon appears beside him, "Yeah, yeah, I know, not too bright? Saw it in a movie once, thought it might work," she explains, peeking over the dune, "did you get any of them?"

Mark slaps her arse, "Yeah I got four and nearly had to bury one little girl, stupid, stupid, stupid."

Elleon gives him a seductive pout, "Ooo, love a man that can take charge, if you weren't married," she says, raising her eyebrows.

Mark gives a grimace, "Cute," he remarks, then shakes his head as he peeks back over the dune, "Oh shit, here they come."

Elleon grabs his hand, "Quick, this way," she instructs, pulling him around a dune, then zig zagging around some more, as if she knows the desert like the back of her hand. She drops to the ground, "Wait here," she says, climbs up to the top of a dune, picks off three more then rolls down, "move!" she says urgently, grabbing his hand again and zig zagging for a while.

She points at the top of a dune, then in the direction they just came from, sticking two fingers in the air as she climbs another dune. Mark climbs the dune to see two Mercs creeping up to about where they just left. He's amazed, "How the hell?" he breathes, whispering under his breath as he shoots the two Mercs then slides back down.

Elleon slides down after taking two shots, "That's another four, only twelve to go," she counts, grabbing Mark's hand to pull him off on another snaky path for a few minutes.

She stops, listens, then rushes to the top of a dune, "Damn, they're bugging out."

Mark rushes to the top of the dune as Elleon drags him to the ground, "Seems that only nine are left," she says, putting a finger over Marks mouth.

They sit there silent for a while, then Elleon looks deep into Mark's eyes. She puts two fingers up and points behind him then one finger up and points over her shoulder, then grabs his hand to run around a few more dunes. She stops dead, pushes Mark to the ground and whispers in his ear, "Won't be long," then sidles off silently.

Mark lies there, scanning the dunes with his gun covering the only two entrances she left him.

A few minutes later Elleon slinks in, wiping a knife on a bit of rag, "Well, they won't be reporting back in a hurry," she says as she slips the knife back in its sheath, "my buggy's this way," she tells him, walking back into the desert.

Mark walks after her, "How the hell do you do that?" he asks as the buggy comes into view.

Elleon taps the side of her nose, "You coming or you want to walk to Tan-Tan?"

Mark climbs in.

CHAPTER 22
THE ROAD TO TAN-TAN

The sun is quickly dropping over the horizon to leave a crimson glow across the desert, as Carl reaches the road for Tan-Tan. He pulls up at the road's edge to stretch his legs, "Oh, thank god for that," he says, turning to look at the desert behind him, "would not like to be travelling across that in the next couple of minutes, even with a compass," he remarks, thinking to himself that he would still probably have got lost, "now all I have to do is find someone else that I actually know."

He scrambles around in the four by four for his canteen, then sits at the side of the road sipping at the cool water, feeling quite proud of himself. Then a set of lights appear, in the desert he just left, "Oh shit, I hope that's Mark," he worries as he scrambles into the four by four, to hide it behind a dune on the other side of the road, "please, please, please God don't let that be someone sent to kill me," he pleads, huddling down in the seat, "I don't want to die alone."

Suddenly, a set of headlights bounce up on to the road to point directly at the dune he's hiding behind as Elleon's voice booms out, "You're not very good at this hiding lark, are you?" she asks, standing with her hands on her hips in the middle of her full beam.

Carl's head pops out from behind his four by four, "Oh, thank God it's you. any sign of Mark?"

Mark steps out of the buggy, "You do realise we saw you hiding from about half a mile out," he says, sniggering at Carl, "you Walter."

Mark walks over to the four by four to rummage through the back, "Ahhh, there you are," he says, pulling the radio from under the seat.

Carl looks in the back of the vehicle, "Where the hell was that?"

Mark points to the back seat, "It got wedged under there, what, you didn't think I would leave you without a radio?" he asks, shaking his head, "numpty."

Carl shrugs then grabs his canteen.

Mark radios Pyah, "Where are you, honey?"

Pyah comes back, "We took the other road back out of Marrakech and are now up towards the coast on the road to Tan-Tan."

Mark looks at the map, "OK dear, you should be with us in about half an hour, we'll wait for you here. Have you heard from Lacey?"

Sarah grabs the map, "That should put them about here," she says, pointing at the map.

Pyah takes a quick look, "No, we haven't heard from her but we do have a small problem. We ain't got much fuel, enough to get to you but not much further. Any fuel station in sight?"

Carl stands in the middle of the road, looks right then left, then back to Mark, "Nope."

Elleon slaps the back of his head, "How the hell you managed to stay alive in Vietnam I don't know."

He puts his hands in the air, "Just a bit out of practice is all," he justifies, walking back to Mark, "that's what I got him for."

Mark radios back to Pyah, "Just keep coming, we'll sort something when you get here. OK?"

Sarah grabs the radio, "Roger wilco and out," she says, then sniggers at Pyah, "just in case that numpty of mine is listening."

Mark turns to Carl, "You know, she's going to have to stop hanging 'round with you."

Carl shrugs, "What can I say."

Elleon walks around him, "Nothing, would be quite sufficient."

Carl looks at her quite sternly, "It's a good job you're who you are, otherwise I would be quite tempted to put you over my knee and give you a good spanking."

Elleon smiles as Mark turns to give Carl a harsh glare, "No you wouldn't, the little nymph likes it."

Carl's eyes close, "Not another one," he moans, then scurries to Marks side, "and just exactly how would you know this?" he asks, whispering from the side of his mouth.

Mark rolls his eyes, "Oh, I slapped her for doing something stupid. Bad move, trust me. All she did was smile and give me a glib remark."

Carl slowly spins, "Oh, I see," he says, cautiously walking away rubbing his chin.

Mark starts to study the map as Carl approaches him again, "So what exactly did she do for you to slap her? I'm presuming of course from this you meant across her arse?"

Mark slowly looks up, "Yes it was her arse and trust me you don't want to know what she did. Suffice it to say I know exactly what she looks like," he says, pausing momentarily, "from top to bottom, all of it."

Carl flicks his head, "Oh," he responds, then starts to walk away, stops dead, then turns back, "whoa, what do you mean all? As in naked?"

Mark nods without raising his head from the map, "Ah ha," Carl stands in front of him, "you mean she," he asks, pointing down at his clothes to mimic undressing, "all of it," he continues, pointing back at Elleon, "in front of you?"

Mark still keeps his head buried in the map, "Ah ha."

Carl leans on the hood to look straight up at Mark, "Why?"

Mark pulls Carl up by his shoulders, "She thought it would distract the Mercs, but it nearly got her head blown off, ok? Now you know. Drop it."

Carl looks at Elleon then back at Mark, "OK, it's dropped," he agrees, then starts to walk towards Elleon.

He stops, turns around to Mark, but before he can open his mouth Mark growls, "Drop it!"

Carl carries on walking, "Dropped," he says, making a zip motion over his mouth.

Elleon jumps into her buggy, "Well, you lot are sorted so I'm off," she says as she starts the engine, "probably see you around," she remarks, then heads off into the desert.

It isn't too long before Mark spots a set of headlights in the distance, "Well, here they come."

Carl shrouds his eyes, "How do you know it's them? Could be the Mercs."

Mark jumps into the four by four for a flashlight, "Since when did the Mercs drive a motor home?" he asks, standing in the middle of the road, waving the flashlight.

Pyah pulls up next to Mark, "Hope you've sorted the fuel situation out because we're running on vapour."

Mark opens the door to look at the gauge, "How long you been on empty?"

Pyah taps the fuel gauge, "About the last ten miles."

Mark shows her the map, "There's a fuel station about six miles down the road," he shows her, pointing at the map, "you think you can make it there?"

Pyah shrugs, "Let's see," she says as she puts it back into gear and drives off.

Mark pulls the four by four out and heads off after her as Carl scrambles into the passenger seat, "So-."

Mark puts his hand over Carl's mouth, "If this question has anything to do with a certain little girl, you're walking to the fuel station."

Carl gives him an innocent look, "Err, no, I, was just going to, err, ask what the plan was."

Mark looks sideways at Carl, "Yeah, of course you were," he sighs, tapping on the steering wheel, "well, when we get some fuel, we head down to Tan-Tan and see what's happening, then take it from there."

Carl shrugs, "What and that's it?"

Mark nods.

About half a mile from the fuel station Pyah runs out of fuel as Mark gently nudges up behind her in the four by four then picks up the radio, "Drop it into neutral dear, we're almost there."

Pyah puts the motor home in neutral as Mark pushes her the last half mile. The fuel station is closed and the pumps are locked, so Sarah takes one of her nail files, grinds it down a bit on the concrete floor, then proceeds to pick the pump lock. Pyah manages to get a window open and climbs into the station to switch the pump on while Mark fills both vehicles up. Pyah puts a note in the register apologising for the missing fuel alongside a couple of hundred dollar bills.

Everything is locked back up and Carl jumps in the four by four with Sarah, while Pyah gets in the motor home with Mark. Mark takes the wheel, "Thank God for that," he remarks, then pulls away towards Tan-Tan.

Carl decides to let Sarah drive just so he can have a rest and a gossip.

Pyah opens a can of soda, "Don't worry, I paid for it," she promises, handing it to Mark.

Mark puts it on his forehead, "Oh, that's nice, that Carl's been doing my head in," he complains, taking a long drink from the can, "I know he's an intelligent man and he's our boss and all that, but sometimes I think we've mothered him too much 'cause he can turn into a stupid little boy so easy." Mark suddenly switches the headlights off and picks up the radio, "going dark," he says into it, then starts to pull over.

Carl picks up the radio as Sarah snatches it off him, "What does he mean going dark and why are we pulling over?"

Sarah switches the lights off and pulls in behind Mark, "That's what he means, going dark."

Mark jumps out of the van as Carl rushes up beside him, "What we stopped for and why are we going dark?"

Mark points off in the distance at a glow on the horizon, "Either that's a town or it's one hell of a big bonfire," he says, lifting some binoculars up to take a look, "and seeing as though there are a dozen or so Mercs left, that's probably where they are."

Carl pulls the binoculars off Mark to look through them, "I can't see anything."

Mark goes back to the van to grab the map, "Well it ain't Tan-Tan, that's a good hour away, must be Rass Oulil."

Pyah steps out of the van and Sarah joins her next to Mark, "So what's the plan? We go 'round?"

Mark strokes his chin, "It's a good chance to try and get the rest of the Mercs, if we can get in there without being noticed, but on the other hand we could go 'round, slip past unnoticed and hope they wait there for us."

Carl steps forward, "That's if they are there waiting."

Mark puts his hand on Carl's shoulders, "You know that's the first sensible thing you've said in ages," he tells him, turning to the girls, "we have to go in anyway, even if it's only to find out if those bastards are there waiting for us."

Mark suggests going so far in the vehicles and leaving Carl to look after them while him and the girls go in to town to check it out. Carl picks up a book when the group go off on foot, "Fine by me. I'll probably do something stupid anyhow and get everyone killed."

He sits and watches the group disappear into the darkness, then switches the interior light on to read by. He's sat there for about three minutes just nicely getting into the book when Elleon's voice booms out behind him, "Bang, you're dead."

He drops the book, then slides down the seat, "I give up," he says, raising his hands before realising he knows the voice.

He slowly sticks his head up as Elleon leans in to switch the light off, "Jesus man, I could see you from a mile out," she says, pulling her sniper rifle around to her front and patting it, "had a perfect shot for, oh, let's say two minutes, could have killed you twenty times over."

Carl leers at her, "Yeah, but I'm one of the good guys so it don't count."

She walks around the vehicle and plonks herself in the passenger seat, "Good job too, because if I could see you from out there then I'm damned sure the real bad guys would have spotted you from in there, eventually."

Carl looks over the steering wheel, "You reckon? Anyway, how do you know they are in there?"

Elleon huffs, "Oh please, I was in there about half an hour ago scoping the place out," she tells him, picking up Carl's book, "what you reading anyway?"

Carl snatches it off her, "It's called '*The Word According to Stephen*'.

Elleon lifts the back to see the cover, "Any good?"

Carl shrugs, "Don't know yet, just starting to get into it, anyway what do you mean you been in there and those Mercs are in there, shit, I better radio Mark."

Elleon grabs the radio, "Oh, that's a really smart move, he's just creeping up behind one and all of a sudden your voice is heard, MARK, yeah not a good idea," she pushes the book back towards him, "just read your book, they'll be fine," she says, sticking her feet up on the dashboard, "so what is it? the book?"

Carl smiles, "It's the Bible."

She spins towards him, "Shit, you're kidding, never would have taken you for a bible basher."

Carl starts to quietly snigger, "Well I'm not and this isn't really the Bible, but it is a humorous take on the Bible and creation and all that shit, another man's perceptions and all."

She looks deep into his eyes, "So it's not the Bible but at the same time it is, sort of?"

Carl drops it on his lap, "Well, it's a humorous explanation in simple terms of how creation could have come about, using the Bible as a loose reference."

Elleon puts her chin in her hand and rests her elbow on her knee, "Fascinating, I'm sure, do you fancy me?"

Carl nearly chokes, "Whoa, just think of who you're asking before you ask a question like that for crying out loud. I was your pop's best mate, I'm your godfather, or didn't you know that? And I'm almost old enough to be your granddad."

Elleon flicks her feet back up on the dash, "Oh, you are funny," she says, giggling like a school girl, "I wasn't asking you for a shag, I was just wondering if you found me attractive? And yes, I knew you were my godfather."

Carl shuffles around uncomfortably, "Well, I suppose you're a, err, pretty, err, little, I mean young, err, girl, I suppose, but I haven't taken that much notice I mean how old are you now? Sixteen?"

Elleon throws her head back in the seat, "HA, you are out of touch, aren't you? OLD man. I'll have you know I'm coming up twenty-two this year," she says, blowing air through her teeth, "Sixteen indeed? I wish," she laughs, running her hands down her hips, "I'm about the same size as your missus aren't I? What is she - five foot three?"

Carl spins to face her pompously, "I'll have you know she's not my missus, she's my fiancée and she's five foot four actually," he corrects, grimacing at her.

Elleon sits forward, "Ooo, we like the tall ones?" she asks, an air of sarcasm ringing through as she pushes her boobs up through her hands, "I'm a thirty-four D, bet her boobs aren't that big?"

Carl puts his hand up to her face, "Don't start with that. I know what you're trying to do-" he starts, then his hand drops suddenly.

CHAPTER 23
RASS OULIL SHOOTOUT

Carl is now starting to feel rather uncomfortable around Elleon. He starts to fumble around on the floor, "Where the hell are they?"

Elleon sticks her head down to his, "Watcha looking for?"

He pushes her back up abruptly, "Binoculars."

She sits up and looks out at the town, "Why, what you spotted?" she asks, then jumps out of the vehicle to grab her rifle, "damn."

Carl finds the binoculars then steps out beside her, "Don't just say damn, damn what?" he asks, looking through the binoculars at a figure skulking over the rooftops, "shit, I can't make out if that's one of ours or theirs."

Elleon lifts her rifle up, "Well, the one crouching down, walking across the back of the roof is your mate Mark and the one coming up the stairs onto the roof is a baddie."

Carl drops the binoculars to reach for the radio. Elleon stops him, "Wait, I got this," she says as she lifts the rifle back up.

Carl looks though the binoculars, "How the hell do you know which is which?"

Elleon taps the sights, "Night sights, now shut up, I got to concentrate," she says as she pulls a silencer out of her boot, spinning it quickly onto the end of the barrel.

Carl watches through the binoculars as the Merc reaches the top of the stairs to enter the rooftop. The Merc walks out and just stands there. Elleon takes careful aim, "Shit, stay where you are, you stupid women."

She shuts out all noises, calms her breathing, steadies the rifle and slowly exhales, closing her eyes momentarily as she musters that last nuance of concentration to squeeze the trigger. Time seems to slow as the bullet leaves the barrel, shooting across the wasteland and into the head of the mercenary. Mark hears the thud as the Merc hits the rooftop, dead.

Carl sees the girls appear from behind a ventilation tower, "Oh, that's who you were calling stupid women," he remarks as the women scurry across to the body, standing up with their arms outstretched, "what the hell they doing now?"

Elleon looks through her scope, "I think that's supposed to be a T and a Y, guess that's a thank you."

Sarah and Pyah pick up the body and carry it to the roof edge to drop it off. Elleon is looking through her scope "No, no, no, you don't want to do that!" she exclaims as she sees the body drop to the ground.

Carl looks through the binoculars, "What? What's wrong with that? It gets rid of the body so no one can see it."

Elleon climbs up on top of the motor home, "Yeah and if they had taken the time to look there is a guard patrolling the perimeter of the town."

Carl scans with the binoculars, "Where? I can't see, oh shit if he comes 'round that corner the first thing he'll see is that body, fuck, fuck, fuck," he curses, banging on the side of the vehicle, "what we going to do?"

Elleon sticks her head over the van roof, "Well, first off, you're going to stop giving our position away with your banging, and secondly I'm going to take out the patrol, then you can get on the blower and get them out of there."

She takes careful aim as the guard rounds the corner. Carl sees him then looks up at Elleon, "Well shoot him then!"

Elleon ignores him, "Just a little further, just a little further," she mutters as the guard spots the body, reaching for his radio, she shoots him straight through the head, "fall forward, please fall forward," she pleads, watching as the guard drops to his knees then onto his face.

Carl climbs up the motor home ladder, "My, you like to cut things fine."

Elleon scans the town, "Yeah, and if there is another one patrolling, he's got to come round the corner to see that one now," she explains, looking back through the scope, "right, get your people out of there."

Carl sits beside her, "And how do you suppose I do that? Fucking semaphore?"

Elleon's head drops, "Use the radio, quietly, and tell them to jump off the back end of the roof, then head east into the desert where you can pick them up," she instructs, waving her hand at the radio.

Carl picks up the radio, "Thought you said it might alert the Mercs?"

Elleon shakes her head, "It's a bit fucking late for that now. Trust me, it won't be long before they are on your people if you don't get them the fuck out of there."

Carl radios Mark, "Looks like they might be on to you, mate. Elleon says to jump off the back side of the roof and run into the desert. Go east, I'll pick you up," he turns to Elleon, "I presume you're going to be covering them?"

Mark comes back, "Due east? And have we got cover?"

Carl jumps down as Elleon sticks her head over the roof again, "There's a lot of activity starting. I think they're on to them so move it."

Carl radios Mark, "Shit mate, they are defo on to you and yes you got cover so get the hell out of there NOW!"

Mark grabs Sarah and Pyah, "Move," he instructs, heading to the back of the roof as a Merc appears on the roof behind them, riddling the roof with gunfire. Mark and Pyah jump straight off into the sand but Sarah drops to her belly on the roof and covers her head.

Elleon takes out the Merc, "Now shift your arse, you dopey cow."

Mark shouts up to Sarah, "Get your arse down here, NOW!"

Sarah lies there, shaking her head in fear, "I can't, it's too high."

Pyah screams at her, "Jump, you stupid bitch, or I'll shoot you myself!"

Mark holds his arms out, "Don't worry, I'll catch you."

Sarah gets to her feet as another Merc on the opposite roof starts to shoot at her. She jumps as the bullets rip around her feet, "SHIT," she yells, landing in Mark's arms, still screaming.

Mark shouts down the radio, "You call that cover?"

Carl shouts back, "Just fucking run!"

Elleon scans for the gunman on the other roof, "Shit, can't get a clear shot," she complains, then she sees another Merc coming around the back of the buildings on Mark's side, "where do you think you're going?" she asks as she shoots him, then turns her attention back to the other rooftop; an R.P.G is sent flying towards her, "Oh fuck!"

She jumps down off the motor home, rolling into the sand as the R.P.G blows the shit out of the van. She runs over a dune for cover as another R.P.G hits the motor home, "Get a funny feeling someone doesn't like me," she remarks, looking to her left she can see Mark, Pyah and Sarah running over a dune in the distance as a Merc appears behind them firing a submachine gun towards them.

They duck down behind a dune as the Merc pins them down. Elleon can just see his head as she takes careful aim and kills him. Her shot gives away her position and an R.P.G hits the dune behind her, sending a plume of sand into the air, covering her, "Shit, some people are so inconsiderate," she complains, brushing the sand off herself then getting up to run using the sand plume as cover.

Mark and Pyah start to run again but Sarah freezes. Pyah stops at the top of a dune, "Jesus, woman, get your shit together," she says as an R.P.G comes hurtling towards her.

Mark drags Pyah down into the dunes as the grenade hits, covering them all in sand.

Elleon sticks her head up to get a bead on the shooter, then randomly fires at where she thinks he is before running further into the dunes.

Mark peers over the dune top to see him fire toward Elleon. He has the perfect shot and, although its further than he's ever fired, he takes careful aim, then shoots. Although he doesn't kill the Merc he hits him in the gut. Mark can see Elleon now. He gives her the thumbs up as Elleon points at two more Mercs heading his way. Mark rushes down to grab Sarah, dragging her by the arm over the dunes and into the desert.

All of a sudden, a vehicle goes hurtling out of the other side of town. Elleon starts to aim at it, but as she is about to fire she hears the other Mercs firing at Mark. She spins around, "Oh, for fuck's sake," she curses, shooting, almost on instinct, the two that have Mark and his group pinned down.

She quickly moves her attention back to the escaping vehicle, "Ooo, moving target, haven't done this in a while," she says to herself, steadying her breathing, making herself comfortable, then closing her eyes as she gives a final exhale to give her full concentration to the shot.

She aims at the driver's seat and squeezes the trigger, sending her round through the air straight into the back of the driver's head. The vehicle skews across the road to plough into a nearby dune. Two passengers jump out, heading in different directions, "Oh, I don't think so mate," she says, putting a round into the one heading in the opposite direction to Mark.

The other one dives into the dunes in Mark's direction. Elleon jumps up proudly, "Now that was a nice shot," she praises, strutting towards Mark's position, "that should be all, except that little shit hiding in the dunes, and he ain't going nowhere."

Carl comes spinning through the dunes, sliding in front of Mark, Pyah and Sarah, "Quick, get in."

Mark saunters towards them, "I think there's only one left, and it looks like our little sniper girl is going to enjoy chasing him down," he says as he slumps into the four by four, "what the hell was that fucking explosion?"

Carl cringes at him, "Well," he starts, rubbing his cheek, "you know that motor home you hired?"

Mark stares at him, "Yeah."

Carl waggles his head, "Well, you ain't got it anymore, BOOM," he describes, making an explosion gesture with his hands.

It isn't long before Elleon tracks the last one down, "Oh, and what do we have here?"

The Merc isn't armed as he puts his hands up to surrender. Elleon shoots him in the knee, "OK, so we're clear on this," she says, aiming her gun at his balls, "I ask you a question, you give the wrong answer and I shoot."

The Merc hold his knee, "You didn't have to shoot me, bitch, I would have told you what you want to know just for the asking."

Elleon prods his balls, "Yeah, but I just needed you to know I ain't kidding. You see I get off on this so, how many more are there? Is the deal going down tonight? Where is De-fuer?"

She prods his balls as he puts one hand in the air, "OK, ok, Christ. Yes, the deal's still going down tonight, twenty-one-hundred, but the bitch lady won't be there, she's sorting a plane out to ship the stuff to Europe."

Elleon prods him again, "Where they flying out from?"

He tries to grab the muzzle, "Shit woman, it's a little airport in Fes, north east of here, and she's flying the stuff down by helicopter."

Elleon starts to walk away from him, "Fes, you say?" she checks, then shoots him in the head.

Carl comes around the dune in the four by four, "Oh, for fuck's sake, we could have interrogated him."

Elleon throws her rifle in the back of the vehicle, "That way please," she directs, pointing off into the desert, "and I got all the information I needed from him, trust me."

Carl heads in the direction she pointed, "So what did he say before you blew the fuck out of him?"

Elleon takes a chewing gum out of her pocket, "Ask me nicely and I might tell you."

Sarah spins in her seat, "Look, you stupid little bitch, this is a matter of life and death, not one of your perverse little games. So, answer him or we just drop you off in the middle of nowhere with fuck all but what you're standing in."

Elleon shrugs, "My daddy used to do that on occasion, I always found my way home."

Mark lifts his finger to Sarah's mouth, "OK, I'm asking," he says, instructing the rest to look forward with a wave of his hand, "please can you tell us what he said?" he asks, moving through to the back to sit next to her, "is that nicely enough for you?"

Elleon smiles, "You should be a negotiator," she suggests, shuffling around to face him, "well, the deal is going down at nine o'clock tonight," she starts, pushing the chewing gum in her mouth, "but you're wasting your time going if you're after Defuer because she ain't there."

Carl stops the vehicle, "What do you mean she ain't there, she's got to be there to oversee the purchase."

Elleon shakes her head, "Nah, she's at Fes airport sorting out transport to Europe. Her second in command, a guy by the name of Renee, is overseeing the deal," she tells them, tapping Marks knee, "and by the way it ain't a purchase, it's a straight swap, five thousand Kalashnikov rifles, amongst other things, for twenty-four VX rockets."

Mark looks at his watch, "Well, it's half eight now, we may still be able to stop the exchange if we hurry," he reasons, reaching back for the radio, "going to call Lacey, see what she's got," he says as he speaks into the radio, "Raven, come in Raven this is Fischer," he says but there's no reply, "shit, I hope she's all right," he worries as Carl puts his foot to the floor.

Carl looks back at Elleon, "So where's this buggy?" he asks as he almost runs straight into it, "Jesus, shit," he curses, slamming the brakes on.

Elleon laughs, "Err, there," she says belatedly, jumping out of the four by four, "anyone want a lift?" she asks, jumping into her buggy, "nope? OK, see you at Tan-Tan," she says, speeding off towards the road as she gives an arrogant wave.

Mark takes the wheel of the four by four and heads off after her but she soon disappears, "You know, I had a feeling that was the last we'd see of her."

Carl shines the torch out of the window, "Don't worry, that one has a habit of turning up at the most unlikely times and places."

Pyah leans through the seats, "Yeah, our main concern should be Lacey and where the hell she is."

Sarah picks up the radio, "Louis to Raven, come in Raven," she tries but still nothing.

Pyah takes the radio and switches it off, "No point in wasting the battery, she's probably gone radio silent. Especially if she's anywhere near her target."

Sarah shrugs, "Suppose," she agrees, tucking the radio in her backpack.

It isn't long before Tan-Tan's lights hit the horizon.

CHAPTER 24
HOT MAMA NINJA

Mark pulls over, switches the lights off, and grabs the binoculars, "OK, let's see. where the hell would that bitch be doing an arms deal with that much armoury?" he asks, scanning the town, "she certainly wouldn't be openly trading that amount of weaponry in the middle of town, so what we have to find, is a warehouse or something."

Pyah taps him on the shoulder, "Maybe it's over there," she suggests, pointing towards a structure, hidden amongst some trees, on a hill, about two miles the other side of town.

Mark looks through the binoculars, "Well spotted, seems to be a lot of activity, you could be on to something there."

Carl walks around the vehicle, "Yeah, and there's a lot of open ground between here and there," he points out, pulling his binoculars out, "can't see a way to it without getting spotted."

Pyah pulls out the map, "Looks like there's a gully running down here," she says, pointing at the map, "it's about half a mile from that hill, we may be able to get down to it by car, but from there on in it looks like we have to go in on foot."

Sarah jumps into the rear of the four by four and starts rummaging around in a bag she's brought. Carl comes around to see what she's up to, "What you doing, hun?" he asks, peeking through the window.

Sarah flips him the bird, "Go and do your planning and leave me alone, I won't be a minute."

Carl shakes his head, "Sometimes I have my doubts about her," he says, walking back to Pyah and Mark.

Pyah puts the map away, "OK, you stay with the vehicle when we get to the gully," she instructs, putting her hand on Carl's shoulder, "while Mark takes the Dragunov up this side of the hill. Then me and Sarah," she says, looking around for Sarah, "wherever she is, go 'round to the side to see if we can find a way in without getting caught."

At that Sarah steps out of the four by four, "OK, I'm ready," she declares as the other three stand, stunned into silence, "what do you reckon?" she asks, pointing down at the all-in-one suit that she is now wearing, "it's a Kevlar and Carbon fibre composite with a micro chainmail lining, completely bullet proof, even against armour piercing bullets," she explains as she gives a twirl, "and stab proof. I designed it myself. Comes with a hood, which should protect me against small explosions too, like grenades," she finishes, giving a firm nod.

Carl walks around her, "You do realise that it fits where it touches and it touches everything?"

Sarah follows his eyes as they look her up and down, "That's the point, I have a full range of movement, it's like a second skin and it's in stealth matt black and camouflage green so no one can see me coming."

Carl huffs, "Yeah, but when they do see you they see EVERYTHING."

Mark circles her, "I think it's kinda cute."

Pyah steps up, "Sexy mamma."

Carl points at Pyah, "My point exactly, anyway, who do you think you are?" he asks, turning back to Sarah with a rather disgruntled look on his face, "THE BAT?"

She pulls the hood over her head and wraps it firmly into her face, "I don't care what I look like, I just know I ain't getting killed."

Everyone gets back in the vehicle as Mark slowly descends down toward the gully. Once there, Mark gives instructions and then sets off crawling towards the warehouses while Pyah and Sarah head around the side of the hill.

Carl just sits twiddling his thumbs in the vehicle, muttering to himself, "Don't know why I have to stay with the damned car. And I should have told her to get that bloody stupid outfit off. Flaunting her all and sundry to everyone."

CHAPTER 25
WAREHOUSE OF WOE

The night is in the grip of a lunar eclipse. The only light in the black night sky is cast by the twinkling of stars. The sheer blackness provides the perfect cover as Mark crawls slowly up between the crags of the rocky hillside. His grey jeans and shirt giving more than adequate camouflage as he silently moves towards the dense tree line surrounding the warehouse. He weaves through the heavy undergrowth to find a perfect perch, giving him a good sniper's eye view of the compound below. Laying down he attaches the night scope Carl procured for him and scans the layout for his intended target. In front of him he sees a line of heavy trucks being loaded with crates as a forklift transfers the VX rockets through a warehouse, disappearing to an unknown vehicle.

Mark spots Pyah and Sarah clambering down from the tree line to his left, "Hold your positions when you reach the bottom, girls," he says as he sees a patrol heading their way, "get behind the container in front of you till that patrol goes past."

Just as he gives the instruction a gun muzzle is pushed into his neck, "Keep your hands where I can see them," a gruff voice instructs him.

Marks head slumps as the guard radios in, "OK, I got the Fischer guy and the women are on the way into the compound-"

He gives a groan as his limp body is slowly lowered to the ground, a knife still protruding from his neck. Mark looks around. Elleon is stood hovering over the body, "You're not very good at this stealth stuff, are you," she remarks, whispering as she pulls the knife from the guard's neck, "I watched you come all the way up from the gully. Then watched this guy creep up on you," she explains, tapping the guy's head with the knife.

Elleon brings a thermal imaging scope up to her eye, "You do realise this is an ambush," she checks, looking back down at Mark, "you got six snipers on the roof, four patrols in plain sight, for your benefit, and a whole load of men hidden in the tree line, just waiting for the word to pounce," she tells him, handing him the thermal imager, "I'd be getting your girls out of there," she advises, pointing towards Pyah and Sarah.

Mark radios Pyah, "Abort, abort, abort, it's an ambush, get the fuck out of there."

Elleon points to the lead truck as it lines up to leave the compound, "I would also take a good look at that truck if I were you."

Mark scans it with the thermal imager, "OK, what's the heat signature in the back? I presume that's what you want me to see?"

Elleon nods, "That, I'm afraid, is your friend, the Raven."

Mark's eyes close as his head drops, "Shit, no wonder we couldn't contact her," he sighs and is about to radio Pyah when Elleon grabs the radio, "they've been listening to your chatter all night, that's how they knew you were coming," she grabs his hand to lead him towards Pyah's position, "ok, we got four coming up the hill behind her. Can you see them?"

Mark looks through the scope, "Yep."

Elleon pulls her rifle from behind a tree, "OK, you take them and I'll get the others coming through the trees," she says, lifting her gun to her shoulder, "let's clear a path for the girls."

Sarah and Pyah weave through the dense tree cover as Elleon takes down two Mercs ascending on their position from their right, "Keep going girls, I got you covered," she says as two more appear straight in front of them. Pyah spots them, but before she can react to shoot them they go down to Elleon's fire, "all clear through the trees ladies," she assures, shouting to Pyah.

Elleon turns back to Mark to find him back at the inner edge of the trees. She quickly runs to him, pushing his rifle down to spoil his shot, "You don't want to do that," she warns, knowing what his target is.

Mark is furious, "What the hell did you do that for?" he demands, pushing Elleon away and taking aim again.

Elleon cups her hand over his scope, "I'm telling you, DON'T."

Mark drops his muzzle, then drops his head in disgust, "I have the perfect shot on De-fuer, we could end this, right here, right now."

Elleon takes her hand away from the scope, "You see the necklace she's wearing?"

Mark raises his gun, looks through the scope, "She ain't wearing a necklace."

Elleon places her hand back over the scope, "Exactly," she says, standing in front of Mark to block his shot, "her brother gave a locket two days before you killed him," she explains as she kneels beside him, "she never takes it off, in fact she bathes with it on. Eats, sleeps, drinks and shite's with it on," she goes on, tapping Mark on the back of the head, "you kill her," she says, pointing at the compound, "and you're just killing a doppelganger." Elleon starts to walk away, "And the real one just goes to ground."

Mark lowers his gun, "OK, let's go and get the girls and get the hell-" he stops dead mid-sentence, hearing a whirring sound, "what the hell is that?"

Elleon walks back to him, "That is your rockets flying off in a couple of Chinook helicopters," she says, putting her hand to her ear, "but if I'm not mistaken, that," she indicates, pointing down to the main entrance, "is a challenger tank."

Mark looks down, "Oh shit," he curses, lifting the radio, "Carl, get the fuck out of that gully, you got a tank coming your way. Pyah, Sarah, get the hell out of those trees and meet where we went in."

Elleon is the first to the edge of the trees. Almost running straight into Pyah, "Here," she says, handing Pyah a key fob, "two hundred yards past the gully, you see those four dunes," she asks, pointing out to a set of strange shaped dunes, "right back one is my buggy, take it. Get into the town and find the hospital," she instructs, tapping Pyah on the shoulder, "they have a helicopter. Do whatever you have to, but get it and try to stop those Chinooks from getting to Fes."

Pyah takes the fob, "What're you going to do?"

Elleon spins and takes two Mercs out as they appear around the trees, "Oh, I got me a little problem."

Mark appears behind her, "And what's your plan for me?"

Elleon points at Carl as he emerges from the gully, "See that big black rock next to Carl? There's a laws rocket hidden behind it," she says, grabbing the radio, "get it and go after the trucks. I'll meet you there after I've taken care of that tank," she tells him, then she radios Carl, "Carl, stop!"

Mark runs down to Carl and grabs the laws rocket, "OK, let's get them trucks," he says as the tank starts to fire on the gully, "and get the fuck out of here!"

Elleon arrives at the tank as it fires on the gully a second time, "OK, let's see how you like this," she says, throwing a grenade down the barrel as it reloads.

The grenade explodes it, the barrel causing the shell to fire prematurely as Elleon waits for one or both of the hatches to open. She covers the firing scope with her jacket, effectively blinding the gunners view, as the driver's hatch cracks slightly open, allowing her to just get a grenade into his compartment. She runs up the tank, pulls the pins on the last two grenades and stands to wait for the main hatch to open, "Come on gentlemen," she says as the grenade explodes inside, causing a panic for the main hatch.

As it opens she kicks the emerging man back down, then throws the two grenades in, slamming the hatch closed to blow all occupants to kingdom come.

Jumping down, she heads for the road after the trucks and Mark. Elleon meets Mark by the roadside, "OK, take out the first truck with that," she directs, pointing at the laws rocket.

Carl scrambles into the back of the vehicle, "I'm sure we can use this," he says, pulling an R.P.G. from under one of the seats.

Elleon kisses him, "Fucking great, we can take the back one out with that, effectively cutting off their retreat,"

she checks through her thermal imager, "yeah, Lacey is still in the second one so we take them all out except that one," she says, lifting her rifle, "ok, take the bastards out."

Mark aims the laws rocket at the first in the convoy as Carl fires the R.P.G at the rear truck. Mark's shot takes the rear of the lead truck into the air, sending it end over end, while Carl destroys the fuel tank on the rear truck, sending it sideways to skew across the road. Elleon starts to pick off the soldiers as they exit their vehicles.

Mark makes a dash for the truck containing Lacey, furiously shooting all that stand in his way. Elleon rushes around the rear truck to catch anyone making their escape, shooting all in her path. As Mark opens the truck a Merc is stood holding Lacey, bound and gagged at gunpoint, "You move, she dies," he says as Carl appears at Marks side.

Mark takes careful aim as Lacey shakes her head, eyes wide. The Merc smiles "I wouldn't do that if I were you," he says, raising a detonator in his other hand, "she's wired - I let go and boom we all go," he explains, opening her jacket to reveal an explosive belt.

Mark notices a knife point slowly piercing the canvas behind the Merc, "OH, YOU WILLING TO DIE FOR YOUR CAUSE EH?" he asks, shouting to cover any noise as Elleon silently slithers through the truck canvas and up behind the Merc.

His eyes dull as she reaches around to calmly take the detonator from him, "I'll take that thank you,." she pulls the knife from the back of his neck and he slowly falls forward onto Lacey.

Elleon reaches into his pocket, brings out a set of keys, and unlocks Lacey's handcuffs, "I don't know, you lot don't half get yourselves into a right mess sometimes."

Pyah and Sarah find the buggy under a sandcloth camouflage and set off for the town. De-fuer has a small army stationed in the town, making it difficult for the girls to drive in and find the hospital, so they sneak in on foot.

Pyah pulls Sarah to one side before they go in the helipad office, "We were told to use any means necessary," she reminds her, unzipping Sarah's suit down the front, "I think your little tush in that should get us what we want, just needed a bit of cleavage is all."

Sarah slinks into the helipad office where four men immediately stop what they're doing, their gazes slowly turning to Sarah. She gives a little girl lost pose in the doorway, "Now which one of you lovely gentlemen would be the pilot of that?" she asks, pointing out to the helicopter.

Two men stood at the counter part as a burly, curvy African lady of about 45 years of age walks through the middle of them, "I would be the pilot, can I help you ladies?" she asks, unwrapping a cheese sandwich.

Sarah's head slumps as Pyah walks past, "Well, we're looking for a lift to Fes airport and we need to get there in rather a hurry."

The pilot shakes her head, "Nah, sorry, can't do it, I might have an emergency here and Fes is about half hour out," she says as she walks out the door past the girls to sit on the bench outside.

Sarah leans in to Pyah, "You clock her on the head and I'll get the keys."

Pyah closes her eyes and shakes her head, "And who is going to fly it?"

Sarah shrugs, "You've had lessons."

Pyah laugh out loud, "Yeah, two!"

The pilot takes the lid of her coffee, then sips at it, "So what's so urgent that you need to be at Fes?"

Pyah walks up in front of her, "OK what's your price?"

The pilot shakes her head, "That bird is for emergencies only."

Sarah stomps over, "This is a fricking emergency, if we don't get to Fes fast some bitch terrorist is going to do something..." she pauses, hesitating for a moment, "well, something really bad, and if we don't stop her she's going to get away."

The pilot calmly takes a bite from her sandwich, "So, this bitch terrorist got a name?"

Sarah grabs Pyah's arm, "We're wasting time here, she probably works for De-Fuer anyway."

The pilot puts her sandwich down and walks in front of Sarah, "You want to watch what you're saying, young lady," she warns, prodding Sarah in the chest, "'cause someone gonna put you on your ass for a comment like dat," she continues, pushing Sarah backwards, "I don't work for dat bitch, ain't no one in dis town work for dat bitch."

Sarah puts her hands up, "OK, ok, I'm sorry, but if we don't catch her..."

The pilot stands back, "You want to catch dat bitch? What for?"

Pyah steps in between them, "We're going to kill her," she says simply, pulling a gun from her belt, "do you have a problem with that?"

The pilot looks down at the gun, then back up at Pyah, "You serious?"

Pyah nods.

The pilot stretches her arm out towards her bird, "I usually save lives but dis time I'll make an exception."

Sarah starts to zip her top back up. The pilot puts her hand over Sarah's, "Oh, I know you did that to get a ride so let's leave it as it is eh?"

Sarah's eyebrows raise. Pyah walks up behind her and taps her bum, "Yeah, you let the lady see your boobs, that's the least you can do."

The pilot turns, "The names Gladys, and she can do more dan dat if she wants," she says, reverting back to her Caribbean roots.

Pyah smiles, "Looks like you've clicked, not surprised in that outfit like."

Gladys turns her head, "Hmm, you got dat right," she opens the door to the helicopter, "you can sit up front with me, if you like."

Sarah shuffles through to the back of the helicopter, "She's got flight experience so I think she should sit up front."

Gladys shrugs, "Suit yourself," she says as Pyah climbs in the co-pilot's seat.

Once they're in the air Gladys slips her hand over on Pyah's lap, "So, you two together?"

Pyah lies her hand on top of Gladys', "Not exactly, and if I had time, trust me, I would probably take you up on your offer," she says, sliding Gladys's hand up her thigh, "but, sadly, I need to go and kill me a bitch."

Sarah slides forward in her seat, "Well, when we have her you might be able to come back this way," she suggests, chuckling to herself.

Gladys reaches back and softly grabs Sarah's lapel

"I'm going to keep you to that," she says, pulling her forward to kiss her.

It isn't long before the airfield is in sight and the Chinooks are on their approach. Gladys flies low and fast up behind them but then she notices a tiger gunship approaching in the opposite direction, "Oh shit, looks like we got company and I don't think they want to talk," she says as she swoops up and dives to her right as a stinger missile comes hurtling towards her, "oh shit, I think they mean business," she curses, making a run for a cluster of trees she's spotted.

She avoids the stinger, but the gunship starts to fire a Gatling gun in their direction. Gladys takes a hit as the chopper starts to plummet into a spiral towards the ground.

Pyah grabs the stick, "Her feet are stuck on the pedals!"

Sarah leans through to pull Gladys's feet clear, "Oh shit, she's dead."

Pyah pulls the stick back hard, "So are we if I don't get this thing level," she yells, throttling up as the ground comes rushing towards them, "I'm afraid this is going to be a hard landing," she says as she gets the nose up to stall.

The tail hits first as the rotor spins off into the desert, then the skids slam into the ground, sending the cockpit forward onto its nose. The girls are shaken up but uninjured. Pyah throws the door open, "We need to get out of here before that thing gets here," she says, pointing toward the gunship.

Sarah grabs Pyah's hand to drag her clear of the wreckage as the gunship fires another rocket at them. Sarah pulls Pyah under an overhanging rock, then lies on top of her as the rocket hits, sending a ball of fire across the surrounding desert, including across the rock that the girls are under. Pyah is pushed against the back of the crevice, "You know, there is a time and a place for this, my dear."

Sarah climbs on top of her again, "Pull your knees up, for Christ's sake."

Pyah pulls her knees in, "You do realise someone is trying to kill us?"

Sarah tuts, "My suit hides heat signatures and hopefully that blast will cover us as well," she explains, pulling Pyah's arms under her, "if they have thermal imaging, they should think we went down with the ship."

Pyah gives a puzzled look, "Ship? It's a helicopter, and it ain't called Enterprise."

The gunship hovers, searching through the wreckage with a spotlight, then, after a couple of sweeps over the trees, heads back to the airport.

Once it's gone quiet Sarah lifts herself off Pyah and crawls out from under the rock. Pyah just lies there pouting, "Aww I was enjoying that."

Sarah stoops down, "Err, bitch to kill?" she reminds her, pointing toward the airfield.

Pyah reluctantly skulks out, brushes herself down, and starts to walk towards the airstrip, "So how far I got to walk and how long is this going to take?"

Sarah grabs her arm, "Come on, it's less than half a mile, should only take about fifteen minutes, tops."

Pyah starts to wriggle, "It's all right for you, I got sand in my knickers."

Sarah stands with her hands on her hips, "Well at least you're not wearing an all-in-one that doesn't let heat out. Talk about sweating. Then some dork pulled the front down and now I got sand stuck to my tits, thank you," she complains, brushing the sand from her cleavage, "so shut up and walk," she says, laughing as she walks in front.

CHAPTER 26
FES

Mark, Elleon, Lacey, and Carl head for the airbase as fast as the jeep will go. As they near, they see an explosion off in the desert. Mark turns to Carl, "I hope that is not my wife, or your fiancée."

Carl puts his hand over his heart, "Probably, but they're ok," he insists, closing his eyes, "yeah, they're ok. If they weren't I'd feel it."

Mark gives him a strange look, "You not going all mystic on me now are you?"

They hurry off to the site of the explosion.

When they get there Elleon jumps straight out and scans the surrounding area while Carl and Mark rush to the crashed helicopter. Lacey stays in the vehicle, praying. Mark and Carl find the charred remains of the pilot, "Shit, I hope one of ours wasn't flying."

Elleon stoops down near the overhanging rock, "Nope, they went that way about ten minutes ago," she says, pointing toward the airfield.

Mark rushes across to her, "Who went that way?"

Elleon points at two sets of footprints, "Size four military style boots, that's got to be Sarah, and Gucci walking shoes?" she says, stroking her chin "I wonder who would be wearing them?" she teases, smiling at Mark.

Mark smiles and shakes his head, "Yep, looks like they went that way. Let's move," he declares, jumping back in the vehicle.

Pyah and Sarah are almost at the perimeter of the airfield when a man appears in front of them, "Evening ladies," he greets, startling the girls.

Sarah draws her gun, "OK bud, what do you want?"

The man disarms Sarah and flicks Pyah to the ground before either of them have time to react, "OK, I'm guessing that all this commotion is over you two? So, let's stop the violence because I think I'm here to help you," he says, letting Sarah go as he steps back cautiously, "I presume that you were in that chopper that's just gone down?"

Pyah picks herself up, "Yeah and who the hell are you?"

The guy holds his hand out, "The names Carl Fisher, Safari Ranger. Saw the blast and came to investigate."

Both Pyah's and Sarah's heads drop as Pyah laughs silently to herself, "Oh, this could be confusing."

The ranger's head jolts back, "What could be confusing?"

Pyah points at Sarah, "Her fiancé is Carl Sinclair and my husband is Mark Fischer spelt with a C."

The ranger laughs, "Is that Fisher with a C or Mark with a C?"

Pyah gives him a sideways look, "Fischer."

The ranger's ears prick then he grabs the girls, throwing them to the ground, "Shhh, vehicle."

Both the girls listen but can't hear anything. The ranger points out towards the crash site as a pair of lights can just be seen coming over the horizon, "Middle name's Ben if that's any good."

Sarah shakes his hand, "Nice to meet you Ben."

Pyah stands back up, "It's ok, I'd recognise that style of driving anywhere," she smiles as the four by four comes bouncing towards them.

It slides to a halt in front of Pyah, "Took your sweet time, didn't you?" she accuses, sticking her head in the driver's window.

Carl looks at the ranger, "And who is that?"

Pyah turns, "Oh that's Ben, he's a safari ranger," she says, then calls him over, "Ben this is Carl Sinclair, Carl meet Carl Ben Fisher, oh, and my name is Pyah," she introduces the rest to him and him to the rest of the party, then tells him what's going on.

Ben walks up to the top of a dune to look at the airstrip, "Well, I'm afraid you're too late to stop that cargo," he says, pointing out to a large plane, "you see they very quickly loaded that Hercules and it's about to take off, looks like its bound for Europe."

Elleon grabs the binoculars, "RAF Hercules. Tag XV 195."

Lacey walks up to Ben, "Don't suppose you have a mobile I could use?"

Ben hands her his phone, "I presume you mean one of these?"

Elleon shoulder charges Lacey down the dune, "SNIPER!" she yells as a bullet whistles past their heads and buries itself into the sand behind them.

Ben dives down the dune, "Where?" he asks as everyone ducks for cover.

Elleon points towards the back of the airstrip, "Muzzle flash from the tower on the crane east corner."

Sarah starts to stick her head out for a look but Elleon drags her back, "Don't give him a target," she warns, then crouches, running to the four by four to grab her rifle, "I don't suppose I could borrow that suit?" she asks, pointing at Sarah.

Sarah hides behind the four by four, "Yeah, I suppose, if you're thinking what I think you're thinking."

Carl rushes around after her, "Hang on a sec," he says, grabbing a coat, "put this around you because it's quite evident you're naked under that," he explains, pulling the coat up in front of Sarah, "she's already flashed her bits to everyone so I don't mind but I don't want you flashing it, thank you."

Sarah gives him a puzzled look, "What do you mean? She flashed?"

Carl's blushing can be seen even in the total black of the night, "Well, she didn't flash to me, she flashed to Mark, in fact she stripped off in front of him," he sputters, stumbling for words, "I wasn't there, he just told me she got naked."

Sarah manages to get out of the suit without anyone seeing her and Carl wraps her in the coat. Elleon comes around the vehicle and strips while Carl rushes away, embarrassed, "Don't know where she gets her arrogance from?"

Sarah helps her into the suit but says nothing about what Carl told her. Elleon's clothes fit Sarah, so she dresses in them and Elleon disappears through the dunes.

Lacey calls Cramer, "Are you still in France?"

Cramer is glad to hear from her, "No, we are checking something out in Spain at the moment, why?"

She walks around the four by four, "Well, I might have something for you, an RAF Hercules may be coming into Spain or France with twenty-four VX rockets. Its tag is XV195 and it belongs to Denier De-Fuer,"

She can almost hear Cramer give a high five to himself, "Yes, we got her! Is she on the plane with them?"

Lacey cups the phone, "Ben, don't suppose you know if a female that looks like this got on the plane with the rockets, did she?" she asks, handing him a photo.

Ben looks at the photo, "Nope, she took the gunship somewhere to the east."

Lacey is about to tell Cramer when she hears him, "Fuck, its ok, I heard him," the phone is silent for a moment then, "ok, you go after the bitch and be careful, I'll stop that Hercules."

Ben notices some soldiers heading their way, "I think you lot better get out of here, I'll wait for Elleon."

Mark fires up the four by four. Everyone jumps in except Ben, "If you head south for about ten miles you'll come to an old building near an oasis, I'll meet you there," Ben says and Mark shoots off into the desert.

Elleon sneaks around some dunes and up behind a clump of rye grass where she has a perfect view of the crane. Looking through the thermal imager she can see the sniper. She picks up her rifle, sets the scope to night and takes careful aim. The sniper spots her just too late as her bullet spreads the back of his head against the crane's ironworks.

Suddenly she hears a sound behind her. Drawing her handgun, she spins, aiming it directly at a rather stunned Ben, "You could get your head blown off, creeping up on a girl like that."

Ben lies down beside her, "Just thought I'd inform you that there is a small army heading this way."

Elleon hands him the thermal imager, "Yeah, I know. Just going to see how many I can get before they work out where I am," she says, smiling, "then let's see if the rest can find me, what you going to do?"

Ben looks through the thermal imager, smiling, "Confident little minx aren't we," he remarks, scanning the area, "got one coming through the hanger."

Elleon drifts her gun across and calmly shoots him. Ben keeps scanning, "Looks like you might have one up on the tower. Not sure."

Elleon swings around a bit, "Yep," she agrees, then shoots him, "oh shit, looks like they got my position. Think it's time to move."

Ben heads off into the desert, "My truck's this way. The others have gone to a safe place I know. said we'll meet them there."

Elleon takes one last shot, shooting the pilot of one of the Chinooks, "That should just about do it," she declares, then runs after Ben.

They soon come across his vehicle, jumping in, they speed off after Mark.

It isn't long before they are at the oasis chatting to the rest of the group. Sarah approaches Pyah, "Did you know that that little tramp stripped off for your husband?"

Pyah smiles at her confidently, "Wouldn't worry about it. He's scared of little girls," she confides, patting Sarah across the bum, "didn't think you were one for gossip?"

Sarah huffs, "I'm not, it's just that she came on to Carl too."

Pyah grabs Sarah by the chin and starts to scrutinise her eyes, "Yeah, there it is."

Sarah's head jolts back, "There what is?"

Pyah sniggers, "That little green-eyed monster."

Sarah rolls her eyes, "As if I would be jealous of THAT!"

Pyah starts to walk away, then turns, "Got to admit she's pretty," she says, seeing if Sarah will bite.

Sarah stomps after Pyah, "She'll be pretty fucking dead if she comes near my Carl again, trust me."

Pyah laughs out loud, "Oh, trust me, I've seen Carl's reaction to her. Talk about the disappointed father figure," she laughs then looks around, noticing Lacey is missing, "where the hell has she gone?"

CHAPTER 27
THE OASIS

Darkness shrouds the oasis as the glistening water reflects the starry night sky. Lacey is taking a walk around the oasis, enjoying the peace and quiet of the night, when Ben strolls up behind her, "You know, it may seem safe out here but there are a few creatures still awake that might eat you out here."

Lacey taps her gun, "Heard you coming," she says, turning to face him, "realised you had two feet so I didn't blow your head off."

Ben sniggers, "That's because I wasn't stalking you as prey," he points out, pointing over to the other side of the oasis, "now that big boy might want to eat you."

A silhouette of young male lion can just be made out drinking at the edge of the oasis, "That's if you're lucky."

Lacey shrouds her eyes, "Why if I'm lucky?"

Ben sniggers again, "Well, in this light he might think you're a possible mate," he suggests, sliding his arms around Lacey from the back.

Lacey looks down, "And I wonder where he would get that idea from," she says, smiling over her shoulder.

Ben kisses her neck, "Well, it may be the bush aroma that you seem to have picked up, or that tantalising perfume."

Lacey spins, wrapping her arms around his neck "I'll bet he hasn't got a silver tongue though?"

He gazes deep into her eyes, "I'm sure I don't know what you mean," he replies, a wry grin glowing all over his face.

He gently lifts her up to walk into a cluster of reeds, laying her softly down on a small grassy clearing in the centre. Lacey shuffles to comfort herself, "What happens if the big cat decides to come 'round to investigate?"

Ben pats Lacey's gun, "I'll have to show him who's the alpha male, won't I?" he says as he unfastens her waistband.

She kisses him then slides her hand down the front of his trousers, "Oh shit, I think I may have found a snake."

Ben slides his hands up onto her breasts, "Looks like I may have found a camel because it certainly isn't a dromedary."

Lacey funnily slaps him, "And why wouldn't it be a dromedary?"

Ben slides his hands up into her bra, "Well, they only have one hump," he says, sniggering to himself.

Lacey takes a knife out, "Well, maybe you need a better look," she says, pushing the blade up under her bra to slice it off at the front.

Ben kisses each nipple softly, "Nope, doesn't smell like a camel."

A small rustling can be heard a few meters away as Lacey tries to sit up to take a look, "What was that?"

Ben carries on, "Oh, it's just Elleon having a perve, wouldn't worry about it, she followed me out here."

Lacey lies back down, "Well, you never know, the little bitch might actually learn something," she says, sighing.

Ben's hands slowly reach around to a roll he brought with him. Unwrapping it and spreading it out next to Lacey as she watches on, "My, I get the feeling you came prepared."

Ben rolls her onto the blanket, then slides his hands down the back of her trousers, "Well, we wouldn't want you to get any grass where it shouldn't be now, would we?"

Lacey lifts her hips to allow him to pull her pants down, "A gentleman as well?"

Ben slides her trousers down, taking her briefs with them, "As well as what?" he asks, kissing her torso as he descends.

Lacey places her hands on the back of his neck, "As well as a comedian," she says, chuckling to herself.

Elleon stays quiet, knowing that they know she is there, she watches intently. Imagining it was her with the ranger as she places her hand down her own pants to play with herself in silence.

Pyah picks up the thermal imager to scan for Lacey. As she scans the oasis she sees Elleon, "What the hell is that dirty little bitch doing," she murmurs, scanning to see what Elleon is watching.

Her scan comes across Lacey and Ben, "Ooo, that's where you are, you lucky bitch," she says softly, staring for a while, "suppose you should have your privacy, now do I go and sort that little minx out or would that disturb you," Pyah wonders then decides to let things lay, "I'll sort this when you're done honey," she says, giving herself an assertive nod as she heads back to the group.

Ben has Lacey naked by now and is slipping out of his underwear as Lacey runs her fingers down his rippling muscles, "Oh, aren't we a big boy."

Ben slips his head down between her legs, kissing the inside of her thighs as she twitches with ecstasy. The door of heaven beckoning her to step into the world of paradise as Ben softly slips his tongue inside her. Lacey moves in synchronization as she realises he is in perfect harmony with her pleasure. He gently replaces his tongue with two fingers as he runs his tongue up her hips, across her abdomen and onto her breasts. Her back arches as she bites her lip, restraining the moans to a dull rumble. The tingle of passion lifts the hairs across her body as he reaches deep into her very soul, caressing the very fabric of her mind with seduction. His voice softly whispers sweet nothings in her ear. She has never felt anything like this as she wonders if she is finally falling in love, true love, the love that only a soul mate could feel for another.

She wonders if he feels the same as he looks deep into her eyes, "Do you believe in love at first sight?" he asks, taking her breath with his words.

She reaches up, pull his mouth down to hers, "I didn't till this very moment," she answers, then kisses him the way she has never kissed before.

Every fleeting moment seems to last for a lifetime, yet is over too soon. Her battle-hardened heart melts as he feels his heart flutter like a nervous child, "Will you marry me?" he asks, trembling through the entirety of his being.

She inwardly gasps as she finds her mouth speaking the word, "Yes," without hesitation.

He hugs her, "Oh, I don't believe you just said that."

She holds him tight, "Neither do I, but I've never been so sure of anything in my life. You make me feel like a small child again."

He pulls back, "Have you felt how much I'm shaking? No one has ever done to me what you are doing to me at this very moment," he kisses her, "I swore I would never do this. Yet here I am falling in love like some schoolkid infatuated with his

French teacher," he says, huffing, "I just want to scream it to the world."

Lacey puts her finger over his lips, "Well, I think, in the present situation, we should just go and tell them," she says, pointing back towards the camp, "in a calm and quiet fashion."

He pulls her hand away, "What, you don't mind telling them?"

She rolls her eyes "Don't mind? Shit, I want to scream it to the world as well."

They quickly get dressed while Elleon scurries back to the group. She runs straight into Pyah, "Did you enjoy that, madam?"

Elleon's head drops, "She wasn't that good, bet I could teach him a thing or two."

Pyah walks away, shaking her head in disgust. Lacey walk back into the camp hand in hand with Ben, beaming with anticipation. Sarah slips past them, "Oh, I wonder what you two have been up to?"

Lacey looks deep into Bens eyes, "Oh, just getting engaged," she says, grinning from ear to ear.

Sarah stops dead, "Whoa, did I just hear you right there? Engaged?"

The rest of the group hear Sarah's comment as heads spin. Ben puffs his chest, "Yes, Lacey has consented to be my wife."

Pyah drops to a crouch, "Jesus, how long have you known each other? About an hour? Damn, talk about love at first sight."

Mark walks over, holding his hand out, "Congratulations."

Carl steps in, "Well, I think we better get this job sorted then, it looks like we might have a wedding to arrange," he says, pausing for a moment, "don't suppose you would mind having a double wedding, would you?"

Sarah saunters around in front of Carl, "Ahem, don't you think you should ask the proposed bride first?"

Carl drops to his knee, "Will you marry me?"

Sarah covers her mouth as the tears flood down her face, "Oh, you stupid old fart, you know I will."

Carl stands up, "Well, that's that then," he says, hugging Sarah, "kill the devil bitch, save the world, then get married. Sounds like a plan."

Congratulations are expressed. A small but quick celebration is had then everyone beds down for the night as an early morning assault is planned on Denier De-fuer.

CHAPTER 28
THE BREAKFAST CLUB

A haze dusts the barren wilderness as the crimson glow of the impending sun mounts the horizon. Its light shears the dunes, casting ghostlike shadows across the desolate sands. A wisp of gentle wind warms the camp, rousing the intrepid troop to a glorious daybreak. Bleary eyed, Mark and Carl gather wood to make a fire while the girls check provisions for a hearty breakfast.

Ben disappears into the wilderness, returning soon with goose eggs and a loin of meat, "Breakfast, if anyone is interested."

Lacey pulls a large knife, "OK, what is it?"

Ben smiles at her, "Goose eggs."

Mark turns to him, "How do you like your goose eggs? Medium rare?"

Pyah stands up, "Prefer mine cooked till it's well and truly dead."

Lacey drives the knife through the heart of the meat, "Smart arses," she says, then pushes a stick through it to hang it over the fire, "ask a stupid question of some stupid people, you're bound to get a stupid answer."

Elleon walks beside her, "Who you talking to?"

Lacey glances up at her, "The only person I seem to be able to get a straight answer from this morning," she says, pointing at herself.

Elleon smiles, "Betcha got the answer you wanted in the bushes last night," she teases, then slopes away.

Lacey grumps to herself, "Oh, you're going to get the answer you're looking for one of these days, madam," she mutters under her breath.

The meat and eggs are cooked. Everyone enjoys their breakfast, then Mark stands up, "Well, we got a bit of a drive in front of us, so shall we?" he asks, heading for the vehicles with his bedroll tucked under his arm.

Sarah helps Pyah tidy up, "Looks like that little minx has upset Lacey again."

Pyah looks around at Elleon, "She better watch what she's doing. I certainly wouldn't want to push Lacey too far and she's my friend."

Sarah whispers, "Well, at the next town I think we should teach her some manners."

Pyah reaches out to shake Sarah's hand, "Deal."

Pyah approaches Mark, "I hear that the little madam stripped for you."

Mark gives a raucous laugh, "You should have been there."

Pyah is stunned by his reaction, "Whoa, hang on a minute," she says, grabbing him by the shoulder, "you and THAT?"

Mark puts his hand on Pyah's shoulders, "No, not me and THAT," he says, smiling blissfully at her, "she jumped up on a sand dune, Naked, yes. But about five hundred yards away from me," he explains, kissing Pyah, "then she nearly got her head blown off."

Pyah is confused. Mark shakes his head, "Trust me, she wasn't flirting. She was stupidly trying to attract the attention of another sniper. Something she apparently saw in a movie."

Pyah's head spins toward Elleon, "Not too bright, that girl," she remarks, turning back to Mark with a smile, "but I bet you still scoped her out?"

Mark hangs his head, "Nope, didn't really get the chance once they started firing at her," he says, a wry grin coming over his face, "mind, what I did see was cute like."

Pyah slaps him, "Dirty old man," she says, chuckling with Mark, "you wouldn't, would you?"

Mark sucks breath over his teeth and shakes his head, "Well, I don't know, you know."

Pyah slaps him again, "Don't you go teasing now, you might get what you wish for."

Mark puts his hand over her mouth, "Don't even go there," he warns, a serious note appearing in his voice as the thought strikes him.

While Lacey is stowing her stuff in the back of the vehicle she notices a holdall tucked under the back seat. She drags it out and starts to rummage through it, "Oh. this looks comfy," she says, pulling a leather biker jacket out.

She puts the jacket on, "Hmm, almost perfect fit," she sighs, then rummages a bit more and finds a rather large watch, "you're a big bugger," she remarks, noticing a USB port at the back, "now what do you suppose you're for?" she wonders as she pulls out a pair of sunglasses with a cable attached to them.

She puts the sunglasses on and feels a small switch under the arm, "Fuck me, talk about James Bond," she exclaims, taking them off to investigate.

She finds that the cable fits the watch but nothing seems to happen. When she puts the glasses back on she can see behind her, "Ah, you have cameras in the arm," she looks at the watch, "so what do you do?" she asks, flicking the buttons.

A recording starts to play on the glasses. A recording of Denier De-fuer giving instructions to some Mercs, "Ah ha, been spying on the bitch. So, what else is on this thing?" she wonders but just then the flat battery icon appears and the whole set-up switches off, "damn," she curses, looking through the bag for a charger, "got to be one in here somewhere."

She moves some tools, then picks a black squidgy object up, "OH SHIT," she yells, dropping it, realising it's an eight-inch black strap on dick.

She looks around for something to wipe her hands on, "Has anyone got any antibacterial wipes or something?"

Sarah walks over, "There's some alcohol wipes in the first aid kit, why?" she asks, handing her the first aid kit.

Lacey takes one out, "Oh, I just," she starts, pausing to think, "err, found some greasy oily tools," she finishes, wiping her hands frantically.

Sarah fluffs the shoulders of Lacey's jacket, "Wow that's smart, where did you get it?"

Lacey points at the bag, "In there with them tools and this," she says, showing her the watch and glasses.

Sarah is intrigued, "You know, this four by four is equipped with a USB port. That might charge it."

They show the rest of the group what they've found, then plug it in to let it charge while they resume their journey. Mark takes point in the four by four while the rest follow in the other vehicles, "I reckon we should head back towards Tan-Tan," he says and everyone agrees.

It isn't long before they hit Tan-Tan to find that De-fuer has flown to the coastal town of Tarfaya. Deciding to push on they head for Tarfaya, arriving mid-afternoon.

CHAPTER 29
WELCOME TO THE GIRLS' CLUB

The midday sun blisters across the town as the temperature rises well above a hundred degrees. The group decide to frequent a small bar near the Tarfaya hotel for some refreshments. Exotic belly dancers are performing as Mark and Carl order a round of drinks while the girls sit their weary bones down to watch the entertainment.

Elleon and Ben decide to scope the town out to see if there is any sign of De-fuer and it isn't long before Elleon comes across the tiger gunship parked under a camouflage net, "Well, she's definitely here, but where is she staying?"

Ben asks one of the locals if he has seen any sign of her. He is told that she is staying in a private residence midtown.

They set off and soon come across a three-story building with guards placed outside. As De-fuer doesn't know Ben he can roam past unnoticed but Elleon slips up onto a rooftop to find a better angle of view. Elleon spots De-fuer through one of the widows, climbs down to find Ben, then they head back to the bar to inform the rest.

When they get back to the bar Carl is up on-stage dancing with a couple of the belly dancers. Ben sits beside Mark, "He does realise they are men he's dancing with?"

Mark covers his mouth with his hand, "I haven't had the heart to tell him," he admits, chuckling to himself, "we are just enjoying the spectacle," he adds, shaking his head.

Ben turns to Pyah and Lacey, "You enjoying the show ladies?"

Pyah buries her head in a cushion as Lacey turns her head away, "Damn, it's funny. He hasn't a clue."

Sarah is stood behind a pillar, "If he wants to make a fool of himself, who am I to stop him," she says, giggling quietly as she sneaks a peek, then moves back in, giggling like a schoolgirl.

They watch as one belly dancer grinds their buttocks against Carl's groin and the other grinds their scrotum against Carl's buttocks. Carl is blissfully unaware of what is transpiring until the music stops. Then he gasps as he exits the stage with his arms around both dancer's waists. He escorts them to the bar, introducing them to the group, "This is Alara and Autisher," he says, turning to them, "and what would you like to drink ladies?"

Before they can answer Mark butts in, "So that's your stage names, but what's your real names, Mohamed and Mustafa?"

Carl gives Mark a rather puzzled look then watches as the rest of the group turn away giggling. His eyes widen as his eyebrows lift. Then it dawns as his head spins to stare straight at the dancer's faces, "Oh shit, you're joking, right?" his head drops, "you are men, aren't you?"

Alara chucks his chin, "Does that make a difference, honey?"

Carl carefully places his hands on Alara's shoulders and cautiously pushes them away, "Err, yes it does, I'm afraid. Well I'm not afraid, that is, that is, err, well, no, no, no, I don't bat that way, sorry," he stammers, backing steadily away from them.

He stands behind Mark, "Oh, shit, they were rubbing their watsits against me and you just stood there," he says, brushing his arse, "some friend you are, oh god, I kissed one of them."

Mark turns to him, "Yeah I know, we saw it. Was she good," he asks, dropping his head in laughter, "sorry, was he good?"

Carl knocks his drink back, "OK, you bastard, I'm going to the hotel, screw you."

As he is leaving, Alara approaches him, "Do you want some company, honey?"

Carl pushes them back, "NO I BLOODY WELL DON'T, THANK YOU," he yells, then storms out, leaving the rest of the group in fits of laughter.

Mark turns to Pyah, "You do realise he will be hell to live with?"

Pyah smiles, "Oh yes, but it was worth it."

Ben summons the rest of the group to inform them of Defuer's location, "The problem is she has more security than Fort Knox. Getting to her will have to be at night. Even then it's going to be darned near impossible," he smiles at Elleon, "but we might not have to get into the hotel."

Elleon stands up, "Yeah, I might be able to take her out from a nearby rooftop, just need a good spotter, my thermal imager and a decent set of night sights."

Mark huffs, "Well, your best spotter just had a hissy fit and skulked back to the hotel."

Elleon rolls her eyes, "Oh, I suppose I better see if I can talk him round then, shall I?"

Back at the hotel, Elleon finds Carl sat having a quiet drink in his room, "What on earth are you doing, big fellow?"

Carl doesn't even look up from his drink, "What do you want? Another dig at the stupid old git?"

Elleon sits next to him, "Err, no. I need a guy who's good with night sights and thermal imaging to go on a night stalk with me," she says, putting her head on his shoulders.

Carl gives her a sideways look, "So why don't you go and ask the ranger?"

Elleon pushes his hands to one side, then straddles his lap, "Well," she starts.

Carl shoves her off onto the floor, "Look, one of these days, all this flirting is going get you in some big fucking trouble," he says as he tosses his whiskey over her before storming out of the room.

Elleon sits there for a moment, "What the hell is it with the men in this troop?" she asks, then gets up, brushes herself off and saunters out after him.

Carl decides to go for a walk before the rest of the group come back to the hotel. Elleon misses him but runs into the group as they enter the foyer, "Anyone seen Carl? The daft bugger stormed off again."

Sarah walks over to her, "What the hell did you say this time?" she demands, grabbing a clump of Elleon's hair, "or should I say, what did you do to him?"

Elleon grins at her, "I didn't say anything, I just sat on his knee and he took the huff."

Sarah grabs her chin with her other hand, "Oh, you just sat on his knee?" she says, pushing her backwards over the counter, "in other words, you were flirting with him again," Sarah starts to drag Elleon towards the stairs "I think it's about time someone taught you a lesson, young lady."

Pyah struts over to take Elleon's arm, "So what we got in mind for this little tease?" she asks as Lacey walks outside to collect the holdall from the vehicle.

Sarah turns to Pyah, "Oh, I think we can come up with something," she says, snarling over Elleon.

They drag Elleon to one of the hotel rooms and throw her in the middle of the floor. Elleon sits there, smiling, "you've worked out I like it rough then?"

Lacey walks in. She walks over to Elleon, drags her up off the floor and throws her over her shoulder, "Trust me, you're about to get it, and I know how to play it rough."

Elleon just slumps over Lacey's shoulder, "Good job you ain't got a dick then, isn't it?" she says while she reaches down to slap Lacey's bum.

Lacey throws the holdall on the bedside cabinet then reaches in to it, pulling the strap on out while she throws Elleon on the bed, "Oh, you'll be surprised at what I've got," she says as she straddles Elleon's hips.

Elleon starts to struggle, "Whoa, hold on a minute bitch," she protests, scratching at Lacey, "if you come anywhere near me with that thing I'll fucking kill you I swear."

Pyah steps forward and pins Elleon's hands down above her head, then straddles her shoulders, "Feisty little bitch, aren't you?"

Sarah just stands against the wall, wondering what she has started and whether she should try and stop it, "Look girls, do you think this is such a good idea?" she asks, debating on whether she should try and stop them, "I mean, I'm all for teaching her a lesson, but this might be going a bit too far."

Elleon bites at Pyah while Lacey undoes Elleon's trousers, dragging them down to her knees, "Ooo, looks like we got us a VIRGIN. Well, I'll be damned," she crows, turning to Sarah and winking, "all that talk and she hasn't even had any experience at all."

Elleon thrashes, "Just because I haven't had some old pervert's dick in me doesn't mean I haven't had any experience, now get off me, you dirty old cow."

Lacey rams her knee between Elleon's legs, then wiggles the strap on in-between Elleon's legs, "Now, this is going to hurt somewhat," she says as Sarah moves in to grab Lacey's wrist.

Sarah shakes her head as Lacey looks her straight in the eye, "She still hasn't got the message yet."

Sarah lets go and turns her back. Elleon stops shouting and growling, her threats become more of a plea, "Please don't do this," she pleads as tears start to run down her cheeks, "I promise I won't flirt any more, just don't," she cries, blubbering, still trying to close her legs, "you don't have to do this please."

Lacey steps off her, as does Pyah. Sarah moves in, "They weren't going to do it, honest," she promises, cuddling Elleon, "but I'm afraid you did need to be taught. If this was three guys you would have had no chance," she says, lifting Elleon's face, "just imagine what would have happened if you had pushed a couple of men past this point," she explains, wiping the tears from her face, "you would be in deep shit, and trust me if any of them had been like her boy," she says, pointing at Pyah, "then that's going to fucking hurt, first time or not."

Elleon cuddles into Sarah, "What do you mean, like her boy?"

Sarah chuffs, "Trust me, he's a big lad," she says, spreading her hands out to about three feet, "I mean a big lad."

Pyah walks back to Sarah and closes her hands to about fourteen inches, "He's not *that* big."

Elleon looks at Sarah's hands, "You're kidding, right? Men don't get that big?" she says as Sarah wipes Elleon's nose with a tissue from the bedside cabinet.

Lacey laughs out loud, "Oh shit, you haven't even seen a man, have you?" she realizes, walking around the bed, "talk about walking a dangerous line."

Pyah sits on the bed, "Talk about living a naive dream."

Elleon looks around at all three of them, "You are kidding me? You're still trying to frighten me, right?" she asks, sniffling, "well its working, trust me."

Lacey sits on the bed, "No dear, I think we have taught you a valuable lesson, but yes, men do get that big on occasion and Mark is one of those occasions."

Elleon takes a deep breath then sighs, "Shit, hang on a second, how do you know how big her husband is?"

Pyah laughs out loud, "Because we have had a threesome," she admits, blushing slightly.

Elleon's jaw drops, then she turns to Sarah, "Have you, err, well, you know?" she asks, pointing at Pyah and Lacey.

Sarah's head drops, "No dear, I haven't been with Mark, but I have been with these two, and yes, I have seen Mark's donger," she tells her, standing up to walk to the window, "while she was sucking it," she adds, pointing back at Lacey.

Elleon starts to relax, "And you lot call me?"

Lacey chucks Elleon's chin, "Yeah, but we haven't told you a load of bullshit or tried to be something we're not. For Christ's sake, you haven't even had a proper orgasm yet."

Elleon takes umbrage at this remark, "Excuse me, but I have had an orgasm," she corrects, blushing slightly, "I do know how to play with myself."

Sarah turns with a proper guffaw, "Trust me, young lady, you haven't had one yet," she says, then turns to the other two, "ladies, shall we?" she asks as they move in on Elleon.

Elleon backs up the bed, "Hold on a minute, you said you had taught me," she says, pulling a pillow over her lap, "and I told you I had learned."

The girls sit on the bed as Lacey leans forward to kiss Elleon, "Relax, we are not going to force you to do anything, but I think it's about time you had some real experience," she says, smiling at Sarah and Pyah.

Lacey starts to kiss Elleon's neck as she slides her hand down onto her breast. Elleon nervously twitches as Lacey comes back to kiss her lips, "Relax, trust me, you will enjoy this if you just let it happen," she promises, bringing her hand back up to stroke Elleon's neck, "a woman knows what another woman wants."

Elleon looks deep into Lacey's eyes, "If I want you to stop then you stop, right?"

Lacey smiles, "Anytime you feel too uncomfortable you just say and we'll stop."

Elleon looks around at Sarah and Pyah as they sit either side of her. Pyah reaches around her back to undo her bra while Sarah starts to kiss her abdomen. Lacey softly kisses her lips with as much passion as she can muster, then slowly slips her hand down on to Elleon's clitoris. Elleon tries to close her legs but her subconscious gives in, allowing Lacey to play. Elleon's body trembles with a mixture of pleasure and anticipation as Sarah suckles on one of her nipples and Pyah flicks the other with her tongue. Lacey runs her tongue down between both of them, across Elleon's abdomen then down onto her vagina. Elleon's legs twitch with uncertainty as Lacey pushes them apart to flick her clitoris with her tongue.

Lacey looks up at Elleon's face, "This might sting a bit but if you go with it, trust me, you won't find a greater pleasure this side of heaven," she says as she forces her finger into Elleon's vagina.

Elleon's hand slams down on to Lacey's head, "Oh, shit, what the fuck," tears come to her eyes, "Jesus, no, that's it, I want you to stop."

Lacey gives another small push and a flick of Elleon's clitoris then starts to retract. Elleon's back arches, "OK no, no, no, don't stop, I can take it," she says, panting frantically.

Pyah brings her mouth up to meet Elleon's, "Oh, you need to be ready for the ride of your life now, honey," she says, kissing Elleon, "there's no turning back now and this is going to be one hell of a roller coaster for you, so hang on tight, here we go."

Elleon's hips start to thrust immediately as Lacey jabs her finger in and out, still flicking with her tongue. Elleon's body goes into spasm as her first orgasm comes swiftly, "Oh shit, urrrgh," she moans, slamming her buttocks back on to the bed, thrusting her pelvis back and forth, "Oh fuck, no, no, no, shit no, urrrgh, fuck, shit," she curses as her head buries itself into the pillow, the groans of delight rumbling from the very pit of her being, "no, no, too much, too much," she pants, grabbing Pyah's face to plunge her tongue inside Pyah's mouth, eyes wide as the veins in her neck are at the point of explosion.

The pressure of blood rising to her head, as she forces every last sinew of pleasure from the orgasm before collapsing back on the bed to pull the pillow over her head in shame. Lacey slides up the bed over Elleon's body, pulling the pillow aside, "Not bad, but trust me, that was just a small one," she says, looking deep into Elleon's eyes, "I think we can do a lot better than that."

Lacey thrusts her lips against Elleon's but Elleon pushes her away, "Let me get my breath at least," she says, taking a deep breath, then pulling her back.

Sarah looks on, infatuated, "Oh, we're getting right into it now, aren't we?" she remarks, sliding her hand down between Elleon and Lacey.

Pyah picks up the strap on, "Hmm, I wonder," she hums, perusing it carefully.

She takes it into the bathroom to wash it under a very hot tap, suds it down, then rinses it, "OK, let's see if you fit," she mumbles, strapping it around her waist.

She looks at herself in the mirror and starts to giggle, then struts back into the bedroom, "Hey, any of you girls want to play with a shemale?" she asks, laughing raucously.

Sarah turns to giggle, "Hope you cleaned that thing thoroughly?"

Pyah gives her a sultry look, "I sterilised it with antibacterial and hot water, why, you want a go?"

Sarah slinks over then drops to her knees, "Hmm, seems to be a bit futile like, but what the hell, I think I need the practise," she says, popping the strap on in her mouth.

Pyah throws her head back and starts to groan as Sarah looks up at her, starting to choke, "Stop it, you're making me gag," Sarah stands up, "damn it, you bitch, stand still," she says as she drops her drawers, then wraps her arms around Pyah's neck to pull herself up, "let's see what you can do with that thing," she says, wrapping her legs around Pyah's waist to slide down onto it, "you do realise that if Carl finds out I've had another dick up me he'll flip? Rubber or not," she comments, laughing out loud, then grunting as Pyah thrusts it up into her.

Lacey looks up from Elleon's vagina, "Ooo, looks like fun."

Elleon sits up to see what's going on, "Jesus, that looks painful."

Sarah spins her head as Pyah walks her over to the bed, "Trust me, this would be painful for you but for us its quite small and most enjoyable."

Lacey goes back to Elleon's vagina, "Let's see if we can make this big enough to fit that," she says as she gently pushes two fingers into Elleon.

Elleon's back arches again, "Oh shit, what is that, your fucking wrist?"

Lacey comes up to kiss her lips, "No dear, that's two fingers."

Elleon claws Lacey's spine, "Oh God, and you think I could take a man's dick?"

Lacey thrusts her fingers in then out a few times, then slips a third in. Elleon reaches down to hold Lacey's wrist, "No, no, oh shit, that hurts," she says, stopping Lacey from moving, "I don't think I can take any more."

Lacey moves her hand very slowly, spreading her fingers, slightly easing her hand into Elleon again. Elleon holds Lacey's wrist, grunting and shaking but not stopping the hand from moving completely.

Pyah rolls down onto Sarah as Sarah drags at Pyah's blouse buttons. Pyah thrusts the strap on into Sarah and starts to fuck like a man, "I think I could get good at this, wonder what would happen if I proposed using it on Mark," Pyah suggests, giggling out loud.

Sarah grabs Pyah's arse, "Don't know but if you don't put some effort into it then I'm going to have to get on top."

Pyah kisses her, "Be my guest," she says, rolling Sarah on top of her.

Elleon watches on as Lacey suckles on one of her nipples, then that feeling starts to come up her abdomen as she starts to reach a climax, "Oh shit, here we go again," she says, but Lacey takes her fingers out of Elleon, then starts to caress her breasts.

Elleon looks into Lacey's eyes, "What did you stop for?" she asks, reaching down to her own clitoris.

Lacey stops her, "No, you don't want to do that," she says, kissing Elleon, "just relax and let it pass. See if you can hold it off for the next couple of times, trust me it will all be worth it in the end," she promises as she starts to stroke and kiss Elleon's erogenous zones, sending a tantalising tingle through Elleon's body.

Elleon relaxes back, "Holy shit, what are you doing to me?"

Sarah starts to bounce up and down on Pyah as Pyah starts to sing, "There were four in the bed and the little one said…"

Sarah interrupts her, "And the little one said shut the fuck up and fuck back while I enjoy this."

Lacey leans across and slaps her arse, "Hurry up and stop whining, I want a go."

Elleon pulls Lacey's hand back, "Thought you were with me?"

Lacey looks deep into her eyes, "Oh trust me, when I get that thing I'm going to be more than WITH you," she says, giving a scary laugh.

Pyah places her hand down on Sarah's clitoris to tickle it as Sarah starts to climax. Sarah twitches, then spasms, then wrenches forward, her hair flailing over her head to shroud Pyah as she drops onto Pyah's breasts.

Pyah spits and splutters, "That's the only problem with long hair," she comments, pulling it from her mouth.

Sarah sits up, "Was it good for you?" she asks, looking deep into Pyah's eyes.

Pyah rolls her eyes, "Funny. All I got was a face full of hair, a body slam and a wet skirt. What do you think?"

Sarah groans as she lifts off the strap on, then giggles as she slurps. Pyah stands up, looks at the wet patch on her skirt and shakes her head, "I look like I've peed myself," she says, getting another skirt off the wardrobe.

She throws the strap on over to Lacey, "Go on then."

Lacey catches it, then pulls a gross face, "Oh, you could have cleaned it again," she says, grabbing a wet wipe from the drawer, then throwing the strap on back to Pyah.

Elleon tuts, "Thought you were going to show me an orgasm I couldn't forget?"

Pyah takes the strap on into the bathroom, cleans it, then throws it back at Lacey. Lacey sits up, "Oh, you have seen nothing yet my dear," she says, strapping the dildo on.

Elleon looks down at it, "Err, I don't know about that like," she says, taking it in her hand, "two fingers hurt like hell. This thing is a chunk bigger."

Lacey smiles at her, "Trust me, I won't hurt you," she promises as Sarah and Pyah come back to the bed to surround Elleon.

Sarah reaches into her hand bag, "Here," she offers, passing Lacey some KY gel.

Lacey takes a large dollop in her hand and smothers Elleon's vagina with it. Elleon twitches back, "Shit, that's fucking freezing," she hisses as Lacey slides her fingers back in and Elleon arches her back, "oh shit, that's nice."

Lacey builds up to three fingers again, then inserts the end of the dildo. She pushes it in about an inch, then retracts it. Elleon reaches up to grab Pyah's face, pulling her down to kiss her as Sarah starts to play with her nipples. Lacey pushes the dildo in about two inches then three then all the way as Elleon's legs twitch, undecided whether to close or not, "Shit, too big, too big, too big."

Lacey pulls it about halfway out, "Is that better?" she asks, flicking Elleon's clitoris.

Elleon nods, "Damn, I thought you were pushing my guts up to my tonsils for a moment."

Lacey starts to move the dildo faster and faster as Elleon spasms and grinds down on to it, "Oh shit, oh shit," she curses, her chin burying itself into her neck as Pyah plunges her tongue into Elleon's mouth to muffle the screams of delight. Not realising that Lacey is now thrusting the dildo in its full length then all the way out, Elleon is in full bloom of an ecstatic orgasm. Every sinew of her body in rapturous spasm as her blood rushes explosively through her veins, adrenaline pumping through her like a freight train, causing volatile tremors up her spine as she claws at Lacey's flesh through the roller coaster of emotions. The perspiration drips away from her every pore drenching the sheets below her. A final push down as the height of the orgasm reaches its complete bursting conclusion, then plummeting into the pillow, exhausted but exalted, gasping for air through the clouds of confused imaginings soaring through her mind.

The flush of crimson abates from her body as she regains reality, "Oh Jesus, I thought I had died and gone to heaven," she sighs, her eyes glistening with a softened bliss, "never knew that sex could do that, I want more but I need to sleep now."

There's a knock at the door as Mark pokes his head in, "Hope you don't mind-" he starts, then averting his gaze, "oops, my apologies," he says as he drifts back behind the door, "but we do need to come up with some sort of plan as to our next move," he remarks, pulling the door almost closed, "so when you ladies have finished we'll be at the bar," he finishes, then he saunters down the stairs, totally aghast at what he thinks he has just witnessed.

Pyah lifts Elleon by the arm, "A good old shower should put you right."

Sarah grabs her other arm, "Welcome to the girls' club," she says as Lacey walks in to turn the shower on.

Elleon's heart is willing but her legs just seem to have given up the ghost, "Shit, my legs won't work and my stomach is killing me. I don't think I'll be having sex for some time," she comments as she wobbles and staggers to the bathroom.

The girls help her in, then soap her down, trying not to provoke sensual response. Pyah suds her abdomen down with a soft sponge but as she is about to reach under her vagina Elleon stops her, "I think I better do that bit," she says, smiling at Pyah, "don't want another orgasm tonight thank you."

The girls all laugh together.

It isn't long before Elleon has regained her composure. All the girls are dressed and heading down the stairs to meet the boys.

De-fuer has been located and its decided that Elleon and Carl should head out after dark to assassinate her. Ben suggests they take his truck as its less conspicuous, a ranger's truck around town. It has a CB radio. He has a mobile CB to keep in touch with them if necessary. The group have an evening meal at the hotel restaurant while Ben recons the area as the night starts to close in.

CHAPTER 30
SKELETONS AND SNAKES

The night air turns chilly as the sun creeps down beyond the horizon. The moon is just a faded smear behind a cloudy sky as the night turns black. The perfect night to hide in the dusky shadows, cast by the few scattered street lamps. Elleon again borrows Sarah's all-in-one stealth suit, while Carl equips himself with a night scope plus Elleon's thermal imager. Ben describes, then gives directions to a perfect place for their endeavours. A rooftop with a similar height and the perfect view of the building's top floor where Denier De-fuer is residing. Elleon picks up her sniper rifle, equips it with a night scope and silencer and they set out to bring this undertaking to its gruesome conclusion.

Carl and Elleon soon find the rooftop, as described by Ben, then poise themselves ready for the kill. Hiding down by a small walled boundary of the roof, Carl scans the building's floors for any sign of life. He counts three armed guards patrolling the roof, one guarding the inside of the front door, one outside and one patrolling the rear of the building. Elleon sets her weapon up atop of the boundary wall then waits for Carl's instruction.

Carl scans the top floor where he comes across two heat signatures in a far-left corner room, "Think I've got her, top left corner got two females," he says as he scrutinises the images, "oh, one of them just slapped the other, I can take it that's our Denier?"

Elleon takes a deep breath, "OK, give me her approximate position from the window."

Carl taps Elleon's shoulder, "I don't need to, she's coming to the window. Looks like you'll have the perfect shot, just about... now."

Elleon's finger hovers over the trigger as she exhales, steadies her aim, then stops, "Hello, who's the skeleton?" she asks, looking at an unknown female in the window.

Carl quickly transfers to his night scope, "Aye, who the fuck are you?" he asks, scrambling for his phone, "if you're not De-fuer, then the other heat signature must be? That means that our Denier is just a little pawn in a bigger picture," he figures, lifting his camera.

Elleon looks up at him, "You think I should shoot her?"

Carl shakes his head, "Nope, just need to find out who the hell she is."

Elleon looks back through her scopes, "You reckon you'll get a good picture with that thing from here?"

Carl can't quite zoom in far enough, "Damn. I know, if I put this against the night scope I might just get her," he does so and gets the perfect image, "hold still now," he breathes as he snaps the shot.

Elleon drags him down, "You numpty, you left the flash on," she says as a barrage of gunfire ricochets off the little wall in front of them, "you gave away our position."

They scurry towards the fire escape as Elleon drags Carl along the ground, "When we get to the car I'll drive you, just take that photo to the rest of the group," she says, pulling him down the fire escape, "I'll drop you off at the end of the alley opposite the hotel, stay there till it's clear then get to the hotel," she instructs.

They jump into the vehicle as Elleon screams off down the road. At the end of the alley she slides to a halt as Carl jumps out to hide behind a dumpster, then she races off for the towns outer limits. She calls Ben on the CB, "Little Fox to Big Bear, Big Eagle has a parcel and he's at the end of the alley."

Ben looks out of the window, "OK, got you," he says, looking down the street he can see one car heading to flank Elleon, "you got one bogey coming to cut you off, what you going to do?"

Elleon speeds for the town exit, "I'll take them out into the desert to deal with them."

Ben watches a Land Rover go hurtling past, "OK Little Fox, that pickup of mine has upgraded suspension and you're going to come to a salt flat on your right," he says, running down the stairs as he instructs her, "take them across that into the dunes. You got about a four-hundred-yard lead on them, you should be able to extend that somewhat across the salt," he says, then he instructs Pyah, Mark and Sarah to get Carl when he's gone and jumps into the four by four to head off after Elleon.

As she reaches the salt flats the guys in the Land Rover start to blast the back of the pickup with gunfire, smashing the rear window, spraying glass all over Elleon. She swerves to avoid them but then just guns it across into the dunes. Heading for the top of a large dune she slides to a halt. Rolling out of the vehicle she sprints through the dunes for cover. About two-hundred-yards away she finds a clump of rye grass and beds in behind it. Lifting her rifle up she can see the Land Rover pull up at the bottom of the dune. One of the men get out and cautiously climbs the dune while the other covers him from the bottom. Elleon has the perfect shot at the one climbing but can only just see the top of the other's head, "Can't risk it, if I lose him then I'm fucked."

At that, the one at the bottom disappears so she takes careful stock of the other. Taking a deep breath, she aims carefully, covers the trigger then exhales to gently squeeze the trigger. As she shoots the man drops to his knees, a knife with a twelve-inch blade can be seen glinting through the air into his back. A lone figure emerges from the darkness dragging a body to the top of the dune. Through her scope she can see its Ben as he stands proud then turns to bow directly at her, "How the hell does he know where I am?" she wonders, standing up as he beckons her.

When she walks over to him he is checking the bodies, "Hmm, no I.D. or labels. Pockets are completely empty," he says as he starts to cut the sleeves of their jacket.

Elleon looks on puzzled, "Now what are you doing?"

He checks both men's arms, "Looking for tattoos or some kind of identifying marks."

Elleon puts her hands on her hips, "And?"

Ben shakes his head, "Nothing. That's the problem. There is no way of identifying who they are," he explains, lifting their hands, palms up, "not even finger prints. They've been surgically removed," he then reaches inside his cab to take out a small vial from the first aid kit.

Elleon crouches down to inspect the men, "So now what are you up to?"

Ben lifts the vial, then pulls out his knife, "Blood sample. Maybe I can get a DNA sample that might be used to identify them," he says, shrugging as he cuts their veins and places a sample in the vial.

Pyah and Sarah have managed to secrete Carl back to the hotel, "Shit, I'm not cut out for this fieldwork stuff anymore," he says, taking his phone out of his pocket, "here, find out who the fuck the skeleton is," he instructs, handing his phone to Lacey.

Lacey looks at the picture, "Skeleton?" she repeats, then starts to laugh, "oh I see what you mean."

Sarah comes around to have a look, "Jesus, talk about needing a good meal," she comments as they look at the picture, "so who is she?"

Carl gives a stupefied look, "Well that's what I want you to find out. Can't you send that thing to your mate in the F.B.I or Interpol or something?"

Lacey Bluetooths the picture to her phone, "What I meant was, what's your interest in her? I presume it is a her?"

Carl walks over, "Well I'm not sure, but what I do know is that she, he, it slapped De-fuer and De-fuer took it without question."

Pyah hurries over to take a look, "So what you're saying is that De-fuer is just a puppet and she's the puppeteer?"

Carl gives a condescending nod, "So who is she and what are they up to? Because this seems to be more than just a vendetta against you two now and I'd like to know why."

At that Lacey's phone rings, "Talk of the devil," she says, answering it, "hi, I was just about to contact you."

Cramer is on the other end, "Well your cargo didn't arrive in Europe. It got out towards Gibraltar, then swung left down the coast of Morocco before we lost it," he says, sitting down, "so what were you thinking of me for?"

Lacey rolls her eyes, "Well, I have a picture of a woman I'm going to send you and we need a name."

Cramer seems disappointed, "OK, send it through and I'll see what I can do," he says, then the leading question follows, "so how are you and have you missed me?"

Lacey cringes, "Yeah," she replies, wondering if she should tell him over the phone or wait till she sees him in person before telling him about Ben.

A silence seems to linger, "And how are you?" she asks, closing her eyes.

Cramer sighs, "I'm ok, sounds like we need to talk, so I'll see you when you get back then, eh?"

Lacey nods, "Yeah, ok, see you soon," she says, ending the call abruptly.

Sarah gives Carl a cuddle, "I think you're getting too old for this."

Carl smiles back at her, "Excuse me, but who you calling old?" he demands, patting her bum, "I'll show you old later."

Sarah gives him a devilish grin, "Oh, so we going to play?" she asks, reaching behind her, "because I got a surprise for you," she proclaims, slamming the strap on down beside him.

Carl gives a puzzled look, "What the hell would I need that for? You trying to say I ain't big enough for you?"

Sarah grins and shakes her head in a naughty schoolgirl manner, "No, I'll be wearing it," she corrects, sticking her tongue out provocatively, then knowingly raising her eyebrows as she taps him in the bum with it.

Carl drags her arms from around him, "Whoa, I don't think so," he protests, taking a couple of awkward steps backwards, "if you're thinking what I think you're thinking, you, can think again. That thing ain't coming anywhere near me."

Sarah slinks towards him, "Oh, it's all right for you to stick yours where you want to but," she starts, looking down at her feet, "when it comes to me sticking mine where I want to, you back off," she finishes, wriggling it in his face.

Carl backs up, straight into Lacey. Lacey puts her arms out around him, "I thought you were one for experimentation?"

Carl jumps out of his skin, "Jesus, what the hell has she been telling you?"

Sarah sandwiches him in between her and Lacey, "Oh, I just told them what a horny little whore you are…why?"

Carl starts to blush, "Fuck this for a lark," he says, then makes a break for the stairs.

Lacey and Sarah are in hot pursuit, "You don't actually think you're getting away do you?" Sarah says, rattling the dildo between his legs, "keep going, you're heading in the right direction."

Pyah is folded over with laughter and can't breathe as Mark collapses on the sofa, "He's shitting himself, poor guy."

Pyah sits on Mark's knee, "Oh, trust me, when they have finished with him I was thinking of having a go with it and you."

Mark lifts her slowly up, stands up gently, then drops her onto the sofa, "Yeah right," he says, then casually walks away to the bar.

Pyah skulks after him, "So I can take that as a no then?"

Mark shakes his head, "Err, yes, that IS a no."

Pyah kisses him teasingly, "You never know, you might like it," she says, taunting him.

Mark orders a drink, "Yeah, I might like heaven but I'm not going to let you fucking shoot me, am I?" he responds, smugly drinking his scotch.

Pyah wraps her arms around him, "I'm teasing," she says, kissing the back of his neck.

Mark smiles at her, "Yeah I know, but are those two teasing Carl or is he getting butt raped?" he suggests, laughing raucously.

Pyah looks away then back, "Nah? They wouldn't? Would they?"

Mark sips at his drink, "Well, you know them better than me, and there are two of them."

Pyah scurries off up the stairs, "Shit, that's the problem," she says with a worried look on her face.

When she gets to the room Sarah and Lacey are outside giggling but Carl is inside with door locked shouting, "You can go and fuck yourselves."

Pyah knocks on the door, "Are you ok in there?" she asks, sniggering to herself.

Carl pushes a chair under the door handle, "I'm fine, just your psycho girlfriends and their rubber snake."

Pyah looks at the girls, "It's not a snake it's just a harmless sex toy."

Carl sits on the bed, "Well tell them they can play somewhere else with their fucking toy because it ain't coming anywhere near my arse."

Sarah leans against the door, "You have to let me in sometime, honey."

Carl coughs, "Don't think so. You go and sleep somewhere else till you get rid of the viper."

Sarah winks at Lacey, "OK honey, I'll go and sleep with Pyah," she says, pausing for a moment, "and Mark."

Carl jumps up, throws the chair to one side, then opens the door, "I don't think so," he says, grabbing Sarah by the arm, dragging her into the room then slamming the door behind her, "his is apparently bigger than yours and you've been eyeing it up," he adds, locking the door behind her.

Sarah puts her hands out to show they're empty, "I ain't got one. Lacey has it, but I don't think Ben will like it," she says, sniggering to herself.

Carl frisks her just in case. Sarah sighs with delight, "Ooo, keep going."

Carl is crouched down looking up at her as she pouts with her eyes closed, "What, you actually think I'm in the mood after a scare like that?"

Sarah looks down at him, "I don't give a shit, just keep searching," she instructs as she strokes his hair, "you never know what you might find. Your mood might just be down there," she says, pulling his head into her crotch.

Carl slowly slides his hand up her skirt in-between her legs as she moans. He looks up at her, "I'm just checking you haven't concealed it up there."

She slaps him across the head, "You cheeky bastard," she says, then pushes him away and opens the door.

Lacey and Pyah nearly fall in with their ears firmly planted against the door as Sarah grabs the strap on off Lacey, turns and throws it on the bed, "Go fuck yourself," she says, then slams the door and struts down the hall.

Lacey turns to Pyah then back to Sarah, "Lover's tiff?"

Sarah carries on walking. looking back over her shoulder "He's not interested in that either," she says as she stomps down the stairs.

Carl sits on the bed twiddling with the strap on, then throws it in the bin. He pours himself a scotch, thinks for a while, "Sod this for a lark," he says, then knocks the drink back, picks the strap on up and puts it in his pocket, "I'm getting too old for this," he sighs as he struts out of the room, holding his head high to walk downstairs.

He walks up to Sarah, "Get packed, we're going home," he says, taking her by the arm, "you two can sort this out by yourselves," he adds, turning to Mark and Pyah, "I'm sick of nearly getting my arse shot off," he says, smiling arrogantly, "one, I'm no good at fieldwork, two, I don't feel comfortable out here and three, I can't do any research without my desk," he elaborates, pulling Sarah back up the stairs.

Sarah turns to stick her tongue out at Pyah, "Told you he could be a man when he wants to, see you at home," she says, blowing her a kiss, "take care now."

Carl stops in front of Ben, "You can have this," he says, handing him the dildo, "she might find some use for it," he explains, pointing at Lacey.

Ben smiles then puts the dildo in his pocket, "Could be fun."

Mark looks at him gobsmacked, "You're joking, right?"

Ben pats him on the shoulder, "When Lacey agreed to be my wife I felt like a dog with two dicks, now I am," he says, laughing out loud.

Elleon jumps up to sit on the bar, "Just the four of us then, now what we going to do?"

Just then Lacey's phone rings, its Cramer, "Hi, I got some bad news and some even worse news, which do you want first?"

Lacey puts the phone on open, "Any."

There's a rustling from the other end, then Cramer speaks, "OK, your woman, we're not sure, but we think she's an ex-KGB agent that died about ten years ago, no name."

Lacey scratches her head, "OK, I presume that's the bad news, what's the worse news?"

Cramer is silent for a second, "Well that cargo arrived but there were only twenty rockets so we reckon four were dropped off somewhere near the Canaries, and we're now tracking a helicopter leaving De-fuer's location carrying your mystery woman."

Lacey's head drops, "How the hell do you know that?"

Cramer laughs, "I have a friend in the CIA who had a satellite nearby and I'll tell you now your friend De-fuer left about half an hour ago, heading due south towards the western Sahara so here's the really bad news, I can only track one of them for you."

Lacey rubs her chin, "OK, can you stay on our Russian friend? We'll deal with De-fuer."

Cramer agrees to keep tracking the Russian then hangs up. Carl and Sarah reappear, "So what's the plan? Apart from us going home?" Carl asks, lifting his case to show everyone.

Lacey informs him of Cramer's conversation as a taxi turns up at the door. Carl links arms with Sarah, "Well, I'm sure you have this all in hand? Good luck. Keep me apprised and I'll find out who the Russian is when I get back."

Kisses and handshakes are exchanged as they leave and a few tears are shed.

CHAPTER 31
SAMARA

A silence unfolds, chilling the African air as the group is left with a sense of depletion.

Mark calls the manager, "Have you got a computer with internet access, please?"

The manager brings them a laptop and Mark thanks him. Pyah takes the laptop, "I got this, I think I know where you're going," she says, opening up Google Maps.

Mark watches her, "You got it in one. Let's see what's out there. Where could she possibly be going?"

Pyah scans due south from Tarfaya, "Well, the only place I can find that she could make on the fuel she has is Samara."

Mark nods, "Seems like a good place to start."

Ben steps in, "I got a friend in Samara, I'll ring him to keep an eye out for her."

Mark hands the laptop back, "Sounds like the start of a plan."

Soon the group are on their way, travelling through the night. Playing catch up. Mark drives while the rest check the weaponry. Elleon strip cleans her rifle, "Do I get to kill her when we find her?"

Pyah pats her on the lap, "We find out what she knows, then you can possibly kill her. OK?"

It isn't long before the moon is overwhelmed by the first light of dawn as Samara's haze comes in to view. Ben's friend sends him a text that someone fitting De-fuer's description has booked in at the hotel in Samara, so he is sent into town to do a little recon. On arrival, he confirms that she is there, finds out where, then instructs the rest of the group on how to descend upon the town unnoticed.

De-fuer is in a small hotel in the north west but Ben's friends have agreed to put them up in his residence on the far south east in the Lezab quarter. It's a small four-roomed residence but seems cosy, unobtrusive and out of the way and there is a place to hide the vehicle. Food and refreshments are brought on the groups arrival.

Ben's friends welcome everyone with open arms, "Welcome my friend, we have prepared a small meal for you and your friends," he greets as he leads Pyah, Mark, Lacey and Elleon to a small table surrounded by cushions, set in the middle of the room.

Fresh fruit is placed on a large platter and another is brought, piled high with rice and meat mixed with herbs and spices then drizzled with a chunky tomato dressing. The man brings wooden goblets with a large jug of wine, "Eat, drink, and rest. For tonight we stalk our prey, yes?" he says, wild-eyed with teeth shimmering as that of a mad man, before sitting in-between the girls, laughing outrageously.

Once the meal is over the man leads his female guests outside to an open-air shower, "I'm afraid this is the best I can do," he apologizes, placing screens around the shower, "these ladies, my wives," he says, nodding towards four women, "will take care of you and make sure you are not disturbed while you bathe," he promises as he turns to walk back to talk to Ben and Mark.

Mark stands up, "We haven't even been introduced yet," he says, holding his hand out to shake the man's hand.

The man touches his own chest then his mouth then his head, "Salaam my friend. My name is Callime I have known Carl or, as he is known to you, Benjamin," he starts, tipping his head to the side, "for several decades now," he continues, placing his arm around Ben's shoulders, "and you are Mark Fischer, American security services," he says, closing his eyes momentarily, "Ben has apprised me of who you are and what your mission is," he adds as he waves to a young boy, "refreshments? A whisky maybe?"

The boy brings a decanter with three glasses.

Soon the girls are refreshed and return. Pyah walks over to Mark in a Moroccan style full length smock, "No pants again," she whispers in his ear.

Mark looks her up and down, then sniggers at Elleon as she fidgets in her smock, "What's up, dear? A mite too feminine for you?"

Lacey flaunts herself, "Quite refreshing, I think. Gives a sense of freedom to the unmentionables, if you know what I mean?" she says with a wry grin.

Elleon stomps around, "Damned refreshing, my ass. In fact, that's exactly what's getting refreshed, as soon as my jeans are washed and dried I want them back. Can't fucking move in this stupid thing," she complains trying unsuccessfully to sit crossed legged, then pulling it back up around her boobs, "Damn thing keeps riding down on me."

The rest of the group just laugh.

Before long the group's clothes are washed and dried. Elleon soon demands her jean, T shirt and underwear back, then sets off for a bedroom to change in private but she is followed by an entourage of Callime's wives. She tries to shut them out but they insist on helping her change. As she is changing they start to throw pillows at the door due to a young man peeking in while Elleon is undressed. One of the wives rushes out to grab the young man then take him to his father. Elleon quickly dresses as she hears a commotion in the yard.

When she arrives in the yard to see what it's all about she finds the young man being strapped to a pole as she is handed a whip then invited to lash the young man for his crime. Elleon walks around to look at the young man's face. He is a twenty-year-old mixed-race boy with the bluest piercing eyes she has ever seen. His complexion is that of a young woman's, delicate and soft. Elleon looks deep into his eyes, "Why were you looking at me?"

His head bows with shame, "I will accept your punishment gladly for I have never seen such a goddess. To gaze upon your beauty will be worth ten thousand lashes."

Elleon drops the lash then proceeds to untie the young man. Callime stops her, "Why are you not punishing him? He has brought shame to you and my family."

Elleon pushes Callime away, "He has committed no crime in my eyes," she says, turning to Pyah for conformation, "a man that is willing to suffer for me is worth ten that are not," she looks at him "would you die for me?"

He drops his head, "Gladly."

Elleon unties him, takes him by the hand and walks him back into the house, to the confusion of every member of his family.

He rushes into a room then reappears with a kukri, "This is for you."

Elleon takes it, draws it from its sheath, then admires its finely engraved blade with its jewelled handle, "This is a fine knife why would you give it to me?"

The man drops his gaze, "When you are done with me you will use it to end me. Yes?"

Elleon places it in her belt, "Nope, but I will keep it."

Callime approaches Mark, "He has fifty horses and two thousand chickens, they are yours," he says, waving his hand toward the young man, "he will make a good husband."

Mark laughs raucously, "Whoa, she's not mine to give."

Elleon struts over to Callime, "I don't think so. I'm a western woman, and free at that to make my own decisions. I say who I marry and when I'm ready," she says, standing with her hands firmly planted on her hips.

The young man walks gingerly over to her then kneels down, "All I have is yours if you will be my wife."

Elleon pats him on the head, "I'm a little too young to be getting tied down to a marriage but thanks for the knife," she says, then kisses him on the forehead, "I will come back to see you after we finish and maybe go out on a date then see what happens. that's all I can promise."

The young man takes her hand, kisses it then thanks her, "That is more than I can hope for, thank you, I will wait."

The wives start to tease him so he retires to the privacy of his own room. Plans are made for an assault on De-fuer, to kidnap her as the group wait for the setting of the sun.

A dark veil consumes Samara, allowing Callime's men to move unhindered across the rooftops while Pyah, Mark, Lacey and Elleon wind their way through the street to within sight of the hotel that gives sanctuary to De-fuer.

A small contingence of soldiers patrols the perimeter of the hotel. Ben travels on the roofs with Callime's men to direct the rest of the group as to the whereabouts of the patrolling guards. Elleon is able to silently pick off the guards patrolling the outside of the hotel while Ben takes care of the guards on the roofs. Pyah, Mark and Lacey enter the hotel via a window on the ground floor while Ben scans for De-fuer's heat signature with the thermal imager. Once he has located her he directs Lacey, Mark and Pyah to her location.

Soon they have her chloroformed, back at the house of Callime where they proceed to interrogate her. Inducing her with a truth serum they ask her about the plans for the weapons she stole and who is the Russian woman.

Before they can get enough information Mark's phone rings. It's an incoming call from Carl's phone but the Russian greets, "Good evening Mr Fischer," in a very English accent.

Mark smiles hopefully, "Good evening Miss Koliakova, it is Miss Anja Koliakova isn't it?"

Anja huffs, "So you have my name? You also have something or rather someone I need, yes?"

Mark smiles again, "Yes we have De-fuer, and can I assume that having Mr Sinclair's phone, you also have him?"

The phone is silent for a moment, "I also have his fiancée. You're at Samara. I will exchange your hostage for mine at Tarfaya beach. You have six hours," she says, then she hangs up.

Mark turns to Pyah, "She's given us six hours to get back to Tarfaya with this shit," he relays, pointing at De-fuer.

They put De-fuer in the back of the four by four with Lacey while Elleon rides along with Ben. Lacey carries on interrogating to find out as much as they can but Def-fuer is relatively resilient to the truth serum. They find out the four missing VX rockets were dropped for pickup via a submarine near Gran Canaria but not their final destination. They also find that Anja Koliakova is an ex-KGB seismologist but has no interest in De-fuer's revenge plot against the world for her brother's death though they learn her brother was working for the Russian. For what purpose, they are unable to ascertain.

CHAPTER 32
BLOODY BEACH PARTY

The sea breeze chills the air as the brisk sea spray dampens the beach and its surrounding dunes. When arriving at the beach of Tarfaya they find they are substantially early with no Russian presence.

Ben and Elleon take up positions in the dunes with their sniper rifles and wait for the arrival of Anja, Carl and Sarah. Pyah, Mark and Lacey wait, with a restrained De-fuer, by the cars at the entrance to the beach. Time ticks slowly by but then a black Russian sedan can be seen heading down the beach towards them. When the vehicle arrives two men with machine guns exit the vehicle to stand by the doors, with guns poised in wait as a helicopter appears on the horizon, from out at sea. The helicopter lands near the water's edge as Mark's phone rings, "You do exactly as you're instructed and no one will be harmed," Anja instructs Mark, then she exits the chopper with Sarah and Carl, hands handcuffed behind them.

Mark watches intensively, "OK, you send them and I'll send De-fuer."

Anja laughs down the phone, "No, my dear, I'll send Mr Sinclair as a gesture of good will," she pushes Carl forward, "when he arrives, you send Ms De-fuer. I have no interest in your quarrel with her," then she puts a gun against Sarah's head, "when Ms De-fuer gets halfway I'll send Miss Louis and that's the end of our business," she taps Sarah's head with the gun, "you deviate in any way from my instructions and Miss Louis dies."

Carl quickly walks toward Pyah and Mark, looking back over his shoulder with worry for Sarah's welfare. When he arrives Pyah quickly uncuffs him as he glares at De-fuer, "I don't know what that bitch is up to but get ready, she has something planned I know it."

De-fuer is sent on her way as Mark instructs Elleon and Ben to get ready, "Carl says the Russian is planning something. If she moves, take the bitch out."

201

De-fuer reaches the halfway point as the Russian sends Sarah on her way. The air can be cut with a knife as Mark anticipates the worst. As De-fuer crosses paths with Sarah the Russian signals to her men at the car, then lifts her gun to shoot De-fuer in the head. Both Elleon and Ben shoot at the Russian but miss as she dives back into the chopper. One of the Russian men open fire on Mark and Pyah while Lacey makes a dash for Sarah. The other starts to shoot at Sarah as Lacey shoulder charges her to the ground. Elleon and Ben concentrate their fire on the Russian's car as the men quickly jump in to make their escape. Mark and Pyah blast the hell out of the vehicle in vain, finding it to be bulletproof as it speeds off down the beach, to disappear around the dunes in the distance.

Everyone's attention is turned to Sarah and Lacey as Sarah struggles to climb from under Lacey's limp, lifeless body. Ben stands up off the dunes to see Sarah kneeling down over her friend screaming to the sky, "No, please God, no!" as Mark and Pyah rush to her side.

Blood pours out of a head wound to the back of Lacey's scalp. Mark reaches down to feel for a pulse, "She's alive but we need help *now*."

Ben arrives on the scene, tears flooding down his face, "Please, please, please, don't let her die."

A call comes through from Cramer on Lacey's phone. Pyah answers it with tears flooding down her face, "We need help *now*," she says, hardly able to speak the words.

Cramer was watching through the satellite feed but is only now realising the horror of the situation, "I have an air ambulance en route it will be with you in five minutes, just hold on," he takes a breath, "how bad is it?"

Pyah stalls, "She's been shot in the head," she gets out, then breaks down, collapsing to her knees.

Cramer manages to hold it together, "The ambulance is nearly there and a trauma team is ready and waiting at Gran Canaria. Just hold on."

The ambulance lands as two paramedics rush across to Lacey. They bind her head then place an intravenous plasma drip in her, stretcher her to the helicopter and rush off in the direction of Gran Canaria.

Cramer arrives at the hospital before them, awaiting their arrival.

Ben spots a seaplane down the beach docked at a jetty. He runs down to steal it but when he gets there an elderly gentleman, witnessing all that occurred, invites him onboard to take him to the hospital. Everyone boards the plane as they set off. MI6 is informed of the situation. They send the best neurosurgeons while the surgeons strive to keep Lacey alive.

Pyah, Mark, Ben and Elleon are met at the hospital by Cramer, "They have her in surgery now," he says, his eyes filled, wiping the tear he cannot hold back, "she's a fighter, if anyone can pull through this I know Lacey can," he reaches his hand out to Ben, "you must be Ben. You just have to believe in her."

Ben takes his hand then pulls him into a hug, "Oh, I believe in her, what have they said?"

Cramer looks deeply into his eyes, "Let's just see what happens before we start making assumptions eh?"

Ben pushes him away "I just want to know what the doctors have said," he says, then grabs a nurse, "excuse me, how is Lacey Raven?"

The nurse puts her hand on his shoulder, "You'll have to wait till the surgeons come out of theatre before I can answer that I'm afraid."

Mark and Pyah reassure him, then take him to a family room as the British surgeons arrive to take over.

After several arduous hours, the surgeon exits the theatre, "Well, we've removed the bullet, she is alive and stable but she is in a coma, so until she regains consciousness we won't know the extent of the damage."

Ben grabs him by the shoulders, "And how long will that be?"

The surgeon shrugs, "Your guess is as good as mine, we'll be moving her to England soon where we can keep an eye on her."

Cramer pulls Pyah to one side, "Am I being paranoid or do Ben's actions seem a little, well overly, err," he stammers, nervously shaking his head "how to put this without seeming jealous. I don't think he rings true, might just be my feelings for Lacey getting in the way but I just don't trust him."

Pyah puts her arms around Cramer, "It probably is jealousy but I'll keep it in mind and keep an eye on him for you. OK?"

Cramer gives Pyah a peck on the cheek, "Yeah, it's probably nothing, but at least I know you'll look out for her."

Pyah stands for a moment, silent, then puts her hands on Cramer's shoulders, "I know she would want to tell you this herself but, well, he asked her to marry him and she accepted," she says, gritting her teeth.

Cramer is stunned into silence for a moment then Pyah's eyes widen as she is helpless to stop him from approaching Ben. She sighs as he reaches out his hand to Ben, "Congratulations Ben, I just heard you and Lacey are to be wed."

Ben stares at him, still flooding with tears, "That's if she ever pulls through."

Cramer laughs, "Oh, trust me, if she has a wedding to go to, she's pulling through. She wouldn't miss it for the world. I know, and now I know she will make it."

Ben thanks him for his words then goes to Lacey's bedside for a long vigil.

CHAPTER 33
RELAXING CAN BE TIRING

Dawn creeps out of the sea as the rising sun fractures the horizon. Dancing shafts of light glistening across a calm ocean view from Lacey's hospital room. George, Lacey's boss, arrives with the rising sun. Walking into Lacey's room he approaches the bed "How is she?" he asks, turning to Pyah.

Pyah shrugs, "They say she's stable, that's it," she chokes out, covering her mouth to stop herself from crying.

George turns to hug her, "Hey, at least she's alive. You know her as well as any. She's a fighter, she'll pull through," he assures, patting Pyah on the back, "not to put a dampener on anything but she would want you out there looking for the bitch that did this."

Ben steps forward, "The problem is we don't have enough Intel on the Russian to go after her. And the only lead we did have was eliminated before we could get anything out of her."

George turns to Ben, "And you are?"

Pyah puts her hand on Ben's shoulder, "This, my dear friend, is Lacey's fiancé," she says, giving George a little girl lost look.

George gazes at Pyah, then gives Ben a sideways look, "So, when was I going to get to know about this?" he asks, putting his hands in his pockets, "and when were you going to ask my permission? You do realise that you need my permission? After all I'm the closest thing she has to a father," he tells him, patting Lacey's hand.

Ben is stuck for words, "Well, err, she never, err, well, we didn't discuss it."

George looks over his glasses at Ben, "Well you better discuss it when she comes 'round, oh, and by the way, I have a gun and I will use it if you don't treat her right."

Ben nods and smiles as Pyah walks past him, "He means it," she says, looking straight into Ben's eyes.

The smile drifts off Ben's face when he sees everyone is looking rather sternly at him. Then George extends a hand of grace, "Suppose it's welcome to the family," he says, smiling at Ben then shaking his hand.

He picks up his briefcase, "Well, I might have something to help," he begins, pulling a file from the case, "this is an extensive file on your Russian, Anja Koliakova. So, study it well and then go and get the bitch. I would appreciate it if you could bring her back alive though, MI6 would pay a handsome reward to have her."

Ben pulls George to one side, "How did you get that file?" he asks, speaking very softly as not to be overheard.

Although George finds Ben's line of inquiry a mite dubious he tells him, "I have a lot of friends in Interpol, the Kremlin, Brussels and the EU, etc., if you know what I mean."

Pyah, Sarah and Mark peruse the file while Carl skulks around, "Don't mind if I just go for a coffee, do you," he says, walking out of the room.

Only George is aware of his exit, "I'll come with, if you don't mind?"

Carl discretely nods then waves George in front of him, "So what was Ben talking to you about, if you don't mind me asking?"

George smiles wryly at him then pushes the button for the elevator. Once inside the elevator George turns to Carl, "You don't trust him, do you?"

Carl shakes his head, "I don't know why, it's just something niggling at the back of my mind. He hasn't done anything but, well, I don't know, he doesn't feel right."

George places his hand on Carl's shoulder, "Must be us suspicious oldies because I get the same feeling. Something doesn't track with him," he pats Carl's chest, "keep an eye on him."

Carl shakes George's hand, "Oh I will, trust me, I will."

After the file has been scrutinised, it's decided that Pyah and Mark should head towards Spain. They have a hunch that's where Anja is heading. Ben insists on tagging along but Elleon decides to stay with Lacey. George goes back to England to do some more investigating while Sarah and Carl stick to their original plan of heading back to the States.

Pyah and Mark travel to Spain with an overnight stop at Gibraltar. They book into the O'Callaghan Eliott Hotel. Once in a room Pyah decides to phone Sarah, to make sure they have caught a flight ok.

Carl is feeling apprehensive, even though he is safely onboard the plane and bunked down for the long-haul. Sarah decides to calm him down the only way she knows how. She lifts his blanket up as he fidgets, "Just lay back and enjoy."

Carl looks at her wide-eyed, "Ahem, what are you up to?"

Sarah kisses his ear then whispers, "I'm going to relax you."

Carl scans up and down the aisle, "You're not doing what I think you're doing, are you?"

Sarah smiles and nods, "Yep. A blow job, so shut the fuck up and relax."

Carl looks up and down the aisle again, "Do you think this is a good idea? I mean really? In the middle of a crowded plane?"

Sarah puts her head under the blanket, "Shut up and give me a tap if anyone is coming, apart from you that is," she says, sniggering to herself as she slips his fly down.

She just nicely gets his penis into her mouth when her phone rings. She pulls it from her pocket and looks at the caller ID. It's Pyah but without missing a stroke Sarah cuts her off then texts back, "*I'm a bit busy at the moment.*"

Pyah reads the text and answers, "*Why? What are you doing? Why can't you talk? Is everything OK?*"

Sarah texts back, "*My momma taught me to never speak with my mouth full.*"

Carl lifts the blanket to see why Sarah is moving about so much, apart from up and down, "What you doing, hun?" he asks.

His phone alerts him of an incoming text from Sarah reading, "*I'm texting Pyah, she wants to know why I can't talk, and I'll tell you what I told her, I don't speak with my mouth full, so shut up and lay back and fucking relax. I'm not doing this for the good of my health.*"

Carl slips his hand under the blanket and gently grasps a handful of Sarah's hair, but soon lets go, as she gently bites down on his manhood, "OK, ok, I'll just lay and relax."

Sarah gives a muffled, "Hm hm."

Mark strolls out of the bathroom after a relaxing shower to see Pyah still texting, "Who you talking to, honey?"

Pyah just hands him the phone and he starts to scroll down the conversation as she pulls the towel from around his waist. He looks down at his genitals as Pyah starts to stroke him, "Works for me," he comments, throwing the phone on the bed as Pyah pulls him into her mouth.

Carl lies back with his eyes closed as a hand gently taps him on the shoulder. His hands come crashing down on the blanket as a hostess reaches out to lift it, "And what have we here?" she asks, forcing Carl's hands away to lift the blanket.

Sarah looks sideways at her as she looks back at Carl.

Carl smiles back, "Her momma taught her to never speak with her mouth full."

The hostess drops the blanket back, "If you wake the rest of the passengers you lose that," she warns, pointing down at his dick, then calmly reaching above him to switch the light off, "best turn this off," she says as she pats him on the head, then struts back to the crew area.

Sarah just carries on as if nothing has happened. Carl is a bit befuddled but accepts the situation and relaxes back. Then that feeling starts to come over him. Remembering what the hostess said about waking the rest of the passengers he grabs a pillow and forces it down over his own face as he grunts into it, trying his hardest to muffle the noise as Sarah finishes him, wipes her mouth then comes up to kiss his sweaty lips, pushing the pillow down to laugh at him.

Pyah is in the middle of deep throating Mark when her text alert rings. It's Sarah, "*All done, I think that Carl is relaxed and dropping off to sleep now. How are you doing?*"

Pyah picks up the phone then places it against Marks pubic region to text back, "*Oh, in the middle of a full on deep throat.*"

Mark looks down "Really? I mean really, texting in the middle of this?"

Pyah cups his balls then gently squeezes.

Mark puts his hand on her head, "OK! You want to text that's fine with me. I just found it a bit strange."

Pyah softens her grip to a fondle as Marks sighs. He starts to reach his tingly feeling when she pulls off him. His head snaps down, "Oh come on, I was almost there."

Pyah smiles at him, "I know," she says, pulling him by his dick onto her, "I need a little relaxation therapy too," she explains, dragging him on top of her, "so get fucking and don't even think of making this last a couple of minutes."

Mark tuts, "Well I can't stick it in yet then because I'll come straight away."

Pyah kisses him, "Suppose you're going to have to use your tongue then," she says, pushing his head down towards her vagina.

Mark stops at her breasts, "Eeny, meeny, miny, mo," he says, deciding which one to suckle on.

Pyah grabs a handful of his hair and thrusts his mouth around her nipple, "Mo, now do something to relax me."

Mark pulls as much of her breast into his mouth as he can, then gently bites down, flicking her nipple with his tongue as he teases her spine with his fingernails, running them from her shoulder blades to the crease in her buttocks. He slides softly into her as he reaches around with one hand to slip one finger into her anus.

Pyah thrusts back onto his hand moaning with pleasure as he plunges into her. She claws at his back while sliding down to penetrate his anus with a single finger. She then reaches around to his ear to nibble while wrapping her legs around his waist, manipulating his hips with her heels. Mark pulls back out then rams into her vagina as Pyah persuades him with her legs, throwing her head back into the pillow with a screech of delight as Mark reaches up to kiss her neck, then drinks the droplets of perspiration that are forming over her body. Her spine arches off the bed as she gasps, throwing her head into his shoulder to grind down into her pelvis, wrapping her arms around him, reaching her first orgasmic delight.

Mark slides out of her then slithers down between her legs to entice her into a frenzy with his tongue. She throws her legs across his shoulders as she pulls his head between her thighs forcing his mouth onto her clitoris. Mark pulls her vulva into his mouth while forcing his tongue inside her to savour the sweet nectar-like juices emitted by her climax. Her hot-tempered body rigid in spasm as she creeps towards an immediate second climactic convulsion. Mark flicks then licks as his wife's temperature rises to a steamy encore of delight, flailing uncontrollably as he grasps at her hips to maintain his position, bringing her to a heightened sense of sexual enlightenment.

Without giving her chance to come down he moves up her body to re-enter her, thrusting for all he is worthwhile still flicking her clitoris with his finger. Her eyes widen as the veins in her neck seem to be at the point of explosion, her face a crimson glow as she pushes down on her breath to grunt through the final spasms of a simultaneously ejaculation with Mark through an explosion of sound and frantic elation.

CHAPTER 34
IN-FLIGHT ENTERTAINMENT

On the flight, Sarah fidgets uncomfortably in her bunk while Carl slips into a quiet slumber. She gets up after a short period and softly slinks down to the crew area. Behind the curtain there is a young man tending to a trolley with a mature hostess drinking a coffee and having a chat. Sarah steps inside, "I don't suppose you have a spare toothbrush handy and some toothpaste please?" she asks, directing her question towards the female.

The young man turns to her, "I'm afraid you're not allowed in here," he says in a soft, rather camp, voice, "if you need assistance you should press the buzzer above your bunk."

The female waves at him, "Ignore him, he's new," she says as she reaches into a trolley to produce an oral hygiene pack, "here, will this do?"

Sarah takes it, then flicks the woman's name tag, "Thank you, Janet," she says, placing the pack in her pocket.

Janet looks down at her tag, "That's me," she says, sipping at her coffee, "if you need anything at all just buzz and I'll be there, oh, by the way, is Mister Sinclair relaxed now?" she asks with a wry grin appearing across her face.

Sarah smiles at her, "Sleeping like a baby, thanks. The problem now is it's left me frustrated." She explains, tapping Janet's tag again, "shame that didn't say Cathy or Pam," she says, then turning to look at the man.

He stares at her, "Don't look at me sweetie, you're not my type, if you know what I mean?"

Janet pulls Sarah's shoulder, "How do you know Cathy and Pam?"

Sarah's head drops, "Oh, a couple of friends of mine had, well, an experience with them, if you know what I mean."

Janet pulls Sarah's chin up, "You're friends with the FISCHERS?"

Sarah's eyebrows raise, "Oh, you know of them?"

Janet nods her head frantically, "Oh, we know of them. We don't know the full story but we get the general gist," she says, licking her lips, "he may not bat that way," she adds, pointing at the boy, "but I might be able to satisfy your needs, if you're willing."

The boy stands with his hands over his ears, "La la la, I'm not hearing this," he declares, turning his back.

Janet pulls him back, "Go and see if the flight crew need anything, and take your time."

The boy scurries off while Janet moves closer to a rather apprehensive Sarah, "We have an emergency bunk," she offers, pointing at a curtain in the corner, "if you're up for it, that is," she adds, pulling back the curtain.

Sarah rolls her eyes, "Oh, what the fuck," she decides, then pulls her panties down, sticks them in her pocket and climbs into the bunk.

Janet flicks her eyebrows "Keen?" she remarks, then drops her panties the same way to sidle in on top of Sarah, "or are you that desperate?"

Sarah hitches her skirt up around her waist, "Desperate? I'm frigging clamming," she says as Janet starts to unbutton Sarah's blouse.

Sarah pulls Janet's head up to kiss her, "The only problem with this is I'm rather audible when it comes to sex."

Janet kisses her, "Not on this flight you're not," she says, pulling a spare pillow from under the bunk, "bite down on this if you have to," she offers, then flicks Sarah's front loader bra open, "wow, you're very pert, aren't you?" se comments as she strips herself to the waist.

Her breasts aren't as pert as Sarah's but Sarah isn't complaining when she pulls one into her mouth. It's soft and delicate, well-toned and ripe without any harshness, tasting of strawberries. Janet reaches down between Sarah's thighs, "Oh my god, you wringing wet. Talk about ready to pop?"

Sarah nods as she suckles on Janet's breast, "Hm hm."

Janet reaches under the bunk, where she has a small vanity case stashed. She fumbles around for a while then produces a female deodorant spray, "Hm, think this should do," she says as she slides the opposite end to the cap into Sarah.

Sarah bites down slightly on Janet's breast as her nails dig into Janet's spine, both girls simultaneously moaning with delight, their torsos crushing together as they both arch their backs, Janet's breast stretching before popping out of Sarah's mouth like a champagne cork to slap back beside the other. Sarah starts to become extremely audible as she slams her spine down on to the mattress. Janet pushes her mouth against Sarah's then thrusts her tongue into Sarah's mouth to muffle the sound of Sarah's orgasm. Sarah reaches down to push Janet's buttocks down as Janet vibrates the aerosol in and out of Sarah to enhance the already gushing explosion of ecstasy through Sarah's climax. Sarah grunts down into her chin as her head recedes in to her neck through the final push, crushing Janet's hips with her legs as she rips into the small of Janet's spine with her nails. Spasm after spasm erupts until Sarah finally drops exhausted back on to the bed, awash with sweat, releasing Janet from her bear-like grip.

Satisfied beyond explanation she reaches up to pull Janet back to her lips, "Thank you," she says, kissing her before looking deep into her eyes, "your turn."

Janet rolls onto her back without a word as Sarah takes the deodorant spray, rolling on top of Janet. she gently inserts it in to Janet's vagina, then softly rubs her clitoris as Janet silently twitches. Janet lies back to reach for the headboard as she wraps her legs over Sarah's thighs thrusting her pelvis in a soft rocking motion. Sarah teases her fingers up over Janet's ribs before caressing her breast to squeeze it tightly between her fingers, tweaking Janet's nipples with her nails. Janet grips the bunk as she bites down on her bottom lip, eyes closed, fantasising in a world of erotic mania. The surge of spine-tingling pleasure rushes through to every nerve, driving a rage of passion through every sinew culminating in a suppressed silent explosion of emancipated lust as Janet climaxes into Sarah's hand, pulling her into a final embrace before relaxing down onto a saturated sheet.

Suddenly a hand comes through the curtain holding a pack of wet wipes, "You may need these," the boys says, dropping them on Sarah's back as the girls start to giggle, cleaning themselves before emerging from the bunk.

Sarah kisses Janet before quietly returning to her own bunk. She silently climbs in without disturbing Carl, then soon drops into a relaxed slumber.

James gives Janet an enamoured look, "You jammy bitch," he declares, his campness dissipating somewhat, "have you seen what you have done to me? Hope it was worth it?"

Janet looks down at the bulge in his trousers, "Whoa, did not see that coming."

James funnily slaps her, "It hasn't come yet, but if anyone needs me I'll be in the loo."

Janet frowns at him, "Why?"

James rolls his eyes back into his head, "I'm going to have to go for a wank, aren't I? You don't expect me to finish the flight with this do you," he says, pointing down to the bulge.

Janet reaches out to it, "You need a hand like?"

James flinches away, "You come anywhere near it and it'll just shrivel and hide," he says, bending his index finger in the air then strutting off towards the toilet.

Janet tuts, cleans herself up, then carries on with her chores before making herself a cuppa. She checks her schedule then James returns, "Did we enjoy that?" she asks, giving him a wry grin.

"Would have been better with a magazine or even a man but I coped," he replies, holding his nose in the air.

Time passes and soon the passengers are awakened with the smell of freshly cooked food. Coffee is served and when Janet comes to Sarah and Carl she takes her time, chatting to Sarah in a provocative manner. It takes a while for Carl to click that something is going on, "OK, did I miss something last night? Because you two seem very intimate this morning."

Sarah smiles as Janet bends down to peck her on the lips, "I'm sure I don't know what you're talking about."

James sticks his head over the back of Carl's seat, "Not one to kiss and tell, but you missed a bloody good show last night."

Carl looks up at him, then his head snaps around to Sarah, "You better not have!" he exclaims, pointing at James.

James taps him on the shoulder, "Not me sweetie," he says, turning to gives a sly glance at Janet, "her."

Carl gives a sigh of relief, "Oh, that's ok then."

James is stunned, "What? You're not bothered with her cheating on you with her, but you are if it was me?"

Carl gives his hand a condescending tap, "That's not really cheating now is it and something tells me she's not exactly your type."

James lifts Carl's hand from his and throws it to one side, "Homophobe!"

Carl starts to stand, "That's not quite what I meant. I have nothing against gay people."

James slowly turns back to him, "Oh, you don't, eh?" he asks, lifting his hand to stroke Carl's face.

The colour drains from Carl's face as he swallows, "Err, well, I, err, don't have anything against them, but it's not, err, exactly my scene."

James looks deep into his eyes, "You can't really know till you've tried," he suggests, raising his eyebrows then pouting.

Carl steps back slightly, trying to figure out how to resolve this situation without offending James, "I am extremely flattered but I'm just not into it and I can't see me ever being into it. I apologise if I have given the wrong end of the stick, sorry but no," he stammers, stumbling over Sarah's bunk.

James smiles, "Your loss," he remarks, then carries on to the next passenger.

Carl wipes his forehead then sighs as he sits back in his own seat, "Thought I was fucked there."

Sarah nearly chokes on her coffee as Janet leans in, "You would have been if he had his way," she points out, then pats him on the head.

Carl turns to Sarah, "Oh, you don't half get me in some situations madam."

Sarah's jaw drops, "Me? You were the one chatting him up!"

Carl nearly chokes on his coffee, "I'm bloody sure I didn't, did I?" he asks, rubbing spilt coffee off his chest, "It didn't seem that way, did it?"

Sarah nods quietly. Carl looks down the aisle, "Shit, I hope I haven't given him the wrong idea," he says as James turns to catch Carl looking then blows Carl a kiss.

Carl jumps back in his seat, "Oh shit, what the fuck have I done?" he asks, looking out the window, "hope this flight is landing shortly."

Sarah buries her head in a book, "If you had tried that dildo you would know what to expect," she points out, sniggering to herself.

Carl slams his hand down on Sarah's book, "Really!? I mean, you really are bringing that up now!?" he demands, a super stern expression on his face.

Sarah can't help but cackle out loud. Janet comes down to their seats, "Are we having fun kiddies?"

Sarah has a cushion over her face as Carl looks up at Janet, "You don't want to know, trust me, you just don't want to know."

Janet can't help but smile, "I'm sorry, but you're disturbing the rest of the passengers so do something with her."

At that Sarah bursts out into a louder cackle as Carl buries her head into the cushion, "Have you got a tranquilliser or something?"

Janet purses her lips, trying to hold back the laughter, "Oh I wish. Is she always as audible as this when she gets excited?"

Carl spins his head slowly, "Well, apparently you should already know," he says, holding back a grin.

Janet turns her head away blushing but can't hold the laughter back anymore. Before long the whole cabin is in an uproar of laughter with only Sarah, Carl and Janet knowing what they are laughing about. The seatbelt sign is lit as the pilot announces their approach. Janet takes a breath, "Oh, thank God for that," she says as she rushes to get everything ready for landing.

When the flight lands Sarah insists they hang back until last. On disembarking Sarah says her goodbyes to James and Janet with kisses and hugs, while Carl hugs Janet but shakes James's hand, "Hope you find the right man."

James smiles, "You never know, I might have already."

Carl moves around Sarah while still looking at James, "Bitch," he says, funnily sticking his nose in the air.

James raises his eyebrows, "I know where you live."

Carl eyes spin to Sarah. Sarah shrugs, "Don't look at me."

Carl's head drops, "Oh shit, I hope he doesn't."

Sarah sniggers then carries on walking down off the plane, "We're home now, so relax," she tells him, taking him by the hand to lead him through Customs.

CHAPTER 35
HOME SWEET HOME

It's a glorious morning in LA. Not a cloud in the morning sky as the sun beams down to a bustling airport. Carl hails a cab, throws the luggage in the trunk, then sits in the back as Sarah snuggles into him to relax while they are driven home in peace.

Once in their apartment Carl quickly unpacks, then changes into his business suit. Sarah has a shower but when she gets out she finds Carl has gone. She phones, him, "Where are you?"

Carl is in his own car, "I just need to get to the office, otherwise I'll just burst," he says, fiddling with his tie, "got to get back to normal or I'll go crazy, so if you want me I'll be down at the office checking on my two best agents."

Sarah tuts but understands, "OK, I'll see you shortly."

She then proceeds to get herself into work mode. It takes her about half an hour to get herself ready then another three quarters of an hour to get to the office. On arrival, she is surprised to bump into Janet, "Whoa, what are you doing here?"

Janet isn't surprised to see Sarah, "I've seen you loads of times. I live here," she says, pointing at an apartment block across the way from the Sinclair building, "in fact, I can almost see into your bosses' office from my apartment. I live on the top floor," she explains, pointing up towards the roof, "small world, isn't it?"

Sarah smiles, "Well, at least I know where to come if I need some tension therapy," she remarks, raising her eyebrows.

Janet picks up her bag, "Well, I have to go, so I'll probably see you around," she says, giving Sarah a peck, "you'll have to tell me what you do up there someday."

Sarah pouts then closes her eyes, shaking her head, "We solve problems."

There's a small pause then Janet takes a couple of steps back, "Sounds ominous," she comments before walking away to her apartment block.

Sarah blows her a kiss then walks into the Sinclair building.

On arrival at Carl's office she announces her arrival then walks in to greet him, "Never guess who I just bumped into? Janet!"

Carl's head lifts slowly, "And?"

Sarah walks over to the window, "She lives just down there," she tells him, pointing at the apartment block, "in fact, there she is," she observes, waving as Janet comes to her window.

Carl comes to the window, "Oh for Christ's sake, she doesn't live with him, does she?"

Sarah shrugs, "Wouldn't know, she never mentioned him."

Carl waves then grimaces a smile, walks back to his seat and drops his head on the desk, "Shit, I hope I don't bump into him or I'm moving offices to another town."

Sarah smiles and pats him on the back, "There, there," she comforts, then walks out with an enormous grin on her face.

CHAPTER 36
TURNCOAT

The warm Gibraltar air is thick and heavy as Pyah's alarm call startles her into a confused state of awareness, reaching out to grasp the phone, "Hello," she says into it, sitting, rubbing her eyes as reality slowly dawns.

A gentle voice on the other end of the phone speaks, "Good morning, this is your five am wake-up call, have a nice day."

Pyah looks out of the window, "OK, thank you," she replies, then puts the receiver down.

Mark's arm is flopping about but his mind is still in a dream when Pyah shakes him, "Come on sleepy head, we have a plane to catch," she says as she walks onto the balcony for some fresh air, "God, it's so warm, and the sun isn't even up yet."

Mark throws the covers back, "Jesus, it's still night-time, what the hell are we doing awake? What the hell is the time?" he demands, sitting on the end of the bed, stretching and yawning.

Pyah walks back in, "It's five am," she tells him, giving an extended stretch before heading for the shower.

Mark slaps his cheeks, "Whose stupid idea was it to get an early flight?"

Pyah turns on the shower, "Yours, dear. You said the sooner we get to Barcelona the sooner we catch that Russian bitch."

Mark grumps to himself, "Oh, I think she could have waited another hour or two."

Pyah steps under the cascade of soothing water, "What was that, honey?"

Mark stands up, "Nothing, dear," he says, then walks into the bathroom.

Seeing his wife soaping herself down brings his senses to life, "Hmm, interesting," he remarks as he steps out of his boxer shorts to step into the shower.

Pyah turns to him, "I don't think so mate, we haven't got time."

Mark wraps his arms around her, "Not even for a quickie?" he asks, kissing her on the back of her neck.

Pyah reaches out for her watch and sets a six-minute alarm, "You got five minutes," she tells him, then places the watch down on the shower shelf.

Mark tries to lift her but the soap suds make her slippery, "Oh, for Christ's sake," he moans, grabbing her ass to wrench her up against the wall.

Pinning her with his legs he bangs his penis into her. Pyah's head slams forward, "Whoa, easy tiger," she warns, clawing into his back, "you'll rip me to bits at that speed."

Mark frowns at her, "You put a time limit on it," he reminds her as he suds the rest of his penis down to help it slide in better.

Pyah shrugs, "Oh well, it'll definitely be clean on the inside now," she says, chuckling to herself as Mark starts to push her up and down while thrusting in and out for all he's worth.

A tingle starts to emerge through her body as she establishes the oncoming of a climax. She bites down on his neck while grunting through the experience. Mark is just getting frustrated as he can see the time ticking by with no results. Pyah's head throws back as she quickly starts through the final stages of her orgasm. Hoping this will spur him on Mark goes at it hell for leather. Pyah clasps her legs around him, screaming with delight as the alarm rings out.

Mark can just feel the onset of his ejaculation when Pyah stops moving, "Oh come on, I'm almost there."

Pyah tuts, "Hurry up."

Mark forces through, "It's no bloody good when you're being timed," he complains as he starts to grunt, then spasm, banging his knees against the tiles uncontrollably.

Finally, he finishes, "Shit, I think I've screwed my knees up," he says, dropping Pyah back down to the floor.

She quickly washes herself down, then rinses and grabs the sponge to wash him down, "Come on, we don't have much time, the limo will be here in ten minutes," she says, flicking his dick from side to side.

Mark grabs the sponge, "Steady on, you're going to snap it wanging it about like that."

Once showered, dressed and downstairs they only just arrive before the limo. Luggage is loaded and it's off to the airport. Once on the plane it's a quick hop up to Barcelona. Pyah settles herself down while Mark orders a drink from the trolley. Both Mark and Pyah hate these short two-hour flights, sitting in a seat that doesn't lie down. First class is such a comedown, but at short notice this is all they could get, so although grumping they decide to make the most of it.

Pyah turns to Mark, "Don't have too many of them," she warns, pointing at his scotch, "I know you're having a meal but go easy because I don't want to have to carry you off the plane in a drunken stupor."

Mark lifts his hand like a glove puppet, "Nag, nag, nag, is that all you're going to do all the way through this flight?" he demands, the tension of a cramped space already getting to him.

Ben has opted to stay in economy class so they won't see him all the way through the flight. On the outskirts of Barcelona, the seatbelt light comes on as the pilot announces turbulence due to a lightning storm hanging over Barcelona. As Pyah looks out of the window she can see the whole of Barcelona covered in storm clouds, "Got a nasty feeling this is where they tell us to put our head between our knees and kiss our asses goodbye."

Mark leans over her, "My, you're a bit of an optimist."

Pyah stares at him, "Don't you mean pessimist?"

Mark smiles, "Can you actually reach your ass with your lips?"

Pyah gives him a wry grin, "No, why?"

Mark pecks her on the cheek, "Like I said, optimist."

The plane reaches the edge of the cloud. then suddenly drops about a thousand feet vertically. Mark drops his head between his legs "Oh shit, you had to open your mouth, didn't you?" he moans.

An announcement comes over the speaker, "Would all passengers please ensure that seatbelts are fastened," Mark checks his, "there will be slight turbulence for a short period but there is nothing to worry about, we will be landing in about three minutes. Thank you."

Pyah sees a lightning bolt hit the edge of the wing, "Nothing to worry about?! Shit, we just been hit by lightning, so when do we worry?!"

Mark reaches up to pull Pyah's head down between her legs, "For Christ's sake woman, stop giving a running commentary on our demise and start praying."

Pyah laughs at him, "Oh, stop being a baby. It's just a bit of turbulence," she says as the plane shakes violently, "but then again," she amends as she crosses herself.

Mark closes his eyes, "Oh, for fuck's sake, don't do that."

Pyah slaps him, "Now, make up your mind, do I pray or do I just take it in my stride?"

The plane starts to skew sideways then jolt around. Pyah cuddles Mark, "There, there," she comforts, patting him on the back, "won't be long now," she says, smiling.

Mark glances up at her, "Won't be long for what!?"

Pyah rolls her eyes, "Before we land, you numpty," she says as the wheels touch the tarmac.

The plane skews again before straightening up, then the front wheel can be heard screeching down on the ground as the pilot applies the brakes. Mark lifts his head, then starts to blush, realising he is the only passenger in the crash position, "You're shitting me, right?" he asks, looking around at all the calm passengers, "what's wrong with you people? We nearly died!"

The passenger in front of him turns to him, "Oh, this happens all the time 'round here. You get used to it."

Mark huffs, "Get used to it? I don't think so. I'm never coming here again."

Pyah laughs at him, "Come on, you wuss," she says as she unfastens her seatbelt.

Mark sits rigid, "I think I'll wait."

Pyah takes his hand, "Come on, the sooner we get off the plane the sooner we get inside the building."

Mark pulls her back, "What do you mean get inside the building?"

Pyah shakes her head, "We have to walk across from the plane to the arrival suite."

Mark's eyes widen, "You do realise it's lightning out there? How far is it to the building?"

Pyah tuts, "It's only about fifty meters. I'll get you a brolly."

Mark drags her back down, "Are you out of your tiny fucking mind?" he asks as he looks out of the window, "Fifty metres with a fucking lightning conductor stuck up above my head? I don't think so. Tell them to park closer or I ain't getting off till it stops."

The hostess approaches, "Is there a problem?"

Pyah pouts at her, "He's scared of a little lightning."

The hostess takes his hand, "It's ok, we'll get you a brolly."

Mark sits firm, "Yeah, she said that," he says, pointing at Pyah, "you might as well stick a lightning rod up my arse. Tell them to park closer, or make it stop or something, because I ain't going out in it."

A rather camp male steward approaches from behind, "What's wrong with you?" he asks, brushing his hand across Mark's shoulders.

Mark jumps up then starts to walk backward down the aisle, "Err, look, I know you're a nice lad and all but you're not exactly my type," he says, trying to not offend.

The young man smiles gently as he follows Mark, "are you sure, you know? I mean how can you know if you haven't even considered it? Unless you truly are a homophobe?" he asks, looking sweetly down at Marks feet.

Mark is soon at the doorway as the hostess hands him a brolly, "If you ask nicely, the baggage handler might take you in his truck."

Mark looks up at the sky, then makes a dash for the building.

The hostess looks at Pyah, "Would madam like a brolly?" she asks, handing her one.

Pyah smiles gracefully at her and takes the brolly, "Thank you," she says, then kisses her hand to press it against a rather shocked hostess's lips before strutting down the steps.

By the time Mark makes the building he is wet through to his underwear. Pyah strolls along with her brolly up but still gets wet, "Quite refreshing this, actually," she comments, flicking the water off her brolly at Mark as the rain runs down her face.

Mark wipes his face, "Typical," he says, then starts to look around, "wonder where Ben is?"

Pyah scans the queues, "Didn't see him get off the plane. Did you?"

Mark shakes his head, then shrugs, "Might have got through Customs before us," he suggests, making his way towards the queue.

Once on the other side of Customs they fail to find Ben, even though they put a call out for him, so they decide to find a hotel, leaving a message for him at the airport information desk.

On arrival at the hotel, while booking in, Pyah reserves a table for an evening meal.

Settled in, showered, and heading downstairs they hear a gunshot ring out from one of the floors above them. Security rush past them on the stairs as they decide to follow. A woman's scream leads them straight to the room from where the gunshot originated.

Security keep them and everyone else back while police arrive, but once Pyah and Mark identify themselves they are allowed to enter the room. A woman's body is lying on the floor in the middle of the room. Pyah confirms that this is the body of one of Denier De-fuer's doubles.

Her body is taken to the morgue while Pyah and Mark help the forensic team to scour the room for any evidence of her assassin. The room is clean but security footage shows a hooded male entering then exiting the room at the time of the gunshot. The footage also shows him entering the lift just before the security arrives, then exiting the lift on the ground floor wearing a wide brimmed hat, walking calmly out of the hotel and getting into a limousine before disappearing. Something about the man is strangely familiar to Pyah, but his face is hidden from shot at all times so an accurate description cannot be obtained.

At the morgue, the woman's body cannot be identified as her fingerprints have been surgically removed, her teeth have been replaced with surgical implants and no DNA sample is on file. The only thing that can be verified is that it most definitely is not Denier De-fuer. Mark and Pyah, for obvious reasons, do not disclose why they know it isn't De-fuer. Pyah and Mark head out into town working on a hunch to see if they can find the limo.

Mark stops the car suddenly, "Nah, can't be," he says, looking at another hotel, "I could have sworn I just saw Ben entering that hotel."

The hotel has a couple of rather large gentlemen guarding the door so Pyah points towards an alley, half a block away from the hotel, "How about we take a peek 'round the back?"

Mark drives into the alley and switches the lights off, then finds an unobtrusive place to park. Sauntering around as if they were just a couple of young lovers out for a stroll they come across two more guards to the rear of the hotel. Pyah kisses Mark on the cheek while whispering in his ear, "Seems someone doesn't want anyone near here."

Mark cuddles her in close, "Yeah, I got that distinct impression. Looks like we may have to use the roof," he suggests, smiling at Pyah before heading back down the alley.

Climbing on an adjacent roof Mark notices guards posted on the hotel roof, "Jesus, something tells me we ain't even getting close."

Pyah pulls a small pair of binoculars out of her pocket, "Good job I was a girl guide," she says, pointing them at a window.

Ben can be seen talking to a female sat in a chair with her back to them. Pyah just has time to lipread Ben before he leaves the room, "You better get you act together, the Fischers are here and it won't be long before they find you," she relays to Mark.

The woman says something back as Ben replies, "And you need to find those other four rockets before anyone else does," then he leaves.

Pyah watches as Anja Koliakova stands up from the seat, slamming a file down on the desk before making a quick phone call. She then leaves in a hurry. The guards around the hotel terminate their posts to meet Anja around the front as a convoy speeds off down the main drag.

Mark and Pyah meander into the hotel, on noticing it has an open restaurant they get a table and sit to order a meal. While they wait for the main course, Pyah slips away to Anja's room for a mooch.

When she returns she shows Mark some photos of the file Anja had. The file contained several different plans for using the VX gas to assassinate different politicians around the globe. All of them were put forward by De-fuer. Pyah points out comments at the bottom of the page, "Seems our Russian declined all suggestions."

Mark studies the photos, "Hmm, wonder what she had or even has in mind for what's left, if she can find them?"

Pyah pulls his head around, "More to the point, what the hell is Ben doing fraternising with her? And why hasn't he mentioned any of it?"

Mark thinks for a moment, "Right, let's not jump to conclusions. Carl and George, Lacey's gaffer can check out Ben thoroughly. I'll give them a call and apprise them of the situation, then I think we should see if we can find those rockets before the Russian."

Mark contacts the bosses, while Pyah contacts Cramer to see if he can help locate the rockets. She mentions nothing of Ben, feeling it would not be prudent at this time. Mark calls the waiter, "Excuse me, but do you provide a limousine service at this hotel?"

The waiter asks Mark's name and jots it down, "I won't be a moment," he excuses, then heads to reception.

On his return he apologises, "I am so sorry sir, but the limousines are for patrons only, plus they are all in use at this present moment in time."

Mark takes a small wad of cash out of his pocket, "Could you tell me if a Russian lady used your service? If she did where was she taken?"

The waiter secretes the money away, "I won't be a moment," he says, then heads back to reception, looks at the log then returns, "it would seem that the lady in question did indeed use the service and is at this very moment arriving at Presa de Sau which is a dam just outside Barcelona."

Mark and Pyah quickly finish their meal, thank the waiter then leave.

CHAPTER 37
DAM AND BLAST

After grabbing some demolition equipment, they set off for the dam. When they arrive at the dam they find that Anja is holding a meeting with most of her organisation in a secluded building. The building is situated about a mile down the valley directly in front of the dam. Pyah turns to Mark, "I guess you had a feeling when you brought the demolition equipment?"

Mark smiles, "Yep, had a plan emerging in my mind as soon as the word dam was spoken," he confides, pointing out to an approaching vehicle, "and here comes the rest of the plan."

Four men get out of the vehicle, greet Mark, then hand him and Pyah scuba equipment, "We have the rest of the stuff you requested in the trunk," they say, opening the trunk to a whole load of explosives.

Pyah looks at the building, then steps back, "You're planning on blowing the dam?" her eyes widen, "I thought you were going for the building."

Mark gives her a wry grin, "The rest of the valley is uninhabited, so why not take them out with that?" he says, pointing at the dam.

Soon Mark's friends are planting explosives inside the dam structure, while Pyah helps Mark with mines under the waterline.

Soon, Mark's friends radio him, "All is set. The detonator is in the trunk of your car. Good luck and we were never here," they say as they leave.

Mark thanks them and tells them they have twenty minutes to get as far away as possible then signs off. Pyah swims over to Mark, "Twenty minutes?"

Mark starts to swim to the surface, "Yeah, my intel tells me they will be having that meeting for at least another hour so in twenty minutes BOOM, no more meeting," he says, laughing out loud.

Pyah grabs his leg, "Hang on a minute," she says, pulling him back down, "we got about fifteen minutes' air and twenty minutes to the big bang? What's your hurry?" she asks, sliding her hand down onto his groin.

Mark looks up at the surface then back at Pyah, "You're kidding, right?"

Pyah shakes her head, "Nope, never given a blowjob twenty meters down," she says, giggling.

Mark shrugs, "Hey, if you think you can get it out down here, who am I to argue?"

Pyah swims around the back of him, unzips his wetsuit, then pulls it down around his knees. She takes his penis out, then unmasks herself and starts to suck him for as long as her breath will allow. She quickly takes a couple of breaths from her mask then starts to suck again, "Screw this for a lark, unzip me," she instructs, turning away from Mark.

Mark shrugs again, "What the hell!! But we got to keep an eye on the time," he reminds her as he pulls her wetsuit down, then slides in from the back, lifting her hips up to meet his groin.

Pyah quickly becomes excited but it's also becoming uncomfortable as she realises he is pumping water into her, "Hang on a second," she orders, pushing him away from her.

As he exits her she forces the water out but gasses escape, causing both Mark and Pyah to fold over with laughter, "You know, I've never seen a woman fart underwater, let alone fart from there," Mark says, unable to replace his dick for laughing.

Pyah spins around and slaps him in slow motion, "Sod this for a lark, when we get back to the hotel we're going to pick this up where you left off," she decides, trying to see where her wetsuit is through tears of laughter.

Mark helps her back on with it, then she helps him as they decide to head for the surface.

Mark climbs out first, "You know, that's the fastest shag we've ever had," he says, still laughing, "and you trying to hit me underwater, what a numpty," he lifts his mask, "is that you?" he asks as the pungent aroma of stagnant algae wafts through his nostrils.

Pyah reaches up for a hand, then slaps him across the leg, "That wasn't underwater, was it?"

Mark laughs at her again, "It's neoprene, takes all the sting out."

Pyah scowls at him, "Later mate, later," she threatens, then follows him back to the car.

Surprisingly, Cramer and Fargo are already there waiting for them. Cramer approaches Mark, "So what's the plan?"

Mark taps the side of his nose, "Wait and see."

Fargo approaches, "We've had strict instructions that the Russian is not to be harmed, so whatever you're planning you better tell us."

Mark sulks, "Well, it seems we have a leak."

Fargo nods arrogantly, "Yes, we know, Ben is working with Koliakova-"

Mark interrupts him, "Not that type of leak," he says, pulling the detonator out of the trunk.

Fargo gives him a puzzled look, "OK, what type of leak?"

Mark turns to the dam, "This type of leak," he says, pushing the detonator, "in that," he adds, pointing at the dam as it starts to crumble.

Cramer quickly grabs a radio, "Move, move, move. Get them out of there," he instructs as three huey helicopters descend on the building, "the dam's been blown," he shouts, screaming into the mic.

A small troop of soldiers quickly assault the building, then rush the occupants to the awaiting choppers. Everyone boards as the wave comes crashing through the valley, ripping trees from the ground and churning the rocks and soil with a deafening roar announcing the imminent onslaught of death and destruction it is about to unleash. Anja is placed in the first chopper with an Arab man and French woman. A south African male, a Spanish male, a Chinese female and an English female are placed in the second chopper. An American male, a Cuban general and an Irish policeman are placed in the third chopper.

The first and second choppers manage to climb above the crashing wave as it rushes down below them but the third chopper becomes caught in the wash of air as the rolling water drags the swirling torrent around its rotor blades. hauling it back toward the turbulent depths that annihilate it with shattering force as the debris slices through it, killing all the occupants with nature's full, unhindered strength.

Cramer lunges at Mark, "You stupid little man," he yells, slamming him against the side of his car, "do you realise what you've done?"

Pyah reaches into the car, pulls her gun out and points it at Cramer, "I know you're a friend but let my husband go or I let you go. If you know what I mean."

Fargo slinks behind Pyah but she pulls a knife from her belt to flick it under his chin, "How about we all calm down, take a breath, talk, and see what can be done to rectify our differences," she suggests, cocking her head to one side, "no one wants to die now do they?"

Cramer lets go of Mark, "Differences?" he repeats, storming away from him, "he just killed six American soldiers and you think we have differences?"

Mark faces Cramer down, "No, you killed them by sending them in to get that scum out mate."

Fargo puts his hands up submissively, "I'm with you," he says, pointing at Pyah.

Pyah walks in-between Mark and Cramer, "Shouting at each other isn't going to help," she tells them, placing the gun under Mark's chin and the knife under Cramer's, "now how about you two boys start thinking like men and sort this out?" she suggests, pouting at both of them, "we should start by disclosing all we know to each other."

Cramer's head bows, "OK."

Cramer makes a phone call. Mark, Pyah and Fargo only hear what he says, "Yes, we managed to extract her but we lost a chopper and six men," there's a pause, "mercenaries?" he slams the phone shut then storms over to Fargo, "did you know anything about this?"

Fargo is flabbergasted, "Know anything about what?"

Cramer points down towards the water, "We're using fucking mercenaries?" his phone rings, he decides to put it on open so all can hear, "this is the commanding officer of the NSA what the hell is going on? I just got my ear chewed off by the president."

Cramer stumbles for words, "Err, well sir, as I don't actually work for you, I don't think I need explain myself."

Mark makes a punching gesture towards the phone, "And why would the president call you about one of our operations?"

The NSA commander huffs, "Because we supplied the FBI with the mercenaries and the president was watching a satellite link of the whole fucking cock-up."

Cramer, Fargo and the Fischers are all silent until Cramer speaks, "Well, if you had bothered to give us this intel in the first place then it probably would have gone down differently. Who the hell gave the NSA jurisdiction on this anyway?"

The commander pauses for a moment, "You'll be getting a call from your superiors shortly. That's all I have to say," he says as the phone goes dead.

Cramer is about to call his superior when his phone rings, "Yes sir?"

His boss interrupts him, "Silence! Not a fucking word, I know what just went down, so just listen. The NSA have rerouted your helicopters to an unknown destination. An NSA clean-up team are en route so I don't want you or the Fischers anywhere near when they arrive. It seems that a lot more is going on than they are willing to tell us so get those two clowns you call friends out of Spain to a secure location ASAP then call me. We'll take it from there!"

Cramer turns to the Fischers, "You heard him. Follow me and no fucking about," he orders as he jumps in his car to speed off towards the French border.

Once in France Pyah calls Cramer, "Where are we going?"

Cramer smiles, "Oh, I have a friend in Monaco. She'll put you up for a while until we sort things out," he says, grinning at Fargo, "I think you'll like her but I won't bore you with details, anyway, you seem to like surprises."

When he hangs up Fargo glares at him, "You're not thinking of hiding them with Madam Rose are you?"

A big cheesy grin comes over Cramer's face, "Oh yes, let's see how they fair with a real sexaholic. Who the hell is going to look for them there?"

Fargo grimaces, "Don't know about sadomasochism though."

Cramer shrugs, "Well, we'll find out, won't we?"

CHAPTER 38
MADAM ROSE

A few hours and a few food and toilet stops later Cramer pulls into a driveway leading to a big, old house. When he pulls up outside the main entrance a rather elegant lady wearing a skintight patent leather outfit slinks down the steps to greet him. Pyah and Mark exit their vehicle rather intrigued, "This looks homely," Mark comments, raising his eyebrow to Pyah.

Pyah puts her arm around Marks shoulder, "At first, I had flashbacks of Calum's place but if I'm not mistaken this is quite the opposite," she says, turning to smile at Fargo "brothel?"

Fargo smiles vaguely at her, "Not quite, but it is a house of ill repute, you might say."

The lady struts over to Pyah, "My reputation is far from ill, my dear," she says, running her hand across Pyah's cheek before encircling Pyah to look her up and down, "nice. Very nice. My name is Rose. Madam Rose. Welcome to my humble abode," she announces as she leads them into the house.

Inside the house there is a grand double curved stairway leading to a walkway making the shape of a heart at the centre of the entrance hall. Pyah swirls in awe, "Wow, now this is what I call a brothel!"

Rose spins at the bottom of the stairs, "This, my dear," she starts, waving her arm above her, "is an adult leisure and pleasure palace, not a brothel!"

She scans Mark, "Hmm, definitely knights and dragons I would say," she hums, slinking around him, "a puzzler and hero complex," she decides, then she turns her attention to Pyah, "you, my dear, look like the fairy-tale type, but not a helpless princess, hmm, more a feisty fighter. I have just the room to put you both in."

Pyah leans on Mark's shoulder, "This could be interesting," she murmurs, then calls after Rose, "can I presume we'll be sharing a room? And is this a dominatrix/submissive house by any chance?"

Rose glances over her shoulder at Pyah, "Oh, we are an observant one, aren't we?"

Mark takes a step back, "Err, excuse me, but I don't go for all that bondage malarkey," he objects, raising his hands in protest.

Rose smiles, "You never know what you like till you try. But you're not here for that are you?"

Cramer moves in, "No, Rose, they aren't. Just keep them out of sight and harm's way, please!"

Rose bows to him, "Your wish is my command, kind sir."

Fargo smiles as he leaves, while Cramer puts his arm around Mark's shoulder, "Don't worry, you're in great hands," he assures then he pats Mark on the shoulder, laughs, then leaves.

Rose walks over to a pull sash on the wall, "Won't be a moment," she says as she pulls it, "then we can inspect your suite."

A gong sound can be heard throughout the house then the sound of doors closing. As the last door closes, a small bell rings above the sash. Rose claps her hands then two girls come to take the luggage as Rose takes Mark and Pyah's hands to lead them to their room. Up the stairs, along a lengthy lavishly ornate passage to the very rear of the house where she opens a sumptuously carved door, then beckons the couple in. The rooms décor is of black over red with a six-poster hexagonal emperor size bed as a centre piece, an eight foot Venus de Milo carved fireplace with ten foot French doors leading to a stone carved veranda. The bed has an opulent black oak canopy draped with black silk and red silk sheets with pillows to match. Each post of the bed has a manacle discretely attached, which Mark doesn't notice until Pyah launches herself onto the bed. Rose opens the French window to step outside onto the veranda as Mark follows her. Pyah gets off the bed then notices a fridge full of soft drinks. She takes a cola, then follows Mark outside drinking it.

Mark is up on his tiptoes, "So what's down there?" he asks, pointing to the rear of the grounds.

Rose gives him a puzzled look, "As you can see, it's a maze."

Mark tuts, "No, beyond the maze."

Rose smiles, "That, my dear, is the Monaco harbour where the elite have their yachts and launches."

Pyah rolls her eyes then takes another drink as Mark's eyes widen, "You're joking, right?"

Rose shakes her head with a smug grin, "No dear, if I were joking I would have said something like, so the judge asks Mickey. You want do divorce Minnie because she has bucked teeth? And Mickey says, no I want to divorce her because she's fucking Goofy."

Pyah starts to splutter and choke as the cola goes down the wrong way then is coughed up through her nose, causing her to projectile spit the cola all over Mark's chest. She bends over, spewing snot and mucus from her nose. Trying to take a breath as she inhales more cola while Mark rubs her back, trying to hold back the laughter. Rose produces a small handkerchief from her pocket then hands it to Pyah, "The ensuite is to your right," she says, pointing just inside the room.

Pyah splutters all the way to the bathroom, baulking up bile by this time. Rose hands her a glass of water as she stands in awe at the size of the bathroom/wet room. It has Greek goddess style reliefs on the wall, a luxurious double bath as a centre piece, a waterfall shower in one wall and a bed shower on the other. Pyah walks over to the bed, "What's this for?" she asks, croaking the question.

Rose sits on it, "It's a shower bed. You lay on it and the water cascades from above but the mattress is porous so the water can be forced up through it giving a massage from below," she pats for Pyah to sit next to her, "most of my patrons will pay extra to perform on this," she says, giving Pyah a dirty little girl smile.

Pyah chuckles "I presume by perform you mean shag?"

Rose laughs out loud, "Call a spade a spade, eh? Whatever. But I can say that it makes for an interesting experience."

Pyah sits next to her, "Seems comfy," she comments, looking up at Mark, "you never know," she says, raising her eyebrows "if we have to be stuck here?"

Mark grumps around, "Do we have to stay here? In this room? I mean, come on, even you'll get bored."

Rose stands up, takes Mark by the hand and leads him back outside, "Down there," she directs, pointing to a doorway to the left, "that's the dining room and just beyond that is the kitchen. Both can be accessed from here," she says, showing him a stone stairway down, "plus if you don't mind wearing something a little more discrete you could always take a walk to the Harbour," she adds, pointing to the rear of the property, "then of course there's always my limo which has privacy glass," she continues, indicating a set of garages just sticking out from the corner of the house, "I mean, who's going to look at an Arab and his western mistress wearing a big floppy hat?" she asks, cocking her head to one side.

Mark closes his eyes, then shakes his head, "You mean a disguise?"

Rose shrugs, "And why not? It could be fun. Bit of roleplay never hurt anyone and no one would bat an eyelid coming from here," she says, giving a little chortle and patting him on the back, "think about it," she suggests, then leaves them to get comfortable.

Pyah decides to try the shower bed while Mark pours himself a scotch to reflect on recent happenings. There is a knock at the door so Mark opens it to a couple of young ladies in French maid's outfits, "Err, sorry, not tonight ladies," he says, assuming they are here to render sexual services, "the last time I had a French maid in the room the wife threatened to throw her off a very high balcony," he adds, trying to usher them back out of the door.

One of them stands firm with her hands on her hips, "Apparently you have a spillage outside on the veranda? We're here to clean it up."

At that Pyah shouts out, "What is it honey?"

Mark pops his head around the bathroom door, "Well, we have maids here wanting to clean up your sick."

Pyah just shrugs, "OK, lead them to it."

Mark scowls, "They're French maids."

Pyah shrugs again, "You said they're here to clean up the sick, not clean up the prick, so what's the problem?" she asks, chuckling to herself.

Mark scowls again, "OK ladies, it's this way," he tells them, leading them out onto the veranda.

The maids do their job then leave without giving Mark a second look. Pyah finishes her shower, "Your turn," she says, then changes into a negligee to climb into bed.

Mark jumps in the shower. While he's in Pyah sneaks over to the door, bangs on it loud enough for Mark to hear, then call out "Who is it?"

She then walks past the bathroom door, "That'll be fine, I think over on the bed will be just dandy."

Mark calls out, "Who is it dear?"

Pyah sticks her head around the bathroom door, "Oh, it's just a guy in a thong come to give me a massage," she says, then quickly closes the door to Mark's objections.

"I don't fucking think so," he shouts, coming hurtling out of the bathroom dripping wet, fully naked only to stop and scan the room, "OK, where is he?"

Pyah is buried in the pillow, fitting with laughter. Mark walks back in the bathroom, picks up a towel, walks back out to her still howling with laughter then cracks her across her behind with a swift flick of the towel. She jumps across the bed, "Whoa, you bastard, shit, shit, shit," she curses, rubbing her buttocks, "Jesus, that fucking hurt."

Mark wobbles his head, "Well, you won't wind me up like that again will you?" he says, turning smugly to strut back into the bathroom.

Pyah picks up a can of cola straight from the fridge, shakes it violently then opens it, spraying the ice-cold contents all down his back, leaving him arching his back, running for cover. Pyah slams the can down, "Well, you won't be flicking my arse any time soon."

Mark waves a white towel out of the door, "Truce? You win."

Pyah climbs into bed, "Just get a bloody shower and come to bed," she says, still rubbing her bum.

The day has taken it out of her, finding her falling to sleep before Mark returns. He tucks her in and nods off into a comfortable sleep.

CHAPTER 39
SWIM AND RIDE

The sound of birdsong flourishes through the garden as the sun breaks the horizon. A haze drifts in on the sea air from the harbour, drawing Pyah gently from her slumber. Stretching on the luxurious bed she smiles inwardly as she gazes at Mark snuggling into one of the soft sumptuous pillows that adorned the hexagonal bed. Wrapping herself in a chiffon negligee, she opens the curtains, opens the French doors, then steps out onto the veranda to take in the fresh sea air. The sky is alive with the sound of seagulls squawking.

The open window allows the sound to penetrate Mark's senses, abruptly bringing him into an unwelcome reality, "Do you have to have that fricking door open," he moans, pulling the pillow over his head, "either shut it or shoot those fucking birds."

Pyah saunters back into the room, gently closing the door behind her, "So you won't want a shag then, grumpy?"

Mark slowly pulls the pillow from his head, "Well, that kind of all depends on how you want it."

Pyah cocks her head, "Well, I was thinking maybe in there," she says, pointing at her vagina, "then we could take a walk down to the harbour."

Mark contemplates for a moment, "Shag? Yeah. Walk to the harbour? No," he says, shaking his head.

Pyah shrugs, "Just thought you might be interested seeing as though I just heard the definite tone of a Ferrari and a Lambo pulling in over there."

Mark gives her a sideways look, "I think the shag can wait," he declares, jumping out of the bed then heading for the bathroom.

Pyah's eyes widen as her jaw drops, "You have got to be shitting me?" she huffs, strutting into the bathroom after him, "I'm being passed over for a fucking car?"

As she turns the shower to the cold setting Mark screams, "Oh, shit, you! You did not just do that?" he shouts, jumping out from under the shower head.

He grabs Pyah by the waist then pulls her under the cold water, "Come on, let's see how you like it? Two can play at that game," he says, shivering as he holds his screaming wife under the freezing cascade of water.

Pyah reaches for the hot tap but Mark pulls her hands down to hold her in a hug, "No, no, no, you don't get away with it that easy," he insists as he lets her go to jump out again.

Pyah steps out shivering, "Oh, you're going to get it," she warns, throwing the drowned negligee to the floor to wrap a bath sheet around herself, "trust me, you're going to get it. Just when you're least expecting it, I'll have my revenge," she threatens, waving a finger at him.

It's not long before he is donning a pair of shorts and a T-shirt, "I'm ready."

Pyah walks out of the bathroom in an airy full-length smock, "Ha, you can't wear that," she tells him, tossing a white smock and Arab head dress at him, "you heard what the FBI said. We have to wear disguises if we want to go out," she reminds him, then she plonks a floppy hat on with a large pair of sun glasses.

Mark looks at the smock, "You're kidding, right?" he checks, throwing it on the bed, "I'll wear the head dress but there is no way I'm going out in that. There's nowhere to put my gun and I'll look stupid."

Pyah lifts her skirt, "And where are you going to carry your gun in a pair of shorts?"

Mark walks over to the wardrobe, "I'll put a jacket on," he says, pulling a bomber jacket out.

Pyah laughs at him, "And you don't think you look stupid with that and shorts?" she asks, placing a garter holster around her leg.

Mark rubs his chin, "You got a spare one of those?"

Pyah drops her head, "You want to wear a garter holster?"

Mark picks up the smock, "If I'm wearing this then I want one of them."

She walks over to a draw, pulls out a spare, then throws it at him, "You won't like it."

He starts to strap it to his leg, "Oh shit, got to be careful I don't get the butt up my butt."

Pyah laughs, "Yeah, and watch you don't dong the barrel with your donger."

She kneels down to adjust it for him then he puts the smock over the top of his boxer shorts, "Hmm, it's quite airy and comfortable actually."

The pair head out onto the veranda to make their way around the maze to the rear exit. Mark starts to wriggle, "Bloody gun feels weird there."

Pyah opens the gate, "Oh, for Christ's sake, if you're going to walk like that you'll look like a proper moron. Which will just attract attention so walk normal."

Mark walks out behind her, "Well its digging into my leg and--," he stops suddenly, "oh my God," he says, looking out across the harbour at all the boats, launches, yachts and exotic cars, "wow, there's some money there," he breathes, drifting unencumbered across the highway, all thoughts of discomfort blown away by the sight of all this wealth.

Pyah walks along beside him, "Here, you might need these," she says, slamming a pair of binoculars into his chest, "and I think you might get a better view from up there," she adds, pointing at a small rock jutting out from the promenade.

The pair head up the rock, "Oh, I'm in heaven," he says as he scans the harbour through the binoculars, "and have you seen the size of that one out there?" he asks, pointing at an extremely large yacht outside the bay, "wonder what they're doing? Probably smuggling," he figures with a little chortle, "I DON'T FUCKING BELIEVE IT!" he shouts, handing the binoculars to Pyah, "quick, look. Is it my imagination or is that Anja Koliakova on that yacht?"

Pyah stares at the boat, "Holy shit, Ben's on there with her and if I'm not mistaken that's a periscope by the side of the boat."

Mark snatches the binoculars from her, "You're kidding, right?" he assumes, but amazingly she is telling the truth, "I thought the NSA had her in custody?"

Pyah starts to phone Cramer, "And what the hell is that traitor doing with her?"

Mark grabs the phone, "I think we should investigate this ourselves before informing anyone ok?"

Pyah gives him a dumb look, "And how are we supposed to do that?"

Mark smiles eerily, "That place," he gestures, pointing back at the brothel, "is a sadomasochist house," he says, nodding knowingly, "right?"

Pyah gives him a blank look, "So?"

He shakes his head and huffs, "They're into leather and rubber and stuff, yeah?"

Pyah shakes her head, "Not following you."

Mark sighs, "I'll bet you they have wet suits and diving gear because some freak is bound to want to do it in one."

Pyah still puzzled starts, "Do what... oh shit, you mean? Hang on, how the fuck do you fuck in a wet suit? It's impossible, we know, we tried it, remember?"

Mark shakes his head, "They fantasise," he says, shrugging.

Pyah smirks, "Yeah, that's about all you can do in one of those things. But you could be right," she says, following him back to the house, "so when do we go and what do we tell Rose about the wet suits?"

Mark laughs, "She'll probably think we're getting kinky. Why tell her any different? Then we go as soon as we're ready."

By the time they get back to the bordello, patrons are starting to frequent the place, the kitchen is all abuzz as breakfast is being prepared, the girls are exercising in the grounds, while staff are showing guests the amenities. Mark and Pyah have to make a discrete entrance then slip up to their room unnoticed. Pyah pulls the sash to gain attention. Almost immediately a young girl comes knocking on their door, "Can I be of assistance?"

Pyah turns sheepishly, "I was just wondering if you had a pair of..." she pauses, hesitating with a definite blush. "ahem, wetsuits?"

The girl turns to walk down the hall, "Certainly. Would you like snorkels with them?" she asks without so much as a bat of an eye, then waiting for Pyah's reply.

Pyah, stunned, coughs, "Wouldn't mind some scuba tanks if that's not a problem?"

Completely unfazed the girl produces a notepad, "Single or twin tanks? Empty or full?"

Pyah shakes her head, "Err, well, twin if you have them and full of course, I suppose."

Moments later the girl returns with two burly men carrying the requested items. The men place the items on the bed as the girl turns to Pyah, "One male for Mister Fischer and one female for yourself? They should fit, but if there is any problem just pull the cord and we will endeavour to rectify it, have a good day," she says, then she closes the door as she leaves.

Pyah is stood dumbfounded but Mark is already stripped, donning the wetsuit, "Bloody hell, they got my size perfect."

Pyah shakes her head, "Not a question as to why we want them?" she asks, her eyes wide, "what the hell goes on in this place? Does nothing faze them?"

Mark scowls at her, "Come on! It's a brothel. A sadomasochist brothel with Subs and Doms. That's what they call them isn't it?"

Pyah shrugs, "Suppose so, but what the hell can you do in a fricking wet suit? Nothing! We know, we tried," she slips into her wetsuit as they both head out, unencumbered by the patrons.

Pyah is still flabbergasted that they attract no attention whatsoever, "Look at them. Too busy shagging and groping to even give us a second glance. And this early on a morning too?" she says, shaking her head in disgust.

Mark sniggers to himself, "And you call me a prude?" he teases, deliberately leering at her.

Pyah slaps him across the arse, "Come on, let's get out of here before you start to like it."

It isn't long before they are in the water swimming out to the launch and submarine. Surprisingly the water is quite warm, no predators even though Mark is being overly cautious. When they come upon the sub its engines are running, ready to leave as the last of the cargo is transferred to the launch. Pyah and Mark surface on the blind side of the sub, then work around to the launch just in time for the sub to leave. Listening they hear Ben's voice telling Anja to get the cargo stowed ready for transfer at midnight.

Pyah uses sign language to convey to Mark, "Wonder where they are transferring it to?"

Mark signs back, "Must be somewhere on shore, otherwise they would have left by now."

They decide to head back to shore, to observe the launch from a safe distance. Donning their disguises, they sit on one of the promenades with a computer pad attached to a hidden zoom camera to observe the vessel. The boat does not move but Anja and Ben can frequently be seen to come up on deck to check their surroundings. On a number of occasions both Ben and Anja look directly at the Fischers so Pyah decides they should take a walk then maybe return to the brothel.

On returning to the bordello they ring for room service, deciding to pop out on occasion to check on their quarry. Pyah is getting bored, "I hate this."

Mark snuggles into her, "Patience, my dear, it's just a waiting game."

Pyah fidgets, "I need something to take my mind off it."

Mark starts to nuzzle into her neck as he slips his hand inside her bra, "Will this do?"

She moans pleasurably, "Hmm, it's a start," she breathes, pushing her neck towards his lips like a cat being stroked.

His other hand gently lifts her smock, then slides down into her pants, "Taking your mind off it?"

Pyah starts to wriggle, "Off what?"

He pulls her mouth around to his, then sweeps her up into his arms, "I think it's about time we tried that shower bed out, don't you?"

Pyah just sighs in agreement. He carries her into the wet room still nuzzling into her neck then places her gently down while lifting her smock over her head. She reaches down to lift his smock over his head, throwing it to the ground as he lifts her up onto the shower bed. Pulling her pants off he teases the tops of her legs with his tongue, then reaches up to loosen her bra while kissing her breasts. She pushes his boxers down as far as she can, before wrapping her legs around him to flick them off with her feet.

Mark presses his lips against hers as he turns on the under shower which bubbles up through the mattress to give a soothing water massage to Pyah's spine. She moans gently as he selects the lowest setting for the overhead shower. A gentle mist drifts down on to the couple as he inserts his penis slowly into her, pulling her hips towards him while caressing her nipples with his tongue. Pyah turns the under shower up one notch as the water vibrates along her back, "Wow you need to try this, it might put some umph into your stroke," she suggests, giggling like a schoolgirl.

Mark rolls her over on top of him, "Hmm, seems a bit strange but I could get used to it," he judges, then rolls her back onto her back and turns the overhead shower to the next level as the moderate rain type feeling cascades down on them.

Pyah turns the under shower up fully then the water seems to be pummelling her spine, but before she can reach up to turn it down Mark turns the overhead to its maximum as a torrent of water cascades down like a waterfall, almost drowning poor Pyah. She coughs and splutters, "Turn it off!" she coughs, trying to reach the knobs as Mark's head is plunged into her shoulder, "for fuck's sake," she pants, trying unsuccessfully to throw him to one side, gasping for air only to get a mouthful of water.

Mark blindly reaches for the buttons then manages to reduce the overhead to a mist, but the under shower is now rushing over Pyah's face. She slides out from under him to sit up on the edge of the bed, coughing and spluttering, water gushing out through her nose, "Jesus, I think this whole place is out to fucking drown me," she groans, retching forwards, being almost physically sick.

She stands over the sink in front of her, turns the cold water on to rinse the flannel out, then wipes her nose and face, still coughing up water. Mark lies on his side, "It's only a bit of water," he says, a jovial tone to his quip.

Pyah takes the toothbrushes and toothpaste from a glass and fills it with cold water, "It's all right for you, I was getting it from all sides," she says, drinking the soothing cold water.

Mark smiles, "So I guess you don't want another go?" he checks, giggling as he drops his head onto his hand.

Pyah fills the glass with the freezing water, "Here, you try it," she says, tossing the whole glass straight in his face.

The shock of the cold causes him to gasp, inhaling a good mouthful as he starts to cough water through his nose, "OK, ok, I get your point."

Pyah is ready for him, sure he will fly off the handle but he just stands up, grabs a towel, and wipes his face, still spluttering water through his nose, "Yeah, I think we'll leave that one alone in future."

Evening drifts in as they descend to the kitchen, cook themselves some food, then sit in a deserted dining room to eat. The conversation turns to what they would like to do to both Ben and Anja before formulating a plan for their next adventure out to the yacht.

CHAPTER 40
FOOD FIGHT

With the conversation, the time passes quickly, so before long they are back up in their room, donning the wetsuits again for a jaunt down through the harbour.

As they are about to plunge into the depths Pyah stops Mark, "I have a funny feeling we won't have to get out there," she says, pointing at a small launch heading their way, "if I'm not mistaken, that looks like our man Benjamin heading this way."

Mark quickly drags Pyah under the jetty, takes off his scuba tanks and hangs them on a nearby hook. Pyah follows suit as the launch arrives. They watch as Ben starts to order a mixed nationality of men to move four crates off the launch then load them into a waiting pickup.

Once loaded, Ben takes the vehicle off down the road. Mark grabs a bicycle, pops Pyah across the cross bar, then pedals for all he is worth after the truck. Luckily for Mark, the truck only travels about a mile down the highway before entering a small warehouse.

Pyah dismounts, "Shit, that doesn't do a lot for your sex life," she comments, rubbing her buttocks.

Mark just smiles, "Yeah, not exactly the most comfortable or dignified form of transport, but it's the only thing I could find at such short notice."

Pyah scowls at him, "There was a Ferrari just down the way."

Mark rolls his eyes, "And by the time I had run to it, hotwired it, then got back here, we'd have lost them."

Pyah shrugs "I can still see the harbour from here."

Mark shakes his head, "But I didn't know that at the time now, did I?" he says, climbing up to a small window, "now you keep a fricking eye out for that traitorous bastard while I figure out what's going on."

As he looks through the window he can see the crates being offloaded while Ben is making a phone call. Soon Ben is locking the door then taking both the truck and men back to the harbour

Pyah starts to pick the lock of the warehouse. Once inside Pyah inspects the crates, "Thought so, these are the missing rockets," she says but Mark is off mooching around the rest of the warehouse.

Pyah tries to lift one of the crates, "We have a problem, honey," she breathes, struggling to even lift one end, "how are we going to move these, because we sure as hell can't leave them here."

Suddenly, Mark appears driving a golf cart he found at the back of the warehouse, "Oh, I think I may have that covered."

Pyah rolls her eyes, "OK, so now tell me what we're going to do with them."

Mark jumps off the cart, taps his nose, then starts to lift the crates onto it, "Trust me, just let's get them out of here before someone catches us."

Once loaded Mark heads back to the harbour, "When we were under that jetty I noticed something that might just do the trick."

Pyah goes along in anticipation. At the jetty Mark offloads, the crates straight into the water, "Yes! that's fucking what I call lucky," he exclaims, pushing the crates across the surface, "they float."

Pyah still has no clue as to his plan but say's nothing. She climbs into the water, then swims under the jetty, "I'm presuming we'll need these?" she asks, handing Mark his scuba tanks.

Mark nods, "Probably," he agrees, dons his, then starts to push the crates toward the rock face that creates a natural cove around the bay.

Soon the crates are gently bobbing against the rocks, "OK, now we need to get down there," he directs, pointing under the water, "looks like an underwater cave if I'm not mistaken."

Pyah dives while Mark stays topside with the crates. Soon Pyah is surfacing in a small cavern with a shelf just large enough to take all four crates. She swims back out to Mark, "OK, they'll fit but how are we going to submerge them?"

Mark produces a crowbar that he secreted from the warehouse, opens the crates, floats out the contents, then smashes the wood against the rocks, "Now if we open these cases they should sink and we can drag them into the cave one by one."

It isn't long before the rockets are safely hidden away and the Fischers are back at the bordello acting as if nothing has happened. Pyah orders some light refreshment to celebrate their victory, "Suppertime methinks. All that swimming has made me hungry."

Mark ponders, "You know what, I'm bloody starving, I could eat a scabby horse between two pissy wet mattresses," he exaggerates, snorting to himself, "in fact, I think I might just slum it a bit and get one of those kebabs with a lashing of chilli sauce, topped off with lashings of garlic sauce."

Pyah drools, "Ooo, in that case I want a chilli dog. One of those massive ones with everything on it, followed by an Eton mess for two."

While they wait for their food they decide to shower and cosy down in a pair of onesies they found in the wardrobe. Pyah giggles at Mark as he twirls in his Batman onesie but then he stops to admire her in her My Little Pony onesie, "You know, it doesn't matter what you wear you always look stunning."

She bows to him, "Why, thank you, kind sir. It's a shame you look like a proper twallock in yours. A cuddly twallock but a twallock all the same."

Mark looks confused, "What the hell is a twallock?" he asks, flailing his arms, admiring himself in the mirror.

Pyah sniggers, "It's a cross between a twat and a bollock," she says as she starts to make a run for the bathroom.

Mark spins and grabs a pillow, "Oh, you're going to get it, my dear," he says, slamming into the door as Pyah tries to lock it behind her, "that's not going to stop me, you cheeky wench," he insists, barging in to pummel her with the pillow.

He picks her up over his shoulder then struts back to the bed, flinging her onto it, "So, I'm not only a bollock but I'm a twat too?" he asks, jabbing a finger down into her neck, "I'll show you who's a twallock," he threatens, tickling her like you would a child, "Mister Wiggly might have something to say about that," he teases, wriggling his finger then pushing it back into her neck.

He's just about to start unzipping her onesie when there is a knock at the door, "Oh fuck. Who is it?" he asks, despite knowing it's room service.

A soft voice replies, "Room service."

He opens the door as a waft of pungent aromas drift into the room, followed by Rose pushing a small maid's trolley, "Hungry, are we? Thought I better bring this up myself and see if you have finished with the wetsuits."

Pyah walks into the bathroom to retrieve them, "Yes, here they are, thank you."

Rose takes them, strokes them, then sniffs them, "Enjoy our little jaunt down at the harbour, did we?"

Pyah tries to look puzzled but Rose smiles, "We don't have salt water on the premises," she smiles and tucks the suits under her arm, "I'll have these cleaned and forget I said anything," she says tapping the side of her nose.

She starts to leave, then spins, "Oh by the way, while you weren't out swimming Cramer called to see how you were holding up. I told him you were otherwise engaged, if you know what I mean?" she teases, winking at Mark, "he said he'll be over in the morning to check on you so don't disappear," she gives a cock of her head then shuts the door, "night, night, have fun," she says, then leaves them to enjoy their food.

Pyah picks up the chilli dog, "Hmm, lovely," she sighs as she takes a bite.

Mark sniffs at his kebab, "Ahh, one thing those Brits got right," he declares then smothers it with the garlic, then the chilli sauce.

Pyah snatches a piece of the kebab from his plate and shoves it into her mouth. Mark gives her a sideways look as she dribbles the sauce down her chin sniggering. Mark picks another piece off his plate, "Want some more?" he asks, then shoves it in her face and rubs it all over her chin and nose.

Pyah drops her chilli dog, "Oh, now look what you did," she huffs, picking the dog up, "oh, you gonna get it now," she warns, slapping it down on his head, then rubbing it into his hair.

Mark jumps back, "Shit," he says, looking down as it comes dribbling down over his shoulders, "so you want to play, do you?" he asks, diving towards her, grabbing her top, then shoving his kebab down her bra to slop it all over her breasts.

Pyah struggles to stop him, "Oh, you bastard," she yells, laughing at the top of her voice.

Mark tries to shut her up, "You'll wake everyone up."

Pyah rolls on top of him so the juice of the kebab runs out onto his chest, then picks up the Eton mess, "Who the hell gives a fuck," she declares, slamming it into his trouser tops, taking a handful down into his boxers, "let's see how you like it."

Mark pushes her backwards, "Oh you bitch, this means war," he says, grabbing a handful then first ramming it down into her pants before slapping it all over her face and hair.

The food is flying everywhere as there is a knock at the door then Rose walks in with another trolley, "This is just going to waste and I thought you might be able to use it," she says, throwing a gateau over to Pyah.

Pyah catches it, "Yes!" she shouts, then slams it into Mark's face.

Two other girls are walking past the room so they stick their heads in, "Ooo nothing like a good food fight."

Mark beckons them in and they don't need a second asking before he has Rose pinned on the bed, leaving the two girls to attack Pyah. He grabs a jelly from the trolley, "So you thought you could instigate without consequences?" he asks, dropping the jelly straight down her top, "well you can think again."

Rose turns from a stern madam into a giggling child as the jelly slithers down her torso all the way onto her vagina, "Oh, you think you have the better of me? Think again, I was doing this before you were even a wrinkle in your daddy's knacker sack!"

She grabs him by his lapel, rolls him onto his back, reaches out to the trolley, picks up two fresh cream croissants, then slams them against his cheeks. Quickly reaching out to grab a large lemon torte, she rolls him on to his front then shoves it down the back of his trousers, "Let's see how you like that, young man," she cries, smearing it right around from back to front, "oh my word, I think I might have to get some more to feed that monster," she adds as she takes a firm hold of his penis, turning to Pyah, "you lucky, lucky girl."

Pyah gives her a wry grin just as the girls force two fresh cream muffins straight down her top, "Well, he isn't objecting so go for it. I'm a little preoccupied at the moment," she says, fending the girls off while trying to get to the trolley for some more ammunition.

She slides off the bed, but as she is reaching for a chocolate gateau it's whipped away from her by one of the girls and rammed up between her legs as the other girl throws her back on the bed, producing two tins of squirty cream, "Hold her skirt," she directs, then she shoves one tin down the back and one down the front to fill Pyah's pants to the brim.

Pyah can't help but just lay on the bed, wriggling and giggling. Mark manages to unzip Rose's catsuit while pinning her down. He grabs the last of the cakes off the trolley to shove into it, smearing it all over her as she lies in submission, "OK you win, do your worst," she says, still holding on to his penis, "but I get a go on this when you're finished?"

Mark realises that she has a very firm, toned body and can't believe that she is sixty-two, "Damn, woman, you must work very hard to keep so trim," he remarks, caressing her bosom, "I'm very surprised, I actually thought these were fake."

Pyah shoots up into a sitting position, "Whoa, you mean they're real!?"

Mark squeezes Rose's boobs through the cream, "Every fucking morsel," he confirms, inviting Pyah to hold them.

This is much to the delight of Rose as she spreads her arms in satisfaction, "And it's all yours."

Pyah confidently runs her hands up over Rose's shoulders to lift the catsuit off, then pulls it all the way down to her feet. The two girls watch in amazement to see their Madam being the submissive for the first time.

CHAPTER 41
EXPERIMENTING SUBMISSIVELY

Pyah can't believe that Rose has no cellulite, no wrinkles, no flab and it's all natural, "Holy shit, I wouldn't mind a body like this when I'm your age."

Rose reaches up to the restraints on the bed, "Good living, swimming, healthy food and lots of good old fashion lust," she prescribes, laughing as she places her hands through the restraints.

She spreads her legs for Pyah to put her feet into the ankle restraints then look up at Mark, "OK I'm all yours, let's see what that monster can do."

Mark stands up, "Not yet, my dear," he tells her as he drops a CD into the player.

A soft bass beat starts to play as Mark struts his stuff, trying to provocatively strip the cake-covered clothes from his body.

Pyah sits on the edge of the bed giggling as Rose lifts her head, "Oh my God!" she exclaims, rolling her eyes then slamming her head back into the pillow.

Pyah walks over to the drinks cabinet, produces a bottle of whisky, then slinks back to Rose, gently pouring it across her stomach so she can drink it from her belly button, "Hmm fresh cream, whisky and woman, what a beastly amusing combination."

Mark slithers up Rose's legs, licking the cream from them as she moans in anticipation. As he reaches her vagina he gives her clitoris a gentle flick with his tongue before proceeding to meet Pyah at Rose's navel. Lapping at the whisky, he picks a strawberry from her hip between his teeth to drop into the whisky, then retrieves it with his teeth, offering it up to Pyah's mouth as she bites it away from him, "Hmm strawberries just top this concoction off nicely methinks," she breathes.

The two girls stand watching in sheer awe as Pyah and Mark feed like two hungry predators off Rose's torso, astonished that their dominatrix has so easily converted to submissive. Mark licks his way up onto her breasts, suckles briefly, then gently nibbles on her neck, while Pyah slowly pulls her legs apart to drop in-between them. The two girls sit on a couch opposite, both on the edge of the seat, completely astonished at what Rose is allowing as they watch and listen to her wriggling and moaning. Rose whispers in Mark's ear, "Jingle bells."

Mark frowns, "Is that supposed to mean something?"

Rose smiles seductively, "It's my safe words."

Pyah sits up, "Safe words?"

Rose bites her lip, "Ah ha, do what you want but if I say jingle bells, you stop?"

One of the girls steps forward, "She means you can hurt her, she likes pain, but just to make sure you don't go too far she has a safe word."

Pyah digs her claws into Roses hips, "So if I do this and she says no or stop I can carry on until she says jingle bells?"

The girl gives a sheepish smile, "You got it," she confirms as she sits back to enjoy the show.

Mark rubs his chin, "Don't know about that like, I was brought up not to hurt a woman."

Pyah leans forward, "I wasn't," she says as she grasps at Rose's breasts, lifting her off the bed by them.

Rose gasps but Mark cringes. One of the girls stands up then walks over to the wardrobe and pushes a hidden button at the back as the wardrobe slides out to reveal a small hidden closet full of sex toys, whips, masks, manacles and chains, "You can use these if it takes your fancy," she says, then she walks to the side of the bed, "this also does this," she adds, pushing a button on the bedpost.

Rose is lifted by the restraints on her wrists and brought to the vertical position, hanging by her wrists. One of the girls slips Rose's feet into the lower restraint, "There you go, you can even flog her," she remarks, throwing a cat o' nine tails to Pyah, "trust me, she'll let you know if she wants you to stop."

Mark slopes over to the closet, pretending to show some sort of interest as Pyah gently lashes at Roses buttocks. Suddenly Mark's head cocks over as he spots something of interest, "So what's this?" he asks, picking up a white object that appears to be made of porcelain, about eighteen inches long with a balled end on it.

One of the girls sniggers, "It's a clit-tickler," she takes it off him then twists the ball as it starts to vibrate, "you push it against the clit," she explains, pointing down at her own vagina.

Mark shrugs then pushes it against the girl's clitoris. She quivers, "The further you turn the ball the heavier the vibrations."

Mark spins it all the way around.

"Jesus, this is like a jack hammer now," the girl grasps his wrist and forces it towards her vagina, "no point in wasting it," she says as her head drops on to Mark's shoulder, then her legs involuntarily clamp around the toy.

Mark gives Pyah an unsure look but she is engrossed in Roses delight. The other girl stands up, struts over to Pyah, relieves her of the cat then lashes Rose so as to break the skin, "Told you she likes it," she says then hands the whip back to Pyah.

Rose slants a look across her way, "Later madam, later."

The girl arrogantly smiles back at Rose, "Is that a promise?" she asks, provocatively sucking on her own finger.

Pyah peeks around to see what Mark is up to then decides to take a look in the cupboard. The girl follows, leering at Pyah's arse, "Hmm, wouldn't mind playing with that."

Pyah reaches into the closet, "What's this?" she asks, pulling two lengths of nylon rope out to reveal clamps attached to the ends.

The girl smiles, "Oh, they are one of my favourites," she says, gently taking them from Pyah, "nipple clamps," she goes on, holding them up to her breasts, "and the string goes up through there," she directs, pointing at the bed's canopy.

Pyah intently watches as the girl reaches up to two discretely placed loops in the bed's canopy to place the thread. She passes one clamp to Pyah then gently places the other on Roses nipple. Pyah mimics her actions to the delight of Roses moans. Once the clamps are secured the girl pulls Rose's foot restraint, "Starfish her first," she says, smiling at Pyah as Rose is now hanging on her wrist restraints, then the girl hands Pyah one of the strings, "gently lift her."

Pyah gives an unsure frown as the girl starts to lift Rose by her nipple, "Together," she instructs, beckoning Pyah to pull on the rope.

Pyah tentatively raises Rose by her nipple but is soon astonished as Rose's head is flung back, gasping in euphoric pleasure with her breasts fully stretched against her foot and wrist restraints. Pyah shrugs "Whatever floats your boat, I suppose?"

Rose's back is arched with arms outstretched, crucified to her own desire. Pyah wanders back to the closet to see what else is on offer. Mark is still propping the other girl up as she twitches and squirms. Pyah's girl reaches into the closet producing a pair of leather wrist restraints. She hands them to Mark and points at a hook on the back of the wardrobe, "Hang her up there."

As Mark restrains the girl, Pyah's girl reaches in once more to produce what looks a bit like a scissor jack, "Put this between her knees."

Mark straps the device between her knees then starts to wind her legs open, "Novel I suppose. Wouldn't mind a set of those nipple clamps like," he says and she hands him a pair.

She sees Pyah lifting a weird contraption from the back of the closet, "What the hell is this thing?"

The girl reaches in, "Ooo, forgot about that," she coos, almost snatching it away from Pyah, "she had this commissioned for herself but never had the courage to try it out," she explains, spinning towards Rose, "I think it's about time we find out if it actually works."

The object consists of a board with a leg strap, a motor with a wheel attached to two eight-inch rubber penises, "It straps to her knees and the rest is self-explanatory," the girl says, placing it on Rose's legs, "one goes in here," she explains, pushing one dildo into Rose's anus, "then the other goes here," she directs, popping the other into Rose's vagina before returning to the closet to retrieve a battery, "now we connect this and switch it on."

Rose looks down in anticipation, "Slowly!" she orders, "I don't know what that thing will do to me."

The girl points at a lever, "This is the speed control but we have to make sure the distance is set," she says, rolling the wheel by hand, "yep that's got enough clearance," she judges, then she slowly turns the control as the wheel starts to rotate pushing the dildos in and out alternatively.

Pyah stands back as Rose's head lurches back over to groans of, "Yes, yes, yes."

Pyah shrugs at the girl, "So now what do we do?"

The girl stands on the bed, "Whatever you want," she says, reaching down to rub Roses clitoris.

Pyah stands arms folded, "That's about all you can do," she sulks, feeling like a spare prick at a wedding watching Rose writhe with ecstasy, "her tits are occupied, as is her muff and ass," she says, reaching around to grasp a handful of Rose's hair, "the only other thing that isn't is her mouth," she says, thrusting her tongue down Rose's throat.

Pyah climbs down off the bed a little despondent, "So what you up to, dear husband?" she asks, watching him strap his girl's waist to the back of the wardrobe.

Mark gives Pyah a sideways look, "Well if I can prise this damned dildo from between her legs I was thinking of giving her a good shagging like."

The other girl with Rose jumps down off the bed, "I hope you have protection?"

Mark smiles at her, "Sort of," he says, patting his sidearm.

The girl gives him smug condescending leer, "You know what I mean," she says, reaching into a drawer to produce a condom, "we don't allow unprotected sexual intercourse."

Mark starts to laugh, "What, that thing," he says, pointing at the standard size condom as he drops his fly to let the snake out.

The girl stands in awe, "Holy shit," she says, then turns to head for the bedroom door, "just a sec, I might have the answer to your problem."

Pyah watches her shimmy out then gives Mark a confused look followed by a shrug, "Suppose we'll soon see."

The girl rushes back in the room holding a rather large red-bobbled balloon-type object, "You're going to love this, it's a vibrating condom," she says, holding it up to Pyah's face, "extra-large."

Mark just about snatches it, "You have got to be kidding me," he says, finding a bit of a struggle but managing to force his penis into it, "so how does it work?"

The girl pulls a small wire from around the rim then attaches a small battery pack, "Now all you do is switch it on," she says, flicking a switch.

Mark's eyes light up, "Oh fuck," he remarks as his erection shoots to attention.

He then struts to the girl tied to the back of the wardrobe, "Here's Johnny," he teases, leering like a psychopath as he pushes into her.

The girl immediately starts to twitch into spasms, "Calvin Klein! Calvin Klein! Shit, too much."

Her friend rushes to pull Mark back, "That's her safe word. I'm afraid you may be too big for her."

The tied girl swoons at him, "It's not the girth it's just too long, you were rattling my pelvic bone against my back teeth," she says, smiling at him, "try again, but not too far in please."

Mark is still having problems controlling his ejaculation as he enters her, "Damn, you know how hard it is to pull back in my state," he says as he thrusts forward.

In all of the excitement no one notices Rose's distress as Pyah turns to see her spasmodically vibrating in her restraints almost inaudibly muttering, "jingle bells."

Pyah and the girl jump onto the bed, "Oh shit, she's blacking out."

Rose's eyes glaze over, "Too much, too much, switch it off."

Pyah switches the machine off, then quickly helps the girl untie Rose while extracting it from her. She flops onto the bed into the foetal position as Mark begrudgingly removes his condom, "So what do we do now?"

He unties the girl from the wardrobe as they go to help. All four carry Rose into the bathroom, onto the shower bed and allow the mist to gently dissolve the brown goo mixed with blood from her buttocks.

One of the girls bring some Savlon to sooth Rose's discomfort as the water brings her back into the real world. "Shit, I thought I was a goner," she breathes, placing her hand between her legs, "oh shit, I'm going to be sore tomorrow," she adds, trying to stand but her legs are too far gone so the girls help her out to her own room.

"It's been interesting," they say as they wave, "see you in the morning."

Pyah closes the door behind them, "Well, that was different, I think it's time for some sleep."

Mark sulks slightly, "Tomorrow night," he suggests, holding the vibrating condom.

Pyah smiles, "We'll see," she says, heading for the shower.

CHAPTER 42
SECRET ESCAPES

The breeze can be heard rustling through the trees as the sun creeps over the horizon. Pyah wakes to watch the first rays of sunlight burnish the French sky. Standing on the balcony in silence she breathes the fresh sea air as the first bird breaks into song. A welcome solitude gives her time to reflect as the warm breeze soothes her naked form. Her mind wanders back to Lacey, sorrow and hope fill her heart as tears well in her eyes. Mark arouses from his slumber without notice. Pyah's mind is far from her surroundings as Mark notices her wiping a tear from her cheek. He reaches down, picks up the vibrating condom, then forces it on to his head. Walking out behind her, making just enough noise to let her know of his imminent arrival, he gently places his arms around her waist then kisses her neck, "Morning, beautiful."

Pyah turns to kiss him on his cheek and notices the condom on his head, "Oh my God," she says, rolling her eyes into her head, "what on earth are you supposed to be?"

Mark gives a wry boyish grin, "I'm Ben."

Pyah shakes her head, "What, a bell end?"

Mark wobbles his head, "Nope, I'm a dickhead," he says, laughing out loud.

Pyah glances up at it, "Actually, you're more of a shithead now."

Mark gives a befuddled look, whipping his hand over the top of the condom, "Well, you got me on that one," he comments as he wipes some seagull muck off it.

Pyah laughs, "That seagull just shit on it."

Mark brings his hand down slowly, "Oh, you have got to be kidding me," he complains, carefully taking the condom off to head back indoors, arms outstretched.

Pyah spins, "Now where are you going?"

Mark scowls at her, "To get some loo paper."

Pyah looks at him, then at the seagull, "Don't be stupid, it'll be miles away and you'll never wipe its arse from here," she says, sniggering to herself.

Mark struts into the bathroom, washes his hands, then throws the condom under the shower. Pyah strolls back in behind him but stops when the sound of footsteps coming up the marble stairs to the balcony peek her curiosity. Grabbing the sheet from the bed she starts back out, "Anyone there?"

Cramer greets her at the doorway, "Thought I would give you a chance to make yourself decent. Hope I didn't interrupt anything," he says, infuriatingly winking at Mark as he exits the bathroom, still completely in the buff.

"Actually, you did. We were having a solemn moment I think," Pyah pats her eyes with the sheet "I was just thinking about Lacey. Any news?"

Cramer's head drops, "Still in a coma I'm afraid, but they say she's stable."

Mark grabs his boxers, "Yeah, if I ever get my hands on that Ben the bullet that enters his head won't leave him alive the backstabbing snake," he insists, dragging his trousers up in fury, "I mean fancy asking her to marry him then doing that? Fucking asshole."

Cramer steps forward, "Speaking of Ben Fisher and a certain Russian," he starts, dropping his hands into his pockets, "it seems they have lost some rockets," he continues, his head cocked over to one side smiling, "you two wouldn't know anything about that would you?"

Pyah steps around him, "Excuse me, but more to the point, how do you know about it?"

Cramer looks at the floor, "Well, it seems that the NSA were tracking Ben and the Russian when all of a sudden the aforementioned article went astray."

Pyah shrug, "Sure we don't know what you're talking about," she says, trying a girlish smile.

Cramer puts his arms around Pyah's waist, "The problem is, the NSA suspect that you two had something to do with the disappearance," he says, tapping his foot, "which means that they now suspect that you're somewhere in this area and it won't take them long to find you, so I suggest you get the hell out of here."

Mark huffs, "So, if they find us, what do they think they're going to get out of us?"

Cramer scowls, "The problem is there is a capture or kill order on you."

Pyah spins, "What!? The NSA wants us dead?"

Cramer picks up Mark's suitcase, "Not just the NSA," he warns, throwing the case to Mark, "the CIA are looking for you and we've been told to hang on to you if we know where you are."

Mark grabs his case and quickly starts to fill it, "So who isn't after us?"

Cramer shakes his head, "Well, your friends in the British Secret Service have been warned not to harbour you, but I can't see them taking any notice. Oh yeah, and Interpol have been asked to detain you."

Pyah drops the sheet, "Seems we better get the fuck out of here, don't suppose you have an escape plan?" she asks, standing buck naked in front of Cramer as he blushes slightly.

"Put some clothes on and I'll lay out a plan," he says, averting his eyes, "I do have a friend with a launch ready down there but he will only wait for another hour," he explains, pointing towards the harbour, "don't tell me where you're going, I don't want to know, but find a clean phone and text this number when you're safe," he instructs, handing them a card, "there's a simple cipher on the back. I'm sure you'll figure it out," he says, then he leaves the way he came, leaving Mark and Pyah to quickly pack.

Rose walks in with a food pack and several different disguises, wigs and make-up, "Thought these may help. Good look," she bids them as she walks them down through the maze.

As they approach the harbour a French sailor introduces himself, "I am Alain, a friend of Rose, I will be taking you to your first destination. Come quickly," he says, taking their luggage, then boarding a schooner, "you will be comfortable below deck where you must remain I'm afraid."

The deck hands get busy preparing for cast off while Alain shows the Fischers to their small cabin, "We will arrive at Porto Santo before nightfall," he plonks their luggage on the lower bunk, "once we get through the straights of Gibraltar I will call you," he says, standing in the doorway, "it should be safe for you on deck then, but until then you will have to amuse yourselves."

Pyah smiles at him, "Oh, I think we can do that," she assures, ushering him out, "so long as we're not disturbed."

Alain winks, "I get your meaning. You have about four hours," he says, smiling, "I think that should be sufficient time for amour," he reasons, subtly closing the door as he pulls his head back through it.

The boat rocks gently in the calm sea as Pyah sits, patting the bunk beside her provocatively. The crew can be heard scrambling around the deck above as Mark looks out of a small porthole, "Do you think that's a good idea with all those sailors up top?"

Pyah throws her head back, "Huh, I was just thinking of a cuddle," she says, holding her arms out "just hold me."

Mark gives her a suspicious look, "If I had said that it would definitely not be taken as I want a cuddle."

The couple sit and reminisce over their times with Lacey, hoping above all hope that she is alright. Mark looks deep into Pyah's eyes, "You know, we could try and make it to England to see how she is?"

Pyah's eyes widen, "Something tells me that's the first place everyone will be looking for us."

Mark sits back, points at her and smiles, "Yeah, but that's exactly why we should try. They won't be expecting it," he says with a big wry grin covering his face.

All of a sudden, the captain rushes in, "Sorry to disturb you but we got pirates closing in on us," he warns as he lifts a small bench to reveal a rocket launcher, "either of you two any good with an MG-34 machine gun?"

Pyah jumps up, "Oh, I'll have a go at that please."

Alain leads her and Mark to the deck, "Hopefully it shouldn't come to it because I have a little surprise for them," he says, pointing Pyah towards a canvas shroud, "your toy is under that. Have fun."

Mark runs up a ladder, "I can't see anyone," he says, looking out to sea.

A mate sticks his head out of the bridge, "We have them on radar closing fast, southeast and southwest," he directs, pointing towards the bow of the schooner.

Two dots can be seen moving fast towards them as Alain raises his rocket launcher, "Here they come," he says as he fires a warning shot across the bow of one of the pirate vessels.

Pyah spins the MG-34 towards the pirates, "Are they in range?"

Just at that Alain looks back to the front of his schooner, "Not yet, but I don't think they'll get here anyway," he says, laughing out loud as a Hercules troop carrier flies low overhead, dropping napalm canisters in front of the pirates.

Alain turns to Pyah, "Think you can hit those from here?"

Pyah smiles, "Ooo, let's have a go, eh?" she replies as she starts to riddle the sea with bullets, "yes!" she shouts, blowing the first canister as the pirate boat hits, "this is better than a bloody orgasm any day," she insists, screaming at the top of her lungs, "come on! Bring it on, you bastards," she screams, watching the boat flip through the air end over end.

The second pirate boat tries to avoid the napalm canister but Pyah riddles it with shells, exploding it as the boats aft skims alongside, blowing the tiny boat into a barrel roll, sending its occupants into the plume of flame rising into the air in front of them.

Alain turns to Mark, "She's rather excitable, isn't she?"

Mark just smiles and nods. Alain points at the Hercules, "That's your next mode of transport by the way," he says, walking to the front of the schooner, "it'll land at that island," he explains, pointing at a small island appearing on the horizon, "I'll put you ashore close to the airstrip where the pilot will come to get you."

Mark puts his arm around Alain's shoulders, "So where is this pilot taking us?"

Alain shrugs, "I haven't a clue. My job was just to get you to Porto Santo," he says, waving his arm out to the island, "and that's exactly what I've done. Welcome to Porto Santo."

Soon they are set ashore to sit on a small secluded beach as an extremely large man walks towards them, "You'll be my bonny wee passengers then?" he checks in a surprisingly quiet Scottish brogue.

Pyah's eyebrows lift, "Is that an Aberdeen accent?"

The Scotsman huffs, "Balmedie me dear, just north of Aberdeen. Are you familiar with the place?"

Pyah shakes her head, "Not really, I just have friends that come from that way."

The Scotsman waves his finger, "Well you need to be staying away from them as the powers that be will be keeping a wee eye on all your friends," he picks up all the luggage then escorts them back to his plane, "I hope you're familiar with a touch of parachuting?"

Mark rushes alongside him, "Err, parachuting?" he asks, attempting to pull the man back by his arm, "why would we be parachuting?"

The Scotsman just brushes Marks arm away, "Because my instructions are to drop you out near Faroe Island, north of Scotland, where you'll be picked up by a Russian sub."

This time Pyah rushes up, "Sub? As in submarine?"

The Scotsman nods but carries on walking. Pyah walks in front of him, "A Russian sub? Why Russian?"

The Scotsman just laughs, "Don't worry, he is a very good friend of mine and his sub is extremely well maintained, he's a little eccentric but a good chap."

Soon the Scotsman puts the plane on autopilot then walks back to the Fischers, "OK, here are your 'chutes," he says, handing them two parachutes, "you just hook up there, then when this green light comes on you jump."

Pyah nods, "Yeah, yeah, we have actually done this before."

Mark shakes his head, "No we haven't, this is on a fixed line, we've only jumped freefall and I've only done that tandem."

Pyah shrugs, "Same thing."

The Scotsman chuckles, then heads back to the cockpit, "Happy landings. You go in thirty seconds."

A red light comes on, then the back door opens as Pyah heads out first, "Geronimo!" she yells, diving out headfirst as the fixed line whips her head back, allowing her feet to whip forward unexpectedly, "Oh shit, I think I might have got that wrong."

Mark watches as he steps to the edge, "Don't fucking like this. Stupid woman went before the green light came on."

At that the green light appears, "Oh fuck," he curses, stepping gingerly off the back door of the plane.

The fixed line drags him back as his chute opens, pulling him backwards then swinging him like a pendulum.

Before they know it, they are in the water swimming towards Faroe Island, when out of nowhere a pink submarine surfaces just in front of Mark, "OH MY GOD! I hope for God's sake this captain isn't a fucking woman."

Pyah swims up alongside, "I don't think so, the Scotsman referred to him as a him but he did say he was eccentric," she says, cocking her head.

Mark starts to climb onboard, "Yeah but PINK, talk about inconspicuous?" he says, giggling to himself.

A voice bellows down from the turret, "Yes, but it's under the water so who the hell is going to see it?" a man says, says, followed by a raucous laugh, "you must be the Fischers? Welcome to my little vessel," the man continues, beckoning them to a ladder, "quickly now, we have already picked up your luggage and I don't like to be surfaced for long times, ya?" he says, his almost perfect English breaking down momentarily.

Pyah climbs in first, "So where's our luggage?" she asks, scanning the cramped vessel.

The captain shrugs, "On its way to Scotland as far as I'm aware."

Mark scurries down into the sub, "Scotland!?"

The captain nods, "Ya, a trawler picked it up and is delivering it to the John O' Groats hotel where you will be given instructions."

Mark places his arm around the captain's shoulders, "Oh, so you're delivering us to John O' Groats?"

The captain lifts Mark's arm, "No, no, no, I take you to coast of Kirkwall where we fire you from the torpedo tube towards shore, you swim for about two-hundred-yards where a small fishing boat will pick you up and take you to the Scottish mainland," he tells him, smiling as he walks away, leaving a rather bemused pair contemplating what he just said.

Pyah grabs Mark's hand, "Did he just say what I thought he said? Fired from torpedo tubes?"

Mark rushes up to him, "You're going to fire us out like torpedoes?" he asks, his eyebrows furrowing.

The captain pats him on his back, "Don't worry, we have done this loads of times, never had a fatality yet," he reassures, popping a pipe in his mouth, "you better follow my man to the torpedo room," he says, pointing at another sailor then shooing Mark and Pyah along.

They follow the sailor, but when Mark tries to talk to him he shushes them, "You listen very carefully, yes?"

Mark looks at Pyah then shrugs as the sailor carries on, "You stay underwater till you see yellow marker from fishing boat. It on line under water, yes?"

Mark stops him, "So we swim under the water until we see a line in the water with a yellow marker?"

The sailor rolls his eyes, "Dat what I say, yes? Now listen, it will save time and life," he says, opening the door to the torpedo room, "lots of patrol boats about so you stay underwater till see marker," he instructs, handing them some scuba tanks, "dis goes on front, not like normal. You lay on back. Water fills tube. Outer door open, then we fire you out," he explains as he hands them both neck braces, "must wear these, if neck snap back you die, ok?"

Mark turns to Pyah, "Neck snaps back, you die," he repeats, his eyes wide.

The sailor points up at a set of lights, "When we near, this red light goes on, you climb in, we shut door. When water flooded this light turn orange, when doors open goes green, we fire you. Takes about twenty seconds, ok?"

Mark nods to Pyah as Pyah gives a worried look. The sailor ushers them in as the red light turns on, "Oh, one last thing. Hold mouthpiece in mouth very tight because very difficult to get back until stop."

Mark takes a deep breath, "Oh shit, here goes nothing," he breathes as he lies on his back, his heart pounding for dear life.

Pyah climbs into the second tube, "I do not believe I'm doing this."

A sailor pushes the mouthpiece into her mouth, "Not worry, be done in no time."

The doors are shut as both are thinking "*no turning back now,*" the chambers fill as Mark start to pray to himself.

As the doors open Pyah is thinking "*who the hell puts me in these situations?*"

Suddenly the water rushes out around them. The pressure forces down on their bodies as they can feel the acceleration through the tube. Their blood is driven to their feet as the adrenaline courses through their veins, the only thing preventing them from passing out. As they leave the tubes Mark loosens his grip on the mouthpiece as its whipped out of his hand by the sheer force of the water rushing along his body. The mass of bubbles completely blinding his total vision as he scrambles futilely to find it then swims for the surface on the little breath that he has, hoping he can make it with the extra weight of the scuba gear dragging him down.

He pops up at the surface gasping for air only to see a patrol boat about four hundred meters away, "Shit," he curses, taking a few needed breaths, then finding the mouthpiece and shoving it back in his mouth to dive as quickly as he can.

Hoping he hasn't been spotted he starts to look around in vain for Pyah as he spots the yellow marker from the fishing boat. He swims towards it looking around, waiting for Pyah to suddenly appear out of the darkness. Rising carefully up the line he is met by two sets of arms dragging him out of the water. He spits the mouthpiece out, "Have you seen my wife?"

Pyah's head pops over the side of the boat, "My, you took your time," she says, rubbing a towel through her hair.

Mark climbs onboard to hug her, "Shit, I thought I'd lost you there."

Pyah smiles at him, "Thought you were trying to get yourself caught when you surfaced," she says, placing her arms around his neck, "well now at least you know what a sperm feels like," she points out, teasing him.

Mark kisses her, "It's a bloody good job submarines don't wear condoms then, isn't it?" he jokes, laughing out loud.

He's handed a towel by the boat's captain, "Better get you two below decks before we start to attract attention."

It isn't long before they land at John O' Groats where the captain hands them a couple of raincoats, "You're lucky it's raining, these will help disguise you till you get to the hotel," he reasons, then he hands them new passports, "you're Mr and Mrs Young," he says, handing Pyah hers first, "you're Annabelle," then handing Mark his, "and you're Joseph. The hotel is straight down this track and it's signposted from there. Good luck," he finishes as he jumps back aboard to sail off into the distance.

CHAPTER 43
THE HIGHLAND RUN

Mark turns to Pyah, "Well, Annabelle, shall we?" he asks, holding his elbow out for her to take.

Pyah looks down at her passport, "I kind of like it. Annabelle Young. Sounds like a Quaker or something," she says, giggling to herself.

Mark flicks through his passport, "Well, Joseph fits as a Quaker," he agrees, grinning away as they stroll down the track.

At the hotel, they are greeted by an elderly gentleman stood behind the reception, "Ah, Mr and Mrs Young. I hope you enjoyed your stroll?"

Mark stares at Pyah then back to the gentleman. He is about to speak when the old man slips him a note. It reads, "The two men in the dining room are NSA."

Mark glances at a reflection then back at the man, "Yes, it was lovely, thank you. What time is dinner?" he asks, looking at the man's name tag, "if you don't mind me asking, John?"

John smiles at Pyah, "It's at the usual time, five thirty, and tonight is casual dress. Here are your keys."

Pyah and Mark head up a stairway, hoping they have it right, then disappear around the corner, looking for the door number on the keys. When they reach the room, and open the door Cramer is laid quite comfortably with his arms behind his head, sprawled across the bed, "My, you two took your time didn't you?"

The sound of a flush from the bathroom causes Pyah to reach for her gun, "That better be Fargo," she says, pointing at the bathroom door.

Surprisingly, George from MI6 walks out, drying his hands, "No my dear, it's just little old me, but I'm not here, I'm in London so carry on," he instructs, waving his hand towards Cramer.

Cramer stands up, "We have a little present for you," he says, reaching for a briefcase, "your boss and myself, oh yes, and a little help from MI6," he elaborates, gesturing towards George, "have put a dossier together, something you may be interested in," he explains, passing Pyah a file marked TOP SECRET, "you haven't seen this and if you're caught with it, we don't know where you got it from."

Pyah takes the file, breaks the seal, then stands reading with Mark hovering over her shoulder, "Holy shit, is this all about Ben?"

Cramer nods quite arrogantly, "Some very interesting reading there?"

Pyah scowls towards George, "So you trained him?"

George puts his hands up in submission, "Whoa, MI6 have absolutely no knowledge of his training, as you can see he is of multiple nationalities," he says, tapping the front page of the file, "father British, mother South African and born in the good old U S of A," he reads out, then he flicks on through the pages, "and if you notice here, he was SAS trained, went over to your motherland to train your troops, became a navy seal and disappeared for seven years, resurfacing as a North African safari policeman one year before you came across him. So, no, MI6 had absolutely no knowledge of him or his training thank you!" he insists, then he flicks through to the last few pages, "but the NSA have records of him being involved with something called the Lazarus project. Where it also mentions his involvement with your friend Anja Koliakova, the Russian."

Pyah sits on the bed to start reading through the file from the beginning while Mark puts his arm around George's shoulders, "Two questions, first and most important, how is Lacey? And second, are those two goons downstairs with you?"

Both George and Cramer's heads snap around, "What two goons?"

Without lifting her head from the file Pyah points towards the door, "The clerk at the desk said they were NSA."

Mark sits next to her, "Yeah, two of them sat in the dining room, black suits and all."

George sneaks a peek out the window, "Nope, nothing to do with us, and neither is the car across the way."

Cramer sidles across, "You do realise this is going to be a problem?" he asks, looking George straight in the eye.

Pyah lifts her head momentarily, "For you but not for us, the clerk registered us as Annabelle and Joseph Young, we got passports to prove it too," she says, smiling arrogantly.

George shakes his head, "I know, but I'm supposed to be in London and Cramer isn't in the country, if you know what I mean?"

Mark laughs out loud, "Oh, we are in a bit of a pickle, aren't we?"

George scowls at him, "How the hell are we going to get out of here?"

Pyah opens a bedside drawer, "How about we go and preach the word," she suggests, lifting a Bible while smiling at Mark, "and while those two morons are distracted you slip through the kitchen?"

Cramer frowns, "Preach the word?"

Mark smiles at him, "Yeah, we just became Quakers," he says, donning a wide brimmed hat then rummaging through his case to pull out a rather dapper beard.

George rolls his eyes, "It's daft enough to work," he opens the door, scans outside then steps back in "well, it's all clear, oh, and to answer your question about Lacey," he says, standing with his arms folded, "she's stable. She's in the secure ward at the National Hospital for Neurology and Neurosurgery at Queens Square, London. If you're interested," he explains, giving Mark a wry, knowing grin.

Pyah finds a lace bonnet and a rather 'olde worlde' plaid dress, then heads down the stairs with Mark into the dining room where the NSA agents are having a quiet drink, "Excuse me sir, but you do realise that is the work of Satan?" she asks, pointing at the whisky tumblers.

She places the Bible on the bar beside him as he tries to ignore her. She walks around in front of him, gives a sultry bat of the eyelids then stares provocatively into his eyes, "Satan works in the most cunning ways," she says, touching the agent's knee with her finger.

The agent reaches into his pocket, "Look madam, I don't mean to be rude and I am a good Christian but first off I'm a government agent and at this moment in time I am on duty," he says, flashing his ID towards her, "so I would gratefully appreciate it if you could please leave before I am forced to arrest you for obstruction of justice."

Pyah cocks her head, "Isn't that an American agency? And aren't we in England?" she asks, smiling arrogantly at the agent.

The agent spins towards the bar, "Yes, well actually no, at present we're in Scotland but we do have jurisdiction by permission of the British government so as I said, please leave."

Mark has approached the other agent, "Oh, what I would give to partake in a tipple of that," he sighs, lifting his finger to his lips, "but don't tell the wife. I haven't been with the Friends for very long. Still have a little temptation to discard," he explains, smiling longingly at the agent's glass.

The agent points at Pyah, "It would seem that your wife doesn't hold with your religion?"

Mark shakes his head, "No. She has been with the Friends a lot longer than I have."

The agent smiles, "Seems she is very friendly, in fact, if I didn't know any better I would say she is trying to seduce my partner."

Mark's head drifts around slowly to see his wife stroking the agent's knee with her finger, "Ah, you misunderstand, that is just her way of communicating. She's partially blind," he confides, putting his hand on the man's shoulder, "you see she feels the need to touch everyone she meets," he explains as he starts back towards her, "dear, I think these gentlemen need their privacy."

Pyah reaches for Mark's lapel, "Oh, husband? Have I intruded on something?" she asks innocently, implying the agents are together sexually.

Mark smiles back at the agent, "Sorry for the intrusion. I can understand you wanting to be alone. Our mistake. You two have a good night."

Both agents look at each other as the confusion dissipates and realisation to the implication dawns.

Both agents' heads drop, "They think we're lovers."

Pyah saunters past the reception as John gives her a sly thumb up gesture to indicate that George and Cramer made it. Mark links arms with her to walk regally back up the stairs, "OK, that was easy."

Pyah kisses Mark, "What a pair of clowns!"

Mark's head spins, "Who, George and Cramer?"

Pyah gently slaps his arse, "No, the gormless twins in the bar."

Mark smiles, "OK, now for the hard part. How to get down London."

Pyah shakes her head, "No, the difficult bit will be getting into the hospital, especially Lacey's room."

Mark puts his arm around her waist, "Guess that means we're off to London then, eh?"

On the way to dine John calls Pyah to the reception, "Just an enquiry as to the length of your stay? If I may be so bold."

Pyah leans in close, "Well that kind of all depends on when we can arrange transport down south?"

John hands her a leaflet, "There is a small ferry, leaves here most mornings, that would take you as far as Moray," he says, in the leaflet is a name and address, "and I'm sure someone would be available to guide you from there. As soon as is convenient of course."

Mark walks into the dining room to choose a table, "Good evening, gentlemen," he greets, bowing to the NSA agents before sitting to read the menu.

Pyah soon follows, "Good evening, sirs."

Both agents stand, then bow in respect as Mark pulls her chair out for her then sniggers slightly, "Neither have a clue," he remarks, whispering in Pyah's ear.

Pyah passes Mark the leaflet, "Seems we have a guide whenever we're ready."

Mark peruses the document, "When then?"

Pyah glances at the menu, "I think we can leave it till morning? Don't you?"

After dinner Mark approaches John, "We'll be leaving at first light if that's ok? Now all we need is some transport."

John smiles, "As I told your good lady, if you head down to the bay you'll find a ferry. I'll inform the captain. He'll be expecting you, ok?"

Mark nods as Pyah links arms with him, "So we have a long night ahead and not a lot to fill the time," she says, pulling him towards the stairs.

Mark looks back at John, "Oh, I think we'll find something to occupy our time," he says, lifting a do not disturb sign off the counter.

CHAPTER 44
SATIN AND LACE

Pyah enters the room and Mark swings her around, slamming her against the inside of the door, "Well, Mistress Young, how do Quakers pass the time without any obvious form of entertainment," he wonders as he slides his hands over her breasts.

Pyah runs her finger over his lips, "Well, sir, methinks that you are the master, what wouldst sir have me do?"

Pushing his lips against hers, he ruffles through the many layers of her skirts and petticoats to eventually reach a garter, suspender belt and silk stockings, "Holy shit, you really went the whole hog with this Quaker outfit, didn't you?"

She places her mouth against his ear, "Would sir care to explore some?"

Mark's hand reaches up to her hips, then fumbling finds she is not wearing the usual modern panties but a rather high waist girdle, "Damn woman, has this thing got a combination lock by any chance?"

Pyah pushes his head down, "Why not look for yourself?"

As he drops to his knees, Pyah throws the dress and petticoats over his shoulder, engulfing him in lace. Mark reaches up around her waist to carefully peel the girdle by rolling it down her thighs until it becomes loose enough to drop to the ground, "Shit, it's warm under here."

Pyah lifts the skirts to waft some fresh sea air under, "Is that better, my love?"

Mark crawls back out, gasping slightly, "If there weren't so many layers, this could be fun."

He spins her towards the door, presses himself against her and tugs against the cord fastener of the corset at the rear, "Lets lose a couple, eh?"

Soon he has the corset free, throws it on the bed, keeping the cord in his hand before starting to alleviate her of her petticoats. Once she is only stood in the bare dress, he spins her back facing him, "Well, now I can go back in," he decides, pecking her on her cheek before dropping back to his knees.

Pyah lifts her skirt over his head, "Is that cooler, sir?" she asks as he starts at her ankle to kiss then run his tongue softly all the way up the silk to the flesh that harbours his prize.

Pyah quivers with anticipation as she slowly widens her stance, "Careful, sir, I'm only a mere lass," she says, her hands clasping at the dress above his head as he teasingly flicks her clitoris with his tongue.

She gives a sharp gasp of air as she throws her head back against the door, then pulls his head into her through the folds. Mark pulls back then reaches into his pocket for the corset cord, pulling the dress from off himself he reaches for her hands to bind them behind her, tying her to the door handle before proceeding where he left off, "That should keep you in line and let me take this at my own pace."

Pyah feigns a struggle, "Oh sir, you're so demanding," she breathes, biting down on her lip, "please be gentle."

Mark takes one last look into her eyes before pulling the dress back over his head, "Oh, I'll be gentle, but if you keep up the backchat I'll be forced to punish you later."

Pyah drops one of her legs across his shoulder, "Oh, I do like a masterful man."

Mark flicks her leg back down, "That does it!"

He stands up to reach around her back, unfastening her from the door handle. He bends down, throws her across his shoulder, then while carrying her to the bed he forces her legs up behind her back to shove her stiletto heels behind her suspender belt, restraining her feet before throwing her on to the bed facedown. He walks back to the door, picks up her girdle and struts back to force it into her mouth, "That should keep you quiet," he says, before taking the loose cord to wrap around her ankles, hog-tying her with a pillow supporting her stomach.

Lifting her skirts, he slaps her across the buttocks as she quietly winces, before pulling her back onto his penis to hear her moan with pleasure through her undergarment gag. Beads of perspiration slowly emerge as her temperature soars through the desire of painful pleasure as Mark thrusts himself upon her. He reaches into his pocket to produce a lubricant he has secreted away. Smearing his fingers, he slides one into her anus as she groans, feebly attempting to pull her knees forward, a futile unconscious spasm causing her to drag at her bindings. He reaches up through her dress, around her to firmly grasp at her breast. Clasping it in his hand, he squeezes then twists as he pulls his hips back to violently thrust into her while heaving her breast away from her body.

Pyah manages to discharge her gag, "Can't breathe," she gasps, gasping for air.

Mark thrusts again, "Would you like me to stop?"

Pyah frantically shakes her head, "No more gag though, can't breathe," she sputters, shuddering through the next thrust as Mark smashes brutally into her vagina, vibrating his finger into her anus.

He clutches at her feet. His grip intensifies. Mouth agape screaming toward the sky, "Aarrgh!!" he yells as he hammers through his climax.

Pyah's head buries into the pillow, biting down as she feels his penis engorge through her, separating her internal organs as she reaches an ecstatic orgasm. Blood rushes through every vein in her body as the adrenaline sends spasmodic exhilaration through to her brain. Her very soul ripples with torturous delight, tantalising her with the gates of both heaven and hell. She feels Mark exude his manhood into her as she spews her love juices around him before slumping down as he exits her to drop on the bed beside her.

"I don't suppose you could at least untie my legs," she gasps, panting through every syllable, "I'm starting to lose the feeling."

Mark releases her bindings then pulls her in to spoon her, rubbing her thighs to get the blood flowing again as they both slip into a well-deserved slumber.

CHAPTER 45
BOAT RACE

A blustery wind washes the Scottish morning with a salt sea air, gusting through the window that Pyah had left open as she stretches across the bed. Her bleary-eyed glance catches a glimpse of the sun caressing the horizon as she reaches for the bedside clock. She can just make out the time in the dim light through her fuzzy morning stare, "Oh my God, its six am," she exclaims as she nudges Mark, "Mark come on! We only have an hour before we're supposed to be at the harbour," she reminds him, now shaking him violently as the gentle nudge received little, if any, response.

Mark rolls over but is forced to break his dream as Pyah slaps his back, "Come on, you lazy sod," she shouts, jumping out of the bed.

Mark reaches around but grasps at thin air, "Now where the hell have you gone?"

Pyah disappears into the bathroom, "I'm getting ready, so up and at 'em buddy."

Mark slowly sits up in the bed, "What, no morning cuddle?"

Pyah's head pops back around the door, "Not this morning, bud," she says, a toothbrush sticking out of her mouth with toothpaste foaming around her lips, "we haven't got time," she explains, giving her teeth a quick brush before standing with her hand on her hip, "I thought you were going to set the alarm?"

Mark smiles through a dazed glare, "Hmm, had a bit on my mind last night," he reminds her, rubbing his genitals, "totally forgot about that."

Pyah enters the doorway, "Well just in case you've forgotten, we're on the run and there are at least four agents that might just figure out we are not the Youngs downstairs," she says, throwing a cold wet flannel at him.

Mark blinks erratically as reality hits him, "Oh, shit, I forgot about them too," he says, jumping up to look out of the window, "damn, that fucking car is still there."

Pyah comes out of the bathroom brushing her hair, "Exactly, now get ready and let's see if we can at least slip out of here alive," she says, reaching into the wardrobe for a T-shirt and jeans.

Mark spins, "Don't think that's such a good idea, hun," he says, glancing down at the prepared clothes.

Pyah gives a confused look, "What?" she asks, then shrugs.

Mark smiles and points at the window, "We came in as Quakers," he says, pointing back at the clothes, "I don't think they're going to believe Quakers would wear those. Do you?"

Pyah picks up the jeans, "Whose stupid idea was it to be fricking Quakers anyhow?"

Mark tips his head downward then looks at her under his brow, "I wonder."

She picks up the plaid dress, "Suppose I have to wear this fricking warm damned thing."

Mark laughs out loud, "Oh I would not call it warm. I would call it smouldering hot."

Pyah throws a shoe at him, "Yeah, that's because you're nothing but a dirty old pervert."

Mark throws the shoe back, "Less of the old, thank you."

He rushes into the bathroom while Pyah slides into the many petticoats before asking him to fasten her corset. Mark finishes in the bathroom then pops out to help her. Once he has laced her up he just can't help but slide his hand up her skirts, "Holy shit, woman."

She just glances arrogantly down at him, "What, you think I'm putting that girdle back on? Think again."

Mark puts his hand down onto his penis, pushing down, "Oh shit, now look what you've done. He's going to be awake all day, knowing you are completely commando under there."

Pyah walks over to the wardrobe, pulls out a pair of baggy suit trousers, "Hmm, think these should do," she throws them at him, "embarrassment trousers," she says, then finishes packing the rest of their luggage, giggling churlishly.

When they reach the foyer, John is waiting at the kitchen door, beckoning them through, "This way," he says, whispering softly, "there is a car waiting out back to take you to the harbour," he tells them, hurrying them along, "the ferry man is expecting you."

As they board the ferry Pyah notices a large black vehicle on the approach road to the hotel, "That looks like trouble," she says, pointing the car out to Mark.

Mark approaches the captain, "Excuse me, but how long does the crossing take?"

The captain glances at his watch, "Oh, about forty minutes, why?"

Mark points across to the car, "And how long would it take for them to reach our destination in that?"

The captain laughs, "Oh, even at full pelt all the way, in that tub your looking at, ooo, about an hour and a half, absolute tops."

Mark looks down at his watch, "So by the time they figure out that we are not what we seem," he says, tapping his watch dial, "and figure we might be who they're looking for, hmm, we might be ashore. So, if they phone or even radio ahead we should be long gone?"

The captain smiles, "I'll open her up a bit, just for you. Never got it under thirty minutes yet but let's see," he sticks his head out of the porthole, "ok you lazy lot, let's see if we can get that record back!" he shouts as he throws the throttle wide and all hands start to scurry around like ants.

The sea is calm as the vessel steams through the water. The captain steers a straight course for the land, holding her true as the engineers work to keep the engines running at optimum efficiency. Mark lifts a pair of binoculars just before the harbour leaves their range of sight, "Well, looks like they're on to us," he comments, watching the black sedan speed to the front doors to pick up its passengers before speeding towards the main drag.

It hurtles down toward the ferry landing, "Oh, the mentality of the agency, ppfft, instead of trying to catch us the idiots have gone to check if the ferry is still in port. Loons."

A man gets out of the vehicle, then slams his hand down on the bonnet before picking up the radio to call ahead.

The captain flicks a scanner on just in time to hear the crucial part of the conversation, "We'll be there in an hour."

The captain turns to Mark and Pyah, "Ah, but we'll be there inside twenty-five minutes at this rate. Told you I'd get you safe."

Mark pats him on the back, "So we need to head to a monastery?"

The captain points up at a church on the hill, "It's more a nunnery than a monastery but yeah that's where you're heading, you should be safe."

At that the scanner picks up the man at the car, "What's your ETA?"

The other men reply, "Still about forty-five minutes."

Then to the disappointment of Mark the man at the car informs them, "Don't worry, I have called in the local constabulary, they have the Fischers' descriptions and will be waiting to take them into custody as soon as they leave that boat."

The captain tells his second to take the helm then rushes the Fischers down through to engineering "looking for passengers? Hmm, let's see what we can do about that," he says, handing the Fischers each a pair of oily coveralls, "you may need to grease your faces and that needs to be up," he says, pointing at Pyah's hair, "but my mechanics need to go ashore for oil and parts," he explains, turning to the chief engineer, "don't you?"

The chief sticks his ear to the engine, "Well, I have been moaning you need a new bearing on this shaft for long enough," he agrees, patting the drive shaft housing, "so long as they only check passengers like?"

Two young constables are stood waiting at the dock, looking at photos, then checking passengers disembarking as Pyah and Mark slip off with the mechanics through the boat yard. They quickly start their ascent to the nunnery before all the passengers have disembarked. Once near the nunnery a friendly face appears, "Well, fancy meeting you two here?" a young nun announces on her approach.

It's Paula Shuanasi. Pyah stands dumbfounded, "Wow, the last time we saw you was on the back of your father's motorbike, dressed in leather from head to foot. Please tell me this," she indicates, pointing at her habit, "is a disguise?"

Paula proudly shakes her head, "No, I decided after my close call I was going to leave all that hairy stuff to pop and follow my own dream," she says, posing then giving a twirl, "always wanted to become a nun."

Mark admires her with his arms folded, "Well good for you."

She grasps their elbows, "Now let's get you out of sight before someone twigs."

Pyah gives her a puzzled look. Paula smiles, "Oh, I know all about you being on the run, your friend Cramer has been here," she tells them as she takes them through a small chapel to meet her mother superior.

The mother superior kindly greets them, "You poor things, you must be starving," she says, leading them down some steps to the catacombs.

She opens a door, "Now don't be alarmed, this dark corridor is the quickest way to the living quarters and ultimately to the kitchen," she says, waving at Paula, "hurry child."

Soon Paula is serving them a broth, "Eat up, then we can discuss your plans," she says as a small bell rings.

Two more nuns rush into the room, "We have to hide you as the local police are at the door asking questions," they say, opening a secret door behind a French dresser, "this way... hurry," they instruct, gently pushing the Fischers through.

The broth is emptied back into the pot, the bowls are washed and everything is tidied away as the police inspect the premises. Once the police are satisfied they leave, then the Fischers are brought back out to a scurry of nuns with spare habits for both Mark and Pyah, "We think that this is probably the best idea while you stay," they explain as they are sat back at the table to finish some more broth.

Soon their meal is finished as the mother superior escorts them to their sleeping quarters, "This one will be yours, my dear," she says, opening a door to a small cell for Pyah, "I know it's not what you're used to but it's all we have," she explains.

Pyah steps in, "Well, it's only for a couple of nights at most, and we're thankful for the assistance."

Mark starts to follow Pyah but the mother superior pulls him back by his elbow, "Ahem, your room is this way, young man."

Mark stands, stunned, "You do realise we are married? And we are both Catholic?"

The mother superior gives him a firm disdainful glare, "Under this roof you will not contribute to your sins by way of copulation. What you do on unhallowed ground is your business but here I am the law and I say you sleep separately," she insists, pulling him firmly down the hall, "this is your room," she says, opening a door next door but one from Pyah's.

Pyah stands in her doorway giggling, "Now you do as you're told and I'll see you later."

The mother superior looks at her watch, "You'll see him in the morning, young lady," she corrects, raising her eyebrows, "it's lights out at ten pm and its five to now."

Mark's head almost spins off his neck, "Ten o'clock!? You expect us to go to bed at ten o'clock?"

The mother superior pushes him into the tiny room, "Yes, and no slipping out through the night, my room is in between you," she says, pointing at the door, "so I'll be listening."

Mark spits and stutters, "But what am I supposed to do for entertainment?" he asks, looking at the bare walls, one chair, a small table and a bed, "there's nothing in here."

The mother superior shrugs her shoulders, "Prayer might help," she says, then shuts the door behind him.

She walks back to Pyah to usher her back into her room then closes the door, "God bless and have a good night," she says, then walks back to her own room to pray.

Mark sits watching the clock for about an hour. Fidgeting and twiddling his thumbs. Suddenly he decides to get up and sneak to Pyah's room but as he comes level with the mother superior's door she opens it. She just scowls at him pointing back towards his room.

Mark points down at his penis, "I was just looking for the loo."

She steps out, "It's back that way on the left," she directs, pointing past his door.

Soon he is back in his room pacing the floor. He takes out his mobile phone but there is no signal as the mother superiors voice booms out, "We don't allow mobile phones here."

Mark's eyes widen as he mouths to himself, "How the fuck?"

He is astonished as she replies, "And it's a sin to use profanities too."

He starts to look for holes in the wall or hidden cameras, "Must be able to see me," he mutters but nothing is found.

Pyah sneaks to her door but when she opens it the mother superior is stood outside waiting. Before Pyah can say anything the mother superior points away from Mark's room, "If you're looking for the ladies they are that way on your right," she instructs, then she stands to wait for Pyah's return, "this building won't allow a mobile phone signal either," she adds as Pyah returns to her room, fiddling with her phone.

The mother superior smiles at her, "You only have to wait another five hours to see him."

Mark steps out after listening at his door, "Five hours? But it's only eleven now, that means you get up at what, four am?"

She turns to him, "Yes, and breakfast is at five. If you're late you do without," she tells him as she escorts Pyah back into her room.

She waves Mark back into his room, "Now go to sleep. Good night," she says, watching him in before returning to her bed.

Pyah submits to the rules then quickly falls asleep but Mark is restless for most of the night. Every time he thinks of heading for the door a subtle knock can be heard from the wall to dampen his ardour.

After approximately three arduous hours he finally tires himself to sleep.

The mother superior decides to allow both the Fischers to sleep through to five am before awakening them for breakfast. As they eat, they are introduced to the gentleman that will guide them through a set of tunnels to start their journey towards the English border.

CHAPTER 46
TICTOC

A hazy red sunrise barely glistens through the stain glass windows as the mother superior brings a slight gentleman to their side, "This is TicToc," she introduces, patting him on the shoulder "he will help you when you're ready to leave," she tells them as she stands in front of them while they eat "I must warn you though, he suffers from Tourette's syndrome," she says, glancing back at TicToc, "he swears at fruit."

Pyah nearly chokes on her oats but then apologises, "Sorry, but why fruit?"

TicToc shrugs. The mother superior's head snaps back at Pyah, "I would have thought that the profanity would be more a concern? DON'T YOU?" she inquires, sternly scowling at Pyah, "don't allow him to become excitable and he is fine."

Just at that a nun scurries into the room, "Excuse the intrusion, but it would seem the local law enforcement are on their way with a search warrant."

The mother superior stands Pyah and Mark up, "Quickly, this way," she instructs, leading them to a small hidden door, "why would they have a search warrant?"

The younger nun opens the door, "It would seem a local fisherman saw them enter our premises and when questioned told them what he saw."

TicToc steps through the door, reaches down to an open grate in the floor, then drops down into a shallow passage way, "This way," he orders, pulling a large torch from a shelf as he opens another small door leading to a dark stairway descending into the darkness.

Pyah follows rather gingerly, "What is this?"

TicToc takes her by the hand, "These are smuggler's tunnels. Before this became a monastery, it was an inn where smugglers brought their ill-gotten gains to sell."

Mark holds Pyah's free hand to follow on behind, "So why TicToc?"

Pyah stares in confusion, "Yeah, that can't be your given name."

TicToc smiles, "My given name is a little hard to pronounce so I've always gone by TicToc," he explains as they reach the bottom of the stairs, "I'm a watch maker so it fits, but my real name is Tiberius Isaiah Coltocavitch. I prefer TicToc."

Mark stops dead, "Ti what ovich?"

TicToc sniggers, "Tiberius Isaiah Coltocavitch. My mother was Scottish but my father came from the Carpathian Mountains."

Before she can stop herself Pyah blurts out, "Ooo, vampires."

TicToc stops dead spits at the ground, "Fucking apples. Fucking apples, fuck. Fuck. Fucking apples," he curses, then glares at Pyah, shining the torch in her face, "not funny!" he reprimands but then starts to giggle himself, "I did it again, didn't I?" he asks, referring to his Tourette's, "Which was it, apples or bananas?"

Pyah holds her hand over her mouth, "Fuck, fuck, fucking apples. Sorry couldn't resist."

TicToc shakes his head, "So long as it doesn't offend you?"

Mark steps into the torchlight, "Trust me, we've said worse. So long as you don't mind us laughing," he says, a big wry grin on his face.

TicToc shakes his head, "Most don't find it in the slightest amusing. It's rather refreshing to know you are not offended but please don't refer to my parents as vampires," he says, spitting at the ground again, "fucking apple," he curses, then stares at Pyah as she is in fits of laughter, "I did it again? Apples?"

Pyah nods through the giggles as TicToc starts on his way again. Mark looks back, "Won't the police come down here after us?"

TicToc stops, "There are hundreds of miles of tunnels heading off in at least fifty different directions," he says, shining his torch at several openings that they have passed, "it's a veritable maze down here. Trust me, the law know they would get lost down here for days and they have no idea where we could come out."

Pyah rubs her chin, "I presume you know where you're going?"

TicToc smiles, "Yes dear, I used to play down here when I was a child," he says, starting off again, "we will be down here for a few hours but there are stopping places along the way with fresh water supplies and I have brought some food, so don't worry, we'll be fine."

After walking down the same tunnel for what seems like an eternity TicToc starts to shine his torch at the entrances to all the tunnels to the right, "Ah, here it is," he sighs, pointing the light to the top of one tunnel that has a B carved into the stone, "this is the one," he leads them down a small gradient, "won't be long now."

Pyah pants, "What, we're finally coming out?"

TicToc shakes his head, "No, but we are near the first stop," he explains as the tunnel opens out to a small room.

There are seats and a shelf with water canteens next to a hand pump. TicToc pumps some water into one canteen and hands it to Pyah, then lights a candle, "Here, dear, rest your feet," he says, showing her to a seat.

Mark flops down beside her, "So how much further before we see daylight again?"

TicToc looks down at his watch, "Oh, about another two to three hours I'm afraid but at least you're safe."

Pyah rubs her arms, "I'm cold and damp, I know that."

TicToc walks over to a hole in a wall, "Well, I could light a fire unless you would rather push on?"

Mark takes his jacket off, "I'm actually quite warm," he says, placing the jacket around Pyah's shoulders.

Pyah pecks him on the cheek, "So long as you're ok."

Mark nods, "I think we should push on just to get out of here as soon as possible."

TicToc hands them a sandwich, "As soon as you're ready we can move then."

Mark helps Pyah to her feet, "Come on old woman."

Pyah slaps him, "Less of the old, you old gimmer," she replies as they push on after TicToc.

A conversation is struck up which makes the time pass. Soon they are stopping again. Pyah sits on a rock, "We don't need another rest, but I could do with some water."

TicToc hands her a canteen, "You'll be happy to know we will be out of here in less than five minutes."

Mark steps forward, "Daylight?"

TicToc nods, "But we have to go through that pipe first," he says, pointing at a valved entrance to a pipe with about a two-foot diameter, "didn't want to alarm you so I thought it was best to keep it to myself until we reached it. You haven't got claustrophobia, have you?"

Mark sighs, "No but I don't like it, isn't there another way?"

TicToc points his torch up another tunnel, "That way but it's about twelve more miles. This pipe is only about seventy-five feet which brings you out at an old ruin. Then we go about a quarter of a mile to a friend's place to freshen up."

Pyah arduously stands, "OK, let's get this over with," she sighs as the pipe is opened and TicToc shines his torch in the direction they must go; Pyah steps in first, "Oh my God it stinks."

TicToc laughs, "Oh yeah, it connects to the town sewage pipe, so we'll have to move fast before the next flush."

Mark steps in, "What do you mean, next flush?"

TicToc scratches his chin, "It gets flushed every fifteen minutes."

Pyah looks back at him, "Flushing what with what?"

TicToc waves her on, "The town's shit with water."

Pyah starts to race up the pipe, "Oh shit. And that's not a pun. If I get flushed with shit someone's going to die," she warns, looking down at her hands as she realises she's crawling in human waste, "oh, you are a fucking bastard TicToc. No wonder you shout at fruit. You're a fucking lemon, an absolute moronic lemon. Trust me, when I get out of here you're going to wish you'd never met me."

Mark turns his head, "Oh dear, you think you're in the shit now pal," he says, smiling, "I would not like to be you when we get to daylight. I hope you can run."

Suddenly TicToc stops, "Oops. Take a deep breath and hold on."

Pyah turns her head to him, "Why!?" she demands, then hears the water rushing towards her, "oh, you are fucking dead meat, trust me, you're dead meat," she says, tucking her head into her chest as the water and shit hit her.

It lasts for about two minutes then Pyah starts to retch as she is physically sick.

TicToc shines his torch in front, "There's the opening, about ten feet in front of you."

Pyah crawls forward, still vomiting, as Mark tries to avoid her vomit behind her. Pyah takes another breath but can't hold it as she reaches up to open the hatch. She crawls out coughing and barking, "Where is the scrawny little bastard," she demands between chokes, "I swear, he's breathed his last breath," she insists as TicToc emerges, she grabs him by the lapels then quickly releases him looking down at her hands, "Jesus, you're worse than I am. What did you do? Roll in it?" she asks, trying to find a clean section of her arm to cover her nose with, "where the hell is this friend's house? So I can get this shit off me."

TicToc waves her on without a word then walks down a bank to an alleyway that leads them to a yard. As they pass through the back gate they are met by a tall dark female walking two men by a leash, donning spiked dog collars. Mark head drops, "Have I got brothel creeper written across my forehead or something?" he asks, shaking his head in embarrassment.

Pyah's eyes widen, "Oh, dear, looks like I might get to take you for a walk," she suggests, sniggering as Mark glares at her in disgust.

CHAPTER 47
PLEASURE PALACE

The sunlight cascades across the old house as the shadows burnish a cobbled yard. The lady of the house approaches Mark, "I'll have you know this is not a brothel and I'll thank you not to refer to it as such."

Mark flings his arms in the air, "Oh? And what would you have me call it? A sexual fantasy garden? Or something to the like?" he asks, sighing to himself. "I mean it's a place where people come, pay money and screw isn't it? Doesn't matter how you sugar-coat it, it's still a brothel!"

The lady lifts his chin, "You were close, it's a BDSM fantasy palace," she says, stroking his face, "can I assume that your attire is not fitting to your employment?"

Mark looks her straight in the eye, "If you're asking if I'm a priest then no. I'm an assassin so don't get in my face missus."

She holds her nose, "I see you brought them through the tunnel of love then," she says, glancing across to TicToc, then gently whips one of her subs, "go and ask Madam Fiona to bring two sets of town clothes," she orders as she unhooks him from his leash.

He starts to crawl towards the door, "Yes mistress."

She taps him across the buttocks, "You can walk," she says, scolding him for crawling, "idiot."

He stands, bows his head, then scurries off, "Thank you mistress," he says, disappearing through the back door.

The lady holds her hand over her face, "This way," she says, directing the Fischers to an outbuilding, "it may be a bit rustic but it will do," she explains, pointing at a shower through the open door, "you can get cleaned up there before that stench infects my premises."

TicToc drops his clothes where he stands then to the amazement of everyone, except the lady, he walks buck naked into the outhouse to shower himself off.

Mistress Fiona appears from the rear exit, "What size clothes were you requesting?"

The lady sizes Pyah up, "Hmm, American six? Maybe a four?"

Pyah stands her ground, "I ain't taking nothing off till he's done and gone thank you," she protests, pointing at TicToc.

The lady rolls her eyes, then turns to Mark, "Hmm, forty-eight-inch chest, thirty-four-inch waist, hmm, thirty-six inside leg and a seventeen-inch collar?"

Mark applauds her, "Spot on all the way," he praises, then he drops his robe next to TicToc's and struts into the shower next to him.

TicToc can't help but stare down at Marks genitalia as Fiona and the lady try following him, peering around at the size of his manhood. Mark stands proudly with his hands in the air, "Is there something I can help you with?" he asks, turning with a wry grin plastered across his face.

TicToc snaps his head away, "Err, no, nothing," he denies, then glances back, "shit man, can't help it. What the fuck is that?"

Mark struts into the shower next to him, "It's a dick, what do you think it is? Why?" he says, lifting it with pride.

Fiona walks around him, "Yeah, that most definitely is a dick."

TicToc rinses himself down quickly, then looks down at his average size penis with shame and walks out blushing while talking to it, "Don't worry little man, I bet he can't do the magic like you can."

The lady takes out her riding crop to whack TicToc across his arse, "Put some clothes on and cover it up for Christ's sake."

This sends him skipping, holding his buttocks, "Yes Mistress Hanna."

Mark leans out towards her, "So that's your name. Wondered when someone was going to introduce us!"

She slinks up to him, "Oh, I was definitely going to introduce myself to you," she coos, lifting his penis with her crop, "does this thing work then?" she asks, giving him a quick crack across his buttocks.

He doesn't flinch but turns to face her down, "I've never raised my hand to a woman in anger but I have put a bullet in a few heads," he says, looking down at her riding crop, "and if you so much as try and tickle me with that thing again," he warns, raising his fingers like a gun to the side of her head, "bang. You get my drift?"

Hanna licks her lips, "Ooo, a take charge man, I like a take charge man," she says as she turns to slink out of the outhouse, "but just remember, this is MY establishment and you go by MY rules," she picks up a set of washing tongs, grabs his cassock with them, then hands it to Fiona, "burn these along with the rest of this shite," she orders before disappearing back into the house with TicToc, crouched in a humbled manner, hard on her heels.

Mistress Fiona quickly picks up the soiled clothes, pops them in a plastic sack then throws them into a small burner stood in the corner. She then rushes back into the house to reappear with fresh clothes for Pyah and Mark. Mark is out drying himself as she stands, shaking her head tutting at him, "Didn't your mother teach you to wash properly?"

Mark glares at her, "OUR parents died when we were only toddlers, so no she didn't," he answers, putting her in her place.

Fiona looks at the floor, "My apologies, it wasn't meant maliciously," she says, walking over to the shower, "may I?" she asks, beckoning him back in.

Mark smiles before stepping back in, "Do your worst. But no pain."

Pyah closes the outhouse door before stripping off but as she steps in the door is flung wide by a small huddle of females, "Can we help?" they ask, most of them rushing to Mark's shower.

Pyah wraps her hands over her private parts, "Ahem, REALLY," she says, pointing at the wide-open door.

One of the girls quickly closes it then glances at Mark's penis but saunters over to Pyah with a sultry look in her eye, "Hmm, dick is all right but I'm more a boob girl myself," she picks up a sponge, "would you like a hand, my dear?"

Pyah gives the wench clad female a once over, "Don't mind if you do," she agrees, nodding seductively.

A couple of the other girls turn slowly, "Oh my word, didn't see her," they say then scurry across to give a hand.

Pyah drops her hands against the wall as three young ladies dressed in all manner of kinky outfits slosh soapy sponges down her body. Not a word is spoken, the only sound that can be heard is the gentle running of water with Pyah's moans harmonically resonating through the steel roofed shed.

Mark suds his torso down while Fiona just can't take her hands from his nether regions, "Sounds like your wife is enjoying her shower."

Mark glances down at her, "She always enjoys a good shower but usually it's either with me or solitary."

Fiona kisses the end of his now erect penis, "Seems like someone else likes a good shower too."

Mark smiles, "Oh he just likes a soft hand."

Fiona stands, "I was talking about you, not your knob. Mind he does seem to be happy."

Mark laughs out loud, "You don't want to call him things like that, he might get a complex."

She looks down at it puzzled, "Like what?"

Mark grins at her, "Happy? Or any of the other six? He certainly is not a dwarf," he jokes, chuckling to himself.

Suddenly the door swings open. Mistress Hanna stands naked in the doorway, tapping her leg with her riding crop, "You three, out," she orders, scowling at the three girls attending to Pyah.

She walks over to Pyah lashing at the girls as they pass her, "And close the door on your way out," she instructs as she struts around Pyah, backwards and forwards, then flicks Pyah's buttocks with her crop, "Exquisite."

Pyah stands fast, unflinching, "Truly exquisite," she gently places her hand between Pyah's shoulder blades, then teases it through the water, down her spine onto her buttocks, "seems you don't mind a little pain? Unlike your husband," she judges, letting her nails grasp at Pyah's skin.

She runs her hand over Pyah's hip then up around the front of her torso, resting to cup her breast before squeezing.

Mark turns slowly to watch, "Wants to be careful what she wishes for that one."

Pyah's head snaps around to glare at him. He puts his hand in the air, then drops it around Fiona's butt. Fiona lifts her leg up around his waist as he blows a kiss to Pyah then lifts Fiona up, gently sliding her down onto him.

Hanna reaches around to Pyah's chin, "Oh, there you are," she says, peering deep into Pyah's eyes, "aren't you a dark soul, hiding deep down in there."

Pyah glares back as her heartrate rises somewhat, "Trust me, you don't want to go there."

Hanna tenderly touches lips with her, whispering, "Oh, I like danger and you are dangerous, aren't you? I can see you have demons. I like demons," she brushes her lips against Pyah's ear, "so why don't you come out to play?"

Pyah pulls her head back, cocks it over to one side and stares right into Hanna's very soul, "You want to play that's fine but I suggest you leave her where she is."

Mark has Fiona pressed up against the cold tiled wall, "Your mistress likes to play with fire but I think she's biting off a lot more than she can chew."

Fiona lifts herself up on Mark then throws herself down, "Who gives a shit? She's a big girl. Now are you going to babysit her or fuck me?"

Mark rams himself into Fiona then thrusts out then back in as hard as he can.

Hanna pushes Pyah against the wall, "Seems like your husband knows how to let go and as they say. I'm a big girl I can handle it."

Pyah grabs her by the throat then spins around, slamming her against the wall, "Trust me, you do not want to go there."

Mark glances over his shoulder, "It's all right playing with fire, but a fire extinguisher won't help when you walk through the gates of hell."

Hanna seductively licks her lips, "Hmm, maybe I should take you to my private play area."

Mark looks deep into Fiona's eyes, "Seems your boss won't take no for an answer."

Fiona grasps at his head, "Don't worry, she won't hurt your baby. We don't like to break our toys."

Mark scoffs, "Oh, trust me, I ain't worried about my baby, as you call her."

She reaches down, thrusting his buttocks forward, "How about you concentrate on what you have in hand and let them deal with their own issues?"

Mark bites down on her neck, "Her funeral," he says as he rams into Fiona.

Hanna takes Pyah by the hand, passes her a robe, then escorts her into the house.

Mark spins out of the shower, dropping Fiona onto a nearby bale of hay, "Been a while since I had a proper roll in the hay," he comments, slicing the cord that binds it. Steam rises from the hay as it sticks to their wet bodies. The pungent odour mingles with the scent of fresh perspiration overcasting Fiona's aromatic sexual juices. Mark gently brushes the straw away from her breasts then flicks her nipples with his tongue while sliding his hand down between her legs to tantalise her clitoris, bringing on her climax, enhancing the moment of his own ejaculation. Both bodies spasmodically twitching in perfect synchronization as their pelvises hold together through the final thrust.

CHAPTER 48
SPRITES AND SERAPHS

A gentle summer breeze dances through Mistress Hanna's house, wafting the lace curtains into a frenzied ballet. Interior fans cool the premises to a bearable temperature, but still the patrons' privacy is put on hold as most of the adjacent doors are wedged ajar, allowing the breeze to drive the blistering summer heat to escape. Mistress Hanna sashays through the house, dignified yet audacious in her state of undress. Parading her trophy as she leads Pyah by the hand to her private boudoir. Hanna pushes an ornate oak door inward to reveal her inner sanctum, "This is my very own private play palace," she says, raising her hands towards the ceiling, "you like? I don't bring just anyone in here," she adds as Pyah gives a cynical uninterested glance around the room with its black lace intertwined blood red velvet drops across the ceiling.

Its chiffon draped shelves housing all manner of whips, chains and torture implementation. Chained anal hooks brazenly hang from a winched rail next to a small gilded human cage hung in the far corner of the room. Shackles scatter rails as stretching racks adorn a black and gold deep shag carpet. The centrepiece is a red and gilded four poster bed dressed in the finest black silk. Pyah strolls through the room, "Nice toys but I don't do submissive."

Hanna saunters up behind her, wrapping her arms around Pyah's waist, "Oh, I think I might be able to change your mind, after all you don't seem to be the type that is a stranger to pain."

Pyah pulls Hanna's hands away, "And you don't seem to be the type that listens," she retorts, spinning slowly to face Hanna, "there is nothing in here that interests me," she insists, glaring into Hanna's eyes, "bondage isn't my thing, unless you're wanting me to tie you up?" she asks, cocking her head slightly, then lifting her eyebrow.

Hanna steps back shaking her head, "No, no, madam, I do the restraining in here," she says, moving towards a rack to run her hands down the manacles, "you should try, you might like it," she reasons, beckoning Pyah to step in, "just pick a safe word and when you're done we stop."

Pyah drops her head then slinks over to Hanna. As she reaches her she snaps out grabbing Hanna by the throat, "You just don't get it, do you?" she says, slamming Hanna's head back against the rack, "if I let her out, nothing in here is going to hold her," she warns, jolting Hanna's head from side to side, "and she don't like any of this shit," she insists, rubbing cheeks with Hanna, "you won't like what she is, trust me."

Hanna's heart starts to race, "Oh, I've tamed many a beast in here," she replies, a nervous rattling in her voice as she tries to stay dominant.

Pyah smiles and brushes her lips against Hanna's, "I can feel the fear rising through your very soul," she says, softly growling as she lets her hot breath out across Hanna's ear.

Before Hanna can respond Pyah strikes down with her teeth, lunging them into Hanna's quivering flesh, biting deep through her shoulder as Hanna reaches up, trying to push her away. Pyah lifts Hanna from her feet against the rack, "I thought you wanted to see the real me?" she asks, her mouth dripping with Hanna's warm blood before releasing her, dropping her to the floor whimpering, clasping her wounded shoulder like a terrified child.

Pyah wipes her mouth, "Thought not," she says, storming out of the room.

Pyah hurries down to the outhouse where Mark is almost dressed, "We're leaving," she declares, snatching up the clothes left for her.

She quickly dresses as TicToc appears half-dressed, "What's going on?" he asks, looking at the remnants of blood still around Pyah's lips, "and what's that?"

Pyah pushes him to one side, "Never mind, how do we get out of here?"

Mark pulls Pyah's face towards him, "You didn't?" he asks, handing her a tissue, "please tell me you didn't kill her."

Pyah gives a smug grin, "NO. She's just met Emily Rose, and trust me she didn't like her," she answers, vigorously rubbing her mouth, "don't worry, I just bit her," she explains, giving a slightly worried laugh.

Mark's eyes slowly close, "Oh, you JUST bit her? Well, that's all right then," he says, sarcasm ringing through his voice, "you know I think we may need to get you an anger management specialist when we get out of this mess," he comments, checking out of the door, "either that or a bloody coffin to hide you in until nightfall."

TicToc looks around confused, then heads to the back gate, "This way," he says, hurrying down an alley and leading them to a gate opening to a storm drain, "quickly, in here."

Pyah stops, "OH NO! You're not dragging me along another shit pipe."

TicToc shakes his head, "It's unused and has been for years but it does lead into another smugglers' tunnel, leading to open countryside," he explains, pulling the gate open, "it's in the general direction of where we're going and you'll only underground for about half an hour."

Pyah stands thinking for a moment, "If I get covered in shit again, you're getting covered in blood."

TicToc smiles then waves her in. The drain is surprisingly clean. So is the tunnel.

It's not long before they're out into open country with TicToc showing them across a field. Pyah stops to check her shoes, leaning against a tree as a bullet ricochets off beside her head. She spins before diving behind the tree, "SNIPER!"

Mark sprints to her side, "Where?" he asks as he covers her body.

TicToc is not far behind him but drops to the ground as a round comes whistling through the air to embed itself firmly into his chest. With his last breath, he points to a small wooded area, "Through those trees, keep heading south," he gasps as his head drops, lifeless.

Pyah turns to Mark, "They're about half a mile out and there are at least two of them."

Mark has a quick peek, "Yep, two," he confirms as a couple of rounds miss him by the hair on his head, "how the fuck did they find us so quick?"

Pyah sneers at him, "Bet that bitch put them on to us."

Mark takes her by the hand, "Well, you will go biting people," he says nervously, smiling as they make a run for the trees.

Pyah keeps her head down, "Yeah, but I didn't think she'd play devil's advocate on us."

Mark leads her quickly into a copse, "Serendipity?" he suggests as a flurry of gunfire rains down, scattering wood pulp through the air.

Pyah covers her head with her arm, "Oh, for fuck's sake, don't they know I just put clean clothes on?"

Once through the clump of trees they hit open fields. Putting the copse between them and the snipers they make a bolt for what looks like a forest edge. About twenty feet before they reach the tree line they hear a familiar voice yell "DUCK!" and they dive into a small gully with the ringing of bullets flying overhead.

One solitary round rings out from the trees in front of them then the voice shouts, "Stay down!" as another round echoes through the meadow from the trees in front.

Elleon stands, throwing a gill net to the ground, "Well, fancy meeting you two here," she greets, strutting out towards them with her rifle poised upon her hip, "seems someone wants you dead?" she remarks, pointing out toward two bodies laid just outside the copse.

Pyah stands up, "Yeah, apparently the NSA have a kill or capture order out on us."

Mark stands, brushing himself off, "Problem is, they seem to be ignoring the capture end of that."

Elleon hushes him, "Yeah, well we're not out of it yet," she warns as a helicopter comes into view on the horizon, "that looks like a gunship," she adds, rushing them into the trees, "this place is riddled with tunnels so let's get to one before that thing rips this place to bits."

Elleon reaches down for a hidden trapdoor then drops into the depths with Mark right behind her but Pyah looks back before dropping in, "Oh shit, there's a small troop of what looks like special forces getting out of that whirlybird," she tells them as she dips into the tunnel to a barrage of gunfire.

Elleon shines a torch down one of the tunnels, "Wouldn't worry about it," she says, starting through the darkness, "if they figure out which way we went I have a little surprise waiting for them," she adds, tapping the side of her nose.

About fifty feet into the tunnel Elleon stops, "See these?" she asks, shining the torch on a small camouflaged device, "These are mines. I set them for three seconds, then when they pass them they activate them and three seconds later, BOOM," she explains, shining her torch at more of them dotted down the tunnel, "the last ones we'll set for immediate detonation, that way they get trapped with no way of communication. So, they'll have to dig their way out," she goes on, showing the Fischers how to set them, "that will give us the time we need to get clear, ok?"

Mark and Pyah rush along setting the mines until Elleon stops them, "OK these last ones leave to me. You just head down there," she says, pointing to an adjacent tunnel.

A few minutes later they reach what seems like a dead end as Elleon brushes past them, "Up. We go up here," she tells them, climbing a small hidden ladder to another trapdoor and lifting it, rather gingerly peeking out, "ok, it's clear," she declares, crawling out on her belly, "keep low though, just in case."

As Pyah gets clear they hear a salvo of explosions, "Well, they were hot on our trail."

Mark turns around, "That's what you call a blowjob."

Elleon crawls up behind a tree, "Yeah, but that tunnel would have taken them about a mile in the wrong direction so they'll be looking for you over there somewhere," she says, smiling profusely, "nothing like a bit of subterfuge to confuse your opponent."

A quick scan of the outlying area and they're off. Soon they come across an old derelict building where Elleon hands them some camouflage outfits she has hidden there, "Here, these should make you a little less conspicuous," she says, sitting in the corner to pull a canteen out, "so, do you have any idea why?"

Pyah pull her trousers up to her knees then drops her skirt over the top, "Why what?"

Elleon's head drops to the side, looking up Pyah's skirt, "Err, you got any drawers on? And why they are chasing you?"

Pyah stops dead, gives her a smile, "No and no."

Elleon stands up, "Jesus," she exclaims, pulling out a pair of boxer shorts, "it would seem that someone stole a few rockets and the NSA have the idea it was you two for some reason, put these on for Christ's sake," she adds, throwing the boxers at Pyah.

Pyah drops her trousers, puts the boxers on and then lifts the trousers back, "So this is about those fricking rockets?"

Mark is changing behind a small wall, "So we tell them where those rockets are and they leave us alone?"

Elleon tries to peek around at him, "Well, not exactly. Seems you have some information they want to suppress."

Mark covers his dignity, "What information? And do you mind?"

Elleon laughs, "Seen it all before and if I knew what info I would tell you, but then I would be on their kill list too, wouldn't I?"

Mark looks at Pyah as Pyah shrugs back at him, "Don't look at me. Your guess is as good as mine."

Once they're dressed Elleon checks the perimeter, "Well, we're good to go. I can only take you as far as the railway station where you can catch a train straight through to London. You are going to London I presume?"

Pyah nods, "Ah ha, but it would seem that everyone is expecting us."

Elleon hands them caps and glasses, "Not much of a disguise but it will have to do for now," she says and as they set off again she hands them a pair of parachutes, "don't know what good they'll be," she says, shrugging, "you never know, you might have to jump out of the hospital and trust me she's up on the top floor."

Pyah stops, "Oh, so you even know why we're heading down there?"

Elleon nods then leads the way, "Give Lacey my regards if she's conscious," she says, smiling to herself.

CHAPTER 49
BASE-JUMPING TRAIN WRECK

With the train station in view Elleon kisses them and bids them goodbye, "This is as far as I go. Wish I could come with you but I got pressing business elsewhere," she hands Pyah an envelope, two parachutes and a small holdall then turns to walk away, "don't worry, I'll find you if you survive this," she promises, chuckling to herself, "and if you don't I'll just kill whoever kills you," she adds, walking off into the distance.

Mark looks at Pyah, "Well, she's full of confidence inspiring frivolities, isn't she?"

Pyah takes him by the arm, "Nah, she knows we'll be ok," she says as they casually walk into the station.

The train to London arrives so they board, still checking behind for a tail. As it pulls out Mark notices a military patrol rushing down the hill towards the station, "Oh shit, looks like we got company."

Pyah rummages through the holdall, "Well, we have weapons and grenades," she says handing Mark a handgun.

The train slows so Mark rushes forward to the driver's cabin. He hears the driver being ordered to back the train up, then puts a gun to the driver's head, "I don't think so, mate. Put it back in forward or lose a few brain cells."

The driver sticks it back into a forward gear then opens it up, "Hey, I'm just the driver, what do I want to be a hero for? Anything you say is fine by me."

The military commandeer another train to give chase then order the station master to get them on the parallel track as soon as possible.

Mark looks out of the driver's window, "You're shitting me right?" he says, turning to the driver, "Is there any way they can overtake us or board us along this track?"

The driver looks out of the window, "Well, there is a place where they can switch tracks about a mile down and that train is faster than this one."

Mark scratches his head, "Is there any way we can make this one go faster?"

The driver shrugs, "The only way would be to unhitch the passenger cars which would slow them down too."

Pyah grabs his arm then drags him back to the coupling, "OK, do it."

The driver unhitches the cars then waits with a look of anticipation across his face. Pyah hands him a wad of money then pushes him back into the unhitched cars, "Let's just say it's your lucky day."

The driver blows her a kiss, "You go girl," he says then skips back through the cars, whistling to himself.

Pyah returns to Mark, "On our own again, my love," she says as they pass the switching point.

Mark points down at it, "Not for long, honey. Especially if those cars don't stop before that."

Pyah watches from the back door as the cars stop right on the switch, "OK, looks like we have luck on our side at the moment."

Starting on an ascent into the hills. Mark taps the speedometer, "Not if we slow down any more," he says as they start to head into tunnels.

The other train gently pushes the cars out of the way then backs up as the switch is made. Pyah walks forward to Mark, "Well it's been nice knowing you but here they come."

Mark grabs the bag, "Here, take these and climb onto the roof," he instructs, handing her the grenades.

She opens a vent to the roof then climbs out, "What the hell am I doing up here?" she asks herself, reaching down as Mark hands her the parachutes, "Freezing my ass off and he thinks were on a plane."

They come into open track as the other train approaches. Mark starts to shoot the other train's windows out from the back door, then throws a grenade in, "Well, that should keep them occupied," he reasons, watching as the soldiers run for cover.

As he climbs up onto the roof the grenade takes out the other train's controls, making it impossible for it to slow down or stop. Mark gets on the roof, "Throw another in," he orders as he reaches for his parachute.

Pyah throws another grenade in, "How does this work then?" she asks, struggling to put her chute on.

Mark pulls her to the back of the train, "Simple. Just before we get to that next tunnel we pull the cord," he explains, pointing down the track, "and poof it pulls us clear," he goes on, taking the rest of the grenades, "we drop these in there and we land nice and safe."

Pyah shrugs, "OK," she says, then stands up.

An onslaught of machine gunfire rips through the engine as they pull the chutes. They drop the grenades as the other train passes while being dragged backwards into the ravine below. As they glide gently down they hear the explosion echoing across the countryside as the trains enter a tunnel.

When they touch down they quickly unhitch the chutes to make a run for it. Mark pulls Pyah from her chute, "We'll have to make use of another escape plan from the hospital, we haven't got time to retrieve those."

At the bottom of the ravine is a small river with a boathouse where Mark finds a boat, "Well that's bloody lucky," he remarks, stealing it then heading downstream.

Pyah sits and opens a water bottle, "I hope we're heading in the right direction."

Mark shrugs "who cares so long as we get the fuck out of here?"

The river widens and quickens as Pyah sits up, "Where do you think we are now?" she asks as they pass a small village.

Mark puts his hand to his ear, "Don't know, but it sounds English," he says listening to the locals at a riverside café.

Pyah grabs the rudder, "I'm starving, let's get off here and get something to eat," she says, heading to a small jetty, "then we can work out where we are and how we get to London."

Most of the locals have an undistinguishable Scottish twang but one-man approaches Pyah, "Can I help you, dear?"

His brogue is fathomable as Pyah tries to answer him in her best English accent, "Can you tell me where we are?"

He moves in close to steer her to an alcove, "You're the Americans. The ones that all this fuss is about, aren't you?" he asks, softly whispering under his breath.

Mark gives a shifty glance around, "How the hell did you work that out?"

The man smiles, "Her Oxford English is excellent but she still need to work on her vocabulary."

Pyah stands tall, "Told you I got the accent right," she says, smugly sneering at Mark, "so where the hell are we and is it far to London?"

The guy titters, "Shit, you're on the River Forth. You're still in Scotland but you're in luck," he says, walking them down a dock, "you see that freighter?" he asks, pointing at a large cargo vessel, "well I'm the captain and I'll be taking it through to Sheerness, which is about fifty-odd miles from London and it's leaving as soon we're loaded."

Pyah watches as the cargo is being loaded, "So how long and more to the point how much?"

The guy scratches his chin, "Hmm, how does five hundred sound? Unless you don't mind making an old sea dog happy, then I'll take you there for nowt," he says, flicking his eyebrows.

Mark steps forward, "Nowt? What's nowt?"

The old guy looks around in confusion, "Nowt, you know, nothing, just a shag."

Mark steps in front of Pyah, "Whoa there tiger. Sorry, but I don't hire my wife out to no man."

The old guy saunters around him, "Who said anything about your wife?" he asks, running his hand down Mark's buttocks.

Mark jumps forward, "Err, five hundred you say?" he checks, reaching quickly for the envelope Elleon gave him, "I think five hundred is a fair price," Mark hands him the money, "so when do we board?"

The old guy checks his watch, "Should be casting off in an hour so if you're not onboard then we go without you, ok?"

Pyah grabs Mark by the hand, "OK, that gives us time for a snack," she reasons, pulling him towards the café, "lover boy," she adds, teasing him.

Mark slaps her across the arse, "Yeah, well I'll just stay out of his way but you have a problem what with all those sailors, you know what sailors are known for," he says, sniggering to himself.

They grab a snack then board the ship but to Pyah's surprise not one sailor gives her a second glance. Mark starts to feel a little uneasy when he realises that he is the centre of attention, "Holy shit, we're on the ship of queens."

Pyah opens her top, showing as much cleavage as she dares but gets no attention, "Oh dear, I think you're right," she agrees, noticing most of them are too busy looking at Mark's arse, "hmm, I think we should have bought some anal lubricant before boarding," she says, slapping Mark's backside.

Mark turns to growl at her, "Don't do that in front of them, shit, it seems to arouse them," he says, looking around to see some of them licking their lips.

Mark approaches the captain, "Excuse me sir, but have you got somewhere we can bunk down?"

The captain laughs, "Sir? I like that. You can call me sir anytime," he says, giving Mark the once-over, "well there are cabins down through the lower decks but you can use mine which is up behind the bridge," he tells them, pointing towards some steps, "would you like some company?"

Mark puts his hand up, "Err, thank you but no, it's a kind offer but we have to sort out how we are getting to the city centre, which may take some time."

The captain blows him a kiss, "Well, anything you need just give a holler, right?"

Mark backs carefully away, "That's ok, we don't need anything, thank you," he says, pious in his sexuality.

Pyah giggles under her breath, "Oh, I have never seen you so uncomfortable where your manhood is concerned."

Mark drags her through the bridge, "It's all right for you," he says, closing in on her ear, "you wouldn't have to take a turn in the barrel."

Pyah scratches her head giving him one of those "WHAAATTT?" looks. Mark finds the cabin, "It's an old joke, I'll tell you later," he explains, locking the door behind them.

Pyah plonks herself down on the bed, "Talk about paranoid," she says, scoffing at him.

Mark paces, "Paranoid? Paranoid? Even you said they were after my arse."

Pyah stands to pose confidently, "Well now you know what it feels like."

Mark's head turns with a scowl, "What what feels like?"

Pyah eyes him up then down, "Being letched on," she answers with a wry, cocky grin.

Mark plonks himself down on the bed, "Yeah, yeah, I get it," he says, putting his head in his hands, "well I'm staying in here for the rest of the trip, and if anyone comes to that door I'm asleep, right?" he reaches out to check the lock one more time, "And I don't want to be disturbed, right?"

Pyah sits next to him, "So it's all right for me to take a stroll then?" she asks, stretching back before standing.

Mark grabs her arm, "Whoa, you're not leaving me, are you?"

Pyah shakes her head, "Lock the door behind me," she says, pulling a chair over, "stick this under the handle," she adds, chuckling out loud, "I'll give a secret knock when I come back."

Mark flings her arm to one side, "Funny. Very funny. Go on, fuck off, leave me to the wolves, why don't you?"

Pyah falls back against the door laughing, "Wolves? I don't think there's an animal amongst them. If anything, I would say they were a bunch of vixens, hmm," she says, placing her hand on her hip, "don't think they would bite if you wanted them to," she goes on, opening the door in case he slaps her, "might give you a good suck though," she adds then quickly slams the door behind her.

Mark opens the door slightly, "You watch what you're doing," he says, tutting to himself, "what the hell am I saying, you're probably more man than all of them put together."

Pyah shoos him back in, "If they hear you calling them that they might scratch your eyes out," she says, clawing the air while growling at him.

Mark locks the door then stands looking at the chair, "Fuck it," he decides as he slides it under the handle.

Pyah struts confidently onto the deck. A few of the sailors tip their hats and bid her good day but to her delight not one is sexually interested in her. She has never felt so free amongst men in her life, "I could stay on this ship forever," she remarks, muttering to herself as she leans out over the bow, "wow, I think I could strip off naked amongst them and they wouldn't bat an eyelid."

Suddenly a rather ripped African walks up behind her, "You should be careful, my dear."

Pyah spins, "Oh, I won't fall," she says, stopping dead mid-sentence to take in the rippling muscles hardly hidden by the torn skin-tight T-shirt and the scruffy jeans that appear to be painted to legs that are wider than her waist.

Her lip quivers as she gently bites down on it. Her heart flutters as her pulse races and her skins tingles with perspiration as she takes in his Adonis like sculptured pose. He reaches around her to look down at the waves crashing against the bow,

"Oh, I wasn't worried about you falling," he says, stepping back to peer into her eyes, "I was more concerned as to your state of mind," he explains, smiling softly, "you were talking to yourself."

Pyah puts her hand to her mouth, "Oh, I was just thinking out loud how safe I feel," she says, giving a girlish titter, "what with all you sailors being, well, you know."

His smile turns to an unashamed laugh, "Gay?"

Pyah covers her mouth with shock, "Err, you are gay, aren't you? No offence meant of course."

He drops his hands on the rail beside her, "Yes my dear, you are safe and yes we are ALL gay. Most of the gay sailors end up on here some time or another," he says, laughing into the air, "it's the only ship that will have us and it's the only ship where we don't have to hide it."

Pyah gives him the once-over, "Shame like? What a waste of meat."

He gives her an admiring look, "I'll take that as a compliment and might I add that you're quite hot yourself. For a woman. No offence."

Pyah smiles, "None taken."

He stands in front of her, "So where is your husband?"

She giggles, embarrassed, "I'm afraid he's hiding."

He frowns, "Why?" he asks, his tone changing to a little discordant.

Pyah places her hand on his shoulder, "Oh, he's not homophobic, in fact he's the exact opposite. Live and let live. He just isn't used to this much attention especially from, well, men."

The sailor laughs raucously, "He ain't got nothing to worry about. We don't bite. It's just that, well he is a hunk, but you can tell him we won't approach him. For crying out loud, he's married," he points out, waving at Pyah from head to foot.

Pyah starts to head back to the cabin then stops, Nah, let him stew for a while," she decides, going back to the handrail.

The sailor takes her by the hand, "My name is Jack."

Pyah shakes his hand, "Pyah, nice to meet you Jack."

They set off for a stroll around the deck, "So how long have you served on this particular ship?"

He pretends to count on his hand, "Oh, I been coming and going for what? It'll be about six years now," he figures, laughing and shaking his head, "so how long have you been on the run?" he asks, smiling profusely at her.

Pyah stands stunned, "Does everybody know our business 'round here?"

Jack chuffs, "The captain warned us all. Told us to be nice because you're dangerous or something like that," he says, walking slowly backwards away from her.

Pyah pulls her jacket open to reveal her gun, "He could be right," she says, smiling provocatively at him, "no, but seriously we were set up and now we have to find a way to right it."

Jack strokes his chin, "Yeah, the captain said that's probably the case. He's a good judge of character," he says, holding his hand out for her to carry on walking, "so is that a berretta?" he asks, pointing to her gun.

Pyah un-holsters it, "You know your weapons," she comments, handing it to him.

He weighs it in his palm, "Now, a dangerous woman wouldn't relinquish her weapon. Nice weight though."

Soon they're coming up on the bridge and Jack makes her put the gun away, "I think it's time we put Mister Fischer's mind to rest, don't you?" he says, leading her to the cabin.

She knocks on the door, "It's OK, it's only me."

Mark unlocks the door then Pyah pushes it open, "Oh and this is Jack."

Mark backs against the wall, "Hi Jack," he greets, trying not to look too uncomfortable.

Pyah places her hands on his shoulders, "Seems they've been ordered to leave us alone, especially you, so get your arse out on deck and take it like a man."

Jack sits on the bed, "Don't worry, there won't be any more teasing, because that's all it was when you came onboard," he says, trying to reassure Mark.

Mark takes a swig out of a decanter from the captain's desk, "OK, let's get this over with," he declares, strutting out of the door, twitching his neck.

Jack shakes his head and smiles at Pyah, "He's really got it bad," he remarks, chuckling to himself.

Mark walks on deck with his hands clasped behind him, trying and failing miserably not to make it obvious that he's hiding his butt. Pyah slaps his hands down, "Behave," she reprimands, chucking his chin, "you should be proud that you've got an admirable butt."

He stops, thinks for a while, then struts out onto the deck, "You know, you're right. Let the fuckers look. I got a nice bum and I know it," he says, opening his shirt a few buttons to blatantly flaunt.

After a short while he notices that no one is eyeing him up, "OK, it would seem that I have lost my allure? Why?" he asks, feeling a little disappointed and pouting at Pyah.

She sniggers at him, "They've been warned off."

At that he notices one sailor taking a sly peek which lifts his spirits again, "Hah, they want me. Look," he says, heading through them, proudly strutting his stuff all the way to the bow.

It isn't long before the port is sighted and the captain tells them to go back below decks until they dock.

Once they've docked and the ship is secure the captain approaches the Fischers, "Well, no one has come to check us but I've sent a couple of my girls, sorry, men, to check the harbour," he corrects, laughing out loud, "if it's clear then you should be able to discretely disembark," he cracks open a bottle of rum, pours three glasses and hands two over, "to a safe journey and I hope you find what you're looking for," he says, lifting his glass to toast them, "cheers," then knocking it back before giving a blissful sigh.

Soon his men re-board, "Well, if there are any agents down there then they're hiding well."

The captain pats Mark on the back, "Looks like you're still one step ahead of them. Good luck," he says, leading them down the gangplank.

CHAPTER 50
BED, BOARD AND A BANG

Its mid-afternoon and the harbour is bustling with trade. They head quickly through the harbour and out onto the streets of Sheerness to find a grubby little B and B. It's down a back street well off the beaten track so they book in for the night, safe in the knowledge that no one will think of looking there for them.

Pyah hugs Mark, "So, tell me again why we're in this pit."

Mark places his finger over her lips, "We're noted for liking our luxury, right? I mean who in their right mind would stay in a flea pit like this if they didn't have to?"

Pyah shrugs, "Suppose so," she agrees, gingerly lifting the bed sheet, "if I get eaten by something during the night you're dead meat though," she warns, running her hand down the bed.

Mark slaps her across the buttocks, "Eh, you never know? But it won't be insects that eat you. If you're lucky," he says, leering at her.

Pyah stands up and turns to put her arms around him, "Oh, I thought you had started to bat the other way for a minute there."

He picks up the pillow, "You cheeky mare," he says, chasing her around the bed while bouncing the pillow off her head.

They fall onto the bed arm in arm as he looks deep into her eyes, "Nope, sorry, there is only one man for me and she's laid on this bed."

Pyah picks up the other pillow, "Oh, so you think I'm a man now?" she asks, battering him around the head.

He grabs her arms and pins them to the mattress then pushes his lips against hers. She groans slightly then wriggles her legs out around his waist, "Hmm, thought I'd lost you for a moment."

He slides his hand up under her blouse, "Nope, but it has made me think," he says, kissing her neck, "I don't have to be ashamed when men look at me. I would prefer them to look at you, but if they want to look at me, who gives a shit?" he declares, nibbling on her ear, "I can't help being irresistible to both sexes."

Pyah pulls his head back, "Oh, aren't we the confident one now," she comments, kissing him, "well that makes two of us irresistible, doesn't it?" she asks, reaching down to unbuckle his belt, "Now you know how it feels to be God's gift, just like me," she tells him, slapping him across the arse.

Mark lifts up, "And you call me confident?"

She flings her arms out across the bed, "I can't help it if I'm beautiful," she says, scoffing at him.

He unbuttons her blouse, "Vain. That's what you are. God's gift?"

She grabs him by the lapels, "Hey you, you're supposed to compliment me, love me and find me the most beautiful thing you've ever seen," she reminds him, sniggering at him.

He rips her blouse open, "Oh, you are that, my darling. You certainly are that," he confirms, lifting her bra off her breasts.

She drags him forward, "So, get on with it and make love to me."

He pushes her legs down so he can drag her trousers over her feet, then rips her panties off, "So you want it fast and you want it now?"

She places her hands on his hips, "Not too fast. A bit of slow passion followed by a warm, oh just fuck it," she says, dragging his pelvis towards her, thrusting him into her as she bites down on her lip in full bliss, clawing his buttocks while pulling them apart.

He grasps her hands and pins them down beside her head. Pulls his legs up around hers to force hers shut, tightening her vagina around his penis, while holding her shins down with his feet. Holding her head still with her own wrists he forces his mouth against hers, plunging his tongue into her mouth. Pummelling thrusts rip into her as she is helpless to stop the onslaught of a pure, primal attack being launched against her senses. An attack that she feigns distress against but wouldn't have any other way. Mark can feel the beads of sweat building up around her lips as she struggles for breath. He retracts his tongue as hers follows it into his mouth. He sucks it up, holding her with his teeth. Her hot breath seethes from her nostrils across his cheek as the perspiration runs down her breasts against his chest. He can feel her heart pound through into his body while her temperature rises almost to boiling point. He clasps both her wrists with one hand then slides the other between her legs to vigorously rub her clitoris, forcing her to climax early. Muffled groans of delight can be heard as he presses his mouth firmly against hers, still thrusting through her climax. His hand dampens but he still holds her, forcing her to ramp up into a frenzy once more. Without rest he grips her breast, squeezing her nipple then claws back down to her clitoris to force her through into another uncontrollable climax. He releases her tongue to allow her to breathe easier before starting another onslaught on her.

She gasps, "No, not yet, I can't breathe," through her gasps for breath as he slams his mouth against hers, forcing his tongue back down her throat to pin her again.

His torso slides against hers, lubricated by the sweat between them as she tries violently to shake him off. Mark just holds her firm, carrying on his consented onslaught, but as she's at her pivotal moment he releases her mouth and hands, grasping a handful of hair to pull her head to one side then biting down gently on her neck as he slides his other hand around to penetrate her anus with two fingers, enhancing the final climax to the point of her almost passing out before rolling off exhausted and unfulfilled himself.

Pyah lies drained, awash with sweat, unable to comprehend her state of mind. Catching her breath, she turns her head, "Holy shit, we got to do that again."

Mark scoffs, "Oh he ain't finished. The only problem is the rest of my body would argue the point."

Pyah struggles up on to her elbow, "You mean you didn't cum?"

Mark shakes his head, "Think I left it too long."

She drops her head onto his stomach, "Give us a sec and we'll see about that," she says, sliding her head gently down to pop his penis into her mouth.

Mark just lies, humming to himself as Pyah's arms start to regain their strength enough to hold her up. She forces down, remembering how to deep throat him. His hand slowly slides onto the back of her head but her hand comes up to take it off then she waggles a finger at him. She tentatively caresses his scrotum before stealthily sliding a finger into his anus. The shock alone brings him to an immediate ejaculation. Unable to do anything through his spasms to prevent her from ass raping him with her hand he just rides through it, pretending to be un-amused by the whole experience.

Once finished, Pyah looks up at him smiling, "enjoy that then?"

Mark looks at the ceiling, "Oh, you know I'm going to get you back for that," he says, pretending to be disgusted.

Pyah crawls up him, "Not tonight though hun, I'm knackered."

He pulls her in to spoon her, "No, not tonight because I'm goosed too," he agrees, pulling the cover over them, "but trust me, when you're least expecting it, bang."

Pyah folds his arms around her, "Oh that should be interesting, because I think you've already done everything imaginable to me that I can think of."

Mark thinks, "Might buy some of those anal beads or one of those anal hooks see how you like them?"

He looks over to see Pyah's eyes closed and lies back with a contented grin on his face as the sea air drifts through the open window to lull them into a well-deserved sleep.

CHAPTER 51
NINJAS IN THE NIGHT

The clatters and bangs of a nearby ship yard, mixed with the hustle and bustle of the loading of ships, is an early alarm for Pyah as she stretches. Realising her bra is still up around her neck she pulls it down, then softly climbs out of bed as not to wake Mark. She looks around at her bleak surroundings and realising there is no ensuite she peeks out of the door, "Oh, for fuck's sake, where the hell do I get a shower in a hovel like this?"

At that, Jack appears, leaning against the wall next to her door, "There is a shower room down the hall," he directs, pointing at a door marked WC, "but you might want to cover yourself up before heading down there," he warns, pointing down at her naked bottom half, "and may I suggest you get fully dressed before coming back to your room?" he suggests, raising an eyebrow.

Pyah slaps her hand over her muff, "Oops, sorry about that."

Jack smiles, "Like I said before, you, are definitely the kind of woman that could make a man like me go straight, but the scum that frequent this place wouldn't think twice about trying something a little less subtle. So, don't give them the opportunity," he pushes the door slightly, "in fact, I would think about taking your husband, just to be on the safe side."

Pyah looks back at Mark, "Hmm, I think I might just do that," she decides, then kisses Jack's cheek, "thanks for the heads up," she says before shutting the door to softly wake Mark.

Mark sits up rather bleary-eyed to watch Pyah slipping her trousers back on, "Oh, kinky."

Pyah scowls at him, "No it's not fricking kinky, it's disgusting. The bloody bathroom is down the hall so you get your arse out of bed because you're coming with me."

Mark shrugs, "Wasn't on about that, I was just saying kinky because you're going commando."

Pyah picks up her ripped panties, "Like I'm supposed to wear these? Remember you tore them off me?"

Mark smiles, "Oh yeah. Some night that."

She throws them at him, "Come on, get dressed, I need a shower. Bad enough I have to put these dirty clothes back on."

When they are out in the hall Jack reappears, "Good morning Mr Fischer, did you sleep well?"

Mark smiles at him, "Oh yes," he says, patting Pyah's butt, "don't suppose you know where we can get some new clothes, do you?"

Jack looks around, "What, around here? The only place is a work ware store at the end of the next block," he says, scratching his head.

Mark rubs his chin, "Was thinking more of a ladies' boutique."

Pyah grabs his hand, "Work ware will do, just get me out of these grubby cammies."

Mark looks at her, then back at Jack, "I'll tell you what, while you're showering I'll go get some new clothes."

Jack shakes his head, "That's not a good idea leaving her alone here, trust me."

Pyah grabs his arm, "Yeah you listen to him. You're showering with me."

Jack shakes Marks hand then bids him goodbye. Pyah drags him into the bathroom, "Quick shower, no hanky panky, then we get out of here to that work ware shop ok?"

Mark agrees, "Yeah, not too comfortable myself. I'm sure something bit me during the night," he complains, scratching his arse.

Soon they are showered, redressed, and at the workware shop. Its full of coveralls and uniforms of all different professions. Pyah mooches around at the nurse's outfits as an old gentleman approaches her, "Can I help, dear?"

Pyah puts a nurse's dress against herself, "Have you got a changing room?"

Looking at her with the dress against her he walks around the counter, "Yes my dear, but I don't think that's your size," he says, handing her a smaller size, "this should be more your fit and the changing room is at the back of the store," he directs, pointing to a small door to the rear.

Mark picks up a black coverall and a donkey jacket. He walks around to Pyah, "What do you reckon?" he asks, holding them up.

The door opens but when the old guy looks no one is there, "Hmm, must have been the wind," he says, turning his attention back to Pyah, "what exactly is it you're after madam?"

Mark freezes as he feels the cold hard steel of a gun muzzle pressed firmly to the back of his neck. A voice whispers, "Nice and slowly, put your hands where I can see them," as Pyah sees a tall, rather buff, young man appear from behind Mark.

She scans for a weapon of some description but then another man appears from behind Mark, pointing a gun at her, "You don't want to do that," he warns, holding a NSA ID up, "we have a capture or kill order on you so don't make us kill you."

The one holding a gun to Mark's head frisks him very carefully while the other walks out into open space, pointing his gun at Pyah.

Pyah slowly struts towards him, an arrogant smile on her face, "Yeah, but you ain't going to kill us when you have a witness present?" she asks, flippantly pointing at the store owner.

The agent points his gun at the store owner, "Who says we have to leave witnesses?" he asks as he looks at the store owner, taking his eyes off Pyah.

Taking the opportunity, she kicks him swiftly in his groin, then blades his hand across his neck before side-kicking him towards the counter. Mark throws his elbow back into the other agent's solar plexus then heel palms him in the nose before grabbing a nearby tent to throw over his head. The store owner grabs the one at the counter then bangs him across the head with a small fire extinguisher, rendering him unconscious as Pyah rushes to help Mark. She grabs the agent's gun then pistol-whips him across his head to render him unconscious.

Mark turns to the store owner, "Have you got any gaffer tape?"

The store owner reaches down for a box, "Oh, I got better than that," he says, pulling two gag balls out, "got these as a mix up with an order. Even came with handcuffs."

Pyah reaches down to the agent's belt, "These will be better," she says, pulling the agent's own handcuffs out, "proper security cuffs. Now all we need is a safe place to stick them."

The store owner fetches some climbing rope, "If we wrap this around them, then hang them from that rafter," he suggests, pointing up to the ceiling at the back of the store, "they won't be found for a while."

Mark binds one while Pyah ties the other, "Best if you close the shop for the rest of the afternoon, maybe go and buy some more stock or something," he says, handing the store owner a wad of cash.

He sets off to the front of the store to pull down the blinds and lock the door before putting the closed sign up, "Yeah, I don't want to be around when they come to," he agrees, grabbing a few essentials, "hope you're not a pair of psychotic killers that I'm going to end up doing time for?" he checks, chuckling nervously as he heads for the front door, "Take whatever you need, there's a back door into the ally, just put the key back through the letterbox. Good luck," he adds, then he rushes out, slamming the door closed behind him.

Pyah frisks the agent. She finds a PDA with the plans for the hospital in one of the files, "Well, it looks like going in as staff is out of the question," she says, showing Mark the agent's orders, "they have to check everyone's ID. But there is a service stairwell that leads straight to the roof," she adds, grabbing some rope "we could abseil down to the adjacent room, looks like they're both empty either side and they have adjoining doors."

Mark picks up some black jeans and a black turtle neck pullover, "looks like we're going in ninja style," he says, rummaging through the boxes behind the counter, "now all we need is a way through the security glass."

Pyah opens a drawer, "Well, would you believe it? The old guy has glass dissolver. Think we'll take a few tins of this," she throws them into a holdall on the ground.

Mark throws a pair of jeans and pullover to Pyah, "Go and get changed while I see if he has any lock picks."

Pyah strips down, "What's the point of changing rooms? No one is going to see me," she says, blowing Mark a kiss "you forgot the underwear," she adds, grabbing a pair of boxer shorts.

Mark shrugs, "Sexy, very sexy," he comments as Pyah slides them on.

Pyah grins at him, "Yeah right, have you checked near the keys?"

Mark walks over, "Yes, I do believe we're in business," he says, throwing a set of lock picks in the air.

Just before they are about to leave one of the agents starts to come around. Pyah pistol-whips him unconscious again, "Eh, don't want him seeing what we're wearing."

Mark turns to smack the other across the head, "You never know," he says, shrugging before they head for the back door.

As they step out of the back-door Mark checks for vehicles, "Oh look, the old guy has a van," he pushes past Pyah, "he did say help ourselves," he reasons, rushing back into the shop.

Pyah stands fidgeting, "Now what's he up to?"

He reappears with the van keys, "Transport," he says, waving them in her face then jumping in the driver's seat, "oh and it's got a satnav," he says, putting the hospital's address in.

Pyah jumps in the back, "We're just going to scout it out, right?"

Mark nods, "Yeah, then we'll come back tonight and burgle the place," he says, smiling profusely.

Pyah kisses him on the cheek, "You're relishing this, aren't you?"

Mark pats her leg, "Ninjas in the night," he scoffs at her.

Taking the most out of way route, they arrive at a block of flats about half a mile away from the hospital. Mark pulls the van into the underground car park, "Well, this overlooks the hospital," he says, jumping out, "should give us a good view from the roof and it's facing Lacey's room."

To avoid detection, they start up the stairs, stopping after every five flights. Pyah hands the holdall to Mark, "Here, this thing's getting heavy."

When they reach the top, they are both exhausted and dripping with sweat. Pyah flops on a nearby vent, "Shit, I don't know why I got changed? I stink just as bad now as I did before I showered."

Mark drops the bags on the floor, "Yeah but I carried these things up the last ten flights," he says, flopping on the floor beside her, "let's just rest here for a while. OK?"

After a short rest and a drink Pyah crouches to sneak over to the wall. Looking over she has a perfect view of the hospital but something else catches her eye, "Mark, come and have a look at this," she says, pointing at the ground, "what do you make of that?"

Mark sidles over, "Hmm, looks like someone has had a tripod up here," he says, examining three indentations in the roof.

Pyah brushes the gravel away, "Yeah, and bloody recent too."

Mark takes a pair of binoculars out of the bag, "Looks like someone else is taking an interest in our friend," he says, pointing the binoculars at the hospital "but who and why?"

He can just see Lacey in her bed. The arm of a guard can also be seen through the door, posted outside the room, "Looks like she's well-guarded so we're going to have to be very careful."

Pyah pulls a second set of binoculars from the bag, "Yeah, I can see this going tits up for some reason."

Mark drops his binoculars down around his neck, "Do you have to be so bloody negative? Think positive, we are going to see Lacey, even if she can't see us. OK?"

Pyah pulls a card out of her jumper, "Well yeah! I even got her a get-well card," she says, smugly grinning to herself, "well, he did say help yourself."

Mark shakes his head then lifts his binoculars, "So the service stairs come out on the far side, then we rope that handrail to drop down to which window? Left or right?"

Pyah points at one, then the other, "Eeny meeny miny mo. The one on the left."

Mark sniggers, "You're mad."

She turns slowly to him, "We're about to assault a heavily guarded hospital to break into a room to deliver a get-well card to someone in a coma," she reminds him, shrugging, "you're damned right I'm mad," she agrees, patting him on the shoulder, "but you're coming with me, so what does that make you?"

He pats her across the bum, "Downright fucking crazy, but would you have me any other way?"

She smiles at him, "What a team," she slumps down against the wall, "so what are going to do till nightfall?"

Mark sits down next to her, "Bit rough to go banging on this," he says, rubbing the gravel with his hands then jumps up to his feet, "I know, we could go shopping."

Pyah grabs his leg, "Sit down, you fucking loon. If they see someone bouncing around on this roof they might send someone to investigate."

Mark sits sulking, "Sorry dear, just trying to lighten the mood."

She shakes her head then rolls her eyes, "I'm sure you get spurts of attention deficit," Pyah slides her hand down his trousers, "maybe this will shut you up?"

Mark pulls her hand out, "Somehow I don't think he wants to play with gravel stuck up my arse."

Pyah's head jolts back, "Whoa, you, refusing sex? I was going to give you a blow job too."

Mark picks up some of the gravel, "Trust me, this is going to kill your knees, and me moving backwards and forward is going to give me gravel rash," he says, dropping the gravel, "the thought of it has sent him into a definitive sleep."

Pyah slumps back against the wall, "So what the hell are we going to do for, what, seven hours?" she asks, looking at her watch.

Mark shrugs, "Can't go shopping, err, can't get a hotel room because all the comfy ones will be watched, can't stay up here in case we're spotted, you decide."

Pyah starts to look around, "Oh shit, never thought of that."

Mark looks into the sky, "Thought of what?"

Pyah peeks over the wall, "Helicopters, you know, police choppers. Shit, we need to get out of here and under cover somewhere," she says, heading for the door.

When they reach the underground parking lot they sit in the van for a while, then Mark starts it up, "Well I ain't sitting here all day," he says as he heads for the exit.

Pyah jumps in the back, "So where we heading then?"

Mark just shrugs, "Hey, I'm just going with the flow, making it up as I go. See what happens," then he slams the brakes on, "Jesus, shit man," he curses, shouting out of the van to have a go at a pedestrian that's just walked out in front of him, "holy shit Jack, you trying to get yourself killed?"

Jack leans over the hood, "Well looks like you're going somewhere in a hurry. Anything I can help with?"

Pyah pops her head out of the window, "Not unless you can suggest somewhere out of the way that we can enjoy a few hours in private?"

Jack strokes his chin, "Depends on what you call private? If you're just wanting to stay out of the way from prying eyes then where I'm heading could be good, but if you want to be alone then I can't help."

Mark grimaces, "Out of the way from prying eyes will do, but I know what you're going to say," he says, swaying his head from side to side "it's a gay bar isn't it?"

Jack slaps his hand down on Mark's shoulder, "No Mister Fischer, it's the best drag house in the city. Don't you worry though, if any of them gay tramps lay a hand on you I'll rip their nuts off and feed them back to them. OK?"

Mark gives him the thumbs up, "So long as they know I'm not that way inclined."

CHAPTER 52
DRAG QUEEN AHOY!

The street is alive with normal everyday people as Jack leads the Fischers through the doors of what looks like a normal drab club, but when they get past the huge bouncers, a set of massive glittery steel doors and a sequin curtain, the place opens up to a vibrant den of shimmering lights, diamante encrusted pillars and a whole bunch of drag queens bustling around a stage full of glistening wardrobe clad divas lip-syncing to Diana Ross. The place is a hive of buzz and fun. Jack places his arm around Mark's shoulders as Mark's eyes widen. Jack stops him, "Trust me, if I got my arm around your waist it means you're available. If I'm holding your hand it means keep off, he's mine," he says, pointing around the room, "but my arm around your shoulders mean you're straight, so don't even think about it."

Mark sighs, "OK, I'll trust you on this one," he says, quivering with fear.

Pyah grabs his hand, "So what if I hold his hand?"

Jack scoffs, "They'll probably think you're a drag queen too," he says, laughing out loud, "but at least they'll know you're together," he shrugs, raising his hand to the barman, "give them whatever they want, on me."

Mark slaps his hand down, "Make mine a scotch on the rocks, if you don't mind?"

Pyah smiles, "Vodka please."

Another patron brushes past Pyah, gliding his hand slowly across her butt, "Hmm, sweet."

Pyah turns to smile at him, "Oh, I am that, hun. I am that."

His eyes shoot wide and his jaw drops, "Oh. My. God. Please tell me you're not a woman?"

Mark turns to sneer at him, "She better be. She was when I married her."

The man rubs his hand profusely, "Err, I am so sorry," he apologises, then holds his hand out, "Jerry, the name's Jerry," he introduces, batting his eyelashes at Mark, "oh, what am I doing?

You two are married," he says, pointing at both Pyah and Mark, "unless you shake it both ways that is?"

Jack places his hand around Jerry's waist, "Run along sonny," he says, pushing him towards the stage.

Just at that the drag queens that are singing finish their number so Jerry rushes up to grab the mike, whispers in the pianist's ear, then turns to the audience, "This is a special song for the one man in the room that I know I can't have," he says, pointing at Mark.

The spotlight turns on Mark as he buries his head into the bar, "Please tell me this isn't happening?"

Pyah puts her arm around his waist, "Wow, looks like you got yourself a fan."

Mark peeks up at her, "Or a stalker."

Jerry bursts into '*I Will Always Love You*', making romantic gestures towards Mark and blowing him kisses. Mark looks up at Jack, "Can't you do something about him?"

Jack just laughs, "Can't stop him looking or singing."

Mark buries his head again, "Someone please shoot me now," he says as the rest of the queens on stage join in.

Pyah pats Mark on the back, "He's bloody good though."

Mark sneers at her, "Don't even think of encouraging him."

The barman approaches Mark with a cocktail, "From the lady at the end of the bar."

Mark looks down to see what looks like an actual woman raising her glass to him, "Oh shit, not another one."

Jack leans on the bar, "Wow, you are honoured, that's the owner, and yes she is a woman and she is a lady," he turns to Pyah, "if you want I could do the introductions?"

Pyah turns to study her, "Hmm, cute, don't mind if we do."

Mark reaches out for Jack's hand, "Are you absolutely sure that's a female?"

Jack places his arm around Mark's shoulder, "Oh, she's female, but she don't take kindly to men, that's why I said you're honoured. In fact, she is so uptight and straight-laced I don't know what she's doing running a place like this."

As they approach, the lady takes out a cigarette case, then as she places one in her mouth Mark produces a lighter to light it, "Mark Fischer, and this is my wife Pyah."

The lady leans forward to light her cigarette, "Hmm, I know who you are," she says, taking a drag, "you're the couple that the

NSA wants dead," she states, blowing smoke in Mark's face, "because they're not sure if you've joined the Lazarus Project."

Pyah steps forward, "My, aren't we well informed?" she asks, facing the lady off.

The lady takes another drag from her cigarette, "Relax honey," she says as four bruisers appear behind her but the lady waves them away, "it's all down to those rockets you stole from the NSA safe house."

Mark's hand snaps up, "Whoa! NSA safe house? What do you mean NSA safe house? We took them because someone we trusted stole them for that Lazarus group thingy."

The lady scoffs at him, "Eh, I'm only telling you what I know," she says, stubbing her cigarette out, "you give them rockets back and your freedom comes with it."

Pyah sits down next to her, "So how come you know all this and who exactly are you?"

The lady orders another drink, "I own this place," she says, pointing around the room, "and my name is Reaches, MISS Reaches," she goes on, taking the glass off the barman, "I was approached several years ago by the Lazarus Project. Wanted me to join. Gave me the low down," she explains, shaking her head, "I told them I didn't need the hassle, so here I am with a different name and a bar full of queens to hide amongst."

Mark scratches his chin, "So you know what the Lazarus project is and what they're doing?"

She takes out another cigarette, "That's the problem. I know too much. Top and bottom of it is world domination."

Mark drops his head sniggering to his self, "Sounds like a bunch of wackos with a supremacy complex."

Miss Reaches lights her cigarette, "That's the problem, there's not just a bunch of them. They have infiltrated the governments, the medical organisations, the military, the utility companies, the banking corporations, the justice systems of most countries. law, judges and all that."

Pyah gasps, "You're shitting me? That means they're, what, thousands strong?"

Miss Reaches flicks her cigarette, "Tens of thousands, if not more."

Mark orders another drink, "So what's their plan?"

Miss Reaches takes a drag, "Oh, that's easy. They intend to cripple certain countries' economies, bringing them to the point of depression, then step in to lend a helping hand so to speak. The problem is they want total control for their services. And they'll get it, due to the fact their operatives are seated at the top of their infiltrated organisations," she explains, blowing smoke across the room, "you know, like president's aides and the monarchies advisors, top surgeons and the health authorities' financial executives, etc," she stubs the cigarette out, "yep, the world's in shit and it doesn't have a clue."

Mark takes a swig of his scotch, "So, do you know who they are? All of them?"

She shakes her head "Nope. Only met a Russian bitch named Anja and an American, but he didn't give his name. Just another suit with a badge."

Mark's ear prick, "About six foot six, maybe six foot eight, a hundred and eighty pounds, platinum blond hair with ice blue eyes?"

She shakes her head, "Nah. Six foot six, about hundred and forty, maybe hundred and fifty pounds, brown eyes with brown, almost black military crew cut. Typical marine if you ask me."

Pyah sips her vodka, "Could be anyone. What was the badge?"

Reaches shrugs, "Didn't get a good look. NSA, CIA or something like that," she stands up, "he was giving the orders though," she adds, then she walks away, turning to the barman, "give them anything they want. On the house."

Pyah follows her, "Whoa, hang on."

She turns, "Look, I told you more than I should. This could get me found and killed so leave it. I'm going for a lie down," she says, disappearing through a curtain.

Jack grabs Pyah's arm, "Like the lady said. Leave it," he says, pulling her back abruptly as four bouncers step in front of her.

Pyah pats him gently on the chest, "Hey, I was just trying to be friendly," she says, spinning to the barman, "think I'll stick with the cola," she orders, patting the bar.

Mark steps up beside her, "He did say she was uptight," he remarks, then turns to the barman, "I think I'll have a good old English pint thanks."

Jack suggests they take their drinks and sit to watch the show, "You never know, you might enjoy it."

Mark shrugs, "Well, we ain't got nowt else to do for a few hours."

Jack sits with them, "So what you two mischievous imps planning then? Apart from brushing up on your English colloquialisms."

Mark scratches his head, then turns to Pyah. Pyah sips at her drink, "Who's he going to tell?"

Mark nods, "Nobody, I suppose."

Jack leans in, "Ooo, this sounds ominous."

Mark is about to unload their plan when Pyah pushes him back, "We're going to break into that big hospital, past all the security and deliver a get-well card to a dear friend."

Mark looks at her, "I think that vodka has gone to your head, my dear," he says, turning to Jack, "but yeah, that's about it."

Jack's jaw drops, "Seriously? How the hell are you planning on all this?"

Mark scowls, "Haven't actually worked out the finer points. Like getting in. But once we're in we're going to the roof then abseiling down to the next room and climbing in through the window."

Jack looks around, "Well, you can't exactly storm the Bastille, but I reckon that was not your plan? You need a distraction while you slip in the back door, yes?"

Mark nods, "It would help."

Jack sits forward, "I might be able to help you on that score," he says, pointing at a couple of drag queens dressed in nurse's uniforms.

Mark throws his hands up, "What the hell, why not?"

After a few more drinks and a chat with the girls, or rather lads, a plan is hatched. The show goes on as queen after queen get up to sing. Eventually Pyah and Mark are so relaxed they are coaxed up on stage to sing '*Who Wants to Live Forever*'.

Jack approaches them, congratulating them on their performance, but he tells them that it's time to leave as night is starting to fall. They head out in a minivan with some of the drag queens, destination: the hospital.

As they get in the minivan, a flock of pigeons fly overhead as Mark looks up, "Holy shit, and I do mean shit, what is it with English pigeons, are they racist against Americans or something?"

Pyah sniggers as she sees him covered in pigeon shit, "I'm American," she points out, looking down at herself, "and they didn't attack me," she gloats, twirling to show a clean outfit.

Jack spins, "Must be your deodorant or something, man," he says, about to pat Mark but changing his mind.

Mark starts to brush himself down but when his hand touches it he stops, "Jesus H, I look like I've been paintballed with French brie and I smell like a bad case of Gorgonzola. I'll give them shit for luck," he complains with his arms outstretched, "that's what you English say, isn't it? Shit for luck. Yeah, bad luck."

Pyah walks over to give him a tissue, "Here, it's the best I can do. Mind, it's good camouflage," she sniggers.

Mark grabs an old rug from the back of the minivan, "Can we just get this over with so I can get out of these clothes?" he asks, rubbing himself down while getting in the back of the minivan.

The driver takes the scenic route to the hospital to avoid any unwanted exposure. The night falls rather quickly so they park in a side street, close to the hospital. The queens in nurse's outfits get raucous with bottles of wine and start to stagger around the back of the hospital. They approach the guards on duty to flirt and chat them up, offering them a drink. The guards chase them but they won't go so the guards escort them to the front of the building at gunpoint.

This is Pyah and Mark's chance. They slip in the back door and head for the roof. Once on the roof, they quickly rope off, then abseil down to the adjoining room to Lacey's. Spraying the window with the glass dissolver they slip in quietly, then pick the lock to Lacey's room.

Once in the room Pyah sits next to Lacey, "Oh sweetie, please come back," a tear runs down Pyah's cheek as she stands to kiss Lacey.

She stands stoking her face as Mark places the get-well card on the bedside cabinet then whispers to Pyah, "You do realise even signed P and M they're going to know it was us?"

Pyah shrugs, "Who gives a fuck?" she asks as she heads to the bathroom to swill her face.

As she's bent over the sink a knife appears at her throat, "Not a movement, not a twitch," she recognises Ben's voice.

She is as still as a statue as he moves around her back, "I know you're probably not going to believe this but I'm not the bad guy."

Pyah keeps still, "Oh, I believe you, but put the knife down and we can talk."

Ben leans in, "I put the knife down and you start kicking shit out of me."

At that he feels the cold steel of a gun muzzle pressed against his neck, Mark has crept up behind him, "She said put the knife down and we'll talk. So, put the knife down and we'll talk."

Ben hands Pyah the knife. She takes it and slowly turns scowling at him, "OK, cute stuff, talk," she demands, waving at Mark to lower the gun.

Mark looks at her befuddled, "Err, he's one of them. You know, that Lazarus shit."

Pyah shakes her head, "No he isn't, are you? What are you, NSA?"

Ben drops his head, "Can't say, but I will tell you as much as I can. Not here though."

At that the door swings open again, "You know you lot are making enough noise to bring the whole of the hospital running?" George walks over to the toilet and takes a pee, "I suggest you do what you're going to do, quickly and quietly then get the hell out of here," he says, shaking himself, then pulling his zipper up, "and I would do it fast because they know you're in the building."

Mark turns to Ben, "So how did you get in here?"

Ben smiles, "Same way you did but the other room."

George checks the coast is clear as the three head back out the way they came to the roof.

Once on the roof Mark turns to Pyah, "If they know we're in the building then all exits will be covered. Won't take them long to work out we're up here either."

Pyah looks over one of the rails, "There's a lower roof here. If we tie the ropes together, double them up, we can abseil down then pull the rope down to abseil to the ground."

Mark looks over, "Good plan, but how do we get off the grounds?"

Ben taps his nose, "I got that covered."

Mark stops him as he ties the rope, "OK, spill before we go any further."

Ben takes out his phone, "Look, I can't tell you much, but I am going to meet one of the head honchos of the Lazarus project tomorrow night and you're welcome to tag along," he sits on the rail, "all that leaves is a matter of four missing rockets."

Pyah steps forward, "OK, we didn't know it was a safe house. We thought you were the bad guy."

Mark pulls her back, "Err, we still don't know if he's a good guy."

Ben smiles, "Well, you know that kill or capture order out on you?"

Pyah nods, "Go on."

Ben wags the phone at her, "I know someone who can rescind it. All I need is the whereabouts of those rockets?"

Mark is still suspicious but Pyah tells him where they are. He makes a quick call then turns to Mark with the phone on speaker. They hear a voice say, "OK, as soon as we locate the items we'll rescind the order. Be about an hour."

Soon they're on the ground when Mark turns to Ben, "OK genius, over to you."

Ben walks towards a waiting morgue vehicle, "Your carriage awaits," he says, jumping into the driver's seat.

Up on the roof where Mark found the indents of a tripod Elleon is listening through a high powered directional mic, "Well that's interesting," she says as she sees them get into the van through binoculars and watches them drive away, still listening to their conversation when another vehicle slips out of a side road to follow them, "hmm, and that's bloody interesting too. Now who are you?"

She hears Ben tell Mark that they are going to the Corinthia hotel just before they get out of range. She packs up quickly then sprints down the stairs where she has a little fiat waiting then heads off after them.

When she gets to the hotel she notices the car that followed parked up, just down from the hotel. She scans the area for a vantage point then climbs up on a roof, "Yes, couldn't get any luckier if I tried," she says, looking straight into the window of the room where the Fischers and Ben are.

She sets up her listening post to sit and wait.

CHAPTER 53
AN AUDIENCE WITH...

A clear sky sparkles with stars above a cold London town. The night air is brisk as the temperature drops around Elleon. She listens intently through her earphones to the conversation between the Fischers and Ben as they plot. Wrapped in a blanket, shivering while stamping her feet as she spies through her binoculars from the cold rooftop.

Ben lays out a plan for the night to follow, informing the Fischers of the pending plan, "I know that there is a mole and I know that most people suspect me, but trust me, I'm not the bad guy," he pours a drink "I don't know who the mole is but I intend to find out tomorrow night," he says, handing Mark the decanter and a glass, "apparently I'm supposed to meet with Anja and one of the top brass of the Lazarus project in this underground car park. Then I'll find out who's been one step behind you and one step ahead of me all the way."

Pyah takes the glass off Mark, "So you mentioned a list?" she asks, sitting on the arm of a chair.

Ben sits opposite her, "Yeah, apparently someone has a full list of the main members of the group. If only I could get my hands on it then I could stop this madness. I just know it," he sips at his drink, "you two can tag along but you need to stay put, of sight. The only way I'm going to get the list is if I can finally convince them that I'm one of them and, in order to do that, I have to be willing to do some rather unlawful things. You get it?"

Mark paces around him, "OK, so let's say we believe you, what do you want us to do?"

Ben huffs, "Nothing, that's just it. Stay out of my way and stop compromising my cover."

Pyah stands up, "Yeah ok, we can do that. So long as this stupid kill thing is lifted?"

Ben smiles, "Trust me, it should be revoked by now. But I would keep your heads down till after this meeting."

Mark places his glass down, "Right. You get it revoked and we see who this top brass guy is, then we're off, back to America. OK?"

Ben lifts his glass, "That'll do for me."

Mark swigs his drink back, "Well, I'm off to bed," he announces, turning to Pyah, "you coming?"

Pyah looks at her glass, "Yeah, in a minute. I just got a few more questions."

Mark takes the glass off her, "I think they can wait," he says, putting her glass on the table next to his.

Pyah picks it back up, pushes him away, then swigs it back, "You think I'm leaving that? Yeah right," she says, then takes his hand, looking sultry over her shoulder at Ben, "night, night," she says, blowing him a kiss.

Mark funnily drags her into the bedroom, "If you're feeling that way out then show me not him."

Pyah dims the lights in the bedroom then starts to close the door. Noticing that Ben can see straight into the bedroom through a mirror conveniently placed against one of the walls, she decides to leave the door slightly ajar.

Ben turns the light off in the living room then sits in a chair opposite the mirror. He realises that Pyah has deliberately left the door ajar, "Oh, kinky bitch. Well, I won't pass up the opportunity," he reasons, mumbling to himself as he settles himself down in a comfy chair with his glass and a bottle.

Elleon watches from her rooftop roost, "Jesus, is she going close them blinds or what?" she wonders, secretly hoping that Pyah likes to show off brazenly with the blinds open.

Mark casually lies on the bed as Pyah slinks around the room, seductively brushing the surfaces of the dressing table drawers. She turns the radio on low then dances slowly at the bottom of the bed. First turning to tease Mark, she then positions herself in the room facing the door where she can just make out Ben's silhouette as she slowly unbuttons her blouse. She winks at him, then pouts to let him know she sees him, before slowly turning to face Mark as she slides the blouse down off her shoulders, still holding it against her breasts. The soft light shimmering across her cleavage casting a warm glow to her flame red hair. She wiggles as she seductively places her finger in her mouth then runs it down her bosom, sliding her hand under her bra strap to lift it off her shoulder. Blowing a kiss to Mark, she drops the blouse to her feet, running her hand teasingly back across her torso, up over her breast to lift the other strap off her shoulder. A girlish smile under her provocative glare. Nefarious wonderings swaying around her mind of how she can tantalise and allure. With a hand holding the bra's front she slowly spins away, unclipping the bra then turning slowly she slut drops to a squat to lower her bra to the ground. Unbuttoning her trousers, she stands holding her ankles to unfasten her shoes, then sliding them off she stands, flicking her hair over her head, cascading like a torrent of flame above her. She wriggles the trousers over her hip to the beat of the music, then turns again to pose to Mark with her curvy buttocks while sliding the trousers over her feet to step out. She gives a churlish glance over her shoulder then drops her gaze to her boxers as she slips them over her cheeks. Bending down, sliding them over her legs till they drop to the ground for her to step out. Turning she slinks around the bed to straddle Mark. She undoes his belt then his button to finally unzip his fly. Teasing his boxers down she gently pulls out his penis and drops forward to kiss him while arching her back to insert the monster into her. Slipping slowly down on to him she licks his lips then plunges her tongue deep into his mouth. She slowly thrusts backwards and forwards across his hips then lifts herself to plunge back down on to him as he grips the wrought iron headboard. Her breath is hot against his cheek. She lifts herself on his chest to arch her back, then swishes her hair above her in a torrent. Craning her neck back, the perspiration runs down her breasts to softly drip from her nipples onto his torso.

Mark places his hands under her buttocks to lift her slowly off then pulls her up towards the headboard. She grips the rail as he lowers her onto his lips, plunging his tongue deep inside her.

Ben sits sipping his drink, watching as she presses herself against the wrought ironwork. He stands up then quietly rushes to the bathroom, "Oh shit, going to need a new set of underwear at this rate," he curses, mumbling to himself as he unzips his fly.

His penis pops out fully erect, "Shit fella, going to have to cool you down before you pop," he says, turning the shower to cold as he undresses to step in.

Elleon is glued to her binoculars as she watches the show unfold, "Oh my God, what the fuck is he doing to her?" she asks, involuntarily rubbing her own breasts as she watches Pyah lift off Mark's face, sitting on his chest to slide down through her own juices to arrive at his penis. She strokes it gently then caresses the end with her tongue, looking back up at Mark with provocative eyes.

Ben looks down at his penis as it dwindles under the cold water, "OK fella, think it's about time we went to bed. Can't handle any more of that tonight," he decides, wrapping a towel around his waist to exit the bathroom.

On his way to the second bedroom he catches a glimpse of Pyah as she slowly engulfs Marks penis with her lips. Ben holds himself, "Oh for fuck's sake!" he curses, rushing back into the bathroom, "I know, I know, we haven't had that done to us for a long time," he says, slapping a cold towel on his manhood, "but it's time for us to go to sleep," he sighs, looking down at himself, "oh, come on," he exclaims, unable to shake the erection as the thought of Pyah's mouth around him invades his consciousness.

He looks in the mirror, "You're going to have to do something," he says, desperately trying to think of something unsexy as an image of Anja's wrinkled face against his genitals pops into his head, "oh hell no," he moans but his erection dissipates rather quickly, "hah, that did the job. In fact, I think it frightened you. Shit, where did you go?" he asks, looking down at a shrivelled mass.

He walks gingerly back to his bedroom with his hands blinkering his eyes. As he reaches for the doorknob he drops the towel, inadvertently unblinkering his eyes to catch it. From the corner of his vision he seizes a reflection of Pyah, "Oh for fuck's sake," he curses again, slumping back to the bathroom.

Elleon stands fixed to her binoculars, unable to pry herself away from the spectacle as she hears Ben's mumblings. Spinning the scopes in his direction she sees him strolling back to the bathroom in his nakedness. His erection stood proud, glaring him straight in the eye. Elleon's hand slips down her trousers as she unconsciously starts to play with herself, "Oh shit," she curses, jumping back from the binoculars as her hand feels the warm juices flowing into it, "shit no," she curses again, unbuttoning her trousers to drop them and her underwear to the ground, "fuck, I don't need this," she complains, reaching into a holdall for a small box of tissues to press against her vagina.

Mopping up her indulgence she grabs some more tissues, "Going to need new undies if I'm not careful," she says, reaching for more tissues to pad her panties as she can't help but peer through the binoculars once more, "no, no, no," she reprimands herself, pulling herself away but then dragging her trousers up to take just one more peek.

Mark grips the bed end as Pyah slide his penis into her throat to completely envelop it. His hips start to jitter as he tenses through the pleasure. Pyah slips her hand under him then slips one finger into his anus to enhance his ejaculation. He spasms and writhes as Pyah flicks her way back up with her tongue to tantalise the end of his urethra. His buttocks raise from the mattress as he convulses, tightening his cheeks around her finger, exploding into her mouth as she plunges back down on to him. She pulls slowly off him then crawls up his torso to kiss his neck then plunging her lips against his as they gasp each other's breath before laying beside him in a pool of sweat.

Elleon steps back from the binoculars, totally aghast at her experience. Flopping to the ground as she feels the sweet sticky juices between her legs.

Mark looks down at his sodden shirt, "Well, I think I need a shower," he says, standing as the clothes on his back cling to him.

Ben sits on the loo to relieve himself, finally giving in to the inevitable before washing himself then returning to his room a satisfied chap.

Pyah helps Mark strip before blatantly walking him naked across the darkened living room to the bathroom. She sets out some towels as Mark steps into the shower, "Oh shit, this is cold," he exclaims, jumping back out as he turns the temperature up, "shit, he must like a cold shower."

Pyah smiles as she knows why the shower's temperature has been lowered. They set it correct then step in together. No sexualness involved, they wash each other down, then quickly step out to dry each other, before returning to the warmth of the bed.

Elleon packs up her stuff then heads down from the roof to her jeep. She rummages for some wipes and cleans herself before changing, then grabs a coat, a blanket and the car rug. She sets a five am alarm then snuggles down for the night to drift off into a quiet slumber.

CHAPTER 54
SHOWER PARTY

Four thirty am and the crisp sunlight pierces the two buildings in front of Elleon's jeep. A shard of blazing light slices through the morning air into her vehicle, dazzling her as she prises open her bleary eyes. Quickly snapping them back shut she rubs them, "Oh, you have to be kidding," she says, looking at her watch through the morning fog that glazes across her vision and blinking intermittently, "four thirty?!" she exclaims, dropping her head back on the bag she's used as a pillow.

She shuffles about, her bones aching with the cold as she tries to snuggle back into the covers, "Nope, this is no good," she sighs, sniffing her armpits, "shit I need a bath."

She drives towards the river then parks up. Stepping out she gazes out at the river. The tide is out as the pungent stench of the black mud engulfs her senses, "Hmm, don't think I'll be going skinny dipping in that today," she gets back in her jeep and starts to drive around the deserted city streets.

Suddenly she spies a fountain, "Ah, fresh water."

Pulling up alongside she steps out, walks over and dips her hand in the freezing water, "Brr, God, the things I do for my country," she says, stripping off to her underwear and glancing around to make sure no one is around.

She steps into the cold icy water then splashes herself, letting out a shrill scream as the water runs down her back. She quickly rubs herself all over then rushes back to her jeep. Jumping in the back she rushes to get clean clothes from a holdall, "Oh fuck, oh fuck," she curses, shivering as she dries herself.

Soon she is dressed, feeling refreshed she uses the jeep's air conditioner to dry her hair as a policeman approaches, "Excuse me miss, but is everything ok?" he asks, tapping on the window.

Elleon nods, dropping the window, "Yes officer. Don't suppose you know where I can get something to eat around here at this time of the morning?"

The officer thinks, "Well, a burger van should be setting up shortly near the market, 'around the corner if that's any good," he replies, directing her.

She finishes drying then sets off for the burger van. When she arrives the cop is there waiting, "Figured you would be along soon," he says, picking up his coffee, "what would you like? On me."

Elleon gives him the once-over, "Hmm, could do with a bacon sandwich and a black coffee, if you don't mind?" she says, thinking to herself "*he's cute*" as she slinks around him, "so, you married?"

He smiles, "Nope, and no, I don't have a girlfriend, before you ask."

Elleon picks up her coffee, "So you are hitting on me?"

He shrugs, "Hey, can't a guy offer a damsel in distress a cup of coffee without her thinking he's hitting on her?"

Elleon sips her coffee, "Ooo that's good," she sighs, closing her eyes to take in the aroma as the coffee warms her through, "so you're not going to ask me out then?"

He twitches, "Well, since you mentioned it, how about dinner? Tonight? Pick you up about seven?"

Elleon scowls, "Sorry, can't do dinner. Busy tonight, but you could take me for lunch. Got most of the afternoon free."

He strokes his chin, "Problem is I don't get off till two."

She pats his bum, "Two is just fine. Where?"

He takes out a notepad, "Where are you staying?"

Elleon laughs then points at her jeep. He walks over and struts around it, "Hmm, seems you might be picking me up then," he says then kicks the tires, "two o'clock, the corner of Avonley road and Old Kent road?"

Elleon jumps into her jeep, "See you at two o'clock then," she says, blowing him a kiss before spinning the wheels in front of him to burn off down the road.

He smiles then wags a finger at her before getting into his police car shaking his head.

Ben is also an early riser. He is out of bed by six am making breakfast. The aroma of eggs and freshly grilled bacon wafts through the apartment, drifting into the Fischers' bedroom, tickling Pyah's senses as she stretches through the warm sunlight cast across her bare bosom, "Hmm, smells like time to get up," she gently shakes Mark but he just rolls over to snuggle back down into the pillow, "suit yourself, but I'm hungry," she says, throwing the sheets back then grabbing a dressing gown before exiting to follow the bacon trail to the kitchen.

"Hope you made enough for me? I'm fricking ravenous."

Ben turns his head slowly, "Figured you would be," he says, unconsciously eyeing Pyah up, the memories of the previous night bouncing around his head, "sleep well?"

Pyah sits at the table, "Eventually. You?"

Ben cracks an egg, "I always sleep well. How do you like your eggs?"

Pyah smiles to herself, "Over easy will do. Did you enjoy the show last night?" she watches as his shoulders tense.

His head lifts slowly, "Oh, what show was that?" he asks, trying to be nonchalant, keeping his eyes firmly fixed on the pan.

Pyah stands and walks over to his side, "Why do you think I left the door open?" she asks, leaning around him, "that mirror is very well placed," she says, licking her lips, "I don't mind. Mark might, but I don't."

His head spins, "And what would he say if he knew?"

She shrugs "Not a lot," she says, turning to walk back to the table, "so long as you don't try and act on it."

His hands had just started to come around her waist, "Oh, right," he says, then he backs off to the pan, "so I'm allowed to look but no touching?"

She sits then pushes the chair back, "Oh, you're allowed that," she says, opening her robe, "in fact he loves it when a man looks at me like that," she goes on, putting her hands between her legs, "makes him proud to walk down the street with me knowing I picked him."

Ben places the eggs on a plate then some bacon and sausages, "Well, he is a lucky man and I admire him for that," he says, turning to bring the plate to the table, "holy shit woman!" he exclaims, dropping the plate as he sees her in her nakedness.

He fumbles to pick up the broken crockery, trying his hardest not to look, "For Christ's sake, do you have to?" he asks, sweeping the eggs up with a cloth, "Put it away before you get us both shot."

The kitchen door opens, "OK, what you doing with my woman?" Mark stands sternly in the doorway, "You better not be shagging."

Ben holds his hand up, "We weren't doing anything. Err. Look mate. It's not what it looks like," he defends, averting his eyes away from Pyah, "tell him it's not what it looks like."

Pyah starts to snigger to herself, "He was just going to show me what kind of man he is."

Ben's eyes widen as he spins to look her straight in the eye, "Whoa, hold on there," he protests, his head spinning to Mark, "I was just ... Err. Well I was. Oh fuck."

Mark can't help but laugh, "Derr I know you were just ... And I know you were just ... last night."

Pyah's head spins, "What, you know he was watching us?"

Mark nods conceitedly, "What, you think I'm stupid?" he asks, picking a piece of bacon of the table, "Poor lad hasn't had any for a while, if that's going to, well, you know, then who am I to take away his enjoyment," he says, smiling then sitting at the table, "so what's for breakfast? Hope you got coffee on?"

Ben stands shocked. His skin white as a sheet. His mind awhirl, then gathering his thoughts he grabs a dustpan and brush as Pyah takes them off him, "You sort out the food. I'll clean this up."

He shakes his head, "You two are a pair of bastards, you know that?"

Mark smiles, "Ah ha," he agrees, munching arrogantly on the bacon.

Pyah sits next to Mark, "Yeah, we had a hell of an audience," she says, biting off a piece of Mark's bacon, "what with you and our friendly neighbourhood Peeping Tom," she goes on, gesturing towards the window, "seems we were covered from all sides," she finishes, laughing out loud.

Ben stops, looks at Pyah, then walks to the window, "What do you mean? Peeping Tom?" he asks, scanning the buildings opposite.

Pyah walks over to the window, "Yeah, seems that someone was up on that roof watching," she says, pointing at a rooftop in the distance.

Ben rushes out of the room, "Shit, you mean we're under surveillance?"

Pyah walks over to pour herself a coffee, "We were but they're not there now," she says as Ben comes back in with a pair of binoculars.

Pointing the binoculars at the rooftop, "Are you sure? What makes you think someone was there?"

Pyah sips at her coffee, "Oh, I saw the glint of a scope or binoculars or something while we were shagging."

Mark turns his head slowly towards the window, "Hmm, maybe we should go take a peek."

They quickly get dressed then head for the rooftop.

Once up there, Mark stands at the wall, "Yep, someone was definitely up here."

Pyah picks up a tissue, "Hmm, sweet," she hums, sniffing at it then pushing it under Mark's nose, "what do you reckon?"

Mark sniffs at it, "Ooo, young," he says, then bends down, "these weren't made by a rifle though."

Pyah bends down, "Told you, binoculars or a scope. Not deep enough to be a rifle."

Ben walks over, "What the hell are you two on about?"

Mark points at three indentations in the roof, "She had a tripod."

Ben huffs, "So what makes you think it's a woman?"

Pyah tosses the tissue at him, "Seems she couldn't control her urges."

Ben sniffs at the tissue, "So you reckon…" he starts, hesitating then sniffing again, "my, that is sweet," he says, turning to look towards his apartment through the binoculars, "so I'm presuming you have someone in mind?"

Pyah and Mark turn to him in unison "Elleon?"

His head rips around "Elleon? Is she here? In London?"

They both nod then Mark walks over to him, "Yeah, we saw her in Scotland, said she had other business but she might catch up with us later."

Pyah walks over, "Seems later has come sooner than we thought."

CHAPTER 55
DATING ADAM

London bells start to chime as noon drifts across the town. At twelve pm Elleon starts to mooch around a boutique., finding a flouncy summer dress. She makes her face up, gets her hair done then sets off for her date.

When she steps out of her jeep the policeman stands aghast at the transformation. "Wow, I thought you were cute before but holy shit woman, you do scrub up well."

She spins, "You like then?" she checks as the dress twirls out.

He places his hands on his hips, "Ah ha, I like very much," he confirms, nodding eagerly, "so, where you taking me?"

She drops into a girlish stance, "Your town, you tell me." He scratches his head, "Hmm, well there is this little place across town, a bistro that serves delightful lunches. Yeah, I think I'll show you off there."

Elleon links arms with him, "Ooo, show me off, eh," she coos, opening the jeep door for him, "I like the sound of that. Mind, I would like to know your name."

He shakes her hand, "Adam. Adam Kent, and you are?"

She shakes his hand, "Elleon Vixter," she says, then kisses him on the cheek, "nice to meet you Adam Kent."

He stands looking at the door, "Aren't I supposed to do that for you? And seeing as though I know where we're going I think I should drive? Eh?"

Elleon sits in the passenger seat, "Why, thank you, kind sir," she says, openly giggling.

He rushes around to the driver's seat then sets off for the bistro. Elleon notices that he keeps glancing over at her, looking her up and down, "Err, excuse me, but eyes on road," she says, pointing forwards.

He looks at the road, then back at her, "Can't help it. I mean, wow," he breathes, looking down at her legs.

Elleon pushes his head back towards the road, "Policeman, remember? Driving without due care and attention and all that," she scolds, smiling to herself.

He laughs out loud, "Oh, trust me, I'm giving plenty of attention."

She slaps his leg, "To the road, not me!"

When they arrive at the bistro Adam jumps out of the jeep and virtually sprints around to Elleon's door. He escorts her into the bistro, strutting with his chest puffed out, "Table for two, my good man. A window seat please for this beautiful young creature, if you would."

Adam wines her and dines her, swoons and flirts all the way through the meal making it abundantly obvious he has a place in his heart for her. The chemistry is overwhelming as Elleon's heart gives a flutter. She knows instantly that he is the one.

When he invites her back to his place she jumps at it without hesitation but when he pulls up outside an old warehouse she starts to become a little dubious and very nervous. He hops out then goes to a large sliding door, "OK, you just stay there, won't be a minute," he says, putting a code in a keypad by the side of the door.

It starts to open as he comes back to the car. He drives in as the lights starts to illuminate, opening up to a beautiful two storey open plan apartment, "You like?" he asks, proudly waving his arms around, showing off his lifelong creation.

Elleon is in awe as she attempts to step out before the jeep comes to a complete stop. Adam grabs her as she is completely oblivious to the danger, "Wow," she breathes, her head spinning, her eyes wide, trying to take in the majesty of the place.

Adam takes her hand, "Well?" he asks, pulling her face towards him.

She looks at him briefly, "Well what?" she returns, pulling away from him to soar through the ambience of light.

Adam stands with his hands on his hips, "Well, do you like it? Welcome to my humble abode."

Elleon drifts her hand across the back of one of two five seated settees, lost in the void of a floor that surrounds them, "Oh my God, this is massive! You live here all on your own?"

He nods proudly, "This is just the ground floor, wait till I show you the upstairs."

Elleon spins around to him, "The bedroom?" she asks, lowering her eyebrows to a sociable scowl.

He wipes his mouth, "Yeah, but I'm not trying to get you into bed, if that's what you think? Well I am, but not just yet. Look, do you want a tour?"

Elleon skips like a child over to him, "OK, lead the way," she agrees, gently clasping his hand, "you're the boss," she says, her head pulled down in a shy girly manner.

All the exterior walls are privacy glass with cream coloured sliding panels. A sliding wall separates the living area to the dining area. When he opens the wall Elleon steps into a small banquet hall with a table to seat twelve placed dead centre, "Oh my God. You must feel like a king or something eating at this," she remarks, brushing her hand along the twenty-foot walnut table.

At the other end of the table another movable wall is slid back to reveal a kitchen that every chef would kill for, an Aga oven plus a conventional gas oven with an American style wide-bodied fridge stood next to a cool room and large floor freezer. A ten-foot pedestal centre piece houses an eight-ring halogen hob and two catering sink units, complete with vegetable cleaning faucets.

Elleon touches everything, "So, do you have a cook that comes in or are you one of these men's men that cooks for himself then serves himself on that big grandiose table?"

He brushes his hand across the hob, "Well I do cook. In fact, I love cooking, but I eat on the sofa next to the TV when I do eat in," he says, tipping his head to the side, "but for the most of it I only use this place for sleeping to be quite honest."

Elleon slinks around to him, "Well, I'm definitely surprised and very impressed," she says, putting her arms around his waist, "this is a nice house," she compliments, looking around, "if that's what you call it?"

He takes her by the hand, "OK, let's get you to the bedroom," he says, wiggling his eyebrows.

Elleon taps his hand, "I'm not that kind of girl, but I will allow you to show me your boudoir."

His head drifts back, "Oh trust me, it's all of that and some," he promises, laughing under his breath.

He walks her up a metal staircase to a steel door, "I know it's a bit clinical but just wait," he says, swinging the door open.

Elleon steps in, expecting a bachelor's pad bedroom dressed in reds and golds, but to her surprise she steps into a wet room with a luxurious round padded bath taking centre stage. The walls are ornate Greek figures with fountains for showers, furthermore, placed right at the rear is a sauna with plunge pool. Elleon swoons, "Now this is what you call a bathroom."

Adam steps over to the controls, "Yep, took me three years to get this how I wanted it," he confides, flicking the showers on to give her a water show as the streams dance to soft music.

Elleon runs her hand around the rim of the bath, "And here's me thinking you just wanted to get me to the bedroom," she comments, sitting on the bath edge, "three years? To build a bathroom?"

Adam switches off the showers, "Hey, finding the right designer and supplies is a long, drawn out process if you want it just so."

Elleon smiles, "Hmm, suppose, if you want it the way you want it. Looks like it was worth it though?"

Adam nods proudly, "Now the bedroom took five years. Alongside the bathroom of course, not consecutive."

Elleon takes his hand, "Of course," she echoes, frowning, "so where is this masterpiece?" she asks, pulling him back onto the landing.

He gives her a playful scowl, "Well I think you may be able to guess," he says, his eyes aiming down the walkway.

Elleon cocks her head to the side as she sees two more doors. One single then further on a large double door, "Hmm, wonder if the master bedroom is behind door number two," she hums, dragging him to the first door, "so what's in here then?"

He opens the door to a bright pastel yellow bedroom, "This is the guest room," he says, stepping inside, "thought I would give it a nice, neutral colour that's bright but not too garish? Yeah?"

Elleon steps in "Hmm, it's big and it most definitely is, err, refreshing?"

He puts his hand on her shoulder, "Excuse me, but I've slept in here and its great waking up to a sunny feel."

Elleon turns on her heels, "OK seen it, show me the other one," she demands, pulling him out towards the master bedroom, dancing like a kid in a candy shop, "if that's the spare I can't wait to see this," she says, standing by the door in anticipation.

Adam slowly turns the handle then pushes the door wide for her to step in. She stands in the door way, "Holy Mary, mother of God," she gasps, her breath taken by an eight-foot crystal chandelier, lost in the mass of a void that he calls his bedroom.

A plush white carpet four inches' thick lies under her feet, stretching forty feet to her right and forty feet to her left, then disappearing off over one hundred feet into the distance. A twelve-foot-high four poster bed is nestled behind the chandelier, covering ten feet wide by twelve feet long, draped in the finest white silk sheets. A dazzling white canopy of the finest soft lace radiates out like a Bedouin's tent around a spire then cascades to the floor in a deluge of pleat.

Elleon rushes to the bed then stops suddenly, spinning on her heels, "Can I?" she asks, indicating the desire to dive on it.

Adam waves an uncaring hand, "Go for it."

She sprints then dives for the middle, rolling onto her back she is lost in the vastness, giving the feeling of a small child's first time in her parents' bed, "Oh my God, this is huge," she says, sniggering to herself, "take you a week just to get out of it," she laughs, waving her arms and legs as if making a snow angel.

Adam nonchalantly swaggers across, then slips onto the bed to lay beside her. He strokes her hair as she looks deep into his eyes, "Am I going to wake up in a minute back in my jeep and find this is just a dream?"

He leans forward, "I hope not because if this is a dream then I don't exist. Hmm, not too keen on being a figment of someone else's imagination thanks," he says, then he presses his lips softly against hers.

His hand drifts down her neck towards her cleavage as she involuntarily twitches, nervously brushing his hand away from her breasts. He pulls back, surprised, "Everything all right? Moving too fast?"

Elleon shakes her head, "It's just...," she stops then pulls his head back to kiss him.

He places his hand on her hip then creeps very slowly towards her breast. She squirms slightly, "Oh, for crying out loud," she says, sitting up then turning to him, tears welling in her eyes, "I want to, oh shit do I want to, I'm just, well, I have never been with a man before. Not like that anyway," she admits, turning away from him, blushing.

He slides up behind her, "You're a virgin?" he asks, wrapping his arms around her.

She holds his arms, "Yes, well, not exactly, sort of."

He kisses her neck, "Not exactly, sort of?" he asks in his confusion.

She turns on the edge of the bed, "It's a long, complicated story but the top and bottom of it is," she starts, hesitating briefly, "the girls showed me, broke me in, if you know what I mean?"

He shakes his head in amazement, "The girls? Broke you in?" he asks, holding her shoulders, "Why?"

Elleon closes her eyes, "I used to be what you would call a cock teaser if you must know, anyway, my friends decided to teach me a lesson."

Adam huffs, "Some friends! And how exactly did they teach you a lesson?"

She pauses, "Well, they pretended they were going to rape me," she confides, dropping her head.

Adam scowls, "Hold on, your so-called friends threatened to rape you? Shit, I'd hate to meet your enemies."

She stops him, "I came on to their husbands ok? Now let's drop it," she says, getting off the bed to walk away in shame.

Adam jumps off the bed and rushes around in front of her, "Whoa, hang on a minute," he says, seeing the tears streaming down her face, "you think I'm going to judge you on your past? Hmm, do I really look that stupid?" he asks, lifting her chin, "Seems to me that we both need to take things a little slower. How about we start again and we move at your pace?" he suggests, wiping the tears from her eyes.

She stares at him in disbelief, "What, you still want to be with me after what I just told you?"

He smiles, "Hey, silly little girls do silly little things but then silly little girls grow up, don't they?" he says, cocking his head to the side.

She pecks him on the cheek then he takes her hand to lead her back to the bed, "Don't worry, I'm not going to seduce you but I just have to show you this," he says, laying her on the bed then bouncing on beside her, "I know it's daytime and all that but you need to see this," he enthuses, pressing a remote control, "it would be better at night," he adds as the canopy slides to one side then the whole roof of the bedroom splits and raises to reveal the blue sky above, "you should see it on a clear night sky."

Her eyes widen, "Wow," she gasps then turns to him, "is that an invitation?"

He props himself up on his elbow, "Well, if you're up for it? We could just lay here and swap stories under a starlight sky, cuddling each other? If that's ok with you?"

She smiles at him, "You're just a romantic softy at heart, aren't you?"

He nods, "Yep, and proud of it."

She looks back up, then at him, "It's a date but I'm busy tonight so how about tomorrow night?"

He lies back and puts his arm around her neck, "Sounds like a plan."

She looks at her watch, "Well. I don't want to but I have to dash," she says, getting off the bed.

He escorts her to her jeep, "Call me," he says, kissing her as she drives away.

CHAPTER 56
CAR PARK RENDEZVOUS

Twilight casts its eerie glow across the darkening London sky as Ben sits cleaning his gun, loading up with extra clips and sipping at a coffee. Pyah and Mark dress down into grey coveralls, guns concealed about their persons. Mark turns to Ben, "So we get to see who is behind this Lazarus project?"

Ben shakes his head, "Nope."

Pyah steps in front of him, "What?"

Ben stands up, "No, I want you two to stay in the van," he says, sliding a magazine into his gun, "don't want to spook anyone. After all, they think I'm one of them and I would dearly like to get my hands on a certain list. So, you two need to stay out of the way, but don't worry there's a boom mic in the van so you can hear every word. For Christ's sake, stay down and out of sight though. OK?"

As they head out of the door Pyah turns to Ben, "I know we want to get there early, but isn't this meeting supposed to be in three hours?"

Ben laughs, "Well I don't know about you but I'm starving so I thought we might go for some food first?"

Pyah stops dead in her tracks, "Hang on a minute. You expect me to go to some fancy restaurant dressed like this?" she asks, pointing down at her coveralls "I mean I'm really dressed for dinner, aren't I?"

Ben softly takes her by the hand, "Well I was thinking of getting drive-through."

Mark gives him an unwelcome look, "Drive-through? As in greasy burgers and stuff?" he asks, then shrugs, "Suppose it's an experience we haven't tried."

Pyah stands fast, "Do you know what that will do to my figure?"

Mark takes her other hand, "OK, you can have the salad."

She cringes, "Have you seen the cheap rubbish they put in those things? And then they smother it in that oil stuff."

Mark shakes his head, "How would you know? We've never tried one."

Pyah drops her head with her eyes closed, sighing, "OK, let's go and get drive-through, but if I have a heart attack and die I'm taking you two with me," she warns, smiling as she follows them out of the door.

Ben checks the coast is clear before the Fischers come out to the van. He opens the door while they scurry across then jump in, "Now just remember, keep out of sight."

Mark pulls a car rug over his knees, "Yeah, yeah, we know the score just get to the food, I'm fricking starving now."

Ben drives for about five minutes then pulls into the drive-through, "So what would madam like?"

Pyah peeks out from behind the curtain, "Ooo that chicken sandwich actually looks nice. I'll have one of those with two lots of fries and a large banana milkshake, thank you."

Both Mark and Ben look at her in disbelief. She shrugs, "What the hell, I'm hungry too."

Ben turns to Mark, "And sir?"

Mark scans the menu, "OK, I'll have a burger with everything on it. No, make that two and one of those king-size fries. Oh, and some onion rings with one of those dips. One of those chicken sandwiches, same as her, but I'll just have the regular coke, better make that a diet coke."

Ben shakes his head, "You're shitting me, right?"

Mark gives him a serious look, "No!" he exclaims so Ben goes ahead to order.

They sit in the car park to eat but Ben is astounded at how fast they consume their food, "Jesus H, you'd think you'd never been fed!"

Pyah puts her hand over her mouth, "Actually this isn't bad," she admits, turning to Mark, "why haven't we tried these before?"

Mark just shrugs then carries on eating.

When they've finished Mark picks up a napkin to wipe Pyah's mouth then smiles rather leeringly. Pyah jolts her head back, "OK, what's going through that dirty little mind of yours?"

Mark flicks his eyebrows, "You know how much that little lot cost?" he asks, licking his lips, "Next to nothing. And have you seen how sloppy the sauce is?"

Pyah looks at him puzzled, "Go on."

He smiles a dirty smile, "We could afford to buy a boatload of this stuff," he says, flicking his eyebrows again, "then I could smother you in it and ooo the thought has just woken him up."

Pyah gives him a stern leer, "That's not the job we're supposed to be on," she scolds, flicking his genitals, "and he can go back to sleep until we're finished."

Mark give a grunt, "Ouch woman, that hurt," he complains, rubbing his balls.

Pyah smiles, "It was supposed to. Now he's asleep. But it is a damned good idea," she adds, smiling a cheesy smile.

Elleon parks down from the car park then scouts around, an hour before the meeting. She finds several entry points but only one entrance/exit for vehicles, "Well that should do me," she murmurs, then bunks down to wait in her jeep.

While she waits she notices a black Rolls Royce pulling up to let two men out. They separate then scout the outside of the car park, just as she had, they then enter as the Rolls drives away. She slips out of her jeep, climbs up to a higher level, then scopes the place out again to see if she can find the two men but they have disappeared, "Hmm, could do with my thermal imaging goggles for this."

She heads back to her jeep to sort out her gear when another car pulls into the car park. Elleon notices Anja is driving but an unknown person hides under a wide-brimmed hat in the passenger seat. Her curiosity peaks. Looking around carefully, she exits her jeep, sniper rifle fitted with night scopes in one hand and a small holdall in the other. The holdall contains a silenced automatic, a pair of normal binoculars and a pair of thermal imaging goggles. She scales the outer wall as she did before, dropping down behind a parked van then shimmies across the floor to the ramp for the lower level. Checking through her thermals she can see Anja's car, still warm parked over on the far side. Anja is standing against a pillar in front of her vehicle but behind her she can just make out a figure. It's the passenger hiding in an alcove ten feet to Anja's right.

As Elleon is about to leave to go back the way she came she notices another heat signature skulking in the shadows about fifty feet to Anja's left, twenty or so feet to her rear. Elleon is careful to back up, "Now who the hell are you? And where did the goons go?" she asks herself, panning around to scope out the rest of the level, "Ah, there you are," she breathes, the unmistakeable broadness of their shoulders gives them away as they hide in another car that must have been pre-parked for that purpose.

She slowly backs up to the van then climbs back out of the car park to wait in her jeep where she can see the entrance in wait for the next arrivals.

Half an hour passes before Ben arrives, Pyah and Mark hidden in the back. He drives slowly down the car park's entrance ramp then turns left as he spies Anja straight on. He drives his van to a secluded spot where the Fischers can observe without being detected. Without turning he passes two pairs of headphones through to Pyah, "That microphone should be quite adequate to pick up everything that is said so just stay down and try not rocking the van. You should be ok here," he says quietly as he slowly steps out of the vehicle.

He slips a hand gun at the back of his trousers then places one in his shoulder holster before starting to walk towards Anja. As he is walking he scans the rest of the car park level, looking for any untoward movements.

On seeing Ben's arrival Elleon slips out of her jeep then starts to scale the wall again. As she reaches the upper level she notices the Rolls Royce returning to park up outside the car park, then looks through her thermals. She notices one heat signature in the back and one in the front. The man in the front gets out and casually walks away in the direction they arrived, "OK where's the driver going?"

She shakes her head then sets off back to the lower level. As she reaches the drop down to take her discretely to the lower level she notices two heat signatures in the back of Ben's van but she also notices the two thugs quietly approaching the van, "Damn, this party's getting a bit crowded."

She realises she is in no position to warn Ben as she watches him stepping into the light in front of Anja. Anja casually raises a gun, pointing it directly at Ben, "Well, I'm actually surprised you turned up."

Ben holds his hands outstretched, "And why wouldn't I turn up?"

A familiar voice echoes from the darkness behind Anja, "Because I told her about your little rooftop rendezvous at the hospital," it says as Fargo walks out of the darkness, a gun firmly fixed on Ben's head, "you see we managed to intercept your phone conversation too," he explains, stepping beside Anja, "you know I said all along you weren't quite right but I couldn't figure out which agency you were working for. Shit, to my surprise, you're a fucking freelancer being fed by a corpse at the NSA," Fargo waves his gun in the air, "Ooo the penny drops," he exclaims as Ben's head starts to dip.

"You killed him?"

Fargo quickly points his gun back at Ben, "Not so fast, just keep reaching for it then slip it out and place it nice and easy on the ground in front of you."

Ben's hand quivers halfway to his shoulder holster. Anja takes her pistol in two hands, "Seems you made two mistakes," she says, pulling the hammer back, "first the phone call, then you brought your two little friends along," she elaborates, pointing her gun behind Ben.

Ben slowly turns. His eyes close as he sees the two thugs leading Mark and Pyah towards him in handcuffs. Mark cringes, "Sorry mate, they got the drop on us before we had a chance."

Ben slides his gun out slowly, "So you're this mystery guy at the top of this thing then?"

Fargo laughs out loud, "No, I'm just a member of the committee," he says, smiling a cocky smile, "you see there are twenty-five of us. Been a member now for fifteen years," he leans against the pillar.

Ben places his gun on the floor, "So you were part of this shit before you were recruited by the FBI?"

Fargo taps the side of his head with his gun, "In fact, let me tell you a story of a young hacker that just got lucky and found this set of lists," he says, taking out a personal data assistant, "and was put in the position of these people either killing me or making me a very rich man. Bet you can't guess which one I chose?" he adds, grinning an arrogant grin, "These people got me into the FBI and I just had to play the fool. Which I did very well I might add," he huffs, "I mean that dope of a partner hasn't got a clue," he laughs.

At that the other figure lurking in the dark steps forward. Elleon watches him through her thermals as he takes something out of his pocket, slips something up his sleeve then puts the object back in his pocket. Cramer steps out from the darkness with his gun drawn, pointing it at Fargo's head, "Yeah well, this idiot might just rectify that problem right now," he says, growling through his teeth.

Fargo turns his head slowly, "Well, aren't we a clever boy now?"

While Fargo is distracted Ben reaches for his other gun then points it directly at Anja.

Elleon shuffles along the back of the cars to get a better line of fire. When she reaches the end, she can see both Anja and Fargo lined up perfectly for a single shot. She takes aim then waits.

Fargo laughs out loud, "One thing you're all forgetting," he says, waving his gun towards the Fischers as the two thugs bring them out into the light, "your two little randy friends. You shoot me and BANG, BANG, no more randy friends."

Surprisingly, Cramer doesn't lower his gun, "Shit, I think they'll agree with me on this," he says, looking at the Fischers, smiling, "if their sacrifice gets me that list then it will all be worth it."

Mark's head drops, "He's got to be shitting me."

Fargo waves his PDA at Cramer, "Oh, you want this list?" he asks then throws it to Cramer, "Won't do you any good. As I told you I'm a computer genius and that's encrypted to hell. You put the wrong password in three times and the whole thing is wiped," he says, waving his hand at the PDA, "so go ahead it's the only full list of all the members."

Cramer slips a memory card from his sleeve, popping it into the PDA without Fargo noticing he transfers the list file over to it, then pops it out to slip it back up his sleeve. Fargo watches him tapping on the touch screen, "Look, stop messing with it, you're not going to crack it so just pass it back like a good boy."

Cramer stands looking blankly at it for a moment then tosses it back, "OK, what's your next move, seeing as though we seem to have a Mexican stand-off."

Elleon watches what Cramer does. Realising he now has a copy of the encrypted list she pulls the trigger. The bullet passes through Fargo's temple, killing him instantly, but glances off Anja's forehead, sending her reeling across the floor, unconscious. Elleon then sprints up the exit ramp, loading another round into her rifle.

Halfway up she sees the man in the back of the Rolls getting out then attempting to get into the front seat, "Oh no you don't," she says, taking aim as he sits down.

She only gets a glimpse of his foot as he is shutting the door then fires, blowing a hole through his ankle. She carries on running up the ramp loading another round. Dropping to her knee she guesstimates where his knee is then shoots again through the door. Loading another round, she runs up to the vehicle, smashes the barrel of her rifle through the side window and points it at the man's head, "And where the hell do you think you're going?" she asks, reaching in to drag him out by the scruff of his neck.

The two thugs that have Pyah and Mark turn their guns on Ben and Cramer but Mark and Pyah shove them backwards before making a dash for the nearest car.

Cramer unloads his gun in the general direction of the two thugs but under the barrage they make a run for the back of the car park. Ben is close on their heels as he drops to his knee to shoot both of them in the back of their heads. Cramer slumps next to Fargo to pick up the PDA but finds that the screen is scrambled. Ben saunters over to the two thugs' bodies, searches them, retrieves the keys for the Fischers' handcuffs, then walks over to unlock them, "My, you two don't half like making life difficult."

Elleon finds that the man in the Rolls is a seven-stone scrawny weakling. She drags him down the exit ramp as he howls and squeals like a wounded animal. As she reaches the bottom police cars start turning up at the entrance behind her. A black saloon pulls up with them. George from MI6 gets out, flashes his badge then starts down the ramp, "It's ok, she's with me," he says, walking casually to Elleon then turning to two men following, "take him for interrogation," he orders then pats Elleon on the shoulder, "nice bit of shooting that, my dear," he compliments, handing her a card, "come down to the office and we'll see what we can do for each other," he suggests, walking off towards the rest of the party.

When he reaches Cramer he sees him sat on the floor resting against the pillar, tapping the front of Fargo's PDA. Cramer glances up at George, "Well, that's fucked it," he says, passing him the PDA.

Elleon walks up and sticks her head around George, "You got the list and another one of those? I can fix that. Probably have it back up and running in, what, an hour?"

Cramer looks down at the broken PDA then back up at Elleon, "You kidding me, right?" he asks as George hands it to her.

She tips it over then back, "Nope, not a problem, just make another back up of that file you stole, just in case."

Cramer stands up, "Oh, you caught that then?"

She grins at him, "Why did you think I shot that bastard?" she asks, pointing down at Fargo.

Pyah walks over to Anja then turns back to Cramer, "So you got the list?"

Cramer turns to look at her, "Would seem so," he says, then realises what's happening.

Pyah points a gun at Anja's head, "So we don't need this piece of shit then?" she asks, calmly pulling the trigger to splatter Anja's head all over the car park floor.

Cramer's head drops, "Well we could have interrogated her and maybe got something."

George turns to head back to his car, "Well, I expect to see you lot in my office tomorrow morning at nine o'clock sharp," he stops briefly, "oh by the way," he says, turning to Ben, "thought you might like to know. Your fiancée is awake and asking for you," he smiles, turning to Pyah and Mark, "she'd appreciate a visit from you two as well I suppose," he adds, smiling then wombling off, "don't worry, my guys will clean this lot up," he calls before getting into his car to drive off.

Mark leans against a car and sighs, "Well, suppose we should be going then," he says, turning back as he hears a rasping noise behind him.

One of the two thugs is barely alive and has crawled toward Ben's van. Mark sees him reaching up under the van as a small red light appears. Mark runs up to take a look before putting a round through the thug's head, "Oh shit, we've got bigger fish to fry now."

Ben walks around, "What's up now?"

Mark points under the van, "Chemical bomb. Looks big enough to take out this whole car park and the surrounding buildings."

A policeman walks up, "There's a cryogenics lab across the way, don't suppose if we freeze it the chemicals wouldn't be able to mix and the bomb couldn't go off? Just a thought like," he says, turning to put his arm around Elleon, "my, aren't we going to have an exciting relationship?"

Elleon's head slowly turns "Adam? Where the hell did you come from?"

Pyah's head pops out from behind a pillar, "Ahem, did I hear relationship in that sentence?"

Elleon places her arm around Adam, "Pyah, meet my new boyfriend, Adam," she introduces,

blushing slightly, "Adam meet Pyah."

Adam swiftly walks over to Pyah, "Nice to meet you but I think that bomb is set to go off in about twelve minutes."

Pyah stands, staring at him blankly, then waves her arms, "Well, go on then, save the day," she says, hurrying Adam away.

CHAPTER 57
BOOM BOOM

Adam rushes over, picks up the bomb then runs across the road, smashing his way into the lab. Finding a vat of liquid hydrogen, he drops the bomb in then steps back. He stands and makes a sign of the cross over his chest, "Oh God let this work," he prays as he hears the mechanism click and grind.

He stands with his eyes tightly shut for a moment then slowly opens them. Looking around, he gently opens the hydrogen vat, "Phew," he sighs, mopping his brow as he sees the liquids frozen solid, "now all I got to do is get this thing somewhere safe to let it thaw out."

He walks out of the lab to applause. Mark pats him on his back, "Well, if it was going off it would have done about a minute ago so I guess it's safe."

Adam nods, "Just need to get it somewhere safe to explode it now," he says as the bomb squad arrive, "it's in there in stasis," he explains, smiling as they give him a funny look, walking into the lab shaking their heads.

Ben walks over to Mark, "Well, don't know about you but I got a date to keep," he says, rushing over to an empty police car.

Adam steps up, "Excuse me, but you might need these," he says, throwing Ben the keys, "and no bloody siren," he warns, waggling his finger.

Ben salutes him then climbs into the driver's seat as Pyah and Mark climb in the back. He rolls the window down then pulls up alongside Elleon and Adam, "You not coming with us?"

Elleon cuddles into Adam, "Nah. Give her my regards and tell her I said I'll see her later when she's better. Tell her to make it quick because I want to show him off," she says, patting Adam on the chest before kissing him.

She looks into his eyes all dopey-eyed, "Don't think me strange, but usually after a fight I have a ritual."

He shrugs, "Hey, whatever. If you want to be alone that's fine by me."

She giggles then starts to drag him by the hand towards her jeep, "No, I usually do it alone but damn it, I got you now," she says, skipping slightly "you're probably going to think I'm a loon but my heart's pounding and the adrenaline rush I just got needs a little something," she pauses, starting to blush, "you see I usually go somewhere quiet and... Well, you know, I, oh shit, how do I put this?"

Adam stops her, pulls her into his arm and kisses her, "You pleasure yourself?"

Her head drops, "Well, yes," she admits, twiddling her finger across his chest, "but like I said, I got you now and I know I was all shy and twitchy before but I would rather do it with you than by myself and we better be quick before I change my mind."

Adam picks her up then runs to her jeep, "OK, I'll drive. I know a shortcut to my place."

She puts her hand over his mouth, "No, no, no, that'll be too late, put me down."

He puts her down at the jeep, where she opens the tailgate and beckons him in, "Just get in before it wears off," she says, looking around while she drops her trousers, "lie on your back and don't say a fucking word," she adds, climbing in to straddle him, "I don't believe I'm doing this but if I don't do it now I may never do it so shut up and let me get on with it."

Adam just lies there while she drags his trousers down. She looks up to the roof then slides herself onto him, "Oh fuck, that's nice," she breathes as she starts to gently lift up and down, then thrust her pelvis back and forth.

She rests her hands on his chest with her eyes closed biting her lips before lowering to kiss him, "OK?"

He nods happily, "Hm hm, you do whatever you have to, dear."

She stops, stares him straight in the eye and cringes, "Dear?"

He raises his hands, "Oops my bad, sorry. What would you prefer? Darling. Love, or maybe honey?"

She starts to thrust again closing her eyes, "Honey, I like the sound of that, yeah, honey, that will do."

He tentatively places his hands on her hips, "Is there anything else you would like?"

She takes one of his hands to place it on her breast, "Yeah, actually there is," she says, pressing his hand hard on her nipple, "you could do some of the work here."

His face beams with a grin from ear to ear, "Yes honey," he says as he starts to play with her nipple.

She shakes her head, "I meant fuck me, for Christ's sake," his hand stops moving then her head drops, "and play with those you dipstick. I mean, this is supposed to be pleasurable for both of us."

He starts to thrust while twiddling her nipple, "Well, I was kind of hoping it would be romantic."

She drops onto his chest, stares straight into his eyes then pecks his lips, "OK, so show me what you want."

He rolls her gently onto her back as she wraps her legs around his waist, "Ooo, didn't think I'd like a man that takes charge but this could be fun."

He looks deep into her eyes, "Seems that someone is losing all her innocence in one go."

She smiles, "Innocence and virginity at the same time, wow, aren't I the lucky one?"

He kisses her neck as she starts to crane. Her eyes close as she wraps her arms around his back, her nails running down his spine. She nuzzles his neck as she grips his buttocks, pushing him harder and faster. He lifts off her slightly to force his mouth against hers as she grabs a handful of his hair. She pulls his mouth away from hers, "No, don't like it," he stops as she looks at him vacantly, "what have you stopped for?"

He looks at her puzzled, "Err, you told me to? You don't like it?"

She pushes his buttocks forward plunging him back into her, "No, I meant I don't like you forcing the kiss."

He drops his head to her ear, "That's because you were groaning and screaming rather loud," he confides, tapping on the side window, "I'm not quite sure whether they could hear you at the station," he says, chuckling to himself.

She pushes his head up, a shocked look on her face, "Oh my God, you're kidding me?"

He shakes his head, smirking, "Trust me, you were making enough noise to wake the dead."

She pulls his head forward, pressing his lips against hers then pulls him back, "You do what you have to keep me quiet," she says, slamming her mouth back against his before thrusting her pelvis while looking sideways out of the jeep window to check no one is watching them.

Adam lifts off her again, "What are you doing?"

She sticks her head up to look out of the window, "Making sure no doggers are about."

He cringes, "Doggers?"

She nods frantically, "Yeah, people that go out dogging. You know, watching couples screw in cars."

He laughs, "Yeah, I know what dogging is, but there are special places for that."

Her head spins as she jolts it back, "Whoa, how do you know that?"

He gives her one of those looks, "Ahem," he says, pointing down at his uniform, "I'm a copper. It's my job to know."

She slaps her own forehead, "Derr, of course. Silly me," she says in a goofy voice.

She relaxes back as she realises the windows are steaming up, "Not as if I'm going to get arrested."

He flicks his handcuffs around the front, "I could restrain you though."

She gives him a stern look, "Don't think so, mate. And if you think I'm doing any kinky stuff that's the end of our relationship."

He throws the handcuffs back behind him, "Anything you say, honey."

She smiles, "I do like that, honey, now fuck, for Christ's sake," she says as she pushes him back into her.

It isn't long before she is howling like a wolf as she reaches her climax. Adam is instantly brought to his ejaculation by the noise that she is making, his body spasms in perfect time with hers. Clinging on to each other for dear life as they bite into each other's shoulder. He grunts incessantly while she groans, trying to keep the volume down by burying her mouth in his neck. One final pulse then they relax together, their clothes sticking to each other.

Adam rolls off her against the wheel well, "Now that was an experience."

She sits up, "So how did I do?"

He looks at her confused. She prods his shoulder, "Come on, I know you lot rate women on performance."

He shrugs, "Wouldn't know. I'm a virgin too."

She picks up her shoe, "You lying little shit," she accuses, slapping him around the head with the sole.

He holds his hands over his head, "All right, all right. I'm not but I don't rate girls, honest."

She lifts his chin, "But if you did, how would you score me?"

He kisses her, "Trust me, you were defo an eleven."

She kisses him back, "That better be out of ten!"

He nods, smiles then starts to put himself away. Elleon wipes the steam from the window, "God, it's bloody dark out there now," she says then spins to stare at him.

He looks up at her, "What?"

She drops her head, "So if I'm an eleven now, just think what I'll be when you've taught me what you know," she says, raising her eyebrows.

He starts to button her bra back up, "Oh, so I got to teach you now do I?"

She strokes his hair, "Well, unless you want me to learn some more from my girls?"

He runs his hand down her arm, "Going to have to meet these girls of yours some day."

Elleon laughs out loud, "You already met one. The redhead."

He points towards the car park, "What, the one with the legs all the way up to her armpits?"

She raises her eyebrows, "Oh, you noticed?"

He smiles at her, "Couldn't help noticing, shit, they were long, but no need to get jealous and all, I like a cute little bundle, just like the cute little bundle I got here."

She slaps his butt, "Oh, you silver tongued devil, you," she says, giving him her best southern sarcasm.

She quickly finishes dressing, "What the hell, let's go. I'll introduce you to the other one. Mind, she's laid in hospital with a bullet hole through her brain."

CHAPTER 58
THE END OF A BEAUTIFUL DAY

The cold night air creeps through the night as Pyah, Mark and Ben cautiously enter the hospital when the receptionist calls them over. Mark approaches her, "Yes my dear, can I help you?"

She looks around him, "Are you the Fischers by any chance?"

Pyah walks forward, "Err, that all depends on your next question."

The receptionist points towards the lift, "They are expecting you. Top floor."

Mark smiles, "It's ok, we know the way," he says, taking Pyah by the hand as she links arms with Ben, "ok, let's get you two back together again," he adds, smiling at Ben.

Ben starts to skip towards the lift, "Oh, we're off to see the wizard."

Mark stops dead, "I don't think so mate. If you're going all gooey on me, you're on your own."

Ben stands with his hands on his hips, "You can't blame a guy for being happy," he says, blowing Mark a kiss.

Mark frowns at him, "OK, that's just freaky."

Ben jumps into the lift, "Oh lighten up, you old fart."

Mark smiles an evil smile then saunters into the lift with Pyah. The door shuts then Mark gives a pleased with himself grin. Pyah turns to him as the lift starts to move, "OK what are you... oh, you haven't?"

Ben spins, "Hasn't what?" he asks as it hits him, "oh, you dirty bastard. Shit, that stinks," he complains, placing his coat over his nose.

Mark just stands there grinning, bobbing up and down on his toes, "Shouldn't have started acting daft then, should you?" he says, laughing to himself, "Now that's an old fart for you," he adds, wafting his arms about.

Pyah holds her hand over her mouth, "Stop it," she says, grabbing Marks arms.

When the lift stops at the top both Ben and Pyah jump out baulking as Ben looks at Pyah, "Does he do that on a regular basis?"

Mark saunters out grinning at him, "All the time mate," he says as he walks past them towards the ward.

When they arrive at the ward, two security guards are posted outside. Mark approaches them with caution. One of them steps forward, pulls out a picture, looks at it then looks at Mark, "OK Mr Fischer, you can go in."

Mark turns to Pyah and Ben, shrugs, then enters the room. The guard steps back to his post, allowing Pyah and Ben to enter. Pyah rushes over to Lacey, her arms widespread, "Oh I've missed you," she cries, carefully hugging her, "shit, I might break you."

Lacey kisses her on her cheek, "Nah, didn't you hear? Bulletproof, me, hun," she says as she reaches her hand out for Ben.

He stands looking at her with tears flooding down his cheeks, "Shit, I thought I'd lost you," he cries, placing Lacey's hand on his face.

She pulls him down towards her, "I don't think so mate, you got a promise to fulfil and I'm calling you on it."

At that Elleon strolls into the room, "Hey, did anyone get that smell in the lift? Oh shit, is he crying? The soft git."

Ben turns to face her, "Hey you, you're not too big to go over my knee, young lady," he says, smiling at Adam.

Adam puffs his chest out, "I think you'll find that's my job now," he corrects, holding his arms out as if he'd lost his carpets.

Lacey pushes Ben to the side, "And who do we have here?"

Elleon links arms with Adam, "He's a copper, and he's all mine."

Lacey waves him over, "Come on then, let me have a look at the man that is finally taking her off my hands."

Elleon slaps the bed next to Lacey, "Cheeky cow, just wait till you're better."

Lacey cocks her head to one side, "Ooo, you're cute," she says, turning to Elleon, "might just steal him off you."

Elleon gives her a funny look, "Don't think so woman, this one is all mine."

Ben steps forward, "So it looks like we got another guest for our wedding?"

Mark turns around giggling. Ben walks over, puts his hand on Mark's shoulders and spins him round, "So what's so funny?"

Mark shrugs, "You two, married," he says, shaking his head.

Ben turns to wink at Pyah, "Yeah, then I'll be just like you," he says, turning back to Mark, "married to mayhem."

The End